C

# BESS*ime*

ISBN 978-1494395360

Front cover artwork by Connie Wicklund

Typeset at SpicaBookDesign in Caslon

Printed with www.createspace.com

*To imagination...*
*Without it, where would we be?*

# SINCERE THANKS TO:

*Ed Griffin,* my mentor, who taught me to avoid the passive verb and write, write, write.

*Alec,* my husband, who gave me the needed push in the right direction.

*Spunky,* the cat who owns me, oversaw every word I transcribed to the laptop. Strategically sprawled on the table, he also kept a watchful eye on the mouse.

*Joyce Goodall,* a co-worker, who said she loved to read a good Christmas story.

*Connie Wicklund,* an artist, a friend, for her expertise, time and patience devoted to the book cover.

*Rick Peacosh,* who came to the rescue when the computer did not.

*Iryna Spica,* who made the publishing of this book a reality.

The makers of lighted, miniature buildings. Without them, there would be no story.

And to *my family and friends,* your interest and encouragement is appreciated.

# The Bess Time

*by Yvonne Pont*

# CHAPTER I

A host of small lights beckoned, a refuge from the storm. Bess looked through the rain-splattered window at the store's Christmas display. As the rain ran down the window obscuring her view, she moved in for a closer look. Her eyes beheld a magical village of long ago. Intricate, little buildings, artfully arranged along a cobblestone street, busy with miniature horse-drawn carriages, and people dressed in costumes of days gone by, seemed to come to life.

Just as Bess became mesmerized by this scene, reality brought her back with a large drop of cold rain water running down her neck. Shaking her head, she noticed a sign across the narrow street, printed in bold letters the word "LIBATEA," encircled by three teapots painted red, white and blue. Noticing a ladder leaning on the building in front of her, she decided to jaywalk rather than go under it to cross at the crosswalk. She sprinted across the street and entered the little tea shop. The warm air and the smell of fresh baking engulfed her.

A voice rang out, "Find a table, hon. I'll be with you in a moment."

Bess looked around the tiny room filled with three occupied and seven vacant tables. She chose a small, round one by the window. Taking off her wet coat and hat, she sat down and tried to fluff her flattened hair with her fingers. She saw her reflection in the window. *Bess Turner, you must do something about all the grey that has invaded your blond locks,* she thought.

"Sorry, hon. I was just taking a fresh batch of scones out of the oven. We have a lovely selection of teas and pastries. I'll leave the list with you. I'll give you a couple of minutes to decide." The waitress gave a friendly smile and went over to help two women, seated at a table in the corner.

Bess picked up the menu. The cover displayed the same colourful logo of three teapots encircling "LIBATEA" with four words written underneath: "The pursuit of happiness." Bess smiled and opened the menu. She soon made her choice and waved at the waitress.

"I'll have a pot of Buckingham Palace and a scone, please."

"Good choice. I'll be right back, and we'll get you warmed up in no time. What a dreadful day out there. At least it's not snowing."

Bess looked out the window and thought *how true.* Across the street, she could see the lights of the window display. Just looking at them made her feel warmer and the rain less intrusive.

"Here you are, hon." The waitress poured Bess a cup of steaming, hot tea. She put down the blue-flowered teapot and a large, inviting scone. Making room on the table, she placed a dish containing three compartments filled with clotted cream, lemon curd and strawberry jam. "If you want anything else, just wave or call me. My name's Libby."

As Bess sipped her tea, she looked out the lace-curtained window at the downpour. The cozy atmosphere inside warmed her soul. She noticed a lone runner dodge the rain. He passed under the old, wrought iron streetlamp with its two glass bulbs lighting his way. Seeing the lights on surprised Bess, being only two in the afternoon. On second thought, she realized the shortest day of the year was only a week away. Her thoughts brought her to Christmas, and ultimately the reason she ventured out on a day like today: Christmas shopping. She swallowed the last drop of tea in the fine china cup and put it gently down on its saucer. Quickly putting on her red coat and matching hat, she searched through her purse for the red change purse. She left four quarters on the table, picked up the bill and made her way to the counter.

"Everything to your liking, hon?" Libby's large, brown eyes searched Bess's face for the expected approval. "Good, that will be five dollars. Thank you. Please come again."

As Bess turned to leave, a chalkboard caught her eye: "Enjoy life sip by sip, not gulp by gulp."

Bess darted across the street, took one more look at the window display and decided to go into the store. Her hand grasped the handle. It would not turn. She tugged. It didn't budge. In desperation, she looked around. Only then did she see a sign on the door window. It directed her around the corner to the front of the building. Once again avoiding the ominous ladder, she ventured out onto the street and skirted around it. As she turned the corner, a large sign over the door proclaimed, "Stewart's Fine China & Gifts."

Her hand opened the door on its first attempt. A bell jingled. She entered. Shaking the the water off her clothes, the tiny drops landed on a glass cabinet. Bess's blue eyes lit up on discovering the interesting contents inside the rain-smeared cabinet. On one shelf, Dresden figurines vied for attention over their peasant countrymen, the Hummel family. Blanketing the shelf above, a kaleidoscope of colours emanated from the tiny Swarovski crystal figurines. Looking around, she found many such cabinets filled with beautiful pieces of artistry. *Oh my, I am a child in a candy shop, but darn, I cannot touch these precious sweets,* she sighed.

Seeing no assistant, she moved to the next room, a room of medium size, perhaps 20 feet by 30 feet. Each foot was filled with numerous things she could cross off her wish list. Moving her head to the right, Lilliput Lane beckoned her straight ahead. China teacups and pots whistled for her attention. To the left, shelves of exquisite linens begged a feel. Turning around, racks of stationery greeted her.

"Good afternoon. May I help you?" a soft voice echoed amongst the first row of cards.

Startled, Bess looked around. "Yes, aah --- Excuse me, but where are you?"

A rustling from the talking cards produced a petite woman. No wonder Bess missed seeing her when she entered the room.

"Sorry, I was restocking the Christmas cards. I must have just bent over to pick them out of the box when you entered."

On closer inspection, Bess saw an attractive, middle-aged woman, smartly dressed in a pale-blue dress. Perfectly arranged, her salt and pepper hair enhanced her porcelain skin. She and the store's contents complimented each other perfectly.

"Yes, I noticed your window display on the side street," Bess looked around, "but, I don't see it in your store."

"They're all in the back of the store." The saleslady smiled. "Follow me."

To Bess's amazement, the saleslady took her through an opening. It looked like a storage area. Indeed, it was the stockroom. Floor to ceiling shelves full of unopened boxes of merchandise, bordered a narrow passageway. An opening on the right, exposed a small, cluttered office. An elderly man sat at the oversized wooden desk. As the two ladies passed by, he lifted his large head and gave a greeting.

Suddenly the magical room, Bess wanted to see, lay before her. Shelves, laden with more buildings and accessories she could imagine, filled her eyes with wonder.

"Oh my," Bess could hardly speak, "this is fantastic."

"Yes, we do have a good selection of the Dickens Village. Take your time. Mr. Stewart will be in shortly. It is his favourite room and he enjoys sharing it with others. I'll just be out front if you need me," the saleslady said.

Left alone in the room, Bess slowly made her way around the village displays. Now, she truly was in the candy store. If she dared to, she could touch everything. No one was around to chastise her.

*Oh, I must have this. What charming children sitting on a fence. The horses look so lifelike. I could just pet them. No Bess, keep your hands in your pockets. I love this antiquarian bookstore. What stories it could tell.* Many thoughts raced through her head. She mentally calculated the price of each item and kept a running total. *Oops, this total is running away from me,* giggled Bess, as she picked up the boxed items, stacked under the shelves.

"Looks like you're enjoying yourself," the elderly man said as he shuffled into the room. "I love this room. It makes me feel so alive. Lord knows , I need all the help I can get," he chuckled. "Can I help you with anything else? This starter kit gives you two houses, figurines and trees." He picked up the large box to show her the inviting contents.

"No thanks, I think I've helped myself enough," Bess said.

"Good choices. I'll get Joyce to come and assist you." He turned with the aid of his cane and made his way out. "Joyce, the young lady needs some help back here."

Bess smiled. *Young lady, eh? What a dear man.--- Okay, I'm a pushover. I'll take the starter kit too.*

In the distance she heard the saleslady's reply, "Yes, Mr. Stewart. I'll be right there."

Arms full and wallet empty, Bess headed for the front door.

"Let me get the door for you." The saleslady rushed in front of her and opened the door. "Do come again."

"Thank you. I'm sure I will."

The door jingled and Bess stepped out into the late afternoon chill. Walking back to her car, she passed a second-hand bookstore. *Darn, I wanted to go in there,* she mused. *I'll just have to come back another day, won't I.* With as light a step she could muster, while laden down with a large shopping bag in each hand, Bess made her way down the street. Funny, she didn't even notice the rain.

# CHAPTER II

*L*ike a metronome, the windshield wipers switched back and forth. The rhythm sped up as the arms reached their boundaries, clicked and slowly returned to their apex. And thus, the movement began all over again. Evan's large hand reached for the wiper control knob. His tight grip turned the knob to the high position. Rain bounced off the hood of the late model Ford. Water sprayed with a vengeance over the windshield as an oncoming truck sped by, causing the wipers to hesitate. Evan squinted. In front, the red taillights came closer and closer. Suddenly upon them, he braked just in time. *Thank goodness for the anti-lock brake system. --- And to think I almost didn't buy a vehicle with ABS.* He breathed a sigh of relief.

The rush hour traffic came to a stand still. Without the road noise, he heard the rain beat on the roof, like the war chant of African drums. Evan took off his glasses and rubbed his weary eyes. A dull ache at the back of his eyes, pounded in time with the rhythm of the wipers. He turned on the radio, and switched stations until he came across the hockey game.

"At the end of the first period, the Canucks and Flyers are tied one all. And now a word from our sponsor----"

Evan's mind drifted off to the day's events. Year end loomed too close for him. Many of his clients' fiscal year ended on December 31. The dreaded taxman cometh all too soon. Business taxation comprised most of his accounting practice, with a few personal returns to round up his over taxed figures. The whole taxation process boggled the experts' minds, let alone the layman's. His work demanded so much of his time and energy. Today he spent six hours going over Lau and Sons' financial statements. Tomorrow, another full day interpreting their journals and ledgers, awaited his scrutiny.

"Two minutes for hooking. There goes Powe towards the penalty box. Does he look angry. The puck is dropped. Ohlund gets the puck. He skates towards the Flyers' goal. He shoooots. Ooooh, he just misses the corner of the goal. ---- The puck hits the boards. Carter gets the puck."

The brake lights dimmed. The cars in front inched their way forward. Each mile of freeway seemed like fifty; stop and go, stop and go. Finally he saw his exit sign and turned on his indicator. He switched to the far lane and exited the freeway. Traffic was still heavy, but at least it moved at a reasonable speed. Visibility still left a lot to be desired, but at least the stress lessened. The muscles in his neck and shoulders relaxed. His head continued to throb, but like the windshield wipers, the intensity decreased.

Evan's thoughts veered off in the direction of his wife. He worried a lot about Bess. Since her retirement two years ago, she changed. He knew fifty-five had been too young for her to retire, but with the lumber mill closing down, she had no choice. She told him her age provided a determinative end for future employment. To her, work meant a purpose for living, never enough hours in the day, and a good night's sleep at the end of the day.

After a lifetime of responsibilities to others, Evan knew she found it difficult to think of her needs first. The alarm clock no longer did its duty; no punching in and out on the time clock. Her time was her own. Time became her biggest worry. Often she asked him if he needed any help at work or home. Evan knew she needed stimulation. Granted, in the spring and summer, she worked in the garden. She enjoyed planning and working their half acre lot. However, wintertime provided few garden activities, and she became bored and withdrawn. *If only I wasn't so busy at work, I could spend more time with my dear Bess. ----- I do worry about you,* he sighed.

"Hartnell shoots. He scooores!" the radio vibrated with the echo of victory horns.

"Damn," shouted Evan, as he beat his hands on the steering wheel.

The traffic disappeared as he wound his way through the dark residential streets. He stopped at the stop sign, looked in both directions along the deserted side street, signaled and turned left. He prided himself on his flawless driving record. He automatically stopped at yellow lights, never rolled through a stop sign and signaled, whether anyone could be seen or not. Over forty years of driving and never an accident or a ticket. However, he did have one fault common to all drivers, frequent lapses in concentration. Fortunately for Evan, police training did not include mind reading, so his record remained untarnished.

About fifty yards from the corner, a rooftop lined with colourful Christmas lights, attracted his attention. *Maybe next year I'll put up a Santa, sled and reindeer on the roof,* he thought and immediately gave a huge yawn. He put on his indicator and turned right into his flagstone driveway. Evan smiled and breathed a sigh of relief *ah, home safe and sound.*

Pressing the garage door opener, he attentively drove the car into the limited parking space. The Ford stopped just short of the pile of cardboard boxes and tools, stored in the overcrowded garage. Another job to add to his to do list when not so tired or had more time. From the back seat, he picked up his battered briefcase and closed the car door. One last time, he pushed the garage door opener. The door creaked as it closed the stormy elements out of his sanctuary.

The enticing smells of Bess's cooking engulfed Evan as he entered the warm house. "Ah, toad-in-the-hole." He inhaled and exhaled with great pleasure. "Bess, I'm home."

Briefcase still in hand, he rushed into the living room and

grabbed the remote, laying on the oak coffee table. Quickly channel surfing, he stopped when the large flat screen featured the hockey game in living colour.

"Sedin gets the puck. He shoots. He scooooores."

"Yes!" Evan dropped his briefcase and raised his arms. Clenched fists pointed towards the vaulted ceiling.

Five minutes later, he looked on the mossy green, plush carpet to recover his discarded briefcase. Beside old Buxton, he noticed two large, green shopping bags with "Stewart's Fine China & Gifts" embossed on their fronts. *Hmm*, he thought, *Bess must have gone shopping. Wonder what she bought? I must ask her.*

"What? Oh come on. That wasn't a penalty."

Supper, served on the well used T.V. tables, covered in vinyl inlaid hardwood, finished an hour ago. The hockey game finished right after. Evan picked up the evening paper and read the headlines. A few minutes later, he took off his glasses and rubbed his weary eyes. In the meantime, Bess retired to the kitchen and washed the dishes. She wiped down the marble counter top and swept the crumbs off the black and white tile floor. She enjoyed her kitchen and kept it spotless.

Bess had been cooking since the age of nine, when her mother took sick. Shortly after her mother died, and Bess became the cook and housekeeper to her younger sister Mona and brother David. Her father relied totally on her to run the household and look after her siblings. He worked at odd jobs, so money was scarce and hired help, out of the question.

No one around to teach her, she quickly learnt, through trial and error, how to cook. She still laughed over the time she made her father's favourite dessert, rice pudding. Nine year old Bess poured the measured amount of rice into the saucepan of cold water. She looked into the large aluminium pot and thought *that won't be enough. They must have made a mistake when printing the recipe.* She poured more rice and took another look. Shaking her head, she proceeded to pour the whole box into the pot. Satisfied, she put the lid on and went about her other chores.

It took only a short time for the rice to do its magic. It expanded and expanded. She heard a hissing noise and ran to the kitchen. Her blue eyes, wide with amazement, beheld an army of rice kernels trying to escape from Fort Saucepan. They had tripled their forces, and with a spurt of steam, pushed the lid high enough to begin their descent down the sides of the pot. The Great Escape well under way, Bess grabbed the handle and moved the pot off the stove. She flung open the cupboard and rifled all the empty pots she could muster. The family ate rice pudding every night for a week.

Bess turned off the kitchen light and proceeded to the living room. The all too familiar, melodic notes of the introduction to "Law & Order," echoed back and forth across the light grey, painted walls. The streetlight on the corner cast a distorted beam of light through the skylight as the rain ran down its slick surface. Bess looked up and spied a cobweb, tucked in one corner of the skylight.

"Sure, Mr. Spider, make yourself comfortable. You think you're pretty smart being on this side of the window. Enjoy it tonight, for tomorrow, I will knock you down from your high perch," Bess threatened.

She dropped her head and looked at Evan. She expected him to make a comment. However, since he was asleep , it would have been difficult to comment on her discovery. Evan, head bent forward, sat snoring on the chesterfield. The newspaper lay strewn half on the floor and half on his lap. His glasses still lay on the coffee table.

"Oh, Evan, darn you. I did want to show you my purchases." She glanced over to the two shopping bags and sighed, "I wanted to share my exciting day with you. I should have told you at supper, but you were too engrossed in the hockey game. Oh, I guess

10

it's just as well. You wouldn't have remembered my ramblings, in the morning, anyway."

She nudged him; no response. She shook him harder.

"Evan, come to bed. Wake up."

"Whhaat? Ooh." He half opened his eyes.

"Time to go to bed," she repeated.

"Okay, I'm coming," Evan managed to say before the snoring started again.

She looked at her once shining knight. His lips quivered with each exhale, and his nose flared with each inhale. From his open mouth, a spot of drool escaped down his chin.

"To think, I used to dream of those full lips touching mine. Aah, the little nibbles I used to lovingly inflict upon your nose. It was such a handsome nose, so perfect. And your mouth, so full of words of love. Oh, how my heart did sing." She sighed, shook her head and said, "What happened?"

She thought *should I wake him again?*

"No, why bother."

Bess turned off the television and switched off the lights. With hands clenched, she slowly went upstairs to bed.

"Goodnight, Evan," she murmured, as she closed her eyes and thought *where will I put my magical village?*

# CHAPTER III

*T*hursday morning came all too soon. Bess awoke to the sounds of banging water pipes. *Every time we take a shower, the pipes make such a horrid racket,* she thought. *Another job on the to do list.* She laid in bed, eyes refusing to open, and legs aching as if they just ran a marathon. She had tossed and turned all night. *Why should I have slept so?* Bess wondered. Nothing earth shattering came to mind, but she felt uneasy.

The bathroom door opened, allowing the scent of Evan's aftershave to permeate the room. Bess slowly opened her eyes. Evan stood beside the king-size bed, buttoning his blue dress shirt. She watched as he swung his dark-blue tie around his neck and effortlessly knotted it. It took Evan many years to accomplish this feat with the ease he now attained. He jerked his neck from side to side and up and down. He groaned.

"If you'd come to bed instead of falling to sleep on the chesterfield, you wouldn't have a sore neck," Bess mumbled.

"I heard that." He turned around and looked at her. "You're right. I should come to bed; I don't fall to sleep on purpose."

"The Myoflex is on the dresser." She motioned with her index finger. "Oh, come here. I'll put some on for you.---- Don't make a face. It's odourless." She sniffed the tube. *Well almost,* she chuckled to herself.

The wifely deed done, Bess put her head back down on the

12

pillow. Evan went downstairs and started making his breakfast. She heard the cupboard doors closing, and utensils clattering on the kitchen counter. Right from the beginning of her retirement, Bess proclaimed she would not get up until absolutely necessary. Evan was quite capable of getting his own breakfast. She rolled over on her side and dozed off.

"Bess, I'm off. Have a good day." He gave her a quick kiss on the lips and headed back down the stairs. "Oh, yeah, we're out of milk," he shouted up the stairs.

Before Bess could reply, the garage door closed with a thud. Moments later, she heard the gentle purring of the car engine as Evan drove up the road.

"Time to get up, Bess Turner. You have a busy day ahead of you."

She eased her feet out of the warm bed onto the beige carpet. Slouched over, she stretched her upper torso and gradually came to a complete, upright position. Bess made her way into the bathroom and looked in the mirror.

"Good heavens. I look like h--- I sure feel like I'm there," she said as her fingers traced the outline of her wrinkles. "Maybe a hot shower will help."

She turned on the taps and the pipe section of the orchestra did its usual warm up, banging and clattering, ending with a resounding whistle from the wind section. In spite of the sound effects, the shower proved beneficial. The face in the mirror looked younger, and her legs no longer ached. She put on a pair of jeans and a blue, turtle neck sweater. Bess never liked walking around without shoes, so when she went downstairs, the first thing she did, was put on her runners. Grooming completed, she went to the kitchen. Bess poured herself some cereal and opened the refrigerator.

"Darn, I forgot; no milk, no cereal." She closed the door and emptied the bowl of cereal back in the box. "Tea and toast, it is."

After a glance of the morning paper, and finding her name absent from the obituaries, Bess began her day. She quickly went through her household chores. A pleasant task awaited her attention. She had spent the past hour, continually glancing over at the two green shopping bags.

Nothing in her way, except to carry out her threat to Mr. Spider, but that matter could wait, she pulled out the first box from the nearest shopping bag. She wanted to rip it open, but common sense prevailed; she carefully opened the box. Protected in a cocoon of styrofoam, an antiquarian bookstore greeted her. She carefully nudged it out of its hiding place and placed it on the coffee table. She took out the light accessory, attached to a white cord and closed up the box. With great anticipation, Bess moved her hand into the shopping bag and brought out her second treasure. A much smaller box, but as important as the first, received her whole attention. Nestled in its confines, a tiny figurine of a young boy and girl, sitting on a split-rail fence, made her smile. Another box in the first bag revealed a horse-drawn carriage and driver, delivering Christmas presents. "Williams & Sons" written on the side of the carriage, delighted her. *Imagine finding this piece with my maiden name in Olde English script,* she thought.

"I wonder if Evan will notice," she said out loud.

The last box in the bag contained an ornate, brick building. *Yes, this tea house will do nicely,* she thought, as she picked it up and looked all around its perimeter. At the side of this building, lay a shovel and a battered bucket beside the coal bin. *Ah, what treats will you conjure up from your oven, and what tales will be spun in front of your fireplace?*

A tea house meant a safe haven, surrounded by all the things she loved: warmth, coziness, delicious smells of baked goods and a hot cup of tea. *A cup of tea would go good right about now,* she thought. *As soon as I empty the other bag, I'll put the kettle on.*

The second shopping bag contained a large box, the starter set, recommended by the store owner, Mr. Stewart. She had taken his word regarding its contents. She hoped a nice surprise lay hidden within the heavy box.

To her delight, Bess found two buildings, "Fowler's Meat & Poultry Shoppe" and "Basil's Spice & Mustard Shoppe." Tucked between the two buildings, a small box caught her eye. Inside, she found two young boys with mischievous faces.

"I bet you two lads are a handful for your mom."

A final search inside the box revealed a couple of cone shaped trees, a vinyl strip of cobblestone road and two light fixtures.

While the kettle did its job, she cleared the mantel of pictures and figurines. She looked at the young couple holding each other tight. She sighed and put their black and white wedding picture in the cupboard face down and placed her little animal figurines on top. As she finished dusting the wooden surface, the kettle whistled.

Bess placed her china mug, full of tea, on the coffee table and picked up the bookstore. She placed it on the mantel. The other three buildings soon filled in her street of dreams. She moved the tea shoppe next to the mustard shoppe. *Exotic teas and spices go together. I'll put the bookstore on the other side of the tea shoppe; nothing like a good book and a cup of tea.* She pondered *hmmh, the meat shoppe? It doesn't quite fit with the other three. ---- Hmm, -- Yes, on the far end of the mantel will do.* She stepped back, avoiding the abandoned boxes strewn on the floor, to take a final look.

Satisfied with her arrangement, she attached the lights to the back of the buildings. She found a suitable extension cord in the laundry room and plugged them into it. White batting camouflaged the cords and thus looked like drifts of snow piled up behind the buildings. The cobblestone roadway, spread in front of the miniatures, gave the scene an authentic touch. The horse and carriage filled in a bare spot between the buildings, along with the trees and a few pine cones, she collected over the years. Lastly, she placed the children and spread a light dusting of snow flakes all over.

She plugged in the extension cord and stood back to view her magical mantel.

Displaying the village on the mantel pleased her. The fireplace stood front and centre in the living room. The television stood just off to the side and the chesterfield faced directly at its rock facade. Bess and Evan took the words "living room" literally and spent many hours in their favourite room. *Yes, I've made the right decision,* she smiled with satisfaction.

Enthralled by the vision in front of her, Bess moved closer. Her sparkling eyes focused on the bookstore. The old tudor style, three storey building had a crooked appearance as if time had settled it into a comfortable stance. Two large brick chimneys protruded out of the steep slate roof, along with a dormer window overlooking the street. A sign over the front window read "Tellaway Book Shoppe." Now within inches of the shoppe, she noticed a sandwich board located outside its door, listing items to entice the passerby:

"Antiquarian Books ** First Edition ** Jane Eyre by Currer Bell
Wuthering Heights by Ellis Bell ----------
Agnes Grey by Acton Bell"

Bess looked directly at the leaded window and saw a small sign in the corner:

"For sale A Christmas Carol by Charles Dickens"

Her face pressed against the window, she looked inside. To her delight, rows and rows of hardcover books lined the tall, dark wood shelves. Her ears caught a distant sound; clop clop. *The garbage truck must be down on the next street,* she thought. Her attention back on the interior of the bookstore, she noticed what she thought to be an arm. On closer inspection, she saw an arm encased in a long, black sleeve. Suddenly the arm moved, exposing a slender hand holding a red covered book. The hand placed the book into an open spot in the bookcase. Surprised, Bess thought *I didn't notice they moved too. I guess there was too much to look at in the china store yesterday. How clever!* Soon a figure of a lady rose from the aisle, holding a stack of books. A dark haired woman, dressed in a full length dress, turned and smiled at Bess.

Startled, Bess stepped back and caught a reflection in the glass. A young man, looking in the store's direction, stood motionless across the street. Once again, Bess heard the distant clop clop, but this time louder and accompanied by a wheezing sound. It seemed to come from behind her. *That's strange; our street is in front of me.* Her thoughts were interrupted by a sudden jolt. She could feel a presence of something very close to her. It touched her; not once but twice.

"Excuse me, miss. I never saw a lady wit' short 'air an' trousers on before." A dirty face appeared beside Bess. "Me name's Bertie Morton an' t'is 'ere's me mate, Artie."

Another, equally dirty face appeared beside her. Bess looked around to see who this young waif was talking to. *My gosh,* she thought. *He's talking to me.* Bess's heart raced.

The young boy continued, "Seen sumthin' ye like in t'is 'ere shoppe, 'ave ye, miss? Me 'n' Artie likes to look in t' shoppe window too. Artie's learnin' to read, 'e is. 'E lives way down t' street . Ye can't see it from 'ere."

Artie nodded his head and motioned with his dirty right hand. The voice and the two small faces seemed so real to Bess. *Surely they aren't?*

The little voice needed no encouragement to continue, "Me mum owns t' tea shoppe next door."

His little arm, clothed in black tweed, pointed towards Bess's left, where coincidently she had positioned her tea shoppe on the mantel. By moving her head slightly to the left, she could see the beige bricked building. A large sign, framed in black wrought iron, hung over the heavy wooden door. It read "The Lotatea Shoppe." Two small bay windows protruded on each side of the door. Bess saw a slight movement behind one of the white lace-curtained windows. However, she was too far away to see clearly. In order to see what or who the movement belonged to, she would have to move. *If I move, what will happen and more important, can I move?* Bess remained standing in front of the bookstore.

"Me mum's not so pretty as ye, but she's okay. Mr. Brown thinks so anyway. Me dad's a sea captain, so 'e's not bin 'ome fer a long time. Mr. Brown keeps me mum company. See that bloke lookin' in t' window? That's me uncle, Tom. 'E works in a countin' 'ouse, but ye can't see it from 'ere," Bertie said as he turned and looked down the street.

Bess looked in the window and once again glimpsed the reflection of the same man, now leaning on a lamppost. However, this time she also saw a young woman looking back at her. She had short blond hair and wore a blue, turtle neck sweater.

"Short, blond hair ----- blue, turtle neck sweater.---- Oh my, it's me ----!"

Clip clop, clip clop--- The sound became sharper, louder.

Ring, ring, brrring----brrring --- brrrrring!

# CHAPTER IV

*R*ing-------Ring-------Ring------
     Startled, Bess heard the telephone ringing and stepped back from the mantel.

CRASH............ BANG........

"Damn," she proclaimed. *I should have moved those discarded boxes. Bess, you know better than to leave them there.* She scolded herself, then attempted to move her body. "Oouch, that hurts." She slowly lifted herself off the floor. "Oowh!" *Don't be such a baby. At least you didn't hit the coffee table.*

Ring----- Ring-----

"Okay --- I'm coming," she bellowed while making her way to the telephone, as quickly as an injured body could move. "Hellooo."

"Bess?" a voice asked.

"Yes?"

"It's me, Lydia. Are you okay?" she asked. I must have let it ring a dozen times. Where were you?"

"I think I'm okay. I stepped back into some boxes and took a tumble. Thank goodness for plush carpets."

"Girlfriend, you better be careful. You're not a kid anymore. Remember when we used to summersault all over the lawn. I never could do a decent cartwheel. You always put me to shame. So, what did you do this time? A cartwheel? Or a summersault?"

19

"A back flip, if you must know." Bess tried to be sarcastic, but even when in pain, her best friend made her laugh.

"Seriously, are you sure you're okay?" Lydia asked.

"Yes, I'm sure. Give me an hour to check out and repair the body parts," Bess replied.

"Okay, I'll pick you up at eleven."

In the silence of the room, Bess eased herself onto the chesterfield and let her thoughts take over. Gone were the sounds of clip clop, clip clop, the endless chattering of a young voice and the constant ring, ringing in her ears. Only the sound of the wheels turning inside her head disturbed the silence. *It must have been a dream.* She looked up at the mantel. The lights in the little buildings gave off a serene glow. Bess hoisted her tender body off the chesterfield, bent over and pulled out the plug of the extension cord. Bess headed up the stairs.

"Another hot shower, as if I need more wrinkled skin; a dab of Myoflex and I'll be as good as new," she muttered.

Suddenly, Bess heard a haunting noise. She turned around, and her eyes focused in on the mantel and the two little lads, standing near the bookstore. Mouths open, they looked directly at her.

"Surely, it couldn't be ----?"

Boong. Boong. The grandfather clock chimed the all too familiar sounds of Big Ben.

"Of course not. Bess, you're going bonkers."

Just as the clock finished chiming, she heard the garbage truck go down the street. She shook her head, turned and eased her way up the stairs to her much needed shower. Seeking reassurance all was a dream, she looked in the bathroom mirror. A familiar face looked back at her.

"Yep, still fifty-seven, Bess."

Seated behind the wheel of her red Explorer, Lydia waved, as Bess opened the front door and popped her head out.

"I'll be right there. I just have to set the alarm." Bess stepped back in the house, picked up her purse, pressed the secret code onto the alarm box, pressed the activate-away button and rushed out the door. After a frustrating search, she found her keys hiding in the bowels of her purse. Just in the nick of time before the alarm went off, she locked the door. With a stiff gait, Bess made her way to the passenger's door.

"Ooooh, you poor thing. Are you sure you want to go out?"

"Of course, don't be silly. If you think this looks bad, you should have seen me an hour ago. A hot shower and an extra strength Tylenol did wonders." Bess sounded more like she was trying to convince herself than Lydia.

"Okay; enough said. Where do you want to go?" Lydia asked.

"I know the perfect place; I went there yesterday." Bess hesitated, "You know me, I eer---forgot to pick up a gift for my garden club's Christmas party tomorrow. I found a perfect gift store in Littleton."

"Littleton! That's an hour away." Lydia squirmed in her seat, as the house faded from view in her rearview mirror. "I should have made a pit stop at your house."

"Some things never change. When we were kids, my dad always had to make an extra stop for you whenever he drove us anywhere," Bess replied. "At least it's not raining. The trip shouldn't be too long. The way you drive, we'll be there in no time."

"And what's that supposed to mean?" Lydia gave a hearty chuckle.

Bess and Lydia had been best friends since the first day of school, fifty-one years ago. They always complimented each other; Lydia the garrulous one and Bess the reticent one. After a good deal of bantering back and forth, which they had perfected to a fine art over the years, they turned right onto Fir Street. They had no trouble finding a parking spot on the deserted street.

"I'm famished. Let's eat first," Lydia said, as she locked the car and looked around. "There's a place, right across the street." She pointed towards the little tea shop, Bess visited yesterday.

Not waiting for Bess to respond, Lydia quickly crossed the street and entered "Libatea." Forced to jaywalk once again, Bess followed. Lydia anxiously looked around until she found the sign to the washroom. She made a mad dash towards the door.

"I'll find us a table," Bess said to Lydia's retreating back.

A young woman directed her to the same table she occupied yesterday. Bess took off her coat and sat down. She automatically turned her head towards the window, looked across the street and noticed the window display. Her thoughts took her back to earlier in the day. It had been so hectic; the opportunity to reflect on her unbelievable experience, evaded her. Seeing the miniature buildings brought it all back. *It is impossible,* she told herself. The village began mesmerizing her once more. *Surely, it was only a dream?* She blinked and looked away.

A moment later, Lydia appeared with a smile of relief upon her face. Bess waved her over and thought *she still looks great after all these years. Thank goodness, her beautiful smile still lights up her face.* Lydia made her way to the table, took off her blue three-quarter length coat and sat down.

"What a charming place. Oooh, it smells so good in here," Lydia said as she looked around. "It's not fair. It shouldn't smell this good when I'm starving to death." She picked up the menu. "It all looks so good.-----Waitress."

As they waited for the waitress, Bess took a quick look out the window. She found it difficult to keep her eyes off the Dickens Village. It enticed anyone passing by to venture into its magical kingdom. She noticed a couple stop and peer in the window. She saw them pointing, and an animated conversation taking place. They smiled as they turned their heads and continued on their way. Meanwhile, Lydia always the observant one, looked around the tearoom.

Never one to keep her thoughts to herself, Lydia said, "Look at that gorgeous plate-rail." She pointed her finger towards the eleven foot ceiling. "My, a lady spider could easily think she'd webbed her way to heaven, weaving in and out of all those antique plates and gorgeous teapots."

"Yes, I know one who would certainly think so," Bess smiled.

Lydia interrupted, "Is that a Limoges?" Not expecting an answer, she continued while turning her focus towards the floor, "Oh, I just adore the tables. What a positively unique idea of using antique sewing machines as the base." She cheekily looked at Bess. "Sew, what else is new?"

Bess smiled, "Well, I aah----"

A brunette waitress came up to the table. "Ladies, welcome to our tearoom. What can I get you? We have a great selection of teas and our scones are to die for." Smiling, she looked at Lydia and then at Bess. Her big, brown eyes grew wider. "Oh, hi, hon. Long time no see; you were here yesterday. Boy what a miserable day. Sure glad it stopped raining. All that rain is bad for business. No one wants to come out in that stuff. I felt sorry for you; seeing you run across the street without an umbrella and then battle with that stupid, locked door. I don't know why they don't close it in completely. I see more people struggle with that darn door than I know what."

Lydia gave Bess a puzzled look and proceeded to look out the window. "You didn't tell me you were in here yesterday."

"She certainly was, and she must have found the front door, cause I saw her walking down the street later with her hands full of their green shopping bags. Not that I'm a nosyparker, but I was just putting the closed sign in the window when I saw her walk by. In spite of the downpour, I swore she had a big smile on her face."

"You don't say," said Lydia looking straight at Bess.

"I'll give you ladies a couple of minutes to decide. My names Libby, short for Libatea." She turned and walked towards another occupied table.

The two ladies looked at each other, shook their heads and giggled. They proceeded to pick up their menus, with teapots swirling around in a circle.

"And I thought I discovered 'Libatea.' Bess, you sly one," teased Lydia. "What's this about hauling a bunch of green shopping bags out of the store?" She looked across the street.

"It's not like you to be a mad shopper.--- And still you forgot to pick up a gift for your garden club, eh?"

"It was only two shopping bags and besides it is Christmas," Bess defended herself.

"Okay, so, what did you buy?"

"Remember, it is Christmas. Don't be nosy; like someone else in here."

"Ladies, have you decided?"

Shortly after they ordered, the waitress brought their food. Bess poured the Creamy Earl Grey into the delicate china teacups. After a couple of sips of the steaming hot tea, the hearty scotch broth and divine rosemary scones were devoured. They lingered over another pot of tea and finally decided the time had come to do some shopping. The two ladies paid their bills and proceeded to exit "Libatea."

Lydia noticed the chalkboard and read aloud, "When friends ask for a second cup, they are open to conversation." She giggled, "Maybe that's my problem. I should never have that second cup."

The two middle-aged jaywalkers headed back across Fir Street.

"This is the fourth time I've jaywalked within twenty-four hours," Bess confessed as she looked at her watch.

"Oooh, wouldn't Evan be shocked," Lydia teased. "Are you going to tell him?"

"Of course not. I don't want to disappoint him, thinking his wife's not perfect," Bess said, "besides, I do have a few dark secrets hidden from him." A smirk spread across her face, and she raised her eyebrows up and down several times. If only she had a moustache to twirl to complete the picture.

24

As they stepped onto the curb, Lydia noticed the window display. She stopped and took in the Dickens scene.

"It is darling; no wonder you kept looking out the window. Did you see it yesterday?" Before Bess could answer, Lydia banged her forehead with her hand. "Daah--- the waitress said you tried the door. My mind is like a sieve at times. Oh, my--" She cupped her face with both hands. "Do you think it's the beginning of Alzheimer's?"

"I truly hope not. Life would be pretty dull without your spontaneous remarks --- Not to worry; give us a couple of hours, and we won't remember this conversation anyways," Bess said with a straight face.

A puzzled look appeared on Lydia's face for a moment and finally the light went on. "Very funny."

"I've heard our reactions slow down too." Bess rubbed it in and started walking up the street. "Come on, Grandma. The front door is just around the corner."

The bell jingled, as they entered "Stewart's Fine China & Gifts." Bess immediately headed for the back of the store. However, Lydia impeded her journey by stopping to look in the display cabinets.

"I can see why you wanted to come back here. Everywhere you look are gorgeous pieces of china. Ooh --- Look; Royal Doulton figurines. The women are so beautiful, and their gowns so elegant. I could just imagine myself in one of these long flowing gowns." Lydia grabbed the bottom of her coat and twirled around in a slow, waltz-like fashion. On the second twirl, she stopped and pointed. "Oh look. There's another room to explore."

Lydia made her way into the second room, leaving visions of fancy dressed balls in the cabinet. She stopped to look at each display. "Bess, look. I've been searching all over for a Lilliput

Lane cottage for Aunt Louise." She picked up a rose covered, thatched roof cottage. "This will be perfect."

Lydia looked around for a saleslady and spied one helping another customer. The lady acknowledged Lydia by silently mouthing, she would be with her in a moment. In the meantime, Bess thought *I'd better look around for a small gift for the garden club.* She picked up a linen tea towel with an assortment of herbs, embroidered on its front. *Yes, that will do,* she thought. *Besides, if I don't buy something, Lydia will bug me, 'How come you didn't buy anything for your club? Isn't that why we came here'?*

"May I help you?" The saleslady looked at them and instantly recognized Bess. "Nice to see you again. Why don't you ladies put your purchases on the counter. I know you want to go into the back," she smiled at Bess.

"Yes, thank you." Bess returned the smile and headed towards the back of the store.

Lydia in close pursuit, asked, "Bess, where are you going? We can't go in there. You're heading for their storage area."

"Don't worry.---- Follow me.---- Remember, I was here yesterday."

Bess continued on her quest, taking wide-eyed Lydia through the narrow passageway. Mr. Stewart sat at his desk and nodded hello as they passed his cubbyhole. A few more steps and they entered the back showroom.

"Who would have guessed this was here?" Lydia looked around in amazement. "Look at all these little buildings and--- look at the tiny figurines. The people look so real. One could almost imagine being there."

Bess stopped her search of the inventory and gave Lydia a strange look.

"Isn't that dress shop darling?" Lydia pointed at a Victorian style building. She leaned into the display and took a closer look. "What's a Haberdashery?" She turned to Bess. "What are you looking for?"

26

"I want to see where Artie lives and where Uncle Tom works," Bess blurted out without thinking.

"Where who works?"

"Uncle Tom works at a counting house," Bess answered reluctantly.

"What's a counting house?" Lydia asked. "What do they count? Sheep? --- Fingers? --- Money?"

Bess now irritated snapped back, "I don't know. Maybe they count to ten.--one--two--"

On the way to the car, Bess spotted a used bookstore. The brilliant colours of red and green caught her eye as they passed its display window. The proprietor's hard work paid off. Front and centre, Rudolph, with his big red nose, stood on the glossy cover of a children's book. On his left, Frosty gave a friendly wave through his cover of snow. On the right of Rudolph, stood three darling raccoons, wrapped in brightly coloured, woollen scarves. Scattered behind, a collection of books featured Santa Claus, a large, leather bound volume of "Disney's Christmas Stories," and an open book exposed " 'Twas The Night Before Christmas." On a tall shelf at the back of the display, away from the eyes of a child, stood various Christmas titled, pocket books to entice the adult reader. Amongst Binchey, Perry, Higgins Clark and Christie, a little, red book caught Bess's attention.

Recognition lit up Bess's eyes. "I'll be right back."

Before Lydia could react, the door to the store opened and closed. A large hand scooped up the little, red book, and it disappeared from the window. Lydia placed her hand on the brass doorknob at the same time Bess opened it from the inside.

Clutching a small parcel to her breast, Bess's face beamed with excitement. "I've just purchased a 1900's bound edition of 'A Christmas Carol.' "

Back in the car with green shopping bags filled with boxes of Stewart's delights, safely stacked in the cargo space, they headed home. Strains of Christmas music permeated the air waves, as the two tired ladies relaxed and enjoyed the drive. Earlier they decided to take the backroads home; a little longer and slower, but less stressful and leave the freeway to the commuters.

"Strings of street lights, even stoplights, blink a bright red and green, as the shoppers rush home with their treasures---"

"Silver bells, silver bells, it's Christmas time in the city." Lydia and Bess joined Dolly Parton and Kenny Rogers in the rousing chorus, "Ring-a-ling, hear them ring, soon it will be Christmas Day."

While waiting for a red light to change, Lydia asked, "Whose Artie?"

Bess mumbled, "Three, four five, si---" She looked at Lydia. "Don't ask. You wouldn't believe me if I told you."

She immediately began singing along with Bing Crosby, "Let's take that road before us and sing a chorus or two. Come on it's lovely weather for a sleigh ride together with you." She breathed an inward sigh of relief when Lydia joined in, "Giddy-yap,giddy-yap, let's go."

# CHAPTER V

The lock made a clicking sound of metal against metal. She turned the key, and the front door opened. Bess heard the roar of Lydia's engine become fainter as her vehicle turned the corner and sped away into the night. As she bent down to pick up her shopping bags, her coat sleeve rose to reveal her watch. *4:30 --- and already dark; one of the downsides of December,* she thought. Hands already full, she managed to pick up her purse and consequently dropped her keys. *Darn, I should have left the outside light on.* Banging the bags on the door frame, she reached inside and found the light switch. Not only did the lights go on, but the telephone began ringing. *Damn!!* She did a quick look and found the keys beside the welcome mat. *Some welcome,* the sarcastic thought crossed her mind. She slammed the door closed with her shoulder, dropped her stash and ran to the telephone.

Out of breath, she answered, "Hello."

"It's me. I thought I'd better phone to let you know, I will be working late, so don't fix me any supper."

"Oh, Evan. Not another night."

"Sorry, Bess, but Lau & Sons took all day. I have to get some paper work done, and the files are all in the office. I tried to phone you earlier. I hope you haven't started supper."

"Lydia just dropped me off after a day of shopping. You're lucky. I haven't started supper. In fact , I haven't even thought of supper."

"Good then. I'll be home as soon as I can."

"Drive carefully and don't fall asleep driving home," Bess said, as she heard the phone click on Evan's end.

Suddenly feeling very alone, a shiver went through her body. She switched on all the lights and turned up the thermostat. "There, that's better."

An hour later, three green shopping bags had taken up temporary residence in the same spot as yesterday's bags. A hot cup of tea and a grilled cheese sandwich sat on the coffee table. Bess turned on the television and watched the news. Unhappy with the depressing events of the day, she switched channels and settled in to watch a rerun of "Happy Days." Soon bored with Howard chasing Marion around the house, she turned off the television. Not a sound could be heard, except for her occasional sigh. The silence made her feel uneasy. *If only Evan was home, I wouldn't feel so lonely,* she shrugged. *Evan could chase me around the house.* She gave another sigh. *In your dreams, girl.* She thought for a moment, *I know, maybe I need a pet to keep me company.* She looked up at the skylight and saw the spider resting comfortably in his web.

"Oh, good evening, Mr. Spider. I saw the perfect home for you today. Don't worry, I'll not move you tonight." She shook her head. "Yes, I definitely need a pet--- the four legged kind." Bess warned the spider, "Your days are still numbered."

Restless, she looked around the living room and spied the green shopping bags. *Perhaps I should start emptying them,* she thought as she continued to stare at them. Finally she decided *I'm just too tired tonight. I might as well go upstairs and get ready for bed.* Just then a thought struck her *maybe I'll check out the mantel to see where I'll place the new pieces, before I head up to bed.* Without thinking, she quickly got up from the chesterfield, groaned and rubbed her back. She immediately slowed her pace to a bent shuffle and made her way to the mantel. She plugged in the lights. Instantly, her aches and pains faded away as her eyes beheld the wondrous sight in front of her.

Like an architect, she started planning the new development on her street of magic. *I could put Lydia's dress shoppe next to "Tellaway Books." Perhaps, another street off to the left of "Fowler's Meat and Poultry Shoppe"? --- Yes, of course, then I could put the counting house on one corner and the tavern on the other.* She took a step back to picture her imaginary street. Suddenly, her legs felt weary. Bess made her way to the kitchen. She picked up a high-backed barstool, carried it into the living room and placed it in front of the mantel.

After she perched herself on top of the stool, she said, "That's better. Now, where shall I put the carthorse and wagon?" She looked at the street in front of her. Her eyes zeroed in on the window of the antiquarian book shoppe.

Brring! Brring! ------ Brring!

"Darn, not the telephone again." Bess jerked backwards.

"Miss, watch out!"

"Whoa--- Sadie girl," a loud voice rang in Bess's ear.

Bess felt her body falling, falling --- Through the darkness, she heard muffled sounds and a jumble of excited voices, speaking at the same time.

"Neigh!" A warm mist sprayed Bess's face.

Something soft as velvet tickled her nose. "Snort, snort."

Bess opened her eyes and two brown nostrils looked down at her. Startled, she uttered a feeble scream.

"Get back, Sadie," the voice commanded. The nostrils disappeared.

"Miss, are you alright?" another man asked, as he knelt beside her.

"Oh, Uncle Tom, is she dead?" a familiar voice asked.

Upon hearing this voice, Bess turned her head. *Oh my, it's what's his name. --- It's ---*

31

"Bertie," she gasped.

"Miss, yer alive," Bertie's frown turned into a smile.

Bess tried to sit up, but the effort proved too much. She laid back down on the hard surface. *Is it cement?---- Asphalt?* She stretched her fingers across the cold abyss. She must know, as if at that moment, it was the most important thing in the world. *It's flakey, but gritty at the same time.* She gathered a small amount in her fingers and slowly moved her hand to her face.

"It's dirt," she exclaimed.

"Take it easy, miss."

"Here, let me help you up." Two strong arms lifted her off the wet ground.

"What happened?" Bess asked, "Where am I?"

"You've had a terrible fall, miss. You backed off the sidewalk and fell off the curb and landed on the lane," replied her rescuer. "The traffic must have startled you. Luckily, old Jim saw you and managed to stop Sadie before she ran over you."

"Shall I fetch t' doctor, Uncle Tom?" Bertie asked.

"Yes, lad. I'll take her to your mum's. It's starting to rain. Go back to your deliveries, Jim. I'll take care of her."

"Right, Tom. Sorry, miss. I 'ope ye'll be okay," answered Jim. Bess heard the clip clop, clip clop grow fainter.

"Artie, you come with us. I need you to run ahead and keep everyone out of our way," said Tom.

"Aye," shouted Artie, as he ran ahead. "Out of t' way, mate."

Bess felt warm and protected in the cocoon of his strong embrace, as the stranger quickly carried her. "Open the door, Artie." A warm breeze brushed her face as they passed through the doorway. "Pull out that chair by the fireplace, lad." Tom's voice softened as he spoke to Bess, "I'm going to sit you down here, miss. If it's too painful, let me know."

He eased her into the chair. Bess felt a pain shoot up her back and groaned. She repositioned her body and the pain subsided. A sudden burst of intense heat caused her eyes to open. Blurred shadows danced in front of her. Waves of red, throbbed through her head. The red started to take shape, until finally, a bed of red hot coals came into focus.

"Coals," she gasped aloud and then thought *a real live coal fireplace. I haven't seen one of these since I was a kid.*

"Miss, are you cold?" Tom asked. "Artie, put some more coal on the fire."

Bess heard the scraping of metal and then saw a small hand, holding a shovel, throw its contents onto the red fire. Sparks flew as the cold coal settled into the hot embers. Her mind still whirling, she became aware of voices and movement around her.

"Uncle Tom, t' doctor's right behind me."

"Out of the way, folks. Let me have a look at the young lady," a mature voice demanded. "Miss, where do you hurt?" the doctor asked as he felt her pulse and proceeded to open her eyelids.

She felt his hands prod her neck, move down to her arms, back and end with her legs. Except for the pain in her back, she felt numb. Returning to her back, he manipulated his fingers up and down her spine.

"Nothing broken. I feel you have given your tailbone a nasty whack, and the fall jarred your body. You are going to be quite stiff and sore for a few days, but you are young, so will mend quickly. I'll give you a small amount of laudanum to dull the pain. Take it only when necessary." He smiled and winked at her. "Could we have a cup of tea for the patient, Mrs. Morton?"

Bess heard the swishing of fabric. A woman's hand appeared, as it put a steaming cup of tea on the table beside her.

"Drink this, my dear," the demanding voice softened.

Bess took a sip of the strong, black tea. A few more sips and her head started to clear. She looked up at the face that belonged to the demanding voice. Surprised, Bess saw a man in his fifties. *My age,* she thought, *but with all that facial hair, it is hard to tell for sure. Don't they call them mutton chops? He looks like he just stepped out of my great-grandparents' photograph album.*

For the first time, she looked around the room. The dark room, perhaps 15 by 15 feet, being poorly lit, made it difficult to ascertain its correct size. The dark, wood-paneled walls did nothing to improve the light. A large, red brick fireplace surrounded the bed of hot coals. Off to the right of the fire pit, the black shovel stood leaning against a large wooden box. To the left, a set of sturdy, iron tongs and poker stood upright beside a large bellows. A number of small tables, covered in white linen tablecloths, dotted the wood-planked flooring. Just about to turn around in the opposite direction, Bess jumped when the doctor spoke.

"Miss, your colour is coming back. I'll be off then. You have a good night's sleep. If in the morning, the pain is unbearable, one of the lads can come round, and I'll give him some more laudanum for you." He took her hand and said, "Goodnight, miss." He put on his top hat and slightly raised it, "Mrs. Morton, Tom," and walked to the door, where Artie and Bertie stood with the door open. "Thank you, lads."

After the doctor left, they all hovered around Bess.

"Oh, ye do look tired, miss. Tom, take 'er upstairs. She can lay down on t' bed in t' vacant bedroom fer awhile," Mrs. Morton said.

Bess tried to get up, but felt weak and fell back down on the chair.

"It must be the laudanum working on you. Here put your arms around my neck and I'll carry you," Tom said.

"Apples and pears, I'll beat ye up 'em," the boys said in unison as they ran up the stairs.

Tom gently laid her on the four-poster bed. The mattress felt like a bed of feathers as she nestled into its surface. It almost felt as good as Tom's arms around her, so she reluctantly slipped out of his grasp. Bess felt little hands unlace her shoes and pull them off her swollen feet. She opened her eyes and saw the two boys exam her shoes. She heard them whispering as they pointed at her feet.

"You go to sleep now, miss," Tom's gentle voice whispered.

Bess opened her eyes and looked into his beautiful, brown eyes. "Bess," she whispered. "My name's Bess."

"Glad to meet you, Bess." He took her hand in his and said, "Tom,--- Tom Evans."

"Bess N--ike," Bertie boldly piped up.

They both looked at Bertie, who moved to the edge of the bed, still holding one of her shoes. Artie stood beside Bertie, holding her other shoe.

"See," Bertie pointed as he turned the shoe around to expose the back of the heel, "N--ike, --l--ike b--ike, M--ike.---- Right, Artie?" He looked at Artie for confirmation.

"T'is right, 'cause sumone checked it. See." Artie pointed to the check mark on the side of the shoe.

Bess was speechless.

"Me mum always writes me name on all me clothes too."

"Goodnight, Bess N--ike," she heard echo, as she closed her eyes.

"Bess,-- Bess,-- Wake up," a familiar voice echoed in her ear, as a large hand gently shook her. The hand became stronger. "Bess, wake up."

She opened her eyes. "Oh, it's you, Evan."

"Sorry to disappoint you; I'm not that handsome stranger you were dreaming about," Evan laughed. "What are you doing sitting on the barstool in the middle of the living room?" He moved his head and looked at the mantel. "Where did this come from? What a great display. Where did you get it? Was that what was in those shopping bags on the floor, last night?" He looked in the direction of yesterday's bags and said, "No, I guess not. They're still here. Bess, have you been keeping them secret from me? Bess?" He turned and faced her, but realized she had fallen back to sleep. "Come on, old girl, I'll put you to bed. ----- Upsy daisy." He put his arm around her and got her mobile.

"Ooh," she groaned as she moved her body. Somehow it felt like she had fallen again. *It must be that I was sitting in one position too long. Yes, of course,* she thought.

"Bess, what's the matter? You're moving like you just got run over by a horse."

Bess's eyes flew wide open. In a moment she regained her composure and said, "I took a nasty fall backwards this morning."

"Oh, my darling Bess, you must be careful. Lean on me and I'll help you upstairs."

"Apples and pears," she giggled, as she put her weight on Evan.

"How many pain killers did you take? You sound like you're on something." Evan shook his head and held her tighter. "Come on old girl, just a couple more steps."

# CHAPTER VI

The bed never felt so soft. Bess felt her body floating on a cloud of fluffy, white feathers. In the distance, she heard her name being called, but didn't want to answer. *Leave me alone. I want to lie here forever,* she repeated over and over to herself.

"Bess, ---- Bess, dear, wake up." Evan gently tapped her shoulder.

She opened her eyes to discover Evan looking down at her. "At least your nostrils aren't snorting."

"Pardon?" Evan looked puzzled. "Boy, that must have been some pill you took last night. Did Lydia give you one from her stash? Honestly, Bess, I know she's your friend, but you must be careful with her. When you two get together, Lord knows what trouble she will get you into."

"Lighten up, Evan. Lydia didn't give me any medicine. I just had a strange dream. I'm awake now. --- What do you want?" She raised her head and groaned.

"That's why I woke you. Before I leave for work, I thought I would rub some liniment on your back. When I undressed you and put you in your pyjamas, I noticed a nasty bruise on your back."

Bess nodded and sat up in bed. "Thanks, Evan. I'm sure it would do the trick, but I would rather get up." She stood up and started to walk. "Boy do I feel stiff. Perhaps the heating pad will help loosen the joints."

"Steady, old girl. I'll help you downstairs." Evan took her arm. When they finally made it down, he helped her onto the chesterfield and said, "I'll just rush upstairs and get the heating pad and liniment ." At the top of the stairs, he shouted, "Would you like a cup of tea?"

"Yes, thank you, Evan, that would be nice. You're too kind to me," and whispered to herself, "Maybe I should fall head over heels backward more often." She laughed and then immediately groaned, "Maybe not."

Evan's hands gently rubbed the liniment on her back. The warmth of the heating pad seemed to loosen her strained muscles.

"Keep the heating pad on and let the liniment seep deep into your muscles. I have to go to work now, but I'll get you another cup of tea before I go." Evan gave her red bottom a little smack. "Take it easy today. I should be home early tonight, so I'll pick up something for supper."

Bess said goodbye to Evan and laid back on the heating pad. She could smell the strong odour of menthol and something else she could not discern. But at that moment, it did not matter that Evan hadn't used the odourless liniment. The pad felt so warm and soothing. She looked up at the ceiling and noticed Mr. Spider busy spinning his web. He mesmerized her with his precision and diligence. Her eyes felt heavy. Moments before she succumbed to slumber, she shifted her body to face the mantel.

What seemed like a lifetime of slumber, turned out to be only a moment. Bess had switched her body back and now laid stretched out on her back. She noticed Mr. Spider, still hard at work. Suddenly, her eyes opened wide. Something was different. *What happened to the skylight?* The ceiling, a solid mass of wooden planks, interspersed with beams of rough timber, lay suspended above her.

"Mum, she's awake," a familiar voice shouted, as Bess heard footsteps running away. "Cum quick!--- 'Urry, Mum."

Bess heard footsteps creaking up the stairs. "Shush, Bertie, I can 'ear ye, so can t' rest of bloomin' London." The footsteps came closer and with a heavy breath, the woman's voice continued, "Good mornin', luv. 'Ow ar' ye feelin' today?" Bess moved slightly and gave out a small groan, while the woman looked concerned. "Tsk, tsk, still a little sore, ar' we? I'll go downstairs an' fetch ye a cuppa tea. That should do t' trick. Nuthin' like a spot of tea to make ye feel better." The woman turned around and a black mass of material exited the room.

Bess looked around the tiny room. She could barely make out a dresser on one wall, a nightstand on the right of the bed and a wooden chair in the corner. From what she could see, the room, about 8 by 12 feet, left little space for anything else. The only light in the room streamed in through the narrow opening, of the heavy drapes. She heard a distant ringing of church bells.

"T''is t' bells of St. Mary-Le-Bow. Ye can 'ear 'em all over London." Bertie moved closer to Bess. "Did ye sleep alright, miss? I've bin waitin' fer 'ours fer ye to wake up. Uncle Tom told me to watch out fer ye an' I did. Do ye need any medicine? I could go fetch it from Doc Morgan."

"Bertie, don't bother t' young lady. 'Ere, miss, a nice cup of 'ot tea." Bertie's mum poured a cup for herself and put the teapot down on the nightstand. "Good heavens. T''is a wonder ye can see t' cup. 'Ere, I'll pull t' drapes back."

She put down the teacup and quickly moved to the small window. Bess heard the swishing noise. As soon as the drapes opened, Bess saw the woman's form in front of the grey light, coming through the window.The woman wore a maroon coloured, long dress, full in the skirt, but tight fitting around the waist and bodice. She had a black and white tweed shawl draped around her shoulders. As she came closer, Bess noticed the shawl had a deep-red thread running through the fabric. Bess took the woman to be in her early thirties. Her brown hair, severely pulled back in a bun, shrouded in a hairnet, made her possibly look older. She came over and stood beside the bed, a rather large four-poster for such a small room.

She gave Bess a lovely smile, and her large, brown eyes sparkled as she said, "There, t'is better, although t' dreary days of December don't bring in 'auff t' light it should. Mind ye, t' fog, 'owever unpleasant, gives more light than those dark rain clouds. Both ar' so damp. It goes right to t' bones." She shivered and pulled her shawl tighter to her ample bosom. " Take a sip of tea, luv; it will warm thee." She handed the cup to Bess. "Sorry we don't 'ave a fire in t'is 'ere room. I put a hot brick in yer bed earlier, when ye were sleepin'. I'll go down an' get another fer ye." She turned to move towards the door.

"No, please don't bother. I'm fine," Bess said.

The woman turned around and looked at Bess. "Bertie, luv, get me t' chair."

Bertie,who had been standing quietly in the corner, ran across the room, picked up the heavy chair and struggled with it, until he deposited it beside the bed. " 'Ere, Mum."

"Thank ye, Bertie. Yer gettin' so big an' strong." She smiled at her son. " I might as well pour another cup fer meself."

Bess hadn't noticed the second cup on the tray until the drapes were opened. Now she could see the walls of flocked paper and a small wardrobe in the far corner. A small miniature, surrounded by a gilded frame, hung in the centre of the pink flowered paper. *What are they: peonies or roses?* thought Bess. She heard the rustling of the woman's dress as she sat down. On a closer look, Bess discovered the dress was made of taffeta. A cameo brooch, pinned on the lapel of her collar, stood out against the dark maroon colour of her dress.

"Aye, I see ye noticed me brooch. T'is a treasure. Mr. Brown, t' baker, gave it to me. ---Aah--- fer bein' such a good customer an' all." Bess thought she saw the woman blush. The woman quickly changed the subject, " 'Ere, we ar' 'avin' a cupper an' we 'aven't bin introduced. Me name's Lottie Morton, an' t'is 'ere lad's me son, Bertie."

"'Er name's Bess N-ike, Mum," interrupted a smiling Bertie. "We's bin introw -- duced before, Mum."

"Yes, we have Bertie." Bess smiled. "Nice to meet you, Mrs. Morton, and thank you for taking such good care of a stranger."

"Call me Lottie, Miss N-ike."

"Bess, please."

Lottie smiled and then looked her straight in the eye, "Tell me, Bess, where ar' ye from then? Although ye 'aven't said much, ye don't sound like yer from 'ere. I mean England that is.?"

Dead silence enveloped the room. Even the noisy street sounds went dead. Time literally stood still, as Bess thought of an answer. She saw the attentive looks on Lottie's and Bertie's faces. *What should I say?*

Finally, Bess managed, what she thought to be a noncommittal answer, "How observant of you. Yes,--er-- I mean no, I am not from here."

"Well, where yer from then?" Bertie persisted.

Speechless again, Bess tried to open her mouth. Suddenly it had become very dry. Fortunately for Bess, Bertie's mind travelled a mile a minute, and he did not wait for a reply.

"I knows. Yer from America. Ain't ye, miss?" Bess nodded, as he continued, "Aye, t'is excitin'. We'd never known anyone from America. Wait till I tell Artie." He stopped jumping up and down and thought for a moment. "'Ow'd ye get 'ere then? 'Ow long did it take?" Bertie's big, brown eyes searched her face for an answer.

"That'll do, Bertie. She needs 'er rest. Ye can talk to 'er later," Lottie scolded her son. Turning to Bess, she said, "Ye can rest as long as ye like. An' if ye feel up to it later, cum downstairs. I'll 'ave sum nice scones bakin' in about an 'our." She got up to leave and as she reached the doorway, she turned back at Bess as if she forgot something, "Oh, I've hung up a clean dress in t' wardrobe. I think ye'll fit into it. Yer-- aah-- clothes were dirty. I gave 'em to Artie to take 'ome to 'is mum. Mrs. Doyle does clothes washin'. 'Every little bit of dirt 'elps,' so she says." She laughed. "Cum on, Bertie." She motioned to him. " Don't worry, t' lads only took off yer shoes. I came up later an' took off yer odd-er--dirty clothes."

The room became silent. Bess tried to arrange her thoughts *I can't tell them who I am, where I'm from or how I got here. I must be very diplomatic; they wouldn't understand. --- Darn ---- I don't understand.*

Distant sounds could be heard through the leaded window, unfamiliar sounds of traffic and shouting. *I must get up and look out the window.* Instead, she put her head down on the feather pillow and closed her eyes. She smelt the scent of lavender as she pressed her face into the pillowcase.

The scent of lavender became stronger. She wondered *what could be the other scent?* Bess moved her head away from the pillow, but still the scent grew stronger. *Lavender and --- peppermint? No, too strong. --- Menthol?* She opened her eyes. On the coffee table, she saw the bottle of liniment. *Where did Evan ever find this old bottle?* She reached over and looked at its label, circled in red: *'A pleasant scent of lavender.' Yah, right,* she thought.

Now aware of her familiar surroundings, she forced herself off the chesterfield. Bess unplugged the overworked heating pad and shuffled into the kitchen. All that time on the heating pad paid off; she actually felt pretty good. Her stomach growled. Immediately the cupboard door opened to display a variety of cereals. She couldn't decide on one, so she put a smorgasbord of cold cereals in a large bowl. Today there was plenty of milk on hand, so a generous amount filled the bowl to overflowing. Bess wiped up the excess milk off the counter and plugged in the kettle for tea. She looked at the clock. *My heavens, it's eleven, and I'm still in my pyjamas.*

Half an hour later, washed and dressed and her stomach full, Bess felt quite human. Taking her second cup of tea into the living room, she noticed her bags of shopping from yesterday. Enthusiastically, she opened the boxes one by one, until all thirteen items were crowded on the coffee table. Moving the tea-cup to make more room, Bess realized not a drop had been drunk. She had been too engrossed in her task at hand.

As she looked at the table and then back at the mantel, she thought *luckily, the mantel is very long and has a good depth.* Bess picked up the counting house and studied its stark brick and plaster front. Tiny windows surrounded an unwelcome, wooden door. A large sign, extending the width of the building, "W.H. Turner, Counting House," made her laugh. *Evan would not appreciate the humdrum of going to work in a place like that every day. The slave driver's name may not sit too well with him either.* She reassured herself *however, he will see the humour in it. Besides, Scrooge is his hero.* She puzzled about it for a moment, then put it back down on the table.

Bess picked up the Victorian house and thought *yes, I'll put this next to the bookstore. I do like the large bay window, on the right side of the building.* She placed it on the mantel, stood back and reached behind for the next building. Her right hand wrapped firmly around a tall, narrow jut-out on a building, and she picked it up. As it came in view, she noticed her hand had a solid grasp on the bell tower of "Firehall Nbr. 8." The striking, red brick building, complete with wobbly ladders, buckets and hoses, impressed her.

*I do want to show them off, but I'm running out of room.* Bess turned around and looked at the coffee table full of buildings. *I still have four more buildings. Darn, what am I going to do?* With a puzzled look, she studied the mantel and then the buildings. Back and forth, her head moved. Finally a smile erased the puzzled look. *I know.*

Fifteen minutes later, satisfied with her accomplishment, she stood back to take in her artistry. Between the Victorian house and the firehall, a magical opening separated them. The bay window looked onto a cobblestone street, and across the street stood the firehall, positioned perilously close to the mantel's edge. Tucked behind the firehall, loomed a tall, drab building. A similar layout stood at the opposite end of the mantel. There were now two side streets, giving the illusion of more buildings and streets behind. With enough depth on the mantel, she managed to place the towns people and carriages in front of the buildings. She made a special point of placing the cart, driver and his horse and a lamp-post in front of the bookstore.

"I'm not going to make the same mistake twice." Bess turned around and picked up the empty boxes.

Finding room in the storage cupboard, she stacked them on top of each other, until the cupboard door barely closed. She made herself a cup of tea, took a couple of cookies out of their box and went back to the living room. Tea in one hand and cookies in the other, Bess managed to plug in the lights. She deposited her back-side on the barstool and sat back to bask in her creation.

The teacup rattled. As if in a dream, a light beckoned her near. She walked towards the obscure ray of light coming from the window. When Bess reached the window, she could not see out. *Something in the way,* she thought and put her hands out in front of her. Bess's knee banged against a solid object. As she pushed down on it, she felt a slight give. Still mesmerized by the light, her body took over, and automatically her knees bent and rested on the rough object. A cold draught made her shiver. She touched the windowpane. Immediately her hand recoiled, leaving behind a wet palm print.

"Oh, it's so cold," Bess shivered. *I haven't felt this sensation since I was a child. The seal must be broken. Another job for Evan.*

Still the light's hypnotic power beckoned her nearer. Her fingers searched the rough, wooden frame. A small metal clasp freed the window from its inward confines and exposed it to the outside world. A vapour of cold air rushed in causing her to gasp. At the same moment, the world outside came thundering in. The undistinguishable sounds almost made her close the window, but slowly, she poked her head outside. Through the fog, she barely made out the view. A building loomed in front; ghostly movements swayed in and out of the fog. Focusing her attention on the muffled noises, Bess lowered her head, but still she could not make out the sounds. Opening the window further, and supporting her body with her hands, she leaned out. The fog kept moving in drifts, but finally she saw a clearing below.

"Clop, clop."

"Pa-a-par! Ainy of t' mornin' pipers," a shrill voice echoed through the fog.

"Red 'ot chestnuts! --- 'Ot coffee t' warm ye on a cooold dye."

"Clop, clop -- Ring, ring, -- Neigh -- Clop, clop."

The all too familiar sounds awakened her senses. She strained her eyes, and through the fog, she made out a hoof, a leg, another hoof, another leg, a body.

"Oh my," Bess said, as she quickly withdrew her head, grabbed the frame and closed the window.

She turned away from the window, and her knees buckled into a sitting position. The cold air soon took the numbness away. Bess began focusing on her surroundings. Her hands were spread out on either side of her thighs. She looked down to notice they lay on top of a dark-green, tapestry pillow. Her feet dangled in front, while her back stood upright, warding off the cold chill from the window. *Ah, that's what I bumped into, a window seat,* she thought back. Looking forward, Bess noticed a familiarity about the room, flocked wallpaper.

"Peonies or roses?" Her eyes opened wider with recognition. "Oh, no, here I am again." She looked around and stopped when she saw the ornate wardrobe. "Well, Bess old girl, it's time we enjoyed this adventure, we've got ourselves into."

She slipped off the window seat, walked over to the wardrobe and opened the door. The door creaked. An aroma of lavender and furniture polish assailed her nostrils. Inside the closet, hung a single dark-blue dress. As she reached forward and touched it, she felt the loose, woollen threads and found them surprisingly soft. She slipped it off its wooden hanger and placed it on the bed. Searching in the dresser drawers, she spied a long, cotton petticoat, something she thought must be bloomers, and a couple of other things she wasn't quite sure of. Bess looked down at her own clothes, which looked so comfortable. *But the less attention paid to me, the better,* she reasoned. She quickly took off her shoes, pants and warm sweat shirt, but stopped at her undergarments.

"Hey, with all these layers, no one will know."

Exhausted after fifteen minutes of layering her body in unfamiliar attire, she breathed a sigh of relief. *Thank God, I didn't have to put on a corset and lace myself up; I'd be in a fine mess.* She giggled. *Mind you, all those buttons up the back may not be in alignment. Come to think of it, neither is my back.*

She looked around and found a woollen shawl, draped across a chair. *This will hide the buttons and keep me warm to boot. Speaking of boots, I'm wearing my N --- ikes.* Thinking of Bertie, Bess smiled. *The dress will cover them.*

She looked at herself in the mirror, hanging on the inside of the heavy, wardrobe door. A slightly, amber-tinted image looked back at her. Swishing her dress from side to side, front to back, Bess decided she could almost pass as a native, except for the hair. Unfortunately, her hair had not transformed into long flowing ringlets. Sighing, she ran her fingers through her blond hair. *At least the grey didn't come along for the ride,* she mused.

Bess opened the door and stepped out into the dimly lit hallway.

"Dickens World. -----Here I Come."

# CHAPTER VII

*E*ach tread creaked as Bess made her way down two flights of stairs. She hung onto the smooth, wooden banister; afraid she would trip on her long dress. On each landing, a small, narrow window afforded a faint glimmer of light to guide her way. Encouraged by the pleasant smell of baking, downward she went, one step, one stair at a time. Straight ahead, she saw her destination getting brighter. Her steps moved a little faster towards the light. Suddenly Bess stopped. Below, a voice sang out in joyous song.

"The tea! ----- The tea! ------ The wholesome tea!
The black, the green, the mix'd, the good, the strong Bohea!
For it's good for the nerves, and warms my heart,
And Death, ----- whenever he comes to me,
Will find me ------ drinking a good strong cup of tea ----- "

Bess smiled and made her way down the last few steps.

"The tea ----- The tea --- Oooh, Bess." Lottie stopped in mid-note. "Oh, ye must be feelin' better, luv. Cum 'ere and sit ye down." Lottie rushed over and pulled out a chair. "Such a dreadful amount of stairs an' ye on t' top floor. Ye poor thing. Let me get ye a cup of tea."

Lottie rushed off before Bess could say a word. She looked

around the room. The fog brought a brightness to the room that had been lacking the night before. The room, much larger in the daylight, had at least a dozen tables arranged around it. Upon each table, covered with a white, linen tablecloth, blue and white china teacups surrounded a small vase holding a single, elegant flower, The mantel, high above the huge fireplace opening, displayed a lovely assortment of decorative plates. A sturdy set of brass and-irons stood guard beside the roaring fire. On either side of the fireplace, a colourful painting of flowers hung suspended from a narrow railing close to the ceiling. The delicate, brass chains glistened as they held their precious cargo securely in place. The dark, wall paneling brought out the rich shades of the flowers, giving them a three dimensional perception. Below the left painting, a large, open-faced dresser exposed stacks of blue and white plates and sparkling cutlery, laid out on a deep-blue, velvet runner.

Turning around towards the front windows, she noticed two small tables, strategically placed in the recesses of the two bay windows. *Nice touch,* she thought. Delicate, white lace-curtains framed the leaded windows, while deep-blue, velvet drapes hung on the sides. On the right wall, a similar dressed, but much smaller window, brought light into the room. A pretty blue and white wall paper of wisteria blooms, covered the two side walls. Tucked into the far end of the wall, close to the fireplace, an upright piano stood silent. The opposite wall, a small counter separated the dining area from what looked to be a door leading to the kitchen. Bess looked closer to see what the sign behind the counter said, when suddenly, Lottie came through the doorway laden with a tray of goodies.

"Sorry to be so long, but I 'ad a batch of scones in t' oven. Didn't want 'em to burn, ye know." A red cheeked Lottie giggled, as she brought the bounty to the table. "Excuse t' Brown Betty, but since it bein' just t' two of us. Owlde Betty makes a much better cupper than those there fancy snouts." Lottie pointed over to the row of fine china teapots, lined up on a shelf behind the counter. She poured two cups of steaming, golden brown liquid, gave one to Bess and set the other one down for herself. "Milk 'n' sugar, luv?" She placed a plate of warm scones in front of them. "Hmm, they smell good. Nuffin like t' smell of bakin' just out of t' oven." She inhaled and slowly exhaled. Lottie turned to Bess, "Now, luv, 'owd'ye?" Staring at Bess for a reply, she finally smiled and said very slowly, "How--are--you?"

Now aware of Lottie's question, Bess replied, "Much better, thank you. A good night's sleep on your feather bed did the trick."

"Trick?"

"Made me right as rain."

"Right as rain?"

"Much better, thank you," Bess hoped this would save anymore clichés.

"We were very worried about ye, Bess. Ye took a nasty fall. Thank heaven, owlde Sadie didn't run over ye. Traffic is so bad in t' streets these days. Ev'ry way ye look, carts, carriages, cabs. 'Eaven forbid if it were an omnibus." Lottie looked at a puzzled Bess. "Sorry, luv, I think ye call 'em stagecoaches." Lottie smiled and Bess returned the smile for a different reason. Moving closer, Lottie asked, "Now tell me, luv, ar' ye married? I see ye 'ave a ring on yer finger."

Bess looked down at her left hand. *Oh Lord, what am I going to say? If I say yes, I may have more questions asked than I can answer. I can't take my ring off. It just wouldn't be right. Think woman!* After an agonizing length of silence on her part, Bess said to herself *forgive me, Evan.* She crossed the fingers on her right hand, conveniently positioned behind her back.

"No," Bess blurted out. "This was my mother's wedding ring." Having the initial lie completed, she took a deep breath and let the blarney flow. "She wanted me to have it. Being so young when she died, I just slipped it on my left finger. You see, she never wore any other rings, so I just assumed that was where I should wear it. Since my father had died the year before, he didn't object. Eventually, I didn't even notice it anymore."

"Oh, ye poor dear. Ye were an orfunt, then. 'Ow sad." Lottie gently patted her hand. "Yes, of course, it makes perfect sense. Wot a good daughter." She smiled. "Well, I mus'int stop any longer. T' shoppe will be openin' soon an' t' tarts 'ave to go in t' oven." Lottie took a last swallow of tea and moved her chair from the table. She began to position her body in the upright position.

"Lottie, can I help?" Bess asked.

"No, luv, ye take it easy. Finish yer tea. Yer welcome to stay 'ere as long as ye like." Lottie smiled and made her way to the kitchen. She turned back at Bess and said, "Go up to yer room an' rest. We'll 'ave a nice long chat later."

"You're very kind. I'll just sit here for awhile," Bess replied.

Bess watched Lottie pass through the doorway to the kitchen. As she removed her hand from behind her back, she released her crossed fingers and breathed a sigh of relief. With a guilty pang, she thought of her bedroom dresser and tucked way in the back of the drawer, the little, gold box containing her mother's wedding ring.

Bess heard Lottie singing in the kitchen. She picked up the remaining dishes and made her way to the doorway. A large off-white, muslin apron completely covered the front of Lottie's ample bodice and full skirt. Flour covered her long sleeves and powdered her face. Drifts of flour lay spread across the flagstone floor. A large cast-iron stove stood along the back brick wall. Two long, narrow windows added light and ventilation to a very warm room. As Bess walked into the kitchen, she felt the intense heat from the stove. Looking around, she found a cleared counter space, laid the tray of dirty dishes on it and turned around.

"Here, let me wash these up for you," she said as she continued to look around for a sink. Finally, she spied a single tap. Directly below it stood a wooden cupboard. *Strange,* she thought. On closer inspection, Bess found a stone sink hidden within the cupboard's counter.

"Thank ye, luv. Fetch that bucket on t' drainin' board an' fill it wit' boilin' water." Lottie noticed Bess looking perplexed. "T' boiler is on t' left of t' stove.---- See t' tap on t' bottom. Draw off t' 'ot water.---- That's it. Mind ye don't scald yersclf. I just bought a new cover fer t' drain, so don't worry about t' water escapin' when ye pour t' 'ot water in t' sink." She thought for a moment and said, "Ar' ye sure ye can manage it? If it's too 'ard on yer back put it down an' I'll get t' water fer ye."

"No, I'm sure I'll be fine."

Bess managed to fill the metal bucket without scalding herself. The heavy bucket almost wrenched her arm out of its socket as she carried it over to the sink, but she didn't want to bother Lottie. She knew the discomfort would go away. Besides, she was quite proud of herself for not spilling a drop of the scalding water. However, lifting the bucket up to the sink presented another challenge. With a burst of energy, she heaved it up to the side of the sink and tipped it in. Steam escaped in all directions, leaving much of it rolling down her face.

"Bess, luv, add sum cold water from t' tap before ye melt away," Lottie laughed. "That reminds me, I must draw sum water from t' tap. The city water works will be turnin' off t' water soon. We only get a few 'ours a day of water before they turn off t' supply. I 'eard ye get endless 'ours in America. Must be nice. Not that I'm complainin'. It wasn't long ago, we had to fetch t' water out of t' cistern outside. 'Ard work and time consumin' it was."

Bess turned on the tap. It emitted a flow of murky water. She immediately turned it off.

"Don't worry. T' 'ot water will kill t' germs from t' tap water. Use a wee bit of t'is 'ere soap. --- Soap is so expensive, even though they've lowered t' soap tax. I usually make me own. Ye know they tax us to death 'ere. Wot about in America?"

"That they do." Bess laughed and thought to herself *some things never change*. She washed and dried all the dirty dishes she could find. She placed the wet towel on the drying rack by the stove. "Is it alright to pull the stopper off the drain?"

"Oh yes, luv. I 'ad a pipe installed to take t' water outside to t' cesspool.-- Don't frown. Mr. Stewart, a special undertaker, cums ev'ry Tuesday night an' cleans it out. ---- Now, I must get t' urns an' fill 'em up wit' water. If ye like Bess, ye can ladle t' water from t'is urn into t' kettles. --- Mind not to get too close to t' bottom; sediment settles there. After yer finished, I'll clean out t' urn an' pour t' sediment down t' sink, so I can fill it wit' more water from t' tap. In t' meantime, I'll start fillin' t' other urns, cause it takes sum time fer t' murky water to clear before I can collect t' clear water an' then boil it. I always boil all our drinkin' water before usin' it; can't take any chances. All London's water is piped from t' Thames, and Lord only knows wot's bin dumped in there. Fer our washin' up water, I 'ad a special water pipe put in right to t' boiler, so I don't 'ave to fill it by 'and anymore, just turn on t'is tap. Now, I only 'ave to clean out t' bottom ev'ry night." She pointed to a small spigot, located under the boiler. "Mr. Brown is always gettin' me t' latest inventions. 'E's a kind an' generous man, --- a good friend." Lottie smiled as her face lit up. "Now, Bess, ye go an' rest. I must tidy up. Me customers will be knockin' t' door down any minute."

Walking through the doorway leading to the dining room, Bess noticed a few large leaves lying on the floor next to the front entrance. Being a gardener by heart, she went directly over to pick them up and discovered they belonged to a sickly houseplant. Housed in a pumpkin-shaped, ceramic pot, it sat on a small table covered in a blue, chenille cloth. *Hmm, what plant is this?*

"I just don't know wot's wrong wit' me aspidistra. Mrs. Pennycroft, a good customer indeed, gave me t'is plant last Christmas. I was ever so pleased to receive it. All t' fancy folks 'ave 'em in their parlours. I thought if I 'ad it by the door, all me customers would think wot a posh establishment I 'ad 'ere," Lottie tsked. --- "Oh, 'ere she is now." She quickly opened the door as a soft jingle announced the first customer of the day. "Good morning, Mrs. Pennycroft. You're here early today." Lottie said slowly and precisely.

"Good morning, Mrs. Morton." The middle-aged woman entered the tea shoppe and looked around, stopping at Bess. "My, who do we have here? A new helper?"

"How do you do?" Bess extended a hand. "My name's Bess, aah, Bess N-ike. I sort of dropped in to see Mrs. Morton."

Reluctantly, the lady extended her limp hand. "Miss N-ike, that is an odd name. Where are you from? You don't sound like you are from here." The white haired lady looked Bess up and down and focused on her hair. "You do not look like you are from here either."

Coming to the rescue, Lottie said, "Mrs. Pennycroft, Miss N-ike is from America."

"Well, that makes perfect sense then," the lady said and turned towards a table. "I'll have a pot of Bohea and a scone. A strong cup of black tea will do my bones good on this damp, foggy day."

Lottie gave Bess a "Yes, Madam" look and proceeded to the kitchen. Whilst en route, she dislodged the iron teapot, door stopper, thus closing the door behind her. Left in the room alone with Madam, Bess looked for an escape route.

"Miss N-ike, such a strange name. Come sit and tell me about America." Mrs. Pennycroft waited until Bess sat down and started drilling her again. "When did you arrive? I hear The Malisking or was it The Malisqueen docked in Southampton a fortnight ago. A fine ship, so I have been told. Did you enjoy the journey?" The jingle of the door interrupted the interrogation. "Oh, Mrs. Willmot, do come and join us." She waved the large woman, wrapped in an enormous dark-green, brocade dress, over to her table. As the new woman enveloped the dainty chair, she took off her gloves and Mrs. Pennycroft continued, "Mrs. Willmot, this is Miss N-ike. She just arrived on the Malisprince, from America."

As Mrs. Willmot untied her green bonnet, she said, "Miss

N-ike, that is a strange name. America you say? They do have strange names there."

At this point, Bess excused herself. She smiled when she heard the two ladies whispering.

"Must be an Indian name.---- Did you see her hair?"

"Oh, you don't suppose they tried to scalp her?"

Leaving the two ladies deep in conversation, Bess wandered over to the piano. She sat down on the round stool, upholstered in a tapestry of the nine muses. Surprisingly, the small, sturdy stool, supported by four bowed legs, felt quite comfortable. She placed her hands on the keys and began playing. She played softly enough not to disturb the ladies, but loud enough to drown out their conversation.

At an early age, Bess learned to play the piano. Fortunately, she enjoyed it and continued to play it almost every day. The past few days she had neglected her piano, so it took her no time to lose herself in her music. Engrossed in "White Christmas," she felt a tap on her shoulder.

A smiling face looked down at her and said, "Oh, what a lovely piece. Is it new?--- No, don't stop, my dear." The face disappeared, leaving a scent of rose water in the air.

Glancing around, Bess noticed at least half a dozen tables full of teapots and ladies dressed in brocades, wools, silks and taffetas of deep-greens, blues and blacks. Some had their hair in buns, twists and ringlets, while others preferred to wear their bonnets, which hid most of their faces. Throughout all the vocal activity, Bess saw Lottie skilfully carry trays of goodies, whilst stopping to chat and laugh with her customers. Bess continued to play, receiving positive comments on her choice of music, until Lottie finally broke her concentration.

"Bess, luv, yer marvelous. I 'aven't seen 'em drink, eat an' linger, then drink 'n' eat sum more like that before. Yer good fer business. We must talk later. In t' meantime, let's 'ave sum tea, before t' afternoon tea crowd arrives."

Bess turned around and noticed the place empty, except for tables laden with dirty dishes. "Let me help you clean up."

Lottie looked at the dirty dishes and sighed. "Okay, luv, just t'is once. Ye bring out t' dishes. Mind, don't ye 'urt yerself. I'll pour t' 'ot water fer washin' up. Between us, we'll get 'em done and still 'ave time fer tea before I start another batch of scones. Ye'd think it be quiet 'ere wit' t' fog so nasty, but t' rich folk ar' out shoppin' fer Christmas presents. That reminds me, I'll be startin' me mince-meat tomorrow. 'Ere, I'll put t' door stopper back to work."

Lottie bent over, exposing a doorway full of maroon taffeta. The taffeta began singing a merry song.

"Let's be merry------
We'll have tea and toast------
An ---- endless host of syllabubs
And jellies---- and mince-pies----
And other such lady-like luxuries----"

Jingle, jingle---- A rush of cold air made the two ladies shiver.

Slam!--- Turning around they met a stampede of four rosy cheeks.

"Mum, we're 'ungry. Wot yer got?"

"Bertie, 'ow many times 'ave I told ye? Cum in through t' back door. Blimey, there could be customers in 'ere," she scolded. "Ye two lads, don't ye run in t' 'ouse."

"Good dye, Miss N-ike," Bertie and Artie said in unison, as they doffed their caps and quickened their steps into the kitchen.

"Wot ever 'appened to yer lunch, I sent ye off wit' t'is mornin'?"

"Blimey, that yob, Percy Evans took it, 'e did. Innit so Artie?"

"Aye, Mrs. Morton, t'is so." Artie looked at her with large innocent eyes. "'Im's a bad bloke. 'Im's one of those orfunts."

"I were just about to smack 'im in t' snout, when teacher came," Bertie said as his little fists clenched. "Blimey, I were."

"Bertie, mind yer tongue. Where do ye pick up those words?"

Lottie turned to Bess. "Ye teach 'em proper English an' then they go outside an' get corrupted, they do. Those sly Cockneys. They live blocks away an' still they corrupt our babies. Wot's a mut'er to do? Mind ye, even unsuspectin', proper Englishmen fall into their wonton ways, an' they drop their h's an' other letters. Bess, if ye 'ave trouble understandin' 'em, just add t' h's , an ye'll be okay. In no time, ye'll pick it up, but don't ye start talkin' like 'em. I don't want to 'ave to scold ye too." Lottie wagged her finger. "Lads, wash yer 'ands an' sit at t' kitchen table. Ye can 'ave tea wit' Bess an' me." Under her breath she said, "Blimey, children."

Bess smiled *blimey, definitely unsuspectin'*. When the boys were seated at the long narrow table, she asked them, "What did you learn at school today?"

Surprised, they looked at each other and Bertie said, "Summut."

"Excuse me." Lottie looked sternly at Bertie. "That's no answer. Tell Bess wot ye learnt, right after ye take off yer cap. Where's yer manners? I know, Percy Evans took 'em."

They both took off their caps and Bertie continued, "Summut to do wit' that owlde bloke, Shake----pear. -- Aye, an' that bloke Dickens, ye know t' one who's bin to our shoppe before. I told t' teacher that. 'E were impressed, 'e was." Bertie's face beamed. --- "Polly put t' kettle on, we'll all 'ave tea----."

"No singin' at t' table, Bertie," his mother spoke sharply and gave Artie a scowl when he giggled. " 'Ere, drink yer tea an' be off wit' ye. I 'ave work to do an' ye'll be under foot. Besides, I want ye to fetch sum more flour from Mr. Brown."

"Mum, can Miss N-ike cum wit' us?"

"No, not today. She needs to rest. Maybe tomorrow. Off wit' ye lads. "Ere's a farthing. Get yerselves a sweet."

After tea, Bess washed up and left the kitchen with Lottie busy baking. As she entered the dining room, she looked to her right and took in the counter. Protected from wishful hands, a glass front showed off two shelves of enticing pastries. *Lottie does herself proud*, she thought. Rows of custard tarts, bright red, raspberry jam tarts, beige shortbread, dark molasses cookies and miniature sponges filled the first shelf, under the marble counter top. The second shelf left a few gaps between the currant buns. *Perhaps, Lottie's bounty, baking in the oven, will fill the shelf.*

Looking up from the counter, she saw a vaguely familiar, black slateboard hanging on the wall. Contrasted in white chalk was written:

Welcome to "The Lotatea Shoppe"

Teas ------ "The finest from reputable warehouses"

Black --- Bohea, Pekoe, Congou, Souchong --- 2d a pot

Medium --- Imperial and Bing

Green --- Hyson and Gunpowder

Pastries --- 2d or 2 for 3d

"Polly put the kettle on, we'll all have tea."

--- Charles Dickens, "Barnaby Rudge"

Knock, knock.

Bess heard the knocking at the door. *Oh, more customers,* she thought. The knocking became louder, more persistent. Startled, Bess turned around to go to the door. She stopped short. Her chesterfield, in her living room, stood before her.

"Oh, I'm back."

Knock, knock.

"I'm coming," she shouted and opened the door to face a young man, carrying a flat, cardboard box.

"Pizza!" He looked at her puzzled look. "Pizza, you did order pizza?"

"Lost for words, Bess uttered, "Aah."

Checking the bill, the delivery fellow continued, "Prepaid by Evan Turner. ----- Deliver to 2141 Chestnut." He looked for the address on the house.

"Oh, sorry, my husband said this morning, he would take care of supper."

Just at that moment, Evan pulled into the driveway; he waved and smiled.

"Good timing, eh--- bloke---aah, young man. Wait a minute. I'll get you a tip." She ran in the house and picked up some loose change laying on the sofa table and noticed the barstool in front of the mantel. *Darn! I don't want Evan to see it here two days in a row,* she gasped and picked up the barstool.

"I'll get the tip, Bess. We don't want to hold him up from his appointed rounds," Evan shouted at Bess. "Thanks and drive safely, young man."

Bess hurried into the kitchen with the barstool, before Evan came in with the pizza. He gave her a quick peck on the cheek and laid the pizza box and another small, white box on the counter. She took down a couple of plates from the cupboard and two sets of cutlery from the drawer, while Evan went up to wash. Five minutes later, T.V. tables in front of them, they sat down to eat and watch the hockey game.

At the end of the first period, Evan closed the empty pizza box and looked at Bess. "How are you feeling? The aches any better?" Bess nodded and opened her mouth to speak when Evan continued, "That reminds me." He jumped up, took the dirty dishes in one hand, the empty box in the other and headed for the kitchen.

A couple of minutes passed and Bess thought *what's he doing in there? It sounds like he's rearranging the whole kitchen.* In the process of getting up to investigate the loud clatter from the kitchen, Bess stopped in mid-rise.

"Bess, how about a cup of tea? Don't you move now. Just sit back and watch the hockey intermission. The colour commentators are great. I'll bring you a cup and join you in a minute."

Bess rolled her eyes and said, 'Yeah, just what I need, two fancy dressed, ex-jocks babbling over what has been."

"Did you say something?" Evan shouted from the kitchen.

A moment later, Evan entered the living room with two mugs

58

of tea and two platesperched upon the little, white box. He put the mugs down on the tables and proceeded to open the box.

"Look, Bess, I bought your favourite, custard tarts and okay my favourite, chocolate éclairs. You looked in such a sad state this morning, I knew these would pick you up."

She leaned over and gave him a kiss. "Thank you. You are a dear."

"Eat up, old girl. You need your strength." He patted her arm.

Their brief moment over, the second period began and they both sat back into their own little worlds.

# CHAPTER VIII

*F*ar-off bells and whistles, muffled sounds and whispers; Bess tried to unscramble these sounds, as her feet moved forward. Her eyes focused on a dim light in front of her. As she moved closer to the light, the sounds became clearer, more distinct.

"Mum, where's Miss N-ike?"

"She's up restin'."

"Can I go wake 'er? Can I, Mum?"

"No, Bertie, let 'er be."

" 'Ere's she be. Good even', Miss N-ike."

"Good evening, Bertie. Please call me Bess." She smiled at him and then at Lottie. Hearing someone clearing their throat, she entered the dark room and looked in the direction of the guttural sound. "Oh, Uncle Tom," she stammered, "Mr. Evans, how nice to see you. I didn't notice you over there."

"Miss N-ike, --Bess." Tom got up from his chair and gave a slight bow. "Nice to see you up and about. You're looking much better, indeed." His face lit up.

A delicate cough turned Bess in another direction, to find a young woman seated in a low-backed chair. For some reason, Bess looked at her long, black sleeves, which ended at her slender hands, neatly cupped over her lap of voluptuous, black taffeta. As her gaze left the hands, it moved up to the white,

60

slender neck, surrounded by shiny black ringlets. The face, very familiar to her, puzzled Bess, and she tried to recall where she had seen it before.

"Bess, t'is 'ere's Josephine Godale. She's our lodger. She 'as t' bedroom next to ye. She also runs t' shoppe next to us," Lottie said.

"I'm pleased to formally meet you, Bess." She smiled. "Please call me Jo. I only work at 'Tellaway Books.' Lottie likes to over emphasize my duties."

"She be too modest, our Jo is," Lottie piped up. "She literally," she stopped and giggled at her own pun, "runs t' shoppe. Owlde Mr. Tell sits upstairs all day an' just cums down to get t' money ev'ry night."

"Now, Lottie, if it wasn't for Mr. Tell, I wouldn't have a job and you wouldn't have a lodger. He's been good to both of us." Jo replied and turned back to Bess. "As Tom said, I am glad you are up and about. You took a nasty tumble. I hope I didn't startle you. You were looking so intently in the window, and there I go and walk right into your thoughts. It would scare anyone, seeing as I had just been stocking shelves. My attire and hair were a mess."

"Oh no, Jo, it was my fault: preoccupied and not paying attention," Bess answered.

"Bess, cum sit beside Tom. We were just about to 'ave our even' meal." Lottie took Bess's arm and lead her in the direction of a stern looking loveseat. "Cum sit on me new tête-à-tête chair. Tom doesn't like it." She stared at Tom, giving him an if looks could kill look. "'E says, it's too stiff an' all those ripples ar'n't natural like. Wot do ye think, Bess?"

Tom got up and allowed her to be seated. Bess lowered herself and kept lowering herself, until she finally sat down with a most ungracious thud, on a most uncomfortable cushion. *Tom is right,* she thought. *What are all these ridges? It feels like I'm sitting on a giant washboard.* Tom gave a mischievous smile and went to help his sister bring up the food. Bess took a closer look at the contraption, she found herself perched upon. Her hand rested upon tapestry upholstery. It reminded her of a succession of waves at the seashore, but without the soft entrance into its folds. The chair continued into another tall-backed seat. A much smaller triangular-shaped seat squeezed in between the two bigger seats.

"There certainly wouldn't be much tête-à-têteing going on in this chair," Bess burst out loud and caught herself. *Even Mother couldn't squeeze in the centre seat, and if she did, she wouldn't stay long. Hmm, maybe that's the idea.*

Across the room, she noticed a similar tufted chair. The single chair looked heavy with ornate mahogany carved around the perimeter of the clam-shaped, upholstered seat. Its stubby legs spread outwards, giving the impression they would soon buckle under the weight of the occupant. Looking about the room, Bess became fascinated by the lack of empty space. Everywhere she looked, clutter abounded. Lace-covered tables of all shapes and sizes, beheld plants, decorative boxes, figurines, vases and knick-knacks of every description. Next to the blazing fire, stood a small, writing table. Above it, a gaslamp, suspended on a goose-necked wall bracket, gave off a mellow glow. The flickering shadows upon the wall, made the busy wallpaper come to life. The horse-drawn carriage seemed to move, whilst Bess swore she heard the young maidens giggle within.

"Tom, don't tease." The creaking of the stairs brought Bess's attention to the open doorway. "Leave Jo alone. Just cause she smiled at Sean MacLeod, don't mean she likes 'im. Ye 'ave a lovely smile, Jo an' so ye should smile at yer customers. Why I'm always smilin' at me customers, be it woman or man. It's good fer business."

"You're quite right, Lottie. Why we've all seen you smiling at Mr. Brown --- and my isn't he a repeat customer," Tom laughed.

" 'Ush wit' ye. Get a table fer Bess." Lottie laid the tray on a large, round table, supported by a solid pedestal, ending in three retracted claw-like feet. "Jo, do ye need a hand wit' t' plates? Bertie, don't ye drop t' spoons."

Tom placed a long narrow table in front of Bess, bent low and whispered, "Hope you didn't miss us. My sister always makes a fuss over mealtime, especially when we have guests. You should see her at Sunday dinner."

"Bertie, take sum bread an' butter to Bess. Mind, ye don't drop it." Lottie cut some more bread and placed it on another plate. "Oh, that Dutch cheese smells soo gooda, Jo," she giggled. "See, Tom, it pays to smile. Mr. Fowler always gives Jo a nice big sample of 'is latest import. I must get ye to buy t' roast fer Sunday's dinner, Jo," she laughed.

As Tom turned to sit down beside Bess, Bertie scurried in and sat down on the triangular seat in the middle. Bertie smiled up at Bess. Tom shook his head, patted Bertie's head and sat down in his appointed seat.

"Bertie, get off there. Cum an' sit on t' ottoman," his mother scolded.

"Leave him be, woman," Tom replied.

"He's no trouble and besides this seat is made for him," said Bess as she smiled and winked at Bertie.

Bertie beamed, moved a little closer to Bess and started in on his meal. Bess thought the bread and butter very fresh; although the bread had a heavier, grainy texture than she normally ate. She noticed the colour of the bread to be a faint yellow and remembered the scones of the same hue. *Of course, it must be the flour.* She recalled earlier when Lottie spread the flour on the marble slab, it looked almost like a light coloured cornmeal.

Reading her thoughts, Lottie said to Bess, "Yer bread is whiter in America, I 'ere tell. If ye get white flour 'ere, it can be poisoned. Accordin' to Accum's book, alum added to flour makes t' bread white, but does in yer bowels. T'is t' carotene in t' flour that gives it a yellow colour, but don't 'arm ye none. 'E also said, 't' dairyman puts red lead into cheese.' Ye can't trust nobody, so I buy white cheese or Dutch cheese. Their reputable. Once I was in t' grocer's in Drury Lane an' I noticed dried blackberry leaves in t' tea, -- an' t' price we pay fer tea. It pays to buy t' best, so I go to "Twinings" or I buy from Mr. Harrod. Why, it's said a grocer swept brick dust into 'is chocolate powder. Oh, don't get me started."

"Aye, it's true, Bess." Tom continued the subject. "When Accum's book came out, it caused such an uproar, the grocers, druggists and especially the brewers, forced the poor fellow to flee the country. Can you imagine the uproar in England when he denounced our publicans. It wasn't bad enough they diluted the beer, but to add copper water. Why copperas contains sulphuric acid, and we all know what vitriol can do to one. To top it off, he accused them of cocolus indicus, to give the beer a nice bitter taste and a real wallop." He looked at Jo. "No offence, Jo, Robert's one of the good blokes."

"I know, Tom. Robert was just as upset as everyone else. He knows it's still being done, but not at "The Goodale." The name alone is good for business, and he doesn't want to do anything to spoil it, especially these days," Jo said.

Tom looked at Bess. "Sorry, Bess. Jo's brother, Robert is the publican at 'The Goodale' down the lane. It was a stroke of luck, their last name being Godale, and Robert owning the pub. You see, Bess, Godale is an old word for making good ale."

"I prefer books to brewing, so when Mr. Tell offered me the position, I left the pub behind and moved in here. It's much quieter and I can read to my heart's content." Jo smiled.

"Mum, can I 'ave a custard tart?"

Lottie nodded. "After ye offer one to Bess." She turned to Bess. "I saw ye admirin' 'em t'is afternoon. I was ever so 'appy I didn't sell 'em all, so we'd 'ave sum fer tea later."

"Ye like 'em too, Miss Bess? 'Ere, ye take t' big one, cause yer bigger." Bertie offered her the plate of tarts.

"I'm getting full, Bertie. Perhaps, you should have the bigger one." Bess looked over Bertie's mop of brown hair and smiled at Tom.

"You mustn't be too full, Miss Bess as I have a special treat for us all." From under the seat, Tom pulled out a small white box.

"Wot is it, Uncle Tom?" Bertie averted his eyes away from his half-eaten tart.

"A client just came back from Paris and brought me a present. ----- 'Ah, mon cheri, sweets for the sweet,' she said." Tom made a convincing female, French accent, while continuing to untie the string.

"She said?" queried Lottie. "Mon cheri?"

"Don't get your knickers in a knot. Mrs. Haversmith is at least fifty years old." Bess choked and Tom said, "Are you okay, Bess?" Bess nodded and pointed to the tart. Tom rubbed his chin, "Mind you, she is a very rich widow, an attractive one at that." He moved his eyebrows up and down.

"Uncle Tom, 'urry," Bertie said, as he stuffed the last of the tart in his mouth.

"Voila!" Tom opened the box to reveal five chocolate éclairs.

A startled Bess exclaimed, "Oh my," and started to cough.

"Sorry, Bess, I didn't mean to startle you. Are you okay?"

"Have some tea, Bess." Jo ran over with the teapot.

"I'm fine. Really, I'm fine."

When tea finished, the dishes had been gathered, and the room vacated except for Bess. She offered to help clean up, but Lottie told her to sit and enjoy the warm fire. Jo retired to her room and Tom disappeared. Bertie was sent to bed with a promise of a goodnight kiss. The silent room felt empty, even though everywhere she looked clutter abided. On the mantel, a clock ticked. An unlit candelabra stood on one side of the old clock, while three vases of different shapes and sizes stood firmly on the other side. Rogue's gallery, stiff and proper in their shiny, silver frames, filled in any remaining space. Below the mantel, a twelve-inch wide strip of light-grey marble surrounded the fire opening. The brass handle of the tongs glistened in the firelight. On the hearth, stood a black, oval coal box resting on four chunky, brass legs. The closed lid opened by an ornate brass handle, shining brightly from the glow of the fire. *All that silver and brass must be a constant chore,* thought Bess. *My heavens, I have enough trouble keeping my silver teapot polished.*

"Goodnight, Bess. I'm off to my room." Tom poked his head in the room. "You look surprised. Didn't my sister tell you I live here? My room's at the back of yours. Don't' worry, I promise not to sleepwalk." He gave her a mischievous smile and left.

"Goodnight, Uncle Tom."

"Goodnight, Bertie, old man." Uncle Tom could be heard climbing the creaky stairs.

"Me mum said I could cum say goodnight to ye. Don't ferget tomorrow. Ye can cum shoppin' wit' Artie an' me." Bertie moved beside Bess and hesitated.

"Would it be alright if I had a goodnight kiss? I sleep better with one," Bess asked.

"You didn't ask me, lass," a male voice faintly proclaimed, at the top of the stairs.

Bertie giggled, gave Bess a peck on the cheek and a surprising bearhug. "Goodnight, Miss Bess."

"Goodnight, Bertie. Sleep tight. Don't let the bed bugs bite." Bertie looked strangely at Bess. "If they do, hit them over the head with your shoe and say, God bless you." She heard two little feet run down the hallway, followed in close pursuit by an echo of a giggle.

A moment later, Lottie came into the parlour carrying a tray. She set the silver tray on the long table, in front of Bess. She plunked herself down, in a most unlady-like fashion , on the seat, vacated by her brother.

"Blimey, t'is good to get off me achin' feet." Lottie gave a large sigh. "I swear, they get sorer ev'ryday." She lifted her skirt and petticoats, revealing her off-white shoes. Bending down, she gave her mound of skirts a flattening with her fists. "Oh, it ain't easy bein' a woman. Men ar' so lucky, wearin' trousers. ----- Blimey, I ain't even able to get to me feet."

"Here, let me help you." Bess leaned over and picked up one of Lottie's feet and gasped. "No wonder your feet ache, your shoes are flat. You don't even have a heel. You need a shoe with better support." As she untied her laces, Bess realized the shoes were made of a stiff muslin. "Can't you get some leather shoes?"

"I 'ave sum nice black, leather shoes, but I wear 'em when I go out. Ye wouldn't last out on t' street two seconds, wit'out ruinin' these." She looked at her feet. "Besides, t' good leather shoes cum all t' way from Northampton an' ar' so expensive. Me last pair cost one pound, whilst these cost a crown, a quarter of t' price. Mind, t' railway 'as 'elped. Goods get 'ere faster, so more to choose from an' t' cost did drop." She sighed, "But still, I 'ave Bertie to buy fer an' 'e's grown like a weed. I just get 'im into a new pair an' 'e's outgrown 'em."

Bess removed her runners. "Try these on."

"Aye, Bertie was talkin' about 'em." Lottie wiggled her feet, as Bess placed them on her feet.

"How do they feel? Comfy, eh." Bess looked at Lottie, as she walked around the room, holding her skirts high.

"My, they ar' so. They even fit. Wot a shame, ye can't get 'em 'ere." She sighed, "Oh well, achin' feet it be." She sat back down and lifted her feet for Bess. "Well, right now I'm glad to just sit 'ere wit'out any shoes.---- "Let's 'ave sum tea, luv."

Bess got up and brought a small footstool over and put it down in front of Lottie. "This should help."

"Thank ye, Bess, luv." Putting her stocking feet upon the round, upholstered stool, she continued, "Ye ar' a 'elp, Bess, an' that's wot I wanted to talk to ye about. Wot ar' yer plans?" Lottie's face took on a serious look.

"Plans?" Taken off guard Bess replied, "Ah--- Oh yes, my plans." She stopped and thought *your on the spot now, girl. Think fast. Use your imagination.* She put one hand behind her back, crossed her fingers and said, "Well, I'm not sure. ---- I had planned on visiting London and perhaps taking your new train service around the country." On a roll, she squeezed her fingers tighter and continued, "Yes, well I lost my luggage, eh. --- The steamship company misplaced it while getting off the ship. Unfortunately, all my clothes and most of my money were in the luggage." She stopped for a plea of sympathy and to get her breath and thought *that's good, Bess.* "Yes, well I had a few pounds in my pocket, along with my train ticket to London, so off I came and here I am."

"My, my. 'Ow ar' ye goin' to get yer luggage?"

"I'm to contact the steamship office here when I have a place to stay."

"Since ye don't 'ave any money an' ye need a place to stay, why don't ye stay 'ere? Ye could earn yer keep by 'elpin' me in t' tearoom. I need 'elp, especially at Christmas. Ev'ryone wants to treat 'emselves to tea. Besides, if ye wouldn't mind, ye could play t' pianoforte fer t' customers. It would bring in business. Why I could put a sign outside.--- Oh, I can see it now." She waved her arms as if viewing a billboard. "Direct from America, Miss Bess performing live on the pianoforte." Eyes wide open she continued, "Oh, wot do ye say, Bess?"

"Why thank you, Lottie. It is very kind of you. Are you sure I won't be a bother? I can't help financially until my luggage is found."

"Yer 'elp will out weigh any monies yer keep will cost. Besides, Bertie is becomin' very fond of ye. Ye could keep 'im out of me 'air once in a while." She laughed. "I noticed Tom rather fancies ye too." She gave Bess a gentle poke. "So that's settled then. Drink up yer tea. T'is gettin' late an' we 'ave a busy day tomorrow."

"Right, boss." Bess saluted.

They both sat in silence for a few minutes and then Lottie slipped her shoes on. "I'll take t' tray downstairs."

"Let me take if for you. Rest your feet."

"No, that's okay. I 'ave to go out to pluck a rose anyway."

"A rose? You can't have roses growing in the middle of winter, do you?"

"Rose? Oh, sorry, Bess." Lottie laughed. "I ferget yer from America. T'is a genteel lady-like expression, to go to t' necessarium or privy."

"Privy?" Finally the light went on in Bess's confused mind. *Now that's a proper Victorian approach; a necessarium. That's a good one.* "Oh, the toilet--- washroom--- bathroom. I believe you call it a water closet." Bess laughed. "Our genteel ladies way of saying, going to the powder room."

Still laughing, Lottie blurted out, "I aint 'eard of those words, but our blokes say they're goin' out to exonerate their paunches."

Bess laughing along with Lottie said, "Ours say their going to sit on The Houses of Parliament or going to the can."

With tears in their eyes, Lottie said, "That reminds me, where is me 'ead? I haven't even shown ye where t' privy----powder room is. Oh, ye poor thing. Cum wit' me."

After putting the tray down in the kitchen, Lottie lit a candle and they walked to the back door. She opened it to a blast of cold, damp air. The candle flickered. Lottie lead the way over a narrow, brick walkway to a small building.

"Oh, we call this an outhouse."

"Outhouse? ----- Aye, that's a good one."

A seatless seat, resembling a large bowl, greeted them, along with a strong unpleasant odour. *I'd hate to be here in the summer,* Bess thought, as she held her breath.

"T'is quite modern wit' runnin' water to keep t' bowl clean. Unfortunately, t' water trickles only when t' waterworks' powers that be, turn on t' water two times a day. Tomorrow, Mr. Stewart's sons, Bill 'n' George, t' night soil men, will unclog t' pipen leadin' to t' cesspool. T'is Bertie's job to keep t' bowl swished wit' turpentine. Sorry, luv, sumtimes 'e fergets."

"Don't worry. I have the same problem. I pay good money for Mr. Clean to do the same job, and he is always running out on me."

Back in the house, the air felt much warmer, and the kitchen smelt heavenly of left over baking. They climbed the stairs with Lottie leaving Bess to climb the next floor alone.

"Goodnight, Bess. Take t'is candle wit' ye," Lottie said, as she opened her bedroom door, at the back of the parlour. "Oh yes, there's a chamber pot under yer bed."

"Goodnight, Lottie." Bess smiled.

Surrounded by flickering shadows, she ascended the dark, eerie staircase. The flickering shadows took on human forms as she tried to keep her eyes open. She heard indiscernible voices in the distance.

"And nowww fooor the loocal news."

Her eyes suddenly wide open, she saw the local anchor man sternly looking back at her. A slight twitch made her turn around to find Evan sound asleep beside her on the chesterfield. She rolled her eyes upward, spying Mr. Spider.

"What a sight, two old humans sprawled out below you. Why, you could very well have nightmares, you poor fellow. ----- Wake up Evan. It's time for bed."

"What?--- Oh, okay, Bess, I'm coming."

"I need to pluck a rose, and you probably need to exonerate your paunches."

"Exonerate what?"

"Goodnight, Evan."

"Bess, I have to go into the office in the morning, but I should be home by noonish. Why don't we go Christmas shopping after?"

"Shopping will be fine. I'm going to bed. I have a busy day tomorrow. I have a lot of shopping to do." She shouted down the stairs, "Goodnight, Evan. Sleep tight, don't let the bedbugs bite."

"Right, Bess. Goodnight, dear."

# CHAPTER IX

*E*van left early for the office on Saturday morning. Shortly after, Bess stirred and thought *I have a lot to do* and bounced out of bed. A quick brush of the teeth, a splash of water on her face and she bounded down the stairs. She gulped down a large mouthful of cereal and immediately began to cough. Trying to get her breath, her eyes rolled around the room. First she saw Mr. Spider escaping from the Cheerios' line of fire, then the mantel covered in fallout, then ---- a slap---- another slap on the back ---

"There, any better?" a soothing voice said. "Went down the wrong way?"

Bess opened her eyes to find Tom standing in front of her. "Ooh --- coough---- cough. Thank you, Tom. You've rescued me once again, Sir Tomalot."

"I have, haven't I. See it proves you can't live without me." The eyebrows did their devilishly handsome, up and downs. "Here, have some water." He poured her a glass of lukewarm water from the blue, china pitcher.

"Aah---- Thank you. That's much better." Bess wiped her face and ran her finger through her hair. "I must look a sight."

"Ah yes, quite a sight." He laughed, as he moved towards the front door. "We're all going to see 'A Christmas Carol' tonight. Would you like to come along? It's a local production on Drury Lane. It should be quite good, so I've been told. It's written by a popular London writer, Charles Dickens. You probably haven't heard of him in America."

"Yes, that would be great." Bess smiled. "And yes, his novels have reached us. In fact, he is quite popular. Some say his works could very well become classics someday."

"Good then, I'll get you a ticket." He hesitated at the door. "Well, I'll be off then, to work that is." He closed the door and disappeared in the morning fog.

"Was that Tom? Darn it. I wanted to ask 'im sumthin' about ----" Crunch,--- Crunch-- "Blimey, wot's Bertie tracked in this time?" Lottie loudly voiced her annoyance. She bent over to investigate the crime. "Crushed bread crumbs all over t' floor. I don't 'ave time to clean up after 'im all t' time."

"Lottie, you get back to your business. I'll sweep it up."

Bess found the straw broom in the kitchen and made her way back to the dining room. Finding the culprits scattered on the wooden floor, she started to sweep them into the dustpan. Looking around to see if any had escaped, she spied a couple of large pieces, which successfully had escaped the enemy's heavy foot. On closer inspection, she stopped in her tracks.

"CHEERIOS."

Still a bit shaken and at the same time puzzled by her discovery, she carried the incriminating evidence into the kitchen and deposited it in the dustbin. *They actually made the journey with me. Hmm -- Wonder what else could come with me?* She watched the foreign Cheerios fall into the dustbin. Turning around, she noticed a cloud of flour around Lottie. She decided not to interfere with the possible brewing of stormy weather and started right in washing dishes. Soon the flour subsided and a smile broke across Lottie's face.

"'E's a good lad, but sumtimes 'e can be a handful. T'is not easy raisin' a boy wit'out a father."

"Bertie said your husband is a sea captain. I guess he doesn't get home very often."

Lottie rubbed her white hands on her apron. "Aye, that 'e

doesn't. Wot, t'is about a year an' 'auff since 'e was 'ere last. T'is 'ard fer t' lad to remember wot 'e looks like. I 'ave a photogenic of 'im in me bedroom an' there's a drawin' of 'im in Bertie's room. Oh, we get letters from 'im ev'ry six months or so, but he usually writes about where 'e's bin an' where 'e's goin' an' not much about 'imself. T'is not much of a marriage, is it? But, at least we don't fight when 'e's 'ere." She laughed.

"It must be lonely for you."

"Aye, it can be. T'is not that I'm alone, 'cause there's always sumone 'ere, but t'is at night, when ev'ryone's gone to bed an' there's no one to keep me feet warm, so to speak."

"You are an attractive woman, Lottie. There must be many men who would like to keep company with you."

"Yer be quite right, Bess," she laughed, "but in t'is day an' age, certain proprieties ar' expected of women. If it wasn't fer our virtuous, Queen Victoria, always settin' an' example, we women would 'ave a lot more fun." She looked at Bess, and they both burst out laughing.

"Speaking of having fun, what's this I hear about a Mr. Brown?" She noticed a sudden blush on Lottie's face.

"Mr. Brown, ah yes ---- 'e's a lovely man. 'E's just a friend, mind ye. Ye'll meet 'im t'is evenin'. 'E's cumin' wit' us to t' theatre. Since it bein' Christmas, t'is quite proper fer 'im to escort us. Of course, Tom will be there as chaperon."

"Mr. Brown is the baker, right?"

"Aye, 'e's that an' much more.--- Don't ye look at me like that. I meant, he owns t' bakery an' t'is 'ere 'ouse."

"He's not married, I assume. My, he must be quite a catch for the young ladies."

"Aye indeed, Miss Bess.--- An' don't ye be gettin' any ideas."

"Right, Mrs. Morton, but we'll discuss this further after I meet your friend, Mr. Brown."

" 'Ere, 'elp me cut up t'is dried fruit fer t' mincemeat, while I go get sum brandy from t' parlour."

The tearoom was a hive of activity. Ladies burdened with parcels, kept coming in and out. No sooner a table became vacant and another group of ladies would be sitting around its perimeter, drinking tea and gossiping. The rose water lady approached Bess and tapped her on the shoulder, as she placed some warm currant buns in the display case.

"My dear, you must come and play for me. I made a special trip over here just to hear you play. My, I am thirsty. Would you be so kind and ask Mrs. Morton to bring me a pot of Pekoe and one of those. They smell so good." She walked away towards a vacant table beside the piano.

Taking in a breath of scented rose water, Bess closed the cabinet and looked straight ahead. The blackboard's quote had been erased and replaced with a new one:

𝕮onfucious say ...
"𝕴f the stranger say unto thee that he thirstieth, give him a cup of tea."

*Right,* she thought and made her way over to Lottie, occupied with Mrs. Pennycroft, and turned an ear towards her. Bess whispered the rose water lady's request and made her way to the piano. The droning of the ladies' voices inspired her to play her first song, and she quietly sang Shakespeare's little ditty.

"Where the bee sucks, there suck I
In a cowslip's bel I lie –
There I couch when owls do cry
On the bat's back I do fli-i-i---"

A whisper in her ear said, "Luv, Miss Rose Water agrees with ye."
Bess looked over at her table and saw the rose water lady wink and smile.
"She requested ye play that Christmas song again."
Pulled by both arms, Bess looked down at her abductors.

74

Artie, the smaller of the two, tugged harder. His brown, woollen cap barely covered his ears, where as his matching, light-brown hair covered them quite nicely. His pale-blue eyes gave a pleading look of let's go. Bertie, the other abductor, dressed in a similar manner of tweed trousers, white shirt and waist length, woollen fitted jacket, took charge of the operation.

" 'Urry, Miss Bess. We must be off. Me 'n' Artie 'ave lots to show ye."

"Don't rush t' poor girl. 'Ere, put me coat on, an' t'is bonnet. Ye can't go out in public wit'out a 'at. T'is not respectable. Let me tie it fer ye." Lottie stood back to inspect the troop. "Lads, put on yer scarves.---- Watch t' aspidistra. One of these days yer goin' t' knock it over," she tisked. "Mind t' 'orses, when ye cross t' street. Watch out fer Bess. She ain't used to our traffic."

The front door opened, and another world opened for Bess. The fog shrouded lane gave an eerie look to the scene spread before her eyes. Tall, old buildings loomed before her. Through the wisps of fog came giant horses snorting as they pulled their carts, laden with cargo. Ghost-like humans pushed and pulled small carts overflowing with their wares; while other spirits ran and walked past, unaware of her presence. Truly in a fog, she left the safety of the tearoom and immediately crashed into a sandwich board. Bending over to pick it up, she noticed the message:

"The Lotatea Shoppe" ----- Presents
Direct from America, Miss Bess on the pianoforte.
Join us for tea and music to warm your soul.

Bess laughed out loud and the street came alive: horses neighed, dogs barked, humans shouted, carts rattled and bells chimed.

" 'Urry, Miss Bess, t'is one o'clock an' we 'ave to get to t' post office before it closes." Bertie grabbed her left hand and steered her up the street.

"Good afternoon, miss." A portly gentleman doffed his black, silk top hat. Without missing a beat, he tapped his walking stick on the brick sidewalk and carried on.

"Flahs fer t' lady." An old woman with a long nose and sunken eyes, pointed at her cart, filled with bunches of dried flowers.

Bess smelt a whiff of lavender as they hurried by the vendor. Unfortunately, she also kept getting whiffs of not such a pleasant nature. They were definitely nature, natural unaltered, horse dung.

"Mind, Miss Bess, 'ere cums Sadie 'n' Jim." Artie clutched her hand.

Clop, clop ----

"Whooa, Sadie! --- Good dye, lads. --- Why, good dye, miss. 'Ow ye be then?' Jim asked, as he looked down at them from his cart.

"I'm fine, Jim," Bess answered.

"Can we give Sadie sum sugar, Jim?" the boys asked in unison.

" 'Ere ye ar', but one piece each. Sugars too expensive to waste on 'orses, but seein' it be fer Sadie." He winked.

" 'Ere, Miss Bess, ye can give 'er mine. Sadie liked to be yer friend, she would." Bertie gave her the lump of sugar.

The beautiful, brown eyes, surrounded by long lashes, looked at Bess invitingly. She slowly lifted her open hand, containing a small lump of brown sugar. Sadie gently picked it up with her velvety lips, and nodded her head in approval. The boys giggled, and the three departed for their destination. Hand in hand, they walked past a number of shoppes, until they came to the corner.

On their right, stood "The Goodale" pub. The peak of the tudor building, shrouded in fog, looked like it could tell a story or two. It reminded her of an old man bent over, with only his memories to keep him alive. Looking back down the lane, it definitely held the honour of grandfather of the neighbourhood. Every board, wall, and although she could only imagine, the roof and chimney stood crooked. Even the heavy timbered, front door, supported by large, iron hinges looked lopsided. The small diamond shaped, window panes, crusted with dirt, were present only for decoration as no light could penetrate years of grime. *No wonder Jo moved from here,* Bess thought as they stood on the corner. Waiting for the traffic to clear, she saw two workmen unloading a wagon full of casks of whisky. By the service entrance, barrels of ale stood waiting to be taken inside.

"Cum on, Miss Bess. T' traffic's clear." Bertie pulled her hand.

As they stepped off the curb, she looked to her left, to catch a glimpse of the streetlamp. On the lamppost hung an ornate sign, pointing in the same direction as them. It read Fetter Lane. Another sign directly above it, but facing in the opposite direction, read Fleet Street.

"Stop, Miss Bess," Artie screamed and pointed to the ground.

"Oh My," Bess replied, as the next step would have had her runner smothered in fresh horse dung.

"Never look up when crossin' t' street. See that yob cumin' t'is way, in front of that there lady. 'E's a crossin' sweeper. 'E sweeps that away, so t' lady can cross wit'out gettin' 'er shoes an' dress dirty. She gives 'im a farthin'. Me 'n' Artie thought of doin' it, but ar mums said no. They didn't want to clean us up after. We said we'd clean arselfs up, but they didn't believe us, did they Artie?" Artie shook his head in disbelief, as Bertie said, " 'Ere we be then, safe and clean." Artie and Bertie puffed out their chests to indicate a job well done.

They turned to the left, passing many gentlemen, dressed in top hats and snug fitting overcoats. The echo of walking sticks tapping a constant beat, drowned out the sounds from the street. Bess thought any moment she would see Fred Astaire come tap dancing down the street and lead the gentlemen in a Broadway number of the tapping sticks. However, each man intent on his business pursuits, hurried down Fleet Street oblivious to all.

"Good dye, sur," Bertie said in a loud voice to an elderly gentlemen walking towards them.

"Good day." He doffed his hat at Bess and took a closer look at Bertie. "Ah, it's Bertie, isn't it?"

"Aye, sur, an' t'is 'ere's Miss Bess N-ike. She's stayin' wit' us. She's from America."

The gentleman slowed down to almost a stop and took a thorough look at Bess. "Welcome to England, miss. Always nice to have visitors from the colonies."

"Uncle Tom's takin' us to t' theatre tonight," Bertie proudly announced.

"Good for you, lad. 'A Christmas Carol,' I believe Tom mentioned. Yes, well have a good time. --- And give my regards to your mother." He smiled and continued on his way.

"That's Uncle Tom's boss, Mr. Turner. 'E's a kind gentleman, 'e is. Me mum says, 'Uncle Tom's lucky to 'ave a boss like 'im. Most don't remember their employees' names, say fer their relatives'."

" 'Ere we ar', Bertie." Artie stopped.

" 'T'is t' post office. Me mum wants me to buy a stamp an' post t'is letter." He brought out a crumpled letter from his pocket.

Each boy grabbed a large, brass handle and attempted to open the double doors. Just as Bess thought she should lend a hand, a man with large hands came to the rescue. The boys turned with a scowl to address the intruder, who foiled their manly gesture. The scowls turned to smiles.

"Thank ye, Mr. Brown," they both said.

"That's alright, lads. --- And this must be Miss N-ike?" He smiled and doffed his cap at Bess. "It's a pleasure to meet you. I've heard a great deal about you. Why Lottie, aah -- Mrs. Morton was just telling me this morning, --- when she came to get some extra flour for tomorrow. She told me, you're coming with us tonight. I haven't seen her this excited in a long time. Well, I must be off. ---- Until five then. The carriage will pick us up at six." He waved and disappeared in the fog.

"Did ye 'ear that Artie? 'E's hired a carriage fer us. Maybe it be one of those new fast phaetons," Bertie said excitedly.

"Naah, Bertie, it'll be a barouche, an' we'll all be squeezed in together so we can't breathe," Artie piped up.

"Well, maybe we can sit up wit' t' driver," Bertie replied.

Awestruck, Bess gazed at the bright shiny marble. Everywhere, white marble streaked with grey, surrounded her. Her eyes had become accustomed to the dark interior of the Morton's house and the fog shrouded streets, so naturally she squinted at the brightness. The walls, at least thirty-feet high, ended at an ornate, plastered ceiling. From the centre of the ceiling, hung the largest cut glass chandelier she had ever seen. *How do they light it, let alone clean it?*

A large, stained glass window, encased in the front wall, gave off a spectrum of gold, reds and blues on the floor of light marble. Craning her neck, she honed in on the intricate design. On the top, a small lion stood on a crown. On the right side, stood a larger lion on his hind legs and on the left side, stood a unicorn in the same stance. Both were leaning on an oval object. *It looks like a shield. What's that writing on the bottom? I can't make it out.* Automatically, her eyes squinted. After a moment's reflection, she thought *of course, dummy, I'm looking at it from the backside.* She knocked the side of her head with her fingers. *Of course, it's their coat of arms.*

"Yes, -- miss, can I help you?" an official voice echoed.

"Oh, sorry. ---- Bertie?" she stammered.

"Aye, a stamp please, sur." Bertie stepped up to the counter and stood on his toes. "An' would ye mail t'is letter, sur," he continued in his manly voice.

The disgruntled looking clerk fumbled in his drawer and withdrew a small stamp. "One penny please. You will have to lick and apply the stamp yourself, sir. The post box is inside the wall, as you exit the building, sir."

Bess picked up the stamp for Bertie as there was no indication the surly clerk would extend himself any further for a mere boy. She gave the clerk a fake smile. *Typical government employee,* she thought. They quickly moved away. As she licked the stamp, she stopped and gasped *my gosh, is this the "The Penny Black" Evan has talked about? Did I just lick the world's first postage stamp? That's funny? --- It's red. I just assumed they were black. Oh, if only I could tell Evan.*

"Ar' ye alright, Miss Bess?" Artie looked alarmed.

"Yes, fine. I was just thinking. Here you go, Bertie." Hands trembling, she stuck the stamp on the envelope and handed it to him. She watched the stamped envelope go through the metal opening and sighed, "It's only a dream."

"Wot, Miss Bess?"

As they left the building, she turned around to look at the stained glass window. From the street, the colours and pattern appeared sharper. Bess could not pick out the printing around the shield, but the scroll underneath she could see clear enough.

Slowly, she said, "Dieu et mon droit.--- That's French."

"Aye, Miss Bess, t'is true," said Artie. "Me 'n' Bertie just learned it in school. Remember Bertie?" He wrinkled his brow. "Ah --- it means, "God an' me --- my right.""

"I remember, t'is t' Queen's Motto," spoke up Bertie. "T'is right. All t' kings an' queens from ever, says it." He looked closer at the stained glass window. "See t' printin' around t' shield, that means, "Shame to 'im who evil thinks." Me mum's always tellin' me that one."

Bess laughed. Hand in hand, the three walked back in the direction they originally came from, stopping at the corner.

"See down t' drag, past t' coffee shoppe, t'is Uncle Tom's work'ouse." Bertie pointed down busy Fleet Street. "It ain't a real work'ouse like t' poor work in, but Uncle Tom calls it so."

Bess averted her eyes from the bustle of men being lead by their walking sticks, and errand boys running down the street while vendors vied for their attention. The first building she saw, she assumed to be the coffee shoppe, from its bold, black lettered sign over the entrance, "Bean Counters." *Of course,* she smiled.

*This is the financial district.* Nothing unique or ornate jumped out at her, but the building fitted its purpose, to provide a simple surrounding without distractions, in order for gentlemen to conduct business over a cup of coffee. Beyond stood another unattractive building, with four tall, narrow windows on the first floor and five on the second floor. A small dormer window on the third floor, suggested a dreary attic. Again, a practical building for a counting house, lots of light for working with figures, but little viewing for distractions. The sign over the doorway simply stated, "W.H. Turner ---- 123 Fleet Street."

"Oh no, see that bloke cumin' out of t' door, that's owlde man Fingers. 'E's Uncle Tom's overseer, at least 'e thinks 'e is. Cum on let's go, before 'e sees us." Bertie pulled her arm and the three stepped off the curb, just as a horse and carriage went whizzing by. "Blimey, look where yer goin', mate."

Brushing off dirt, sprayed up from their close encounter of hoofs and wheels, they made it across the street and continued back along Fetter Lane. They stopped in front of "Fowler's Meat & Poultry Shoppe." Through the window, Bess saw an assortment of fresh meats and fish. The door bell clanged as they entered. Unlike her butcher shop, Bess got a strong whiff of fresh blood and ripe meat. Taking a step backwards, she noticed chickens plucked and unplucked, hanging from the ceiling. Their limp necks attached to menacing looking, large metal hooks.

"Don't worry, Miss Bess. They won't 'urt ye. They's dead." Artie assured her.

"Wot can I do fer ye, lads, miss?" a loud voice asked.

"Good dye, Mr. Fowler. Me mum wants fer ye to put aside a roast of beef fer Sunday dinner. Miss Jo will pick it up about four," Bertie told the large, middle-aged butcher. "Oh, me mum wants another slab of Dutch cheese like ye gave Miss Jo yesterday. A might delicious it was, weren't it, Miss Bess?"

"Aye then, lad, I'll put it away right now before t' blokes cum in wit' their Saturday pay." He wiped his hands on his bloody, full-length apron. "Nothin' much good left, after they're in 'ere. Yer mum knows that." He turned to put a slab of cheese on the scales. "Right then. See ye tomorrow. Mrs. Fowler is lookin' forward to it."

Leaving the shoppe, Bertie pointed to an add-on, at the back of the building. "See that shed, t'is an ice 'ouse. It keeps 'is meat 'n' stuff fresh. In summer, me 'n' Artie sneak in there to keep cool. Mr. Brown, next door, keeps 'is milk 'n' eggs in 'ere, too."

Passing "The Brown Bread," their nostrils were treated with the aroma of fresh baked bread. Further restoration of their sensory organs continued when they entered "Basil's Spice & Mustard Shoppe." The smell of cinnamon, nutmeg and ginger sweetened the moment, while mustard, crushed peppers and dried thyme, basil and sage awakened their senses. Small wooden barrels of spices covered the floor. A small fire in the red brick, fireplace heightened the aromas.

Bess took in a deep breath. "Oh, it smells heavenly in here."

"Why thank ye, miss. Especially after bein' in Fowlers, hey." A jolly man with rosy cheeks laughed. "I just stepped out to t' pub fer me daily rations of pigs ear an' saw ye three cum out of 'is establishment."

" 'E means beer," Artie whispered in her ear, as he pushed in his nose and wiggled his ear.

Without noticing Artie's translation skills, Basil continued, "If it weren't fer me spices, 'is meat 'n' poultry wouldn't taste an' especially smell auff as good." He laughed even louder.

The boys giggled and Bertie said, "Me mum needs one penny each of cinnamon, nutmeg, ginger and cardamom, ---- an' a 'apenny of mace fer 'er Christmas bakin'." The boys licked their lips and smiled.

" 'Ere, lads, ye can 'elp me fill these bags." Basil gave each boy a bag and took them over to separate barrels. "Ye be t' lady from America. I'm cumin' over to 'ear ye play tomorrow. T' missus is lookin, forward to it. Right then. That will be four an' auff pence, Bertie."

Bertie clapped his hands, spreading a cloud of cinnamon in the air and reached in his pocket. " 'Ere's a tanner, sur."

" 'Ere's yer change, Bertie, one pence, 'apenny." Basil gave Artie the bag of spices, while Bertie put the change in his pocket.

Bess looked at Artie and rubbed the nutmeg off his nose. "Here, I'll take some of them Artie."

Back at the tea shoppe, one look from Lottie and all three immediately went to their rooms to change. Covered in specks of dried dirt, cinnamon and nutmeg, Bess looked in the mirror. She discovered she looked as bad as the boys. She began rubbing smudges of cinnamon off her cheeks and nutmeg out of her hair, only to find the spices settling on her pyjamas. *Pyjamas?*

"Pyjamas, yes indeed they are." Bess brushed the flannel top, releasing the spices into the air. Her eyes followed the spicy particles to the floor. "My lovely carpet, it's covered with Cheerios, cinnamon Cheerios."

"Bess, aren't you dressed yet? It's one o'clock." Evan looked at his watch and walked over and gave her a kiss on the cheek. "Hmm, cinnamon Cheerios." He brushed one off her cheek. "Did you have a Cheer—i—o party for me, when I left this morning?" He laughed. "They're all over the floor. They're even on the mantel." He shook his head.

"I choked on a mouthful. I guess they sort of exploded all over the room."

"Okay that explains the Cheerios, but what about the afternoon pyjama party?" He looked at her and waited for an explanation. Suddenly, his face took on a look of concern and he said, "You're okay, aren't you? Is your back bothering you?"

Feeling guilty, Bess put her hand behind her back, crossed her fingers and made up an excuse as she went along. "No, I'm okay. I just slept late. I thought I heard a noise downstairs." She stopped and looked at an unconvinced face. "So, while I was here, I decided to have some breakfast and read the paper. Before I knew it, well here you are." She gave a sheepish laugh. "I'll just run upstairs and get dressed. I'll only be a moment." As she uncrossed her fingers and put her hand on the railing, she shouted, "I'll clean up the mess when I come down."

"Right-e-o, my Cheer-i-o." He laughed and bent down to pick up the spicy debris.

Ten minutes later, she found Evan staring at the mantel; his cupped hands full of Cheerios. It should have taken her five minutes, however, she noticed the unmade bed and decided one guilty explanation was enough.

"I meant to compliment you on your arrangement on the mantel. I noticed it yesterday morning, but I forgot to tell you. I don't remember seeing these buildings before."

"I bought some the other day, but I didn't have a chance to show you. I was going to show you the other night, but you fell asleep right after supper."

"Oh, now I remember, all those green shopping bags on the floor. How could I forget? I almost tripped over them a dozen times. And to think, I thought they were all my Christmas presents." He laughed. "Really though, I meant to ask you about them, but I guess it slipped my mind." He gazed intently at the scene. "Hey, Bess, look at this horse and carriage. Why your name's written on the side of the carriage, Williams & Sons. Mind you, it should read Williams & Daughter; today, it would." Evan smiled at Bess and quickly went back to looking at the display. His head moved closer to one of the buildings. "Now isn't this a coincidence, even back then, we Turners were great accountants. Mind you, the building is a wee bit shabby for my taste." He laughed. "They are all so authentic. Why I could just imagine working in that building, slaving away over figures, with only a candle to guide my worn pencil. Why there we are, walking arm and arm down the street. What a good wife

84

coming to escort your weary husband home after a busy day of work."

"Speaking of walking down the street, I guess we better get going, if we want to get some shopping done," Bess said as she put on her coat.

Several hours later, arms laden with bags, a weary Bess and Evan arrived back home. The local mall, a height of activity, made them appreciate the quiet of home. Evan flopped down on the chesterfield.

Give me those parcels before you break something." Bess took the brightly coloured bags and deposited them on the floor.

"Yeah, they'll be safe there, Bess." Evan managed a sarcastic laugh.

"Hush, give me your coat and take off those wet shoes."

"You can have my shoes, but I don't want to take off my coat. It's getting cold out. The rain could turn into snow if the temperature drops any further. We're only a few days away from winter, you know."

"Don't be a baby. It's warm in here. ----- Don't shudder. ---- I'll turn up the thermostat." Bess picked up his shoes and on the way to the closet, turned the thermostat to seventy-five. "There. ---- Want some cocoa?"

"With marshmallows?" He perked up and without hearing Bess's answer, he asked, "How about some of your delicious Christmas cake?" Satisfied, he took off his coat and laid it on the arm of the chesterfield.

"Ouch, that's hot," Evan exclaimed, as he lifted his white mucky mouth from the mug. He licked the gooey marshmallow off his upper lip. "Where's the cake, woman?"

"I'm coming. I've only got so many hands, Lord and Master," Bess said, as she brought in a plate of rich, dark fruitcake. Placing the plate in front of Evan, she said, "I like the Christmas tree we got. --- Well, I think I do. It's so hard to imagine what they really look like, after being piled up for weeks. We pull their tight branches apart, stand back to view them, only to have their frozen limbs spring back into the fetal position. We've been fooled many times before."

"I suppose we could always buy one of those suicidal, cultured trees, we see hanging from the rafters. See, they don't even like themselves. They're too perfect for their own good. Besides, who wants to pay eighty dollars for a tree, when you can have a genuine Charlie Brown tree, oozing with character, for twenty dollars?" Blowing on the hot cocoa, he took another cautious sip and looked at the cake plate. "Anymore?"

Bess went into the kitchen to cut some more cake and heard Evan say, "We'll put up the tree tomorrow. I'll put it in a bucket of water later."

"I'm so pleased we found that lovely star for the top. We've been looking a long time for a new one. Our old one wouldn't guide a donkey, let alone a wise man," she said.

"How come you spent so much time in the toy department? We don't have anymore kids to buy for, do we?" Evan asked. "How come you were looking at all those different types of runners? I thought you liked your Nikes."

"I can't buy her a pair with my name on them, can I?" she muttered.

"What did you say? I couldn't hear you," he shouted from the living room.

"Don't shout. I'm right here," she snapped back. "Here's another two pieces of cake for you."

"Great." He smacked his marshmallow, powdered lips and forgot his previous question.

His stomach full, Evan started to nod his head. Soon, his chin dropped onto his chest and the snoring began. Bess sat back with the remains of her cocoa and recalled Evan's questions. *Yes,* she thought *I did spend quite a bit of time in the toy department. What can I get Bertie and Artie for Christmas? --- And more important, will I be able to get them there. It will have to be something small that I can carry.* She sighed *I'd like to get Lottie some comfortable shoes, but without a name branded on them. I don't want the boys picking up on it. I'll keep looking ---- or think of something else.* She looked up at the mantel, hoping for inspiration to get the grey cells working; nothing came forward. Disappointed, Bess leaned back and closed her eyes.

"Can I 'ave sum more chocolate?"

Startled, Bess looked at the cup in front of her. A small hand held tightly to the handle.

"Oh, cum in, Bess. Don't ye look pretty. I'd 'oped me blue gown would fit ye. 'Ere turn around. ---- Let's see." Lottie got up and checked out her dress. "Oh 'ere, let me get t' buttons fer ye. I always 'ave trouble wit' 'em. T' arms ain't long enough. --- Oh fer a lady's maid," she sighed.

Bess looked down to find cleavage looking straight up at her. *My heavens, I haven't seen them exposed and proud of it for a very ---- very long time. My, wouldn't Evan be pleased.* She giggled.

"Sorry, luv, did I tickle ye?" Lottie asked. "Yer probably not used to wearin' sumthin' t'is tight. Wot wit' t' clothes we saw ye cum 'ere in. That reminds me, Artie, do ask yer mum if Miss Bess's clothes ar' ready. --- Not that ye'll 'ave an occasion to wear 'em 'ere, Bess, but all t' same, they're t' only clothes ye 'ave an' they remind ye of 'ome." Without taking a breath, she continued, "On Monday, ye must go round an' inquire about yer luggage. Blimey, they should 'ave found 'em by now. T' shipping companies ar' as bad as t' government. Takin' their sweet time, they do."

"Now, don't get started," interjected Tom.

"Yer quite right, Tom." Lottie poked her head from behind Bess's back. "There, yer all buttoned up. Cum an' 'ave sum supper, Bess. Mr. Brown brought sum delicious buns. An' would ye believe, Mr. Fowler gave us a sample of 'is newly imported cheese from Italy. 'E especially wanted t' young lady from America to taste it.--- Watch out Jo, ye 'ave sum competition." She laughed and winked at Bess.

Not playing favourites, Bess decided to sit between Bertie and Artie, whose well-scrubbed faces shone up at her. She manoeuvred her voluminous skirt onto the tiny triangle in the centre of the tête-à-tête. Suddenly, she became aware of Tom staring at her. *Oh no, he's noticed them too.* She blushed, then smiled at him and received a wicked one in return.

Mr. Brown looked very dapper in his green suit and wine coloured waistcoat, made of silk. The green, silk cravat gave his outfit an appropriate Christmas look. Beside him, sat Lottie in an emerald green, silk gown, which brought out the rich dark-brown colour of her hair and eyes. Like Bess, she wore the bodice of her dress very low, exposing them for all to see, especially Mr. Brown. He looked quite satisfied, indeed. Jo, dressed in a pretty crimson gown of taffeta, looked stunning. Her soft, white skin looked so delicate against the deep colour of her gown and the black lustre of her hair. Bess noticed Jo kept looking at the clock on the mantel.

"Tom, would ye go down an' bring up t' other pot of chocolate, I left warmin' on t' stove?" Lottie looked at her brother and motioned to Bertie. "Pass t' buns around, please son. Artie, luv, ye can carry t' cheese."

A few minutes later, an echo of footsteps ascended the creaky stairs. Two male voices spoke loudly, and soon laughter filled the room. A muscular, young man with curly, sandy coloured hair entered the room. His pale-blue eyes lit up when they rested upon Jo's blushing face. He too did blush.

"Why, good evening, Sean. We wondered what was keeping you," said Mr. Brown.

"Aye, I dinna think I'd make it in time. My landlord wanted a wee chat with me. Sorry, Mrs. Morton."

"Sean MacLeod, yer welcum 'ere anytime. It wouldn't 'ave bin t' same, if ye missed t' play. Would it, Jo?" said Lottie with a wink directed at Jo. "Cum sit beside Jo an' get ye a plate. Bertie, give Sean a bun wit' a good slab of that cheese."

"Chocolate, Sean?" Tom asked, bringing a cup to him." While I'm up, anyone else like some chocolate?"

"Me---Me," piped up the boys as they raised their hands.

"Just a auff cup, mind. I don't want it to be a necessity to take 'em out to t'necessarium at t' theatre." Lottie pinched her nose and the boys giggled.

The clock struck six and they made a dash for the stairs. Mr. Brown went first with the boys right on his heels. He to alert the driver of the impending entourage, while the boys went in the opposite direction, through the back door of the kitchen, for a quick trip to the necessarium. Slowly, the ladies managed to contain their gowns down the narrow staircase. Their escorts treaded lightly behind, in fear of stepping on the ladies' skirts. The boys were back by the time the last lady reached the bottom stair.

"Did ye wash yer 'ands?" Lottie scowled at the guilty faces. "Get ye in there an' wash 'em." She turned back to the others. "Those lads never seem to learn."

The night air, cold and damp, made them shiver as they stepped out of the warmth of the building. Drifts of fog enveloped them as they made their way in the direction of their waiting carriage. A solitary black mass loomed large in front of them. The side door opened and each lady received a gentlemanly hand into the carriage. The men followed and squeezed themselves in between the folds of taffeta. Lottie sat between Mr. Brown and Tom. On the seat facing them, sat Jo, Sean and Bess. Happy with her seating arrangement, Bess sat by the window, directly across from Tom. She hoped to see the sights. The boys sat up front with the driver, and with much gusto they ordered the two horses to depart.

The ride left something to be desired in the way of comfort. The seats, stuffed with horse's hair, did not give at all when the occupants bounced up and down. Bess thought *perhaps the horses are getting even, when they deliberately trot beside every pot hole.*

*Obviously, suspension hasn't been invented yet.* Her teeth shuddered. Clop, clop, --- creak--- squeak could be heard with each turn of the wheels. Impossible to hear any conversation, Bess looked out at the eerie scene. Fog shrouded figures walked quickly down the gaslit streets and dark, scary lanes. Bess envisioned toothless men and women, dressed in dirty, torn clothing, hiding and waiting to pounce on the first unsuspecting stranger, who wandered into their lair. She shivered.

"Aye, Miss Bess, are ye cold, lass?" Sean asked. "Ere, I'll give ye my coat."

"Thank you, but I'm fine. I was just leaning too close to the window. I'll move over out of the draught," answered Bess moving an inch closer to Sean, which happened to be all the space left between them.

"Ah, here we are and not too soon," laughed Tom as he tried to stretch his leg, touching Bess's in the process.

He looked at her. She could have sworn he winked at her. To avert eye contact, she looked out the window. Fortunately, the fog had lifted somewhat, and Bess saw a long line of carriages in front of their coach. People lined the sidewalk. Men in tight fitting overcoats and women in tightly wrapped shawls climbed the wide stairs to a brightly lit entrance. A tall overhang, supported by ornate columns, sheltered the patrons whilst waiting to enter the building. The carriage door opened and out jumped Tom.

"Me lady." He stretched out his hand for Bess to take and began to help her out. She lowered her foot down on the step and noticed a sudden smile spread across his face. "Ye can take the lady out of the country, but ye can't take the country out of the lady."

Bess followed his glance downward and noticed her white runner. She quickly covered her shoe with her skirt and without skipping a beat, took his hand, smiled and descended the coach.

"Innit excitin', Miss Bess." Bertie came up to her, leaving poor Artie struggling to get down. "Cum on, Artie, just a bit farther, mate." Bertie grabbed her hand, and a flustered Artie slipped his clammy hand in her other hand.

"Well, I can see I've got some competition." Tom laughed and turned back to help his sister.

Inside, the crowd chatted and made their way to their seats. The noise level forced Bess to observe rather than listen. Women dressed in evening gowns, with their hair done up in ringlets and curls and cheeks brushed with blush, looked beautiful. Even Mrs. Pennycroft, who incidentally acknowledged them by a feeble smile, looked quite stunning, in her own prudish way. The gentlemen looked almost as dapper as Mr. Brown and definitely not as handsome as Tom or Sean. Unfortunately, the cigar smoke inside, competed puff by puff with the fog outside. With the smoking ban in public buildings, Bess had forgotten how smoke affected her. She began coughing.

"'Ere, let's find our seats," said Lottie, just at the right moment.

Needless to say, the boys sat down on either side of Bess and with a quick response Lottie said, "Bertie, cum sit beside me an' let yer Uncle Tom sit on the aisle seat beside Bess. Now don't ye pout. Ye an' Artie can change seats at intermission."

No sooner did they get seated when the orchestra conductor tapped his stick and the music started. Everyone rose to sing "God Save The Queen." Barely seated, the lights went dim and the red velvet curtain opened.

On the dark, empty stage, a deep voice resonated, "I have endeavoured in this ghostly little book, to rise the ghost of an idea, which shall not put my readers out of humour with themselves, with each other, with the season, or with me. May it haunt their house pleasantly, and no one wish to lay it."

"Ladies and gentlemen, thus begins 'A Christmas Carol.'"

The stage lit up. A man sat with his head bent forward at a desk, while another man sat further away, head down, frantically writing.

The deep voice continued, "Once upon a time---- of all good

days in the year, on Christmas Eve old Scrooge sat busy in his counting house. It was cold, bleak, biting weather: Foggy with all."

A yes murmured through the audience and Artie snuggled a little closer to Bess. The clerk looked longingly at the coal bin and put a white comforter around his shoulders.

"A Merry Christmas, Uncle! God save you." A dapper young actor entered.

"Bah! ---- Humbug!"

The male audience cheered. The play went on at a steady pace. His nephew left the stage and two gentlemen entered, soliciting funds for the poor.

Scrooge asked, "Are there no prisons?"

"Plenty of prisons," replied a portly gentleman.

"And the union workhouses? Are they still in operation?"

"They are still. I wish I could say they were not."

"The treadmill and the poor law are in full vigour, then?"

"Both very busy, sir."

"Oh I was afraid, from what you said at first, that something had occurred to stop them in their useful course --- I'm very glad to hear it."

At that point, the audience broke out with resounding cheers and conflicting boos. Eventually, the theatre fell silent and the play continued.

The first act ended with Scrooge saying to his clerk, "You'll want all day tomorrow, I suppose?"

"If quite convenient, sir."

"It's not convenient and it's not fair. If I was to stop half-a-crown for it, you'd think yourself ill used, I'll be bound?"

"You're right there, Scrooge," shouted the male audience.

"And yet you don't think me ill used, when I pay a day's wages for no work. ------ A poor excuse for picking a man's pocket every twenty-fifth of December. But I suppose you must have the whole day. Be here all the earlier next morning."

Once again, the audience participated, with the fancy-dressed cheering and clapping, while the simpler-dressed booed. Without delay, the curtains closed, the audience's vocals petered down to whispers, and sounds of moving objects could be heard behind the curtain. Five minutes later, the curtain opened and the audience saw a large canopied, four-poster bed. Scrooge, in nightgown and cap, sat in front of a fake fire, eating a bowl of gruel.

"Humbug."

The sound of bells clanged loudly, startling the sleepy members of the audience. All eyes opened wide with the clanking sound of a chain being dragged up a flight of stairs. The creaky door flew open. The audience jumped. A wispy shadow came through the doorway.

"I know him! Marley's ghost," shouted Scrooge.

Artie grabbed Bess's arm and hid his face in her sleeve. Tom grabbed the other arm and winked.

"You will be haunted by three spirits."

Artie looked up and said, "Three ---- spirits?"

"Expect the first tomorrow, when the bell tolls one."

"Couldn't I take 'em all at once, and have it over with, Jacob?"

"You tell 'im, Scrooge," a male voice hollered from the audience.

The orchestra began using their instruments to make a howling, haunting noise, while voices wailed. Soon ghostly figures floated across the stage, while others, bound with chains, shuffled. The sound of chains clanging and mournful wails overwhelmed the stage. Scrooge looked all around with a look of horror upon his face. Suddenly, the sounds and ghostly apparitions faded off the stage, leaving only Scrooge, in dead silence. The theatre stood silent as the audience held its breath. Scrooge shaking, walked over to the open door on stage right, slammed it shut and bolted the lock. It made a loud grating sound, and the patrons almost jumped out of their seats. The curtain closed.

Intermission found them in a smoke filled room, filled with a crowd of theatre patrons looking for the coveted, brown liquid, be it of the spirit type or the tea type. To most, the scene on the stage had been as real as real could be, and consequently left them speechless and their mouths dry. Tom and Sean made their way through the crowd with cups of tea for all. Surprisingly, they had not spilt a drop on the small, china trays. Finding a small alcove by a bay window, they managed to drink their much needed tea without being pushed and shoved by others. A breeze came in one of the small, side windows, allowing the stale air to circulate, and make its way out of the small window on the opposite side of the bay window. This arrangement pleased Bess as one of her sensory glands was on overload. Too many excited bodies confined to close quarters, gave her nose a real workout. Perfumed ladies and cigar smoke could not mask the underlying natural odour of the human body. *What year did they invent deodorant? --- Obviously, not in 1847,* she gathered. A loud bell wrung, beckoning them back to their seats and Act III.

The lights went dim and the curtain began to open.

BONG! ---- One o'clock.

An all white, ghostly figure appeared in the middle of the stage.

"Are you the Spirit, sir, whose coming was fore told to me?"

"I am!"

And thus began the parade of the three spirits and their entourage.

The seating arrangements had changed slightly. Artie still sat on Bess's right, but Bertie now sat on her left, between Tom and her. Throughout the remaining acts, both boys took full advantage of her arms and body. When the scene appeared on the stage with the two wretched children clinging to the Ghost of Christmas Present, Bess felt like a kindred spirit, having her own two, clinging tightly to her sides.

"Bob! Make up the fires and buy another coal-scuttle before you dot another i, Bob Cratchit!" a reformed Scrooge announced.

The curtain began to draw closed and a man, of medium height, walked briskly to the centre of the stage and began to speak in a full, clear voice.

"Scrooge was better than his word. He did it all and infinitely more. ----- And it was truly said of him, that he knew how to keep Christmas well, -----May that be truly said of us." The speaker stopped and looked at the audience and smiled. "And so, as Tiny Tim observed, ---- God bless Us, Every One!"

"Ladies and gentlemen!" The man who first spoke at the beginning of the play came on stage and extended his arm straight out to his side, "Charles Dickens!"

The ride home remained a blur for Bess, except for the occasional comment she heard.

"I weren't afraid was ye, Artie?"

"What a surprise to see Mr. Dickens there."

*Yes indeed. What a wonderful surprise, indeed,* thought Bess, as her heart beat fast.

Needless to say, as soon as they entered the tea shoppe, the coals were stoked and the kettle put on the stove. Lottie remained behind to fuss in the kitchen, and the rest proceeded up to the parlour. Coats were flung on an empty chair and chatter continued. Tom put some more coal on the fire.

"Aye, stoke it up 'arty, Tom. Soon as this fog lifts, we could be getting some snow."

"You are quite right, Sean," Tom answered, rubbing his hands together.

"Snow? Me 'n' Artie, we luv snow. Don't we, Artie?"

"Snow? What's this I hear about snow?" Mr. Brown asked, as he entered the room carrying a tray full of cups, plates and a teapot.

Right behind him came Lottie with a smaller tray full of food. *Is it my imagination? Her cheeks, are they not rosy? --- And --- My, is that a ringlet gone astray?* Bess observed to herself.

"Here, let me help you Lottie."

"Mr. Brown 'as brought us a perfect sprig of mistletoe." Lottie cleared her throat. "Tom, be a luv 'an 'ang it up over t' door."

"Aha, mistletoe! Beware my young pretty maidens." Tom wiggled his eye brows up and down and gave a mischievous smile, while the boys giggled.

After a long day, their bodies warm and full, the yawns began in earnest. They all said their goodnights and made their way to bed. Just as Bess reached the top step of the stairs, she heard a small voice below.

"Mum, me 'n' Artie thinks ye might be scared, after all 'em ghosts, so we thought we'd sleep wit' ye."

"Why thank ye, lads fer yer concern. Cum on then. Let's go to bed."

"Come on, let's go to bed. Bess, it's time to go to bed."

"Pardon?" Startled, Bess turned around expecting to see Tom. Instead , Evan stood over her, touching her shoulder. She breathed a sigh of relief and muttered, "Bed? Sleep? --- Yes, Evan, good idea. Let's go to bed. You can protect me from all those spirits."

"Spirits? Honestly, Bess, lately I could swear you've been into the spirits."

# CHAPTER X

Sunday, proclaimed by many idealists as a day of rest, but there would be no rest at the Turner house. Bess opened her eyes when the call of nature squawked outside her bedroom window. *Darn those jays. --- Don't they know it's Sunday morning, a day of rest,* she mused. *Yeah, get real, Bess.* She looked over at Evan sleeping soundly with the covers pulled over his face. Only a tiny, snore-escape hole reassured her, Evan was indeed alive and survived another night. Realizing sleep had come to an abrupt end, she slipped out of bed and went over to the window. She parted the crack in the middle of the drapes and looked out. A dreary sight beheld her eyes. The bare maple tree looked like an apparition, swaying back and forth against the back drop of a grey, early morning sky. Only the brilliant blue of the pesky jays brought colour to the dismal scene. She closed the crack and went downstairs.

*First things first,* Bess thought, as she made her way to the garage. ---- *Things are definitely looking brighter. Evan, my sleeping prince, you didn't forget to put the Christmas tree in water.* Still pleasantly surprised, she filled up a can with peanuts and sunflower seeds and opened the door to the outside world. A cold blast of air made her shudder.

"Come and get it, you pesky jays," she shouted as she quickly threw the birdfeed on the deck. "Every bird for herself. Enjoy, I'm going in before I freeze my b----"

Back in the house, she put on her red velour housecoat and snuggled up on the chesterfield. She noticed the little, red book abandoned on the coffee table. Bess picked it up and flashes of last night's encounter of the strange kind flooded her thoughts. Scenes of ghosts and characters of Scrooge and Tiny Tim danced before the mantel, obscured in darkness. Deciding to bring a little light to the subject, she strolled over to the mantel, slipped the little, red book in her ample pocket and using both hands plugged in the lights. Returning to the chesterfield, she tucked her legs under her and snuggled up once more. Feeling cozy, she bathed in the lights of her magical street. Her eyes caught sight of a pile of books on the coffee table. *I must clear these off before Mr. Spider has his own emergency staircase from his loft.* She smiled, as she looked up at him, nestled in his web of warmth.

Looking through the books and magazines, she saw a garden book. *I've been looking for that; no wonder it wasn't in the bookcase.* Leafing through it, she stopped suddenly. Flipping back, she found what she thought she saw, an article on popular Victorian houseplants. Sure enough, under the A's, aspidistra stood out in bold, red print. Bess read the article *'The iron plant likes warmth: keep away from draughts: can tolerate low light.'* She reasoned *that's why Lottie's isn't doing well by the door.* She kept on reading *'Symbol of middle-class respectability.'* She smiled. *Of course, now I understand why she fusses over it. Also, it makes sense why it was/is a popular houseplant; it tolerates low light.* She laughed. *What other light did they have?* Bess looked up at the tea shoppe and imagined that poor plant suffering a slow death.

"Tsk, tsk. Wot am I goin' to do wit' ye?"

Bess found herself at the foot of the stairs looking at Lottie hunched over by the front door. She turned when Bess's foot made the bottom step creak.

"Good mornin', Bess. I'm so upset wit' me aspidistra. I did want to show it off to me neighbours. Look t'is dyin'." She put her hands on its yellow, limp leaves. Lottie watched as one fluttered to the floor.

"Now don't fret. Coincidentally, I recently read an article on aspidistras. Apparently, they don't like draughts." Bess surveyed the room. "Why don't we move it over by the pianoforte?" Noticing Lottie's dubious expression, Bess continued, "Besides, who wants to enter a place expecting warmth and laughter and be confronted with a pot of lingering death?"

"Well, when ye put it like that, yer right, luv." Lottie shuttered. "Right then, let's move 'er."

Their outstretched arms made a circle around the heavy pot. On a count of three, they lifted the patient off the table. Dry leaves tickled their faces as they carefully maneuvered it over to the piano. They started to laugh when they almost walked into the piano. The aspidistra's huge leaves made visibility very difficult.

"Put 'er down 'ere, while I go an' get t' table," Lottie puffed.

"I'll get it ladies. You just stand there and hold it." Tom laughed. "It gives a man such pleasure to see his women flexing their muscles."

"Tom, don't ye joke. T'is heavy."

Tom brought the table over and put it down by the piano. He strategically placed his arms around Bess's shoulders.

"I've got it Bess, you can let go now," he whispered in her ear. "Ah, you too, Lottie."

*Too close for comfort. Hmm, that's odd; I am actually enjoying this close proximity,* Bess thought, as she reluctantly slid under his embrace. Suddenly, she felt extremely warm as she watched Tom put the plant on the table. *He does have a nice back and his bu----No, I'm not going there.* She blushed.

"Bess, ---- Bess? Would ye be a luv an' put t' 'olly in t' vases? Tom, ---- Tom? Would ye cum 'n' 'elp me in t' kitchen? Since yer so strong, ye can fill up t' buckets wit' water. T'will be lots of water needed fer tea." Lottie started for the kitchen. Not hearing her brother's heavy footsteps on the wood floor, she ordered, "Tom, cum on wit' ye. Church will be out wit'in t' 'our an' our neighbours will be thirstin' fer tea an' starvin' fer scones. 'Twill be a fine thing, if we're not ready fer 'em."

"I'm coming, sister dear." Tom saluted and muttered, "I thought Sunday was a day of rest, so the good book says."

" 'Ow would ye know wot t' good book says?" Lottie retorted. "When was t' last time ye read a book, let alone t' good book? Right, Jo?"

"Well it has been awhile since I have seen him in the book shoppe," Jo answered from behind the counter.

Jo stood on a chair and continued to erase the saying off the slate board. Definitely not wanting to get drawn into their family bickering, she made several swipes with the clean cloth leaving the lower part of the board black as coal. With a piece of white chalk she wrote:

𝔚𝔢𝔩𝔠𝔬𝔪𝔢 𝔣𝔯𝔦𝔢𝔫𝔡𝔰 𝔱𝔬 𝔬𝔲𝔯 𝔠𝔥𝔯𝔦𝔰𝔱𝔪𝔞𝔰 𝔗𝔢𝔞
𝔄𝔩𝔩 𝔦𝔱𝔢𝔪𝔰 𝔥𝔞𝔩𝔣 𝔭𝔯𝔦𝔠𝔢 𝔬𝔯 𝔱𝔴𝔬 𝔣𝔬𝔯 𝔬𝔫𝔢
"𝔓𝔬𝔩𝔩𝔶 𝔭𝔲𝔱 𝔱𝔥𝔢 𝔨𝔢𝔱𝔱𝔩𝔢 𝔬𝔫. 𝔚𝔢'𝔩𝔩 𝔞𝔩𝔩 𝔥𝔞𝔳𝔢 𝔱𝔢𝔞." _____
𝔠𝔥𝔞𝔯𝔩𝔢𝔰 𝔇𝔦𝔠𝔨𝔢𝔫𝔰 "𝔅𝔞𝔯𝔫𝔞𝔟𝔶 𝔑𝔲𝔡𝔤𝔢"

Jo stepped off the chair and studied the board. Tilting her head from side to side, she said, "Bess what do you think? Does it look straight?"

Bess stood behind Jo and scrutinized the board. "Yes, very professional. I didn't realize you were the artist of this masterpiece."

"Yes, I do it every morning before I go and open the book shoppe. Lottie asked me for my expertise. Since I ran the shoppe, she thought I would know volumes of suitable sayings for her board. Not that I mind, for she is so good to me. Besides, it keeps me alert searching for the perfect ones."

"I noticed you had this same saying on the board the other day," Bess said.

"That is very observant of you. Normally, I try a new one each day, but since many of our friends will be children, they can relate to this simple saying. Actually, Lottie asked for this saying for today. She hardly ever asks for one."

Bess went over to the sideboard, where a large bundle of holly lay awaiting her artistic touch. She picked up a branch full of red berries and immediately pricked her finger.

"Ouch!"

"Thank goodness that is your job. Use the little knife--- next to the holly. It is very sharp, so don't cut yourself."

Cautiously, Bess picked up the piece again and made an angle cut through the branch. Soon she had a number of pieces laid out in front of her. Carefully, she picked up each piece and arranged them in the small, blue pottery vases. She took her artistic creations to the tables and placed one in the middle of each linen tablecloth. She stood back and thought *nice touch*.

Lottie interrupted Bess's self-admiration of her creations, "Bess, can ye cum an' 'elp us bring in t' bakin' from t' kitchen?"

Bess hurried into the kitchen, to find a scene of busy elves preparing the Christmas goodies. The room smelt heavenly. Bess inhaled the aroma right through to the bottom of her stomach. Her stomach growled.

"Hey, noisy one, take these out and don't eat them," Tom laughed as he handed her a tray of jam tarts. "I'll carry the mince tarts. With all that growling going on, I don't trust you with my favourites." He shouted back towards the kitchen, "Did you give Bess any breakfast this morning?"

"Sorry, luv, no time fer breakfast. Where's me mitts? T' scones 'ave to cum out of t' oven."

"There they are behind you, --- on the draining board," said Jo, as she went through the doorway with a tray full of currant buns in one hand and a tray of fancy cakes in the other.

"Jam. I fergot t' jams. Bess, luv, can ye put t' jams in t' glass bowls on t' sideboard? Tom, 'elp t' poor thing. Open t' jars fer 'er."

The bell on the door jingled and in ran a breathless Bertie. "Sorry I'm late, Mum. T' choir master," puff puff, " kept us after church. I tried to tell 'im I 'ad to 'elp ye, but 'e wouldn't listen. 'E said 'e only answers to Gabriel."

"Well, 'e'll answer to me next time I see 'im," said Lottie rather sharply. "Cum in 'ere an' take off yer coat 'n' wash yer 'ands. Ye can 'elp Bess take out t' bowls of jam. --- An' don't ye put yer finger in 'em either."

The church bells started ringing.

" 'Tis eleven o'clock. They'll be 'ere any minute. Put yer jacket on, Tom. Jo, there's flour on yer skirt." Lottie took off her soiled apron and blew a lock of hair out of her eyes.

Bess smoothed out her dress and ran her fingers through her hair. *Maybe I should wear an apron. I've worn this dress everyday and it's starting to show the dirt. On the other hand, if I sit on the piano stool, maybe they won't notice.*

As if reading her mind, Lottie said, "Bess, luv, if ye don't mind would ye play t' pianoforte fer our guests? Tom 'n' Jo will 'elp me serve." She turned and looked at Bertie, who just happened to be tapping on her arm. "An' aye, Bertie will 'elp too."

The door bell jangled and in walked Doctor Morgan, followed by a young family.

"Good morning, Mrs. Morton." He took off his top hat. "I have come early before you get busy. I can only stay a half-hour. I have to stop by and see Mrs. Dudley. She is not well. Her son will be there, so I shall have a serious talk with him." He tsked and took a seat.

"Oh, poor thing, she is a lovely woman. What can I get you Doctor Morgan?" Lottie said in rather a formal manner as she smiled sweetly. When she left his table, she said, "Jo, would you serve the other table? Constable Hunter is going on duty soon."

"Jo, I'll get Charlie's table," said Tom, as he strode over to the table of four. "No we wouldn't want to hold up The Great Hunter from flushing out the pickpockets on Fleet Street. How's it going, you old dog? How about a biscuit?"

Bess heard the laughter of the two young men. The bell rang

again and the tables started filling up. She walked towards the piano and stopped. She looked at the lone occupant of a table laden with scones and mince tarts. Drinking his tea, his eyes looked up at Bess and he put down his cup.

"Miss, nice to see you up and about. You young people bounce back so quickly," he said and hesitated, "I am sorry. You may not remember me. I am the old Doc who looked after you the other night. Doctor Morgan, Miss----?" He stood up.

"Bess N-ike, yes I vaguely remember you. Whatever you gave me worked very quickly. Thank you." She smiled and continued to her appointed duty. She sat down on the stool and noticed a couple of books on top of the piano. She reached up and picked them up. The first book read "Popular Music for the Pianoforte" and the second read "Christmas Music." Thumbing through them, she thought *I didn't notice them before.* A tap on the shoulder made her turn around.

"I thought they might come in handy, since you are probably not too familiar with our music," Jo said softly. "There's a pianoforte at the pub, so I borrowed them. In fact, keep them if you like. They will not be missed."

Bess said a silent thank you and positioned the "Christmas Music" on the stand. *Isn't this interesting. I didn't know these songs were that old. Well that's good; I know them and they know me,* she mused. She started off with "The Holly And The Ivy." In the background, she heard much laughter coming from the neighbours. Once in awhile, she turned to see ruddy faces, clean scrubbed faces, bearded faces, wrinkled faces, pretty faces, but always happy faces. Busy concentrating on a song, unfamiliar to her, she felt a tug at her arm.

"Miss Bess, 'tis me, Artie. Cum an' meet me mum 'n' dad."

Glad for a chance to rest her fingers, she made her way to Artie's table. The room overflowed with folks in their Sunday best. Most of the women probably had only one good dress. The men looked uncomfortable in their only suit and bow tie. Many of the vests, stretched to the limit, gave buttons an impossible task. Over the years, the vest remained faithful, but not the expanding waistline. After indulging in all the goodies spread before them, definitely many buttons would succumb to forces beyond their control.

One such set of buttons belonged to Basil Pepper. As Bess passed by his table, she became aware of the pleasant aroma of spices invading her sense of smell. Out of the scent of survival, she quickly learned to block out most of the unpleasant odours emitted from excited, nineteenth century people, enclosed in small areas. She slowed down to give her sense of smell a brief moment of enjoyment.

"Good dye, miss. I'd like ye to meet t' missus. I told 'er all about ye." Basil's stomach jiggled as he gave a jolly laugh.

"Nice to meet ye, miss. I am enjoyin' yer playin'. 'Tis such a clever thing to play an instrument," said a full-figured woman.

"Bess, please call me Bess. I love the heavenly smell of your shoppe. It must be difficult for you to leave it and venture out into the street."

"Yer quite right, Bess." She poked her husband, and they all laughed. "Rosemary, Rosemary Pepper is me name."

"Me spicy little missus, she be," Basil added and the Peppers laughed some more.

"Nice meeting you, I must go and meet Artie's family," said Bess as Artie held her hand tighter and pulled her along.

The Doyle family sat at the table in the charming alcove of the bay window. As the two approached, Bess noticed the fog had lifted, leaving a light drizzle to spread its cloak of dampness across Fetter Lane. The packed ground looked smooth and slick. A horse and carriage drove by, leaving fresh hoof and wheel designs on the hard surface. For the first time since arriving, Bess saw the buildings on the other side of the lane. Dirty brick and mortar giants, akin to battle scared sentinels, stood guard over the genteel tea and book shoppes across the lane.

"Mither, Father, T'is Miss Bess," shouted Artie as they came closer to the table.

A short, solid built man stood up and said, "Pleased to meet ye, miss. I'm Michael Doyle and t'is is my wife Maureen and our wee daughter Patty."

"Artie never stops talkin' about ye. 'Tis so nice to finally meet ye," Maureen Doyle said, "Please sit down in Artie's chair."

"You have a delightful son and a true gentleman," Bess replied. She noticed Artie's beaming face.

'Tis not easy raisin' t'em in a new country. Back in Ireland, we lived in a small village and raisin' children was easier. We both work long hours, so have not met many neighbours. Fortunately, Artie met Bertie and his family. Mrs. Morton has been a Godsend, what wit' her kindness to Artie and bringin' me lots of laundry." Maureen looked over at Lottie. "Oh t'at reminds me, I've brought yer laundry."

"I hung it up in yer room, Miss Bess. Mither, I knows where 'er room is."

"Know where her room is, Artie," Mrs. Doyle corrected him. "T'is one of the problems livin' in t'is part of London. Children pick up the language so quickly. We try to teach him proper Irish, but he keeps slippin' into Cockney." She shook her head and smiled.

"Why did you move to London?"

Mr. Doyle looked at his wife and said, "Oh, we've asked ourselves t'at question many times. As Maureen said, back in Ireland, we had a small farm, which put food on t' table and a few shillin's in our pockets. We t'ought of makin' our fortune in t' Colonies, but wit' two wee children to support, we couldn't take t' chance. All changed in 1845; the potato famine hit Ireland. Our crops were destroyed by t' potato blight and so was our meager income. A mate of mine moved to London a couple of years before and kept writing for us to join him here. In September of t'at year, we got another letter from him sayin' bricklayers were in high demand in London. I had done a fair amount of bricklayin' as a lad, so I knew the trade. Maureen and I talked it over and decided to quit t' farm and move here. My older brother Seamus had the farm next to ours, so he offered to farm ours too. Between t' two farms, t'ey would support one family, but not two. So wit' heavy hearts, we left our green Ireland, on October t' second."

" 'Twas t' fourt', dear husband," the wife corrected.

Ignoring her correction, he continued, "We moved in wit' our friend in a small lodgin' in T' Rookeries. T' next day, I got a job as a bricklayer. Shortly after, we moved two buildin's down, in a larger ground level lodgin'."

"T' lodgin' was a former laundry, so we fixed it up and decided to make use of t' old laundry tub and space out back for dryin'. Michael managed to find a used stove like Mrs. Morton's. Not so grand mind ye and has no oven, but at least I can boil more water faster," said Mrs. Doyle.

"It's heavy work for you," Bess sympathized.

"True, but so was pickin' and plantin' potatoes," she said. "We have two grand children, our healt' and each ot'er, a roof over our heads and food in our stomach."

"On a day like today, we look around and see all t'ese happy faces and it makes us happy." Mr. Doyle smiled. "As Maureen said, 'Mrs. Morton is a true blessin'.' We are t'ankful for such friends."

"Wot about Bertie 'n' Uncle Tom?"

"Aye, t'em too, son. Tom and I have a pint toget'er now and t'en. Mostly at 'T' Goodale,' but once in awhile, we wander over to 'Ye Olde Cheshire Cheese.'"

"We love Bertie. He is such a delight. Michael and I t'ink of him as our wee London Leprechaun, a mischievous face t'at never stops talkin'," Mrs. Doyle laughed. "Oh, if only he would talk in proper English. He does influence Artie so. I rue t' day Artie starts calling us Mum 'n' Dad." She tsked, as Artie gave a sheepish, little grin. "Where's our manners? Would ye like a cup of tea?"

"I'd love one, but I'd better get back to the piano. Nice meeting you," said Bess.

Bess made her way back to the piano and started playing "White Christmas." Lost in her music, she played a few modern songs and then a few early carols. While playing "Frosty The Snowman," she felt someone watching her. She moved her head and spied two large, green eyes staring up at her.

"Hello there. Patty, isn't it?" asked a smiling Bess.

"Aye," the shy, little girl quietly said.

"Would you like me to play anything special for you?"

The mop of red hair bobbed up and down and whispered, "Wot ye were playin' p'ease."

Bess continued with Frosty, but decided, in the interest of children, words were needed. She tried to sing quietly, as not to disturb the adults, but Frosty always brought the kid out in her and she became louder. Soon, a young audience surrounded the piano. They giggled and attempted to sing along. In no time, they memorized the first two lines and in tune.

"Fros----ty, the snowman was a jol --- ly hap --- py soul with a corn cob pipe and a but -- ton nose -- and two eyes made out of coal-------"

The children giggled at Rudolph, but looked puzzled when Santa was mentioned. "Jingle Bells" had them singing in an off-beat chorus or two.

"I luv t' fast ones; don't ye, Artie?"

"Aye, me 'n' Patty luv 'em too, Bertie."

"Okay, if you want a fast one, here's one for you." Bess flexed her fingers and did a fancy intro.

"Jingle bell, jingle bell, jingle bell rock ------"

When she finished playing, she received a hearty clap from the children and to her surprise, from the adults. She turned to bow and noticed the tea saying on the board.

"For my last number ------ "Polly put the kettle on, kettle on-------"

"-----an' we'll all 'ave tea------" the children sang loudly.

"Now, my dear children, on that note, tea sounds like a good idea." Bess played her last note, and the children went back to their tables.

"My dear, young lady, I thoroughly enjoyed every song," a manly voice said in perfect elocution, "especially the last one." He laughed. "A few years ago, I dabbled in music and wrote a small piece 'The Libretto' for a play. My sister Fanny studied at the Academy of Music and is really the musician of the family."

Bess smiled at the man and thought *where have I seen you before? And --- the voice sounds so familiar.*

"Bess, luv, I see you've met Mr. Dickens," said Lottie. "We all went to your play last night. I was ever so surprised to see you there. Our dear Bess was so awestruck by your appearance, she did not say a word all the way home."

Mr. Dickens took her hand and said, "Honoured to meet a fellow musician, Miss Bess." He smiled and lightly kissed her hand.

Flustered, Bess didn't know if she should curtsy or sit there like a dummy. She decided to attempt a curtsy, got half way up, stepped on her skirt and fell right into Mr. Dickens' arms. To make matters worse, she attracted the attention of everyone in the room, especially when a solid object fell out of her pocket and crashed to the floor. Thoroughly embarrassed, she plunked back down on the piano stool. At the low height of the stool, she hoped no one would see her flaming red cheeks.

"Here, miss, you dropped this." Mr. Dickens was about to hand her the little, red book when he noticed the title. "Why, it is 'A Christmas Carol.' I'm flattered."

Trying to get a modicum of composure back, she weakly said, "Would you autograph my book, Mr. Dickens?"

"My dear, I would be delighted." He smiled and took a small straight pen out of his pocket. He reached into his overcoat pocket and came out with a small bottle of blue ink. "I never leave home without it."

Spying space on a nearby table, he put the bottle down, opened it carefully and dipped his pen into the bottle. He began to write on the inside cover, stopping a few times to dip his pen in the ink-well. Mr. Dickens looked around for a blotter, but finding nothing appropriate, he blew on the paper. Satisfied with the result, he gave it to Bess.

She read the inscription:

"Bess, thank you. I had 'The Bess Time.'

Charles Dickens.... 1847"

He gave Bess a wink, nodded his head, went over to Lottie, said a few words, put on his top hat and walked out the door.

Bess sat on the stool clutching the little, red book when Jim Button approached. She half expected Sadie to be trotting behind.

"Good afternoon, miss." Jim smiled at her with his rosy cheeks brushed to a high sheen; no doubt due to all that scrubbing necessary to rid them of layers of caked on, street dirt. "We're enjoyin' yer music. If ye can spare a minute, Mrs. Button would like to meet ye. She be right at t' corner table." He pointed to a woman covered in a black shawl.

"Of course, Jim. Where's Sadie? Is she waiting outside? If so, I'll get a lump of sugar."

"No, bein' Sunday, t' owlde girl gets a dye of rest." As they approached the table, another woman dressed in a mix match of colours and fabrics, walked up and sat down. "Miss Bess, Mrs. Button." He turned to the older woman, "And t'is 'ere's Lily, t' flahs lady."

The thin woman gave Bess a toothless smile and said, "I saw ye before. Yer t' lady t'at fell in front of Sadie. Mind ye, wi't t' trousers ye 'ad on, I thought ye were one of t' lads. I can see now yer not." Her watery, pale-blue eyes looked Bess over. "I liked yer playin'. I could 'ear it outside. When I were a young girl back in Lambeth, I luved to dance a jig---just ax t'Pearly King 'n' Queen, they'll tell ye 'ow good I were. 'Ere t'is fer ye, fer makin' me 'appy an' rememberin' t' good times." Lily lifted her bony fingers and handed Bess a small nosegay of dried lavender."

"Oh, I couldn't."

"Aye, ye can an' will, quoz I'll be gettin' me own back in coind. Ye can play fer me."

"Lily, did ye get yer tickets fer t' goose club, t'is month?" Jim interrupted. "Ye knows we only got a couple of dyes left."

"Aye, Jim, I'm goin' to win t'is year. Blimey, ye can bet on it, Jim Button." She gave a husky laugh.

"That's wot ye say ev'ry year, Lily," Jim laughed, "Besides t'is year, t' Buttons ar' goin' win t' goose. Right Mary?"

For the first time, Mrs. Button spoke, "Miss Bess, don't take no mind of 'em. Ev'ry year, they say they're goin' win an' ev'ry year they don't. Why auff of London joins t' goose club to win t' goose. We could 'ave a turkey, wot wit' all t' money we spend on tickets."

"Nice to meet you, ladies," Bess said. "Thank you for the flowers. Lavender is so soothing for the soul." She hesitated for a moment, looked at Lily, who was beaming, took a deep breath and bent down and gave Lily a hug. Not surprising, the woman smelt like lavender fields.

Lily shouted at Bess's retreating back, "Don't ferget. Did I tell ye I like 'T' Last Rose Of Summer'?"

Reaching up for "The Popular Music For Piano," Bess thumbed through the pages until she came to "The Last Rose Of Summer." She sat down and played Lily's request. When it finished, she turned towards Lily, who gave her a big, toothless smile. *She truly is the last rose of summer, even if she is a lily,* Bess mused.

"I want to 'ear 'T' Death Of Nelson' I tell ye," an elderly voice demanded.

"Shush, Captain!"

"Don't shush me, woman. I want 'er to play 'T' Death Of Nelson.' God rest 'is glorious soul."

Bess turned around to see Mr. Fowler attempting to quiet an elderly man. Two women at the same table, joined in the conspiracy. Mr. Fowler looked at Bess and mouthed a silent sorry. To appease the elderly man, Bess quickly thumbed through the music book. *Yes, there really is such a song.* Pleased with her find, she started to play the piece.

"Faster, girl, if ye play any slower, Nelson will think t'is 'is funeral march all over again."

"Hush, Father, she be from America. She doesn't know t'is song."

Bess picked up the tempo and the elderly voice shouted, "That's it, girl." He started clapping and stomping his feet.

Fortunately, when the song finished, so was the captain. Bess turned her head to see his head bent forward. The high seas had petered out on the shores of Slumberland.

Bess noticed a gentleman in a clerical collar, so decided to find a more fitting song.

*That will do,* she thought as she saw "Drink To Me Only With Thine Eyes." *Well it sounds more respectable than "Sally In The Alley,"* which happened to be on the opposite page.

Stopping to flex her fingers, she looked around the room. Only five tables remained occupied. The Buttons had left, leaving Lily and a tall stranger at the table.

"Sam, I need ye to cum an' look at one of me chimneys. I've got no draft. It needs a sweep," Mr. Fowler said as he looked back at Lily's companion.

Over in the corner, two, nicely dressed gentlemen sat talking to Jo and Tom. *Where have I seen that gentleman in the green and brown tweed suit?* Bess gave her memory bank a visit. *I know, it's Mr. Turner, Tom's boss. How could I forget a man with a name like Turner?* The older gentleman, Bess did not recognize. He shifted in his chair as if to get into a better position to extract something from his vest pocket. His protruding stomach forced him to give up the futile attempt. He slowly rose from his chair and pulled out the elusive object. A silver pocket watch sprung open.

"My, my, look at the time. I must be off. I have a two o'clock appointment with a man interested in a couple of my antiquarian books. William, are you going to the club tomorrow?" He looked at the other man who said something Bess did not catch. "Fine then, one it is." He picked up his cane and top hat. "Thank you, Mrs. Morton. As always, everything was delicious. I'll see you in the morning, Jo. Get a good night's sleep. We have that big shipment to unpack and get on the shelves. I'm sure we are always the last on their route on Saturday afternoon. It makes for a bad start for the week. I must make a note to tell them of my displeasure." He shook his head. "Not that it will do any good." He put on his top hat and said, "Right then. Tom, don't let Scrooge Turner work you too hard." He laughed and with the aide of his cane, walked out with a shuffle.

A very attractive woman sat laughing at a table occupied by a handsome gentleman. Bess noticed they both had the same infectious laugh. A blond woman sat with her back facing Bess, and a young boy sat between the woman and the man. *All four immaculately dressed; actually seem over-dressed for the occasion,* thought Bess, especially when she looked over at Lily, her poor dress wet with tea stains. Lily slurped as she inhaled every last drop of tea from the china saucer. The attractive woman waved at Bess and beckoned her over to their table. This time when Bess got up, she did it very cautiously. *Complete humiliation would be landing on the floor once more and having this perfect lady staring at me. I can only hope, the lady didn't witness my tumble into Mr. Dickens' arms.*

"I see you have one of my dresses on," said the lady as she moved her head a little closer. "My, is that a stain ---- or two?" She tutted. "Dear, you must come in to our shoppe, and I will make you a new one." She smiled sweetly and her face lit up. "Where are my manners? I am Lydia Taylor. My brother Lawrence and I own 'Taylor & Sons Haberdashery' on the corner. Before you say anything, I am one of the Sons, Number Two Son as Father always referred to me. However, I accept that ranking as my twin brother, Lawrence here, was the first born." She gave a fake smile to her brother and continued, "Our father was so excited about having twins, he just took for granted they would be boys. So upon hearing the joyous news, he had the painter add & Sons to 'Taylor Haberdashery.' Fortunately for Father, we both followed in his footsteps. Lawrence dresses the men and I the women. Mind you, I would make an exception if Tom were to come into my side of the shoppe." She laughed and let her eyes wander in Tom's direction.

Mr. Taylor stood up and said, "Please forgive my better half. Lydia never stops once she starts talking and believe me, it does not take much to get her started." He shook his head. "I'm Lawrence Taylor and this is my other better half, my wife Beatrice Taylor. As you can see, it doesn't leave much of the piece left for me and certainly even less peace." He laughed. "My son Peter and I find life quite challenging with two Taylor women trying to mend our ways."

Mrs. Taylor, also a very attractive woman, said, "I did enjoy your playing, miss. You must be new here. I haven't seen you before."

"Yes, I just dropped in for a short visit with the Mortons. Please call me Bess."

"Well, Bess, do drop in to our shoppe. It is not too late for Christmas shopping."

"Oh, miss--- could we have another pot of tea?" asked a male voice behind Bess.

Bess searched for the servers, but found only Tom engrossed in a conversation with Mr. Turner. So, she said, "Yes, right away, sir."

"Blimey, 'Arry. She's t' pianist." A woman's voice scolded.

"Sorry, miss."

"No bother. I'll take your teapot and be right back."

Bess walked into the kitchen and saw Lottie hunched over a roasting pan. The cook turned around and said, " I'm just puttin' t' roast in t' oven fer dinner. An' soon as our guests leave, we can rest while t' roast is cookin'. Luv, ye must be gettin' tired. Blimey, I knows I am. I'm goin' up to me room an' put me feet up. Bertie went over to Artie's, so I don't 'ave to worry about 'im till dinner time."

"Maybe later, but right now I'm going to have a cup of tea with the young couple out front. Ar--? Harry asked me to join them."

"Oh that be 'Arry 'n' Millie Topham. 'E be our postman an' she cums an' cleans t' 'ouse ev'ry Wednesday. Nice young couple indeed. I might even join ye fer a cuppa."

Bess took two cups and saucers, stacked on top of each other, in one hand and the heavy teapot in the other hand. As she went by Tom, he winked at her.

"Not bad, you might make a waitress yet." He gave a cheeky laugh. "Oh, don't trip."

"Don't ye take a mind to Tom. 'E's always teasin'," said the young woman.

"So I'm finding out," Bess said as she put down the china, and ignoring Tom's laughter she continued, "Lottie said she might come and join us. Thank you for inviting me to join you." She extended her hand. "I'm Bess."

"Nice to meet you. This is my wife Millie and I'm Harry Topham." He took Bess's hand and gave it a light shake. "Millie comes in and cleans for Mrs. Morton once a week. Because of her recommendations, Millie is busy five days a week."

"It ain't easy gettin' steady work, wot wit'out an education. 'Arry t'is a grand scholar. Bin to Oxford, 'e 'as. I were ever so pleased when 'e axed me out. Blimey, I couldn't sleep fer days. I were ever so nervous when we went dancin' at t' Vauxhall. When 'e took me in 'is arms an' we did t' polka, I thought I were goin' pee me pantaloons." Millie put her hand to her mouth. "Oh, pardon me language. I do get carried away. I still fer t' life of me, don't understand wot 'Arry sees in me."

"Millie, I am sure Miss Bess has heard worse." Harry gave his wife an adoring smile. "Miss Bess, Millie is giving you the wrong impression. Her schooling may have been very limited, but her wit is sharp, and her heart flows beyond any university's walls."

"Oh, Bess, don't ye just luv'ow'e talks. It makes me 'art flutter, it does." Millie gazed dreamily at her husband's face.

"Don't mind 'er; Millie's got blinders on when it cums to 'Arry." Lottie laughed, as she sat down at the table. "Ow about that cuppa tea now, Millie, luv?"

" I must confess, Mrs. Morton you are right. I did go to Oxford, but only for one year. Sadly, my father passed away unexpectedly, and I had to abandon my education. However, my one year helped me get a job at the post office. I was posted in London so left home, and here I have been since 1840. I am luckier than most, I get a variety of jobs. I usually work in the post office in the morning and deliver mail in the afternoon."

"Mr. Topham, I was in the post office yesterday. What a grand building. It was so bright in there. The stained glass window, what a spectrum of colours it exudes. Oh, and that enormous chandelier, how do they clean it?"

"Very carefully," piped up Millie, "and not very often."

They all laughed and Bess continued, "Tell me, Mr. Topham, when Bertie, Artie and I bought a penny stamp, it was red in colour. I thought it was supposed to be black, especially since it is known as The Penny Black?"

"As an Oxford scholar," Harry glanced at Millie and laughed, " I was privy to the distribution of the world's first postage stamp. I had just started working at the post office when rumours started circulating. The postmaster called me into his office. Along with four others, we were informed of the impending postage stamp. As of May 06, 1840, any letter, a half ounce or less, mailed and delivered in England, would require a stamp."

Harry took a breath and continued, "In the weeks that followed, we were given bits of information. Already in production, the stamp, engraved on steel plates and printed on gummed paper, would be forwarded to us in a fortnight. We eagerly waited in anticipation of its arrival. We even took bets on the design and size. Since we already knew the cost to be a penny, we thought it would take up most of the envelope. Hardly enough room for the address, we thought. What a surprise, when we discovered the stamp was no bigger than a man's thumb print and it cost a penny. What would the public think of such an exorbitant price? Needless to say, no one won the bet. We were all off on the size and design."

Harry laughed. "They came in rectangular sheets of two hundred forty stamps to a sheet. The young Queen Victoria's profile stood out from the black background. 'POSTAGE' was printed on the crown of her head and 'ONE PENNY' under her neck. We were handed little scissors and a straight ruler for cutting out the individual stamps. On May 01, we cut out our first postage stamp. Although the stamp, officially would not be valid until May06, the public could purchase them as of May01."

Bess interrupted, "But as I said, the stamp we bought yesterday was red."

"The Penny Red came into circulation in 1841 and is still in circulation today."

"Can you still get The Penny Black?"

"No, they were discontinued when The Penny Red came in."

"Oh what a shame. I hoped to buy some. I have a---- friend back home who would love one." Bess looked disappointed.

"I bought a couple to put away. Perhaps, they may fetch ten times their amount in the future," guessed Harry.

"Blimey, ten times t' amount? Do ye really think so, 'Arry?" Lottie asked. "When I bought 'em fer Bertie's birth date, I just thought they'd be a reminder of two important cummin' outs, sort of speak." She laughed.

"Well, my friend will just have to be happy with a Penny Red."

"Miss Bess, I am in the post office tomorrow morning, so come and see me. I'll sell you a Penny Red and a Two Penny Blue," said Harry.

"A Two Penny Blue?"

"Any letter over a half ounce needs a Two Penny Blue. We don't sell many of them." He thought for a moment, "If you like, send yourself a postcard. You lick the stamp, and I will stamp the cancellation mark on it. The Black Maltese Cross looks quite striking on The Penny Red. I will make sure it gets posted and sent on the first ship to America. You can trust our post to get to its destination in a timely manner."

"I wouldn't bet on it." Bess looked at Harry. "Look what happened the last time you bet on something in the post office." They all laughed.

"Right then, up an' at it. 'Tis two o'clock," Lottie announced as she stood up.

Mr. Turner pulled the gold chain, hanging from his vest pocket and out came a pocket watch. He pressed the clip and the face opened. "You are right, Mrs. Morton, it is two o'clock. I must be off." He picked up his walking stick and nodded at Lottie, "Lovely gathering, could not be better. See you tomorrow, Tom." He opened the door, pulled up the collar of his overcoat, tapped down his top hat and left.

"Cum on, 'Arry, luv. Mrs. Morton needs sum peace 'n' quiet." Millie grabbed her husband's arm. "See ye Wednesday then."

"Lovely tea, Mrs. Morton. Nice meeting you, Miss Bess," said Harry as they walked out the door.

"Blimey, 'tis pourin', 'Arry."

"Cum on, ye two. I've got to put me achin' feet up." Lottie went over to Lily's table.

Reluctantly, the two got up and slowly made their way to the door. They hesitated when Sam opened the door. Lottie came out of the kitchen with a small package.

" 'Ere Lily, I 'ad a few extra scones left over."

"They got jam on 'em?" Lily looked at Lottie who nodded. "Good then, I'll be takin' 'em. 'Ere, Lottie." She gave her a nosegay of lavender.

"Lily, take t'is umbrella. Ye can bring it back tomorrow."

"If you don't need me, I'll be off to the pub," said Tom as he put on his coat and followed Lily and Sam to the door.

"Tom, will ye pick up Bertie on t' way 'ome? 'E's at Artie's," shouted Lottie. "Thanks, luv. Dinner at six."

"Cum up an' 'ave a nap, Bess," Lottie shouted down the stairs as her skirt disappeared up the stairs.

Bess walked over to the piano and plunked down on the stool. "Ouch! What's that?"

She put her hand underneath her skirt and brought out the little, red book. Caressing the cover she said, "I can't believe it." Just then her stomach growled. "Blimey, I am hungry."

"So am I."

Bess looked up to see a disheveled Evan peering down at her. He looked as if he had just gotten out of bed. His blue, rumpled pyjamas confirmed the observation.

"No wonder you didn't wake me. You're engrossed in your garden book. Hmmh --- As-pi-dis-tra? I know, that's the plant that English woman with the funny voice used to sing about. "It's the biggest As-pi-dis-tra in the world." --- Oh, what was her name?"

"Gracie Fields."

"That's right, Gracie Fields. I haven't thought of that song for a very long time.---- That reminds me, I haven't eaten for a very long time." He pounded his chest. "Woman, get off chesterfield and get food for man," he growled, but it wasn't from his manly voice, but his stomach.

Bess gave his stomach a poke. "If you wouldn't lay in bed until almost noon, you'd have dined on pancakes. As it is, it is much too late for breakfast. I'll make lunch in an hour."

"An hour? What time is it?" He squinted at the grandfather clock. "Why, it's almost eleven. Okay, you win." He turned with shoulders bent forward and lumbered up the stairs.

Looking down at her own attire, Bess thought *t'is getting to be a habit* and promptly followed Evan. The groaning of the water pipes echoed down the stairwell. *Darn, there won't be any hot water left by the time Evan finishes.* She shrugged. Bess quickly dressed and headed downstairs to finish her toiletries in the guest bathroom.

Evan snuck up on Bess bending over the bottom, kitchen cupboard and gave her tempting bottom a light smack. "Couldn't resist," he laughed. "So, what's for brunch?"

"I was deciding when you so rudely interrupted me. Now I've lost my train of thought."

"Yes, I've still got it." Evan pumped out his chest and moved his eyebrows up and down. "Well, while you're deciding, I'll get the Christmas decorations down. I hope the tree stand isn't at the back of the attic. Damn, I hate those spider's webs."

Bess peered out into the living room and looked up at the skylight. She could have sworn she saw Mr. Spider smile. Back in the kitchen, rummaging through the cupboards, she heard the doorbell ring. Remembering Evan would be in the attic cursing Mr. Spider's relatives, she hurried to the door.

"Bess, we hope you don't mind us dropping in, but I wanted to give you this box of old books. Bruce, put them on the floor by the sofa table."

"Lydia, Bruce, what a surprise. No of course, we don't mind. Here, me let me have your coats."

"Thanks, Bess. Bruce, can you pull my sleeve? I wore an extra sweater, cause it can be so cold in the old church. I think we should try a newer church. They're bound to have heat."

"At least our old church doesn't have to worry about the opposition eavesdropping. Hell, it's too cold for The Old Devil." Bruce gave a hearty laugh.

"Bruce, is that you? Come on up and help me bring down the Christmas decorations."

Bruce raced up the stairs and burst out laughing. "Hell, Evan, what you been doing up there? You been fighting with Spiderman again?"

"Spiderman? Damn, there's a whole army up there. Quick, take these and I'll close the hatch before they advance any further. Damn, I hate those webs."

The men retreated down the stairs; Bruce in the front, shielded by two large boxes, and Evan entwined in cobwebs, brought up the rear. Bruce's bald head teetered on top of the box as eight pudgy fingers and one and a half thumbs, spread around the brown cardboard. At the other end of the box-man, two brown legs, attached to size fourteen shoes, gingerly took one step at a time. The girls laughed when they saw battle-webbed Evan, carrying his trophy, the tree stand.

"I was just going to make some lunch. Why don't you join us? Nothing fancy, just macaroni and cheese," asked Bess.

"Well you know, Bess, you don't have to twist my arm." Bruce said, "Besides, I can help Evan put up the tree."

"While you are making the macaroni and cheese, I can make some of my famous, baking powder biscuits," Lydia said as she made her way to the kitchen.

"Do you want the tree in the same corner as last year?" Evan shouted.

"Yes, that's fine."

"Good. At least when we put it in the corner, I can guy-wire it. Bruce, you wouldn't believe the number of times our trees have fallen over."

"Yeah, I do as a matter of fact." They both burst out laughing. "All I did was walk over and look at your lights."

"Right, but you're supposed to pick up those big clod hoppers; not trip into the lights fantastic."

"Okay, okay, I know. I'll never live that one down."

*Busy hands make short work of it; yeah,* thought Bess as she kept running into Lydia in the kitchen. *Where's the salad bowl? Of course, in the cupboard, right in front of where Lydia is standing in a pile of flour.*

*Busy hands; yeah,* thought Evan as Bruce kept grabbing the tree and tilting it in the wrong direction as he tried to tighten the bolts. *What can I expect with nine and a half digits?*

"I think you need to level the bottom, Evan. Can you find your saw in all that stuff piled in the garage?" Bruce said innocently without malice of fore thought.

"Of course I know exactly where my saw is. Come on, Superman, bring it in the garage and I'll level it." Evan said, but thought *or someone else.*

After a lot of groaning and banging, the tree stood straight, the strings of lights securely fastened, the table set and the food prepared. The four sat down and ate a hearty brunch.

"That was damn good, Bess." Bruce pulled his chair back and smacked his stomach. "What's for dessert? Heh, you don't have any of your famous Christmas cake, do you?" Bruce smacked his lips and smiled.

"Yes, and if you three would retire to the living room, I'll bring coffee for the men and tea for the ladies," said Bess, "And yes, I'll bring the cake."

"I'll turn on the fireplace. Do you want your village plugged in, Bess?" Evan shouted, as the women took the dirty dishes into the kitchen.

The four sat in the living room enjoying their hot beverages and munching on fruitcake when Bruce said, "Good cake, Bess." He took another bite and eyed the plate of sliced cake. He looked up and saw the mantel. "Wow, does that look good. You're a lucky man, Evan old boy. Not only is Bess a good cook, she is artistic too."

"Oh, that looks as good as the display in Stewart's," said Lydia as she rose from the chesterfield to have a better look. "In fact, it's much better. I can tell you put a lot of thought into it." Curious, Lydia looked at each piece and remarked, "There's 'Turner's Counting House.' Right up your alley, hey, Evan?" She laughed. "There's our tearoom, the bookstore and the haberdashery. I looked it up in the dictionary. The dress shop is darling. I'd love to shop in there."

"Hey, I'd go along with that. At least you wouldn't spend any money. Shop to your heart's content, Lydia, my sweet," said Bruce. "On that thought, I think we'd better be off. We have some shopping to do."

"I just put a roast in the oven. Won't you stay for supper?" asked Bess.

"Sorry, Bess, we'll have to take a raincheck. Besides if we stay, Evan will have me decorating the whole tree while he sits back watching the hockey game." Bruce punched Evan's shoulder.

Bess got their coats out of the closet and Lydia said, "Thanks for lunch. Sorry we have to run." She bent over to put on her boots. "Oh, about these books, I was searching for the dictionary and came across them. The dusty old things were taking up room in the bookcase. Since you were so interested in old books the other day, I thought you might find another treasure or two in here.' She pointed at the discarded box.

"Thanks a lot, Lydia. Goodbye, Lydia." Bess hustled her out the door. "Bye, Bruce." She closed the door, glanced over at the box and shook her head. "Later."

Bess smelt the roast cooking in the oven as she sat down on the chesterfield. Her eyes wandered over to the tree. It looked lovely, especially with the new star glistening from the light's reflection. Evan sat watching the game, so she put her head back, but not before she gazed at the mantel. *Oh, the roast smells so good.*

"The roast smells so good."

"That's just what I thought," said Bess.

122

"Bess, cum in. Don't be shy. I was about to 'ave Bertie go up an' get ye fer dinner," said Lottie.

Bess, startled by her entrance into the dining scene, automatically stepped forward. Her foot missed the bottom step. She stumbled and landed in Tom's arms.

"Bess, you are going to get a reputation, always falling for handsome men. You don't suppose it's those fancy shoes you wear?" Tom burst out laughing.

"Tom, a gentleman never insults a lady, after rescuing 'er." Lottie scolded, "Where's yer manners?"

"Me lady." Tom helped Bess to a long table and pulled out the chair. "Please have a seat. Dinner will be served in a minute, me lady."

Bertie giggled and said, "Miss Bess, ye sure play t' pianoforte good. Me 'n' Artie enjoyed yer songs. Can we sing sum more after dinner?"

"Bertie, don't ye be botherin' Bess. She's played enough today." Lottie's hurried into the kitchen.

Tom moved over to the corner, where Mr. Brown and Sean stood conversing. Bertie moved over to a nearby table and started shuffling a deck of cards. Bess noticed the new placement of the tables. Five tables had been positioned lengthwise to form one long table. The table, set for seven, looked quite elegant with two candelabras flickering amongst the cut glassware. In the centre, Lily's posy stood in a vase.

"I 'ope ye didn't mind me usin' yer posy. I saw it on t' pianoforte an' thought it would look nice fer t' centrepiece."

"Of course not. That was sweet of her. I'm sure she can't afford to give her flowers away."

"Aye that she can't, but fer all 'er wrongin's she done in 'er life, she's got a good 'eart." Lottie shook her head. "Poor Lily's 'ad a rough life. She was practically born an orfunt an' lived off t' streets, beggin' an' stealin'. She's a scrapper, she is. An' 'ere she is today, a business woman, sellin' 'er flahs. I 'elp 'er out now an' then by givin' 'er me extra sweets an' buns left over at t' end of t' day."

"Are Sam and Lily a -- er -- couple?"

"Well, I suppose ye could put it that way. Ev'ryone needs sumone an' they seem to enjoy each other's company." Lottie smiled and looked over at Mr. Brown. "Yes, indeed they do. -- Now, I must get t' food on t' table." The swishing of her skirt grew fainter as she passed through the open doorway to the kitchen.

Jo came through the doorway seconds later carrying a covered, china serving bowl. "Bertie, your mother needs your help bringing out the food."

"Let me take that, Jo." Bess grabbed the hot serving bowl. "I'll come and help."

"Thank you, Bess. The cook's got so many dishes in there, it will take an army to carry them all." Jo laughed and headed back through the doorway.

Within minutes, the table, now laden with food, did look like it certainly would feed an army. Lottie came in carrying the roast on a large, white platter. She laid it on the table and called everyone to dinner. After much scraping of chairs on the bare floor, all sat silent in anticipation of the food set before them. Mr. Brown said grace and Lottie carved the roast. By the time the plates were heaped with vegetables, Lottie sliced the last piece of beef . She passed the platter around, closely followed by Yorkshire pudding and gravy.

"Did ye 'ear t' captain carry on about 'is favourite song? I could see poor Mrs. Fowler's face gettin' redder."

"Crazy old blighter. Still thinks he's back in the navy."

After the laughter subsided, Lottie said, "Mrs. Fowler invited us all fer dinner on Boxin' Day." A groan went around the table. " 'Tis our neighbourly duty, besides she always puts on a good feast. Maybe the captain will sleep through t' dinner."

"We can only hope," said Tom.

"I shall have to extend my apologies as I promised Robert I would help out in the pub that night," said Jo.

"Sure, Jo and Sean is going to tell us, he is also helping out." Tom laughed and looked suspiciously at the two of them.

"Well, Tom, I guess that just leaves us two men, reliving The Battle Of Trafalgar with the captain," said Mr. Brown.

"I like t' captain. 'E tells interestin' stories about t' battles wit' t' pirates," piped up Bertie.

"'Ark, is that singing I 'ear?" Sean put his hand to his ear and looked towards the door.

"Aye, Sean, 'tis t' carolers." Bertie jumped up and ran to the door. "Cum quick, Miss Bess," Bertie shouted as he opened the door.

"God bless ye merry gentlemen," The rousing voices filled the room, "May nothing ye dismay." A group of seven young children, dressed in shabby clothes, continued caroling.

"Go get sum more cups of warm wassail. Ye poor dears, ye must be cold." Lottie rushed back to the table, filled some buns with meat and handed them to the children.

The three men rummaged around in their pockets and gave the urchins a few coins and sent them on their way.

" 'Ow lovely. I do enjoy t' carolers." Lottie turned and started to clear the table. "Let's all take our dishes into t' kitchen. We girls can wash up while ye men put t' tables back.--- Tom could ye start t' fire in t' parlour so 'twill be warm when we 'ave tea 'n' Spotted Dick wit' custard."

" 'Urry, Uncle Tom. I luv Spotted Dick."

Half an hour later, the ladies trooped upstairs carrying trays full of hot tea and dessert. Bess took the rear position as not to embarrass herself by tripping on her skirt, whilst carrying a tray full of cups and plates. She found the whole procession most awkward and preferred to hike up her skirt in one hand and carry the tray in the other hand. However, the tray proved to be too heavy, so it warranted both hands. *Where are those men when you need them,* she thought as she reached the top of the stairs. She heard giggling.

Tom stood in the doorway. "Hmmh, hmmh," He cleared his throat and looked up.

Bess followed his eyes. To her surprise, mistletoe hung directly above them. *That's why all the giggling,* she surmised as she saw the other two men beaming and the ladies' cheeks turning red. *Oh, what the heck, it is Christmas.* Bess lifted her head and gave Tom a quick kiss on the lips.

"Very nice, me lady. Would you like to try for a second."

"In your dreams, Sir Tomalot."

"Me thinks me lady protests too much." He gave her a wicked smile and raised his eyebrows up and down.

Bess puzzled over a similar scene she encountered earlier. *No, can't be; another time, another world.* She gave Tom a strange look and shook her head.

"Bess, luv, don't stand in t' doorway all night. Tom 'elp 'er. Bring t' china over 'ere. It ain't easy drinkin' tea wit'out a cup an' eatin' puddin' wit'out a plate 'n' spoon. Not that our Bertie would 'ave a problem." Lottie laughed.

"Can we play cards, Mum?" Bertie sat at a table holding onto a deck of cards. "Do ye know 'ow to play w'ist, Miss Bess? Miss Jo is teachin' me."

"Sorry, Bertie, I don't."

"Well, when I learns proper like, I'll teach ye."

"Cum on, Bertie, old man, we'll have a game with you," said Tom, as Jo, Sean and Mr. Brown sat down at the card table.

" 'Tis good to put me feet up. Could ye be a luv and slip me shoes off me swollen feet? Aah---- thank ye, Bess."

"I'll get you another cup of tea," said Bess, as she finished pulling off her shoes. You need to put your other shoes on. It's alright if you're a lady of leisure, they can wear flimsy shoes, but you're not. You need good solid shoes that give you support.---- Are you listening to me, Lottie Morton?"

"Yes, luv, but t'is so expensive."

"They are not too expensive for Mr. Brown; perhaps he could help?" said Bess.

"Don't ye tell Mr. Brown. I don't want' im to think I'm not perfect." Lottie laughed half heartedly.

126

"I won't tonight, but if you don't look after your feet, I'll tell Mr. Brown, for your own good."

"Tell him what?" Mr. Brown asked from across the room.

"None of yer bui----er --- concern, Mr. Brown," shouted Lottie.

"Bertie, my man, are you cheating?" Tom gave him a stern look.

"Oh no, Uncle Tom, but I think Sean is."

"Bertie, I thought I was yer friend.' Sean sounded wounded. "Aye, ye've 'urt me deeply, laddie."

"Ah, ha! If anyone of you cheated, it did you no good," said Jo as she laid down her cards. "Another treat! I win," she said smugly as the groans echoed around the table.

"Right, off to bed wit' ye, son. -----Don't w'ine. School tomorrow."

"We men will look after the dishes. Off to bed, ladies. Work tomorrow," ordered Tom.

The ladies needed no second commands. They said goodnight and plodded off to bed. Bess opened her bedroom door and received a blast of cold, musty air. Shivering, she closed the door and looked for the sweater, Mrs. Doyle laundered for her. She quickly took it off the hanger and put it over her dress. Feeling a touch warmer, she thought *now, if only I could get rid of this musty smell. Oh, for central heating.* She walked over to the window and decided to open it for a few minutes. She hoped the musty air would escape and leave only fresh air. Unfortunately, the air outside did nothing to improve the air inside, except make it colder. The smells of the city permeated her nasal cavities and left a strong scent of "Odor de Sadie." In fact, the whole perfume de stable had to be situated right outside her window. Quickly, her hand moved to close the window, when she heard the faint sound of carolers.

"I saw three ships a sailing ------ " Their voices became louder.

"Bess, hurry, you're going to miss them."

"We heard them earlier. They must still be hungry."

"When? I didn't hear them, and I've been right here watching the hockey game. And --- speaking of hungry, when's supper. The roast smells so good. It's making my stomach growl."

"Oh, Evan." Bess felt a cold breeze pass by her feet.

"The weather outside is frightful ------"

"Right on." She shivered. "I'm coming, Evan. Is there any wassail left?"

"Wassail what?"

# CHAPTER XI

Strewn across the arm of the beige, lounge chair, laid the red velour housecoat. Bess's hand caressed the folds of the soft fabric. With both hands, she scooped the housecoat up into her arms. Something fell out of the pocket and hit her foot.

"Ouch!" She looked down to discover the little, red book lying face-up. "I forgot I put it in this pocket."

Bess picked it up, put it on the dresser and proceeded to the closet. She hung the housecoat on a hook next to Evan's green and blue plaid one and closed the door. The little, red book in hand, she walked down the stairs and dropped it on the coffee table. Bending over to retrieve her runners from the closet, she almost tripped over Lydia's box of old books. Laying the runners on top, she picked up the box and groaned. *Darn, I forgot how heavy a bunch of books can be,* she complained. *There is more than one way to move them.* She dragged and pushed the heavy box to the chesterfield.

"Well, what treasures do we have in here, Mr. Spider?" said an exhausted Bess as she plunked down and reached for the first book.

Twenty minutes later, three piles of books stood on the floor. The pile of romance paperbacks she put back in the box. *I'll drop them in the charity bin in the mall. Evan might find something interesting in these reference books,* she thought as she hauled them over by the television. She tapped the last pile of hard cover novels with her finger tips and decided to look at them later. Bess spied the little, red book off to the left of the pile, reached over and picked it up. She opened the cover and gasped.

"Bess, thank you. I had 'The Bess Time.'

Charles Dickens…. 1847"

Her hand shook as she gently touched the inscription. Her eyes looked up at the mantel and focused on "The Lotatea Shoppe."

"Oh my gosh. This can't be real. ----- Oh my gosh. ----- This is amazing."

"What's amazing? I know, we men did a great job cleaning up last night, but really, Bess, amazing?" Tom noticed Bess's puzzled expression and continued, "Okay, if it makes you feel better; yes, we are quite amazing." He gave her his devious smile and the flexing eyebrow routine.

"Sorry, Tom, I was --- er --- noticing the weather. It's a-ah-mazing the fog has lifted, and I can actually see across the street." She moved to the window and peered out. "What's that building over there?" She pointed haphazardly.

"If you would keep your finger from moving all over, I could tell you." Tom moved close behind her, and brushed her shoulder as he grabbed her hand. "Point to the building, me lady." His hot breath teased her neck and ran tingles up and down her spine. "Steady, girl. ----- Oh, I see where you are pointing. That is the old Clifford Inn. Since 1345, there's been many a traveller spent the night spinning his tales." Moving her arm to the left, he brought his other arm around and held her tight. "Don't want you to lose your balance. The big brick building is The General Records Office and see the red brick one down there," Their cheeks touched, "that is the home to our literary artists, printers, publishers, stationers and engravers."

"Tom, yer still 'ere. Ye best be off. Ye'll be late fer work," said Lottie. "Wot yer lookin' at outside?"

Tom loosened his grip and stood straight up. "I was showing ----"

"Bess? I didn't see ye," said Lottie as Bess quickly moved away from Tom.

"Yes, Tom has been kind enough to tell me about the buildings across the lane," she rattled on, "This is the first time I've noticed them as every day has been foggy, until the rain cleared up the fog yesterday. I had no idea Fetter Lane was as narrow as it is and yet so overcrowded with buildings. I ------ "

"Steady, girl," Tom whispered in her ear. "Well, ladies, I'll see you later." He grabbed his overcoat and hat, opened the door and shuddered. "Blimey, it's a cold one today." He buttoned his coat and headed up the lane.

"Bess, luv, would ye be a dear an' put t' pastries in t' dispay case. I'm expectin' me tea merchant to drop by shortly, an' I want to be ready fer 'im. There's no time after 'e leaves before t' customers cum in."

The door bell jingled. A gentleman, carrying a large wooden case in each hand, entered the tearoom. He put the cases down and took off his top hat, exposing a receding hairline. His black hair stood on peaks where his hat brushed against it. He quickly rubbed his hand across the top of his head, flattening the obstinate strands of unruly hair.

"Oh, good morning, Mrs. Morton," said the startled gentleman. "I didn't see you standing there."

"Good morning, Mr. Harrod. A nasty day out there."

"That it is, Mrs. Morton, but it feels warm in here," he said as he made his way to the fireplace and rubbed his hands near the blazing fire.

"Take off your coat; it must be wet. I'll hang it over the chair by the fire. Would you like a cup of tea?" Lottie asked, pronouncing each word very slowly and precisely.

"Yes, that would be most gracious of you. I hardly ever get asked if I'd like a cup of tea. I guess people think if I sell it all day, I won't want to drink it too."

Mr. Harrod bent down and opened the first case and lifted out an apothecaries' scale and put it on the empty table. Next came various measuring devices, and silver scoops to fill the empty, wooden chests. As he opened the larger chests of tea, the air filled with the scent of tea leaves.

Bess stood mesmerized by the precise procedures the merchant undertook to arrange his precious cargo, until Lottie awakened her senses, "Bess, cum an' meet Mr. Harrod."

"Thee Mr. Harrod?"

"Aye, I suppose 'e's a thee. 'E's well known 'ere as a reputable tea merchant. I've bin dealing wit' 'im since I started t'is tea shoppe, wot four years ago. 'Ave ye 'eard of 'im? Surely not in America?" Lottie walked towards him. "Mr. Harrod, here's your tea. I would like you to meet a young lady from America, Miss N-ike. Bess seems to have heard of you."

Mr. Harrod stood up and gently took Bess's outstretched hand. "It is possible, I do have one or two customers from America. Mind you, 'The Boston Tea Party' did not help sales in America. Hopefully, they will come around to drinking tea once more. Fortunately, we all have short memories."

"Now, Mr. Harrod, show us what teas you are selling today," Lottie said in a business like tone. She sat down at the table and motioned for Bess to take the other seat beside Mr. Harrod.

Somewhat surprised at the change in Lottie's vocabulary and demeanour, Bess took awhile to follow their conversation. "My, the aroma is divine." She inhaled, hoping they hadn't noticed her moment of distraction.

"Yes, this shipment of Bohea does have a unique aroma. Why at the auction last week, I auctioned off most of it. I barely kept enough for my regular customers." He smiled at Lottie who surprisingly blushed. He scooped a generous portion of the black tea leaves into the large metal container and adjusted the scales. "How many ounces was that? Two pounds? My, you have been busy."

"Yes, that I have. What with Christmas and of course, I opened yesterday for my annual Christmas Tea for my neighbours," she said. "But, Bess, Miss N-ike has really helped. She plays the pianoforte for my customers, and they love to linger and drink more tea. I think we are in for another busy week, so I hope you will call on me bright and early next Monday morning."

"I will indeed, guaranteed a little slower from all that turkey and Christmas pudding, but I will be here. Perhaps someday, I will hear you play ." He smiled at Bess and turned to Lottie. "Will there be anything else, Hyson? --- Eight ounces. --- Fine. Another two pounds of Pekoe --- Excellent. How about a pound of Imperial, always nice at Christmas?"

They finished their business, said their goodbyes, and he opened the door as Miss Rose Water entered.

"I see there will be plenty of tea for me, today." She laughed. "It smells so divine in here. I always try to get here early on Mondays so I can enjoy the pure pleasure of the aromatic tea leaves. Once the others come, my senses are dulled by the invasion of the body odours, perfumed or otherwise." She giggled.

"Good morning, Miss Water," Lottie said cheerfully.

"Where are my manners? Good morning, Mrs. Morton, Miss Bess."

"Good morning, Miss R--- Water," stammered Bess.

"Do call me Rose. Through your music, I feel I have known you for a long time. My dear, while Mrs. Morton gets me ----- Oh surprise me. Will you play for me? I'd love to hear some more of your songs."

To Miss Rose Water's delight, Bess sat down, played a string of songs and softly sang. Pleased with Lottie's selection of tea and pastry, Miss Rose Water munched away and enjoyed the moment. Unfortunately, it did not last long before the invasion of the body odours and their accompanying mouth pieces destroyed her little bit of heaven. Rose finished her tea, smiled sweetly at the enemy, got up, put on her heavy woollen coat and made her way to the piano.

"My dear, would it be possible for you to write down the music and words for, I believe you called it 'White Christmas'? You see, my great-niece loves music and like you, is very good at the pianoforte. It would please me if I could give Harriet your music for Christmas." She put her gloved hand to her mouth. "Where are my manners today? I am being too bold to ask you, a visitor and at this busy time of year. Please forgive me."

"Do not trouble yourself. I will be pleased to do this for you and Harriet. I shall do my best to have it ready for you by tomorrow. Have a nice day, Rose." Bess smiled.

"Thank you, my dear. You have a nice day too." Miss Rose Water giggled and walked towards the door, saying mainly to herself, "Have a nice day. I like that."

Bess pulled the red tartan scarf tightly around her neck. She shivered as the dampness welcomed her to Fetter Lane. *Which way shall I go?* she puzzled as she ventured out into unknown territory. Lottie had reminded her to enquire at the steamship company about her luggage. Lottie gave her directions to the office on Fleet Street, bundled her up to ward off the inclement weather and sent Bess on her way. Obviously, Bess had no enquiry to make, so for the next couple of hours, she would have time to waste. She put her hand in her pocket and searched into its depth. *Nothing there; not even a hole,* she sighed and looked to the left. *Yes, that's it. What better place to spend time when one has no money? A bookstore.* She smiled and started towards "Tellaway Books."

Bess stopped dead. A tall ladder leaned on their building. Its legs firmly planted on the edge of the sidewalk. *Now what do I do? Do I cross under the ladder of misfortune or do I step off the curb and misfortunately step into a Sadie dropping?* She puzzled over her dilemma. *Where are those crossing sweepers when you need them? But, since I don't have any money, they'd probably attack me with their brooms.* She looked once more at the ladder and walked over to the curb. She checked the surrounding road surface for evidence of Sadie and her stable mates' recent departures. To her surprise, the ground looked safe. She hiked up her skirt, gingerly lifted a foot and noticed a small piece of silver. Bess retracted her foot, bent over and picked up the object. *Darn, I forgot I'm wearing gloves. Now I've got one dirty.* Still holding the object, she put one foot down on the road and then the other. Four steps later, back on the sidewalk, she had solved her dilemma without any disasters, except for one soiled glove. Bess opened her clenched hand to find her treasure sparkling against the brown of the glove.

"Bess, do come in out of the drizzle. What are you looking at?"

"Jo, I was on my way to your shoppe when I found this." Bess opened her glove.

"Bess, you lucky girl, you have found a half-crown."

"Half-crown? That's good? --- What's a half-crown?"

"Sorry, I keep forgetting you are a foreigner. A half-crown is two and a half shillings." Jo noticed Bess's perplexed expression. "A shilling is twelve pennies."

The light went on. "Oh, that's thirty pennies. I can buy a lot of stamps."

Jo laughed. "I suppose you could."

"I always knew it was bad luck to walk under a ladder, and by walking around it, I had good luck." Bess smiled and then suddenly frowned. "But, it wasn't good luck for the person who lost it."

"Look at it this way. If they had a half-crown to lose, they probably won't miss it. Besides, you certainly had your share of bad luck, what with losing your luggage and falling like you did. You deserve some good luck." Jo smiled, winked at Bess and said, "What would you like to buy? I have some nice little Christmas books." They laughed.

Bess spent the next hour in literary heaven. Everywhere she looked, first editions of famous authors and poets stood erect, patiently awaiting her perusal of their virgin pages. Her hands trembled as she lifted the first book from the safety of its strong, wooden shelf. She caressed the navy-blue cover and gently opened the book to the first page. No dates, no inscriptions, no auto-graphs, no history, only a blank start to perhaps generations or even centuries of touching and reading. Feeling she invaded for-bidden territory, she turned to the next page. She gasped. Her hand started to shake.

Simply written in olde type, "𝕵𝖆𝖓𝖊 𝕰𝖞𝖗𝖊" and written under-neath, "𝖇𝖞 𝕮𝖚𝖗𝖗𝖊𝖗 𝕭𝖊𝖑𝖑."

Bess peaked at the first few pages and closed the book. She eased it back on the shelf. With her finger tips, she traced the titles, "𝖂𝖚𝖙𝖍𝖊𝖗𝖎𝖓𝖌 𝕳𝖊𝖎𝖌𝖍𝖙𝖘" and "𝕬𝖌𝖓𝖊𝖘 𝕲𝖗𝖊𝖞." Above her head, the "A' s contained volumes of Jane Austin peering down at her. I *must ask how much they are.* She made a mental note, as she reluc-tantly moved down to the "D's. The colourful hard covers included the complete selections of Charles Dickens, from "Sketches By Boz" to "The Battle Of Life." *Oh, how I want them all, but I shall only be able to afford one. ----- I hope.* She agonized over which one it would be.

The poetry section contained as many volumes as the novels. This surprised Bess, until she thought about it. In the eighteenth and nineteenth century, almost every man wrote poetry. I couldn't imagine Evan or Bruce writing poetry, she laughed.

"What is so funny, Bess?" Jo asked, as she poked her head around the shelf.

"I was just imagining something back home which is impos-sible to imagine."

"Speaking of back home, I have something you might be inter-ested in. Follow me. I put a display of Christmas books by the door, and while I was organizing it, I remembered an American book, we had in stock," said Jo as they made their way to an attractive display. "Ah, here it is, 'A Visit From St. Nicholas' by Clement C Moore."

"'Twas the night before Christmas," said Bess. "I'd love to read that to the boys. How much is it?"

"It has been on the shelf for more than one Christmas. I

don't think it is a first edition." Jo looked at the first page. "No, it is the fourth edition since it was first printed in 18 --- 1823. Unfortunately, England has not acknowledged St. Nicholas in the same way you do. However, I've heard he is beginning to appear in some of the wealthier homes on Christmas Eve. I do hope he becomes popular in England. I think he is a lovely character and deserves a place in every child's heart. What do you think Bess?"

"Oh, I agree. Every child in the world deserves a visit from Santa--- ah -- St. Nicholas. If I could read this to Bertie and Artie, perhaps Santa, where I live we call him Santa Claus, will pay them a visit. It could be the beginning of his yearly visits."

"I agree. Denmark and Germany have a fantasy father figure." Jo's beautiful, dark-brown eyes opened wide. "Why shouldn't we? We could call him 'Father Christmas.'"

"Yes, I think that would be a perfect name."

"I got so excited just thinking about it, I forgot to answer your question. Let me ask Mr. Tell. In the meantime, I will put the book aside."

"Thank you, Jo. Let me know tonight. I must be off. I still have to go to the steamship office." Bess waved at Jo and walked out into the cool air, a complete contrast to the warmth she felt from her exhilarating experience.

She headed back in the direction of Fleet Street, thankful the ladder no longer blocked her way. She passed the tearoom, noticing the front windows shrouded in steam. *Must be all that hot air circulating from mouth to mouth*, she laughed. On her left, the street smells tried to invade her nostrils. Instinctively, she turned her head to the right. This quick reaction rewarded her with the enticing smell of exotic spices as the door to Basil's shoppe opened. A light in the second storey, dormer window lit up Bess's imagination. She heard Rosemary Pepper laughing as the jolly lady entertained a neighbour, perhaps Mrs. Fowler. Smoke belched out of the large, red bricked chimney. *Basil must be drying his spices.* She captured a whiff of sage.

The growling of her stomach tempted her to enter "The Brown Bread." She changed her mind when she peered in the window. At least six customers stood in line to buy his delicious bread and buns. Sean, in his flour encrusted apron, had been summoned to help alleviate the queue. A smiling Sean handed a loaf of bread to a lady, dressed in a grey and red tweed coat and matching hat. He motioned to the next in line and spied Bess looking in the window. He waved and his lips moved, where upon Mr. Brown looked up and waved. They both motioned for her to come in, but she shook her head and mouthed the word, later.

Passing by "Fowler's Meat & Poultry Shoppe," she shivered when she saw the ice house. At the corner of Fleet Street and Fetter Lane, she stopped, looked in both directions and cautiously stepped off the curb. At the last second before her foot touched the ground, she remembered to look down. *No money, but also no* ----- she smiled and continued across the street.

She just stepped on the sidewalk of herringbone patterned, red brick, when a large wagon, pulled by four horses, charged past. Sitting next to the driver, a man repeatedly rang a loud bell. Other uniformed men with helmets, hung on tightly to the sides and the back. A large, metal cylinder took up most of the space on the wagon. Through the men, Bess made out the words, "Firehall # 8" written on the cylinder. A long ladder hooked onto its side. As it thundered down Fleet Street, Bess saw a large hose wound around a wooden handle and buckets swaying between the men.

"Another fire. Those poor blokes are kept busy twenty-four hours a day," Bess overheard a tall gentleman say to his companion.

"Let us hope they get it under control before half the city burns down again."

Bess put her hand in her pocket and touched the silver coin. *I'm going to the post office,* she decided. She walked up the four steps to the 6 by 10 foot landing and made her way to the door. As fate would have it, a gentleman opened the door for her. *When was the last time a man opened a door for me, let alone doff their hat? Manners? They must have remained in the nineteenth century. Well, enjoy it while you can, girl.* She smiled and walked in the building.

Still in awe with the interior, Bess stood in the middle of the busy room and reflected on the architectural beauty that surrounded her. She felt the close proximity of the people as they hurried by, but still she did not move. All around, the tapping of heels kept in time with their owners' canes. *Any moment,* Bess thought, *the sparkling chandelier, hanging in the heavens, will burst out with a holy choir singing "Glory, glory, Hallelujah."*

"Bess, ---- ah, Miss Bess."

Breaking her imaginative train of thought, she looked around to see to whom the voice belonged. "Oh, Harry --- Mr. Topham. Sorry, I hope you weren't calling me very long. I was distracted by the beauty of your building."

"Yes, it is beautiful. Many people are in awe of it, and yet many are too busy to stop and look at its beauty. I was keeping an eye out for you. We have just received a new shipment of Christmas postcards. With the overnight success of the Christmas card, the post office decided to produce a Christmas greeting on a postcard. Only the rich can afford to send Christmas cards. The postcard only costs two pennies, where as the card is at least twice as much. Have a look at them, Bess."

"They are lovely. Did I hear you right? It costs two pennies and a penny for the stamp?"

"Two pennies, includes the stamp. I know they are only to be mailed in Britain, but if you want to write yourself a greeting, I'll make sure it gets to America."

"Oh, Harry, that is kind of you. I'll take the one with the street scene; I can show everyone back home where I've been. And a cancellation stamp with the date and place?"

"Of course. I'll make sure the date and London, England is clear."

"Harry, this is so exciting. I wonder if it will make it to America."

"We are proud of our mail service. It may be a little slow, but it will get to you."

Bess thought *if it ever gets to me, slow will have a whole new meaning. Miracle would be more appropriate --- Hey! Maybe that's the problem with our mail; it goes through a time-warp.* She laughed.

"Something funny?"

"Actually, I was thinking of the mail service back home." She shook her head. "I would like a Penny Red and a Two Penny Blue, please. My friend back home will love to add these to his collection."

"He collects stamps? Surely he doesn't have many? They have only been out a few years."

"Ah --- yes that is true, but he collects all sorts of things." *In the garage,* she thought.

"I thought these stamps would interest him. However, I am sad I will not be able to give him The Penny Black."

"I will make enquiries to see if anyone wishes to sell one. Most of our employees bought a couple."

"Thank you, Harry. How much do I owe you?"

"Five pennies, please."

Bess proudly slipped her coin through the metal opening. "My pleasure, Harry."

He slipped the two stamps and the postcard to her. "Your change, miss, two shillings, one penny. There is pen and ink behind you." He pointed at the tall, wooden counter. "When you have written your postcard, bring it back to me."

With her precious purchases in hand, she walked to the counter. Bess slipped the change in one pocket and the stamps in the other and picked up the straight pen. *My, I haven't touched one of these since I was a child.* She smiled and dipped it into the inkwell. An abandoned piece of paper lay on the counter, so she picked it up and started practicing. The first few strokes were awkward and messy. Immediately, her fingers acquired random blotches of ink spots. After a few more attempts, she got the hang of it. Cautiously, she wrote her real name, Mrs. B Turner and address, on the right side of the postcard. Pleased with the result, she moved the pen over to the left and wrote:

*To Bess,*
*December 20, 1847*
*Having the Bess Time!*
*Wish you were here.*
*Miss N-ike*

Reluctantly, she took it over to the wicket and handed Harry a postcard that would definitely get lost in time.

Back out in the street, Bess shivered. In her pocket, she found the dirty gloves and the three coins. The silver shillings reminded her of quarters. However, the copper penny made a twenty-first century penny look like small change. Except for its colour, it resembled a half-crown. *Such a big coin for such little value,* she thought. She examined the copper penny. A profile of a young Queen Victoria, faced left with an inscription arched above her head, and underneath her profile, the date 1845, clearly visible. Concentrating, she looked at the inscription.

"VICTORIA DEI GRATIA," she said as she flipped the coin over. "BRITANNIAR REG FID DEF" -----Okay," she mused as she saw the lovely maiden, Britannia seated facing right. The maiden held, what looked to be a pronged fork standing straight up.

"Miss, may I help you?"

"What? Oh, sorry, no thank you." Bess looked up at the young man in a uniform.

"Constable."

"Constable Hunter, miss. Yer t' young lady from America."

Bess looked at him closely and said, "Of course, Tom was giving you a hard time at 'The Lotatea Shoppe' yesterday."

141

"Aye, Tom does quite regularly, but I take no notice. Besides, I get back at 'im on t' football field. I saw ye lookin' at yer coins an' I thought ye may 'ave bin cheated out of sum money."

"No, I was looking at your coins, and I thought how different they are from ours. When I go to buy something, I want to be able to identify what I'm giving and what I'm getting back."

"Aye, yer wise. One can never be too careful, especially when they know yer a foreigner. Get Tom to tell ye about t' money. Accountants know all about money, at least they think they do." He laughed. "Nice meeting ye , miss. If ye need any 'elp, I'm always around this area," Constable Hunter said as he smiled and walked in the other direction.

Money safely tucked in her pocket, Bess headed back. She stopped at the intersection, looked both ways and even up and down for good measure and ventured across the street. Instead of heading back to the tearoom, she kept walking down Fleet Street until she came to "W.H. Turner Counting House." She hesitated, then stood on her toes and peered in the window.

"Yes, may I help you?"

Embarrassed, Miss Peeping at Tom turned around to find herself, face to face with Mr. Turner. "Oh, oh ----ah---"

"Why, it is Miss Bess from America. I just mentioned to Tom how I enjoyed your music. It is too cold to be ah --- standing out in the cold. Come in. Tom will be pleased to see you. He deserves a break anyways, but do not tell him I said so." He took her arm and opened the door. "Tom, guess who I met passing by the building?" He winked at Bess.

"Sorry, Mr. Turner, you asked me something?" Tom replied as he put his pencil down and looked up from his desk, covered with ledgers and papers. "Bess? --- Bess." Tom stood. "Why, Bess, what a nice surprise."

"Where's your manners, Tom? Get the young lady a chair," ordered Mr. Turner. "Excuse me, miss, I have work to attend to. I will be in my office if you should need me." He took off his hat and walked passed a row of ten empty desks to a windowed office in the back.

"You are lucky you caught me. Everyone has left for the day. I was just finishing up."He looked at the large clock on the wall. "My, it is past five. What are you doing out alone?"

"I didn't realize the time, and I guess I didn't notice it getting dark. I had such a busy afternoon. Let's see ---- I found a half-crown. I stopped at Jo's book shoppe, went to the post office, chatted with your friend, Constable Hunter," Bess rambled on as she put her hand behind her back and crossed her fingers. "Oh yes, I went to the steamship office."

"Slow down, girl. You are making me exhausted just listening to you." He laughed. "Sit there while I quickly finish up and we can walk back home together."

Silence prevailed, except for the scratching noise Tom's pen kept making as he jotted down figures. Brief moments of silence returned when he dipped the nib in the inkwell. The pendulum on the clock kept time to the strokes of the pen. Bess looked around the large, dreary room. Each desk, similar to Tom's, had an oil lantern on one side and a candle in a brass holder. Quill pens stuck out from the inkpots, as if a flock of fine-feathered birds made a nose dive into the depths of the wells of ink. Journals and ledgers, piled high on each desk, made it difficult to see anything else on them. She stretched her upper torso and caught a glimpse of Mr. Turner bent over his desk.

Mr. Turner picked up an envelope and placed a folded letter inside. He picked up a red stick of cinnamon and ran it through the flame of the candle and quickly positioned it over the back of the envelope. A red drop fell from the stick onto the envelope. *Cinnamon doesn't melt*, she thought. *Of course, dummy, it's wax.* Mr. Turner picked up a stubby, wooden spindle. The flat end glistened like gold in the candlelight. He pressed it down hard on the puddle of red wax and let it dry a moment, before placing the envelope on a pile. *Now, that's what I call a sealed envelope.* She laughed.

"What's so funny? Sure, be ruthless to the poor slaves of this world," Tom said, as he blotted his page and put his pen into its appointed hole in the inkpot. "I'm finished. I'll go in and say goodbye to Mr. Turner." He lifted his coat off the rack and handed Bess his hat.

Mr. Turner acknowledged Tom's departure and waved to Bess. She handed Tom his hat and took his arm as he helped her up. They left the counting house with Mr. Turner bent over his desk. A lone candle flickered in his office, while the light of the fireplace grew dim.

Tom extended his arm to Bess. "Thank you. I'm not used to the uneven cobblestones. And ---- before you say anything, no I don't intend to fall into your arms."

"Blimey, and I was so looking forward to it." He laughed and stopped at the intersection. "Across the street is Jo's brother's pub."

They crossed the street, guided by the flickering light of the gas, streetlamp. The door of the pub opened. Bess slowed down to peer inside. The large room seemed crowded with men having a drink before heading home.

She searched the crowd. "I can't see any women in there."

"Very observant. Women hardly ever go into the pub. It is not that we don't welcome them, but society frowns on a lady frequenting the public houses."

"But Jo ----"

"Aye, but she is permitted as her brother owns it, and she helps out from time to time."

"What a shame. I'd love to go in there."

"Would you really, Miss Bess?" Tom rubbed his chin. "Perhaps it can be arranged. After I change clothes, I am going to meet Sean here. Say, why don't you put your fine, fitting trousers on . I'm sure we have a coat and cap that will fit you. I'll pass you off as one of my mates.---- Mind, woman, you have to promise to keep quiet, and when you do speak, it must come from way down deep."

"Oh, Tom, what great fun." Catching his dubious look, she

changed her tone and said as deep as her voice would go, "Right, Tom."

"That will have to do, but remember, we cannot tell Lottie. She would skin me alive, and you would be forced to do kitchen duties or worse."

When they entered the tearoom, sounds of laughter came from the kitchen. Tom opened the door just wide enough for both of them to poke their heads in to discover the source of the merriment. Bertie's stark-naked backside walked reluctantly to a round, tin tub.

"Mum, do I 'ave to. T'is too cold fer me."

"Bertie, don't ye be a baby. Feel --- t'is warm. I put two buckets of boilin' water in there. Ye should be a man like yer uncle. 'E bathes in cold water." Lottie looked up and saw two faces, one on top of the other, jammed in the crack of the doorway. "Bess, I were worried about ye. Ye bin gone fer 'ours."

"Oh!" screamed Bertie and he jumped in the bath. "She didn't see me naked, did she?"

"No, of course not. I was standin' in front of ye," Lottie said as she gave them a cheeky smile. "T'is bath night, 'cause Saturday 'n' Sunday we were busy."

"Mum, t'is still cold."

"Well, that's all t' 'ot water yer gettin', so ye best 'urry up an' wash yerself good 'n' clean. Mind, ye wash behind yer ears," she ordered and turned to Tom, "Would ye be a luv an' empty t' bath water before ye go to t' pub. I want to 'ave a bath after Bertie. Bess if ye would like one after I'm finished, I'll save sum water fer ye."

"No, that's okay, Lottie. You relax and enjoy your bath. My day's outing has left me very tired. I think I'll go right up to bed. Good night, I'll see you in the morning."

Bess slipped her head out from under Tom's and made her way up the two flights of stairs to her room. She changed into her jeans and sweater and hung up her dress in the wardrobe. She stood facing the door, anxiously waiting for Tom's secret knock.

Knock, knock, knock.

Bess opened the door to find a stranger holding a parcel. "Oh, you're not Tom."

"Sorry, ma'am. I'm Don," replied the young man. "Please sign for your parcel." He handed her a clipboard and pen.

Bewildered, she signed the piece of paper, and they exchanged items and Merry Christmas'. She stood motionless in the doorway, a large box in her arms, as her eyes followed his retreating body to a dark-brown, delivery van. A moment later, UPS letters flashed across her eyes as the van sped up the street.

"Well, so much for pub crawling."

She shut the door and put the parcel, addressed to Evan, on the hall table. Heading for the kitchen, Bess stumbled. *What did I trip over this time?* she tsked as she looked down to find the little, red book on the floor. She picked it up and put it on the coffee table covered with piles of Lydia's books. *I'll clean them up later.* She shook her head and continued her journey to the kitchen.

Waylaid by the sight of the piano, she remembered her promise to Miss Rose Water and went in search of the sheet music. Up went the piano seat. Uprooting sheets of neatly piled music, her busy hands flipped through them. Finally, at the bottom of the pile, "White Christmas" made its appearance. Snatched out of its seasonal home, whisked away, slapped down on a cold, hard surface, the sheet lay flat out as a lid came down and crushed it into darkness. Strange sounds, flashing lights, momentary darkness and finally the lid lifted. Back in familiar surroundings and smells of glorious old papers, the sheet stood upright on the piano.

*I shall have to cut the bottom of the first page. There mustn't be any dates or publishing information. I don't want to confuse anyone, or more to the point, asking any questions.*

Bess spent the rest of the day baking and putting the final touches on the Christmas decorating. Evan came home at a reasonable time, so supper finished before seven. In front of the fire, they ate custard and fresh baked, shortbread cookies. Evan looked through the pile of reference books.

"Anything of interest?"

"Yes, this one is interesting. 'Tips for the Handyman.' I can use this." He glanced at Bess. "Don't look at me like that. One of these days, I'll have time for handyman stuff." He grunted a manly grunt and flexed his muscles.

"I'd like to see that."

"Oh, you would," said Evan, as he lunged for her. Interrupted on route, he said, "What's this? 'The Last Of The Mohicans.' Why I read that when I was a kid. Great adventure for a young boy's imagination." Evan picked it up off the coffee table and skimmed through the pages. "I see it was published in 1826. I didn't realize how old it is, and I certainly don't remember it being so many pages and --- such small print." He squinted, took off his glasses and rubbed his eyes.

"No kidding," Bess chided.

"Come to think of it, I believe Dad read it to me over a winter. He made it so interesting. Besides, kids pick out the good stuff from a story, and let their imaginations block out the unnecessary jargon." He put his head back and said, "Poor old Dad."

Bess picked up a couple of the books and like Evan, reminisced *"Little Women," such a feisty girl, Jo, and such antics the little women got into.* She smiled and recalled getting the hand-me-down from her godmother. She looked at the second book *"Gone With The Wind," my first torrid love story.* Bess remembered reading it in library class in high school. *No, actually, it was study period, held in the library, and I just happened to be seated by the M's. It took me the whole year to get through the classic saga.*

"Look, Evan," she said, and he replied with a rousing snore. Disappointed, Bess said, "Okay, be a party pooper." She grabbed "The Last Of The Mohicans" out of his hand before it fell on the floor and put it on top of the other two books on her lap. She looked at the mantel and stated, "Tom's not a party pooper."

Knock, knock, knock.

"Bess, are you there?" whispered a male voice.

"Yes, I'm coming." Bess grabbed the glass knob and turned it. "Tom, it's you." Startled, she dropped something on the floor.

"Hush, we are supposed to be sneaking out, not announcing our departure," said Tom. As an afterthought, he asked, "And --- who else were you expecting at your bedroom door?"

"Aah ---"

"Don't answer. Here put this cap and coat on."

"I'll be right there." Her foot felt something by the door. Bess looked down to find three books. She picked them up and exclaimed, "Oh my, 'Gone With The Wind,' 'Little Women' and 'The Last ---- '"

"Women? Is Jo in there?"

"Literally speaking, yes, but figuratively speaking, no." She put the books on the bed and put on her coat and cap as she rushed through the doorway.

Tom shook his head and rearranged her attire. "You'll pass as a mate, but don't bend over. We don't want any of those fancy blokes checking you out." He made a devilish laugh.

They crept down the stairs, making sure they missed the creak in front of Bertie's room.

Tom motioned to Bess to miss a step or two on the lower flight of stairs. Without a skirt to hinder her movements, she accomplished this with ease. However on the last step, Bess miscalculated and caused a rather loud creak. Fortunately, at that precise moment, Lottie sang a high note and drowned out the creak. They crept to the kitchen door and peered inside. Lottie, with her back towards them, lay submerged in the tub. In order to get her whole body in the small bath, she had tucked her knees up to her armpits. Bess groaned inwardly *how uncomfortable.* Bess put a hand on her back and stretched. *But then again, she is a young woman and still supple. Besides, she's happy; perhaps a little out of tune, but happy.*

They closed the door and Bess looked over to the left and noticed the chalkboard. Curious to see what the saying of the day read, she perused it and found it most appropriate.

"𝔒ne sip of this will bathe the drooping spirits or delight beyond the bliss of dreams." ---- by 𝔐ilton

"Remember, keep your head down and don't talk until I say so."

The latch clicked. The door creaked. The door swung open, revealing a dim lit cavern, swirling in a haze of smoke. Bodies stood and sat everywhere. Voices whispered, shouted and laughed loudly. The air smelt of stale smoke and strong spirits of ale and whiskey. Tom lead the way straight ahead as Bess followed close on his heels. In fact, she only saw his heels as she kept her head down.

"You don't need to follow that close, not that I don't mind, but the blokes might start talking. Besides, we don't want to draw attention."

"Sorry, Tom," said Bess in her normal tone, then remembered. "Sorry, Tom," Bess repeated in a deep voice and followed a few steps further back.

At the opposite end of the door, stood a twenty-foot bar. They sat down on a couple of vacant stools at the far end. Curiosity forced Bess to lift her head and survey the surroundings. Tom's choice turned out to be perfect as they sat deep in the shadows of the room. Most of the patrons seemed intent on listening to their fellow drinkers, so Bess felt safe in perusing the crowd. Most wore their caps and coats as if at any second they would have to make a hasty retreat. Even a few gentlemen, seated at small, wood-planked tables, kept their top hats on as they indulged in a glass or two of bitters.

On the other side of the bar, worked two men, dressed in white shirts and green aprons. One had dark hair and the other a carrot top of unruly curls. The latter's head bent forward, as his muscular arms swung the handle back and forth as mug after mug of beer filled to overflowing. The dark-haired fellow, in his mid-thirties, poured glasses of spirits to the patrons, lined up at the bar. To Bess's surprise, a buxom, young woman came from behind, carrying a pewter tray full of empty glasses.

"Thanks, luv, I'll give you a tray full of dirty ones to take back to the kitchen." The dark-haired fellow looked in their direction. "Tom, the usual?"

"Aye, make it two and two steak and kidney pies while your at it, Robert," Tom shouted, as he turned and watched two fellows vacate a table in the corner. "Grab that table; I'll settle up with Robert."

Bess jumped off the stool and sprinted over to the table, snatching it out of the hands of an approaching giant. "Sor ---" Bess stopped briefly and took a deep breath. "Sorry, mate. Ye snooze, ye lose." Bess quickly lowered her head to look eye to beer belly as the belly moved closer.

"Simon, I see you've met an old mate of mine." Tom came to the rescue.

"Feisty, little bugger. Where'd ye pick 'im up, mate?"

"Ben just dropped in from the country. We are old schoolmates. Right, Ben, old mate?" Tom slapped Bess on the back, almost landing her in the seat, face first.

"Two ales, two steak 'n' kidneys," announced the buxom barmaid. "Whose yer cute, little mate, Tom?"

Tom laughed. "That's for me to know and you to find out, Sal. Besides, I thought I was your fellow."

"Of course, Tom, but a girl's got to keep 'er options open," she said as she winked at Bess. "See ye, luv."

"Eat up," ordered Tom. "By the end of the night, we're both going to need our strength."

They relished their meal in silence. Tom washed his pie down with large gulps of the dark lager, while Bess took small sips of the bitter liquid. The small table, in the dark corner, kept them isolated from the lively occupants of "The Goodale." Feeling no recognition of her gender, she sat back and observed her surroundings. The large room, divided into smaller alcoves, gave off a sinister appearance. The dim gaslights enhanced the overall scene of plots being born and nurtured into full blown crimes and uprisings. Off to the left, constant traffic kept passing by. Laughter and sudden shouts echoed from that direction. Bess leaned forward in hopes of catching a glimpse of the mysterious destination.

"Drink up, Bes-- Ben. Sal likes a man who likes his ale." Tom laughed as Bess stuck her tongue out in his direction. "Now, now, other mates should be so lucky."

Bess leaned closer to Tom and quietly asked, "What's all the excitement over there?" She pointed to the left.

"Oh, the public room? Ah yes, that is where we play billiards. Do blokes play it in America?"

"Why yes, we call it pool. Poolhalls are big business. Unfortunately, they do attract a not so gentlemanly clientele. However, there are a few nice ones and I have played a few games myself."

"You constantly surprise me, Ben. What a shame, no billiards tonight. There's a special event going on in there. When Sean comes, we will pop in and take a look."

"Another one, Tom, luv?" Sal said as she wiggled up to the table. "Wot sumthin' wrong wit' t' ale, luv?" Sal looked at Bess who immediately dropped her head. "Don't ye be gettin' shy on me, luv. One night wit' me, luv an' ye'll never be shy again." Sal poked Bess's arm and gave a cheeky laugh.

"Sorry about the ale, luv. We've been too busy catching up on old times. Thanks, Sal, but we'll wait for Sean," replied Tom.

Sal turned and wiggled her way to the next table as Tom watched her retreat. "Our Sal's quite a cockney miss. Don't you agree, Ben? --- Ben--- Bess, did you hear me?"

"Sorry, Tom. Sal reminded me of something I've been puzzled about," said Bess and leaned forward. "Sal speaks with a real cockney accent, --- like Jim Button, Lily and the postman's wife -----"

"Millie. That is correct, they all do. Most people raised here, speak like them."

"Yes, that's what puzzles me. You don't speak like them."

"True, but I was not born in London. In fact, I wasn't even born in England. I'm from Wales."

"Was Lottie born in Wales?"

"Aye, she was. She came to London as a young bride. I followed a couple of years later when our parents died. Lottie's husband went off to sea, and she wrote and asked me to come stay with her."

"So, if she wasn't born in London, why does she have a cockney accent?"

"That is a good question, Bess. You can imagine how surprised I was when I arrived to be greeted by my sister speaking in a foreign tongue. I think she just adapts wholeheartedly to her surroundings."

"That is true, Tom. I noticed when she is working in the tea shoppe, she loses all traces a cockney accent. She fits right in with her proper English patrons. And, then on Sunday, she spoke as cockney as her cockney neighbours."

"Aye, Lottie fits in anywhere, so I guess it is only natural her voice follows suit," replied Tom. "Besides, it is quicker to drop the g's and the h's. It gives her more words to use to fill a sentence before she runs out of breath." He laughed. "Now, if only we could solve the mystery of her passion for her wandering captain. ----- But, that will have to wait until another day. Here comes Sean. ---- Sean, me mate, I was beginning to wonder, if you were coming." Tom got up and moved another chair over.

Two mugs of ale slopped over as Sean banged them down on the table. "Aye, Tom, late as always; mind, I dinnae loaf around." Sean laughed and glanced over at Bess. "I saw Ivan Williams outside, and we stared talking, so I asked 'im to join us. I dinnae think ye'd mind, seeing 'e's a countryman of yer's. --- Aye, 'ere 'e comes."

A short, stocky man of thirty, holding a mug of ale, made his way to the table. His ruddy complexion and broad smile competed for attention. " Tom, bach, good to see you," he said as he pulled up a chair.

Tom moved his chair closer to Bess's, giving her knee a nudge. "Ivan, old man, it's been awhile. Busy making money, no doubt. Aye, the Welsh are almost as bad as the Scots when it comes to money." The three men laughed.

"Don't forget where you come from, Tom, bach."

"Ivan, I saw ye pass by 'The Brown Bread' this morning. Yer carriage was loaded with parcels. Ye must be stocking up the money. Aye, a poor Scotsman like me cannae compete with the likes of ye." Sean laughed and turned to Tom. "I fergot to tell ye, I saw yer bonnie lass peaking in our shoppe window today. Tom, ye should introduce 'er to Ivan, what with 'is singing and 'er playing the pianoforte. Aye, what sweet music they could make."

Tom ignored Sean and said, "Ivan, lots of parcels to deliver to the rich folks?"

"Aye, Tom, bach, Christmas is becoming a busy season for 'Williams & Sons.' Back home in Cardiff, my dad never used to deliver parcels. Even when we came to London, our service mainly delivered small supplies to merchants. Now, we can't keep up with it. We've had to hire extra help. Tom, Sean, you don't know of anyone I could hire for Thursday? He'd just have to run the parcels in for me. That way I can stay on the carriage, minding the horse and the parcels."

Tom thought for a moment and said, "My mate Ben here, might be able to help out. What do you say?" Tom asked a startled Bess.

"Ah----Me?" Bess deepened her voice, "What about Lottie?"

"True. ---- Ivan, Ben could help you in the afternoon."

"Aye, Tom, bach, that would work out fine. By the time I pick up the parcels from the merchants, it will be about one."

"Good then, it's settled. Ben will meet you in front of 'The

Goodale' at one on Thursday." Tom turned to Bess and gave her a slap on the back. "You won't be disappointed. Ben may look small, but he's a feisty, little bugger. Ivan, old man, he will jump off that carriage before you've checked your next delivery. Why, only a couple of years ago, he won the famous Oxford Race in the hundred-yard dash. ----- OOW --- " Tom groaned as Bess gave his leg a heavy wallop from under the table.

"Good, I'll see you on Thursday, Ben." Ivan gulped down his ale. "I'll be off then, mates. Nosta."

"Goodnight, Ivan," Tom and Sean shouted in return.

"Ben, I be Sean MacLeod." He extended his arm across the table and shook hands with Bess. "Aye, for a fellow with small 'ands, ye've got a mighty grip." Bess smiled and Sean looked intently at her. "Ye remind me of someone."

"Sean, I promised Ben we'd go into the public room," said Tom averting his attention.

The three followed the crowd into a smoky room, hot with the bodies of over excited glands. A circle of men stood solidly in front of them. Staying close behind Tom, she caught a glimpse of billiard tables lined flush with the wall. Tom grabbed her elbow and pulled her to the left. Bess saw only the back of jackets, smelt the sweat of excitement and heard deafening cheers and jeers. Tom gradually pushed her in front of him. Before her, stood two bare-chested men, a foot apart. With clenched fists, they raised their arms and started to box.

"Oh my," Bess uttered, as the blows vibrated in the air. Each punch resounded off the opponents chest, making her knees weak. "Tom --- "

He bent over and whispered in her ear, "Steady, Ben. You wanted to come."

"You're right." Bess stood straight and composed herself. In a few minutes, she had her fists clenched and raised in unison with the two boxers.

The boxers waltzed around the ring of human bodies. After

ten minutes of this, the spectators became restless and started booing the two contenders.

"Our Sal could do better. She'd beat t' pants off t' both of ye."

"She probably 'as---- more than once."

Gales of laughter resounded through the room, as Tom whispered in her ear, "Come on mate, it's time to go." Tom put his hands on her shoulders, spun her around and guided her through the crowd. "Keep your head down. I'll lead you."

Back in the street, Bess breathed in the cool, clean air. Even the smell of the horse dung felt inviting to her smoke filled nostrils. The clip clop of the horses hooves on the cobblestones, sounded like music to her ears.

"Ben, Tom, I'll be off; my turn to fire up the ovens tomorrow morning. If I dinnae get 'em lit by 'alf past three, there'll nay be any bread for the wee lasses and laddies for their school meal tomorrow. --- Tom, I'll be around at seven on Wednesday. Should be a grand dance. The bonnie lasses will be all decked out in their finery. Bess is coming? --- Ye did ask 'er?" Sean looked at Tom who shook his head. "Mate, ask 'er tomorrow morning. Jo will be very disappointed if ye dinnae ask. Besides, since Lottie's not coming and if Bess dinnae come, Jo won't come." Sean looked crestfallen. "Aye, Ben, good to meet ye. ---- I still cannae place that smile." He shook his head. "It will come to me. Goodnight, mates."

They watched Sean turn the corner and they headed back home. "Ben, old man, you did good."

"It was a most enjoyable experience, and one I shall remember a long time. Thank you."

"Right then, so how about the dance on Wednesday night? Being Christmas; it should be a grand ball."

"I have nothing to wear."

"Not to worry, Lottie will dress you up just fine. Good, then that's settled."

He whistled a little tune as they walked past "Basil's

Mustard and Spice Shoppe." Tom entered the tea shoppe first. Instantaneously, he reached up and deadened the sound of the bell by wedging his fingers between the striking pieces of metal. Silence prevailed, except for the beating of their hearts.

Tom whispered, "I've got a couple of things to do in the kitchen before heading up to bed, so I'll say goodnight."

"Thank you, Tom; a memory to cherish." She gave him a kiss on the cheek. "Oh, Ben thanks you too." She kissed the other cheek and headed for the stairs.

"Mind the creaks and especially the one in front of Bertie's room. Lottie has ears like a hawk."

Carefully, she climbed each step until she heard the dreaded creak. "Darn."

"Bess?"

"Damn." Bess stood still and thought *now, what do I do?*

"Bess, I can't find 'The Last Of The Mohicans.' Where did you put it?"

"Pardon?"

"I was looking at it when I must have dozed off. I thought I might read it," said Evan.

"Oh, Evan ---- It fell on the floor, so I picked it up and ----"

"Not to worry. Put it in the bookcase. When I have some time, I'll read it," said Evan. "Apples and pears, I'll race you up the stairs." Evan grabbed her around the waist and tried to pass her. "Phew, you smell smoky." He sniffed her hair and as she turned her face towards him, Evan said, "Bess, have you been into my bottles of ale? You smell like a brewery. If I didn't know better, I'd swear you'd been drinking at the pub."

"Of course not, I've been here all night." She took a whiff of her smoky sweater and crossed her fingers behind her back. "I can't smell anything. You must still be dreaming."

Evan beat her to the washroom. As soon as he came out, she burst in, closed the door, stripped off her smoky clothes and jumped into the shower. Hair and body washed, she brushed her teeth and gargled with a heavy duty mouthwash. *There,now he won't notice.* Satisfied, she opened the door to face accusations head on, but found him curled up in bed fast asleep. *Well, he certainly won't notice now.* Bess went back in the bathroom and picked up her discarded clothes. She put them in the clothes hamper, closed the lid and thought *maybe I'd better check the pockets of my jeans. I'm always leaving Kleenex in them.*

Rummaging through them, her fingers touched a small piece of paper. Lifting it out, she saw a flash of red. *Red?--- Red --- stamp. It's the Penny Red.* She thrust her hand back in the pocket and brought out a second piece of paper. She breathed a sigh of relief. *Yes, ---- it's the Two Penny Blue.* She caressed them with her fingers. *Evan's present. I'll put them away in my nightstand for safekeeping.*

Tucked into bed, she turned off the light and put her head on the pillow. She fell asleep with a smile of satisfaction on her youthful face.

# CHAPTER XII

"'Tis the first day of winter, my fair lady. The day is too short, so arise and rejoice in the daylight hours. Nightfall will come too quickly."

"Huh? --- What?" Bess slowly opened her eyes. "Evan, what are you babbling about?"

"Bess, my love, my life. I must be off, for there is much work I must do." Evan bent down and gave her a warm kiss.

"You're off alright, off your rocker," she sneered and threw the covers over her head.

"I love you too, dear," said Evan, as he headed down the stairs.

Bess struggled with the covers. Suddenly, she sat up. "Was I dreaming, or was that really Evan?"

The room, shrouded in darkness, confused Bess. *Am I still under the covers?* She felt for the light switch beside her bed and flicked it on. The digital clock on the nightstand showed 08:00A.M., December 21. *Evan wasn't kidding when he said it was the shortest day of the year,* she thought as she shivered and pulled the covers up to her neck.

"Evan ---- That reminds me, I'd better check." Bess opened the drawer of the nightstand and to her relief, Queen Victoria's red head stared up at her. She picked it up and found her twin, the blue head, right underneath.

Bess bounced out of bed and ran down to the study. Opening

the desk drawer, she found a small, glassine envelope of stamps, which she dumped out and took the empty envelope upstairs. The Penny Red and The Two Penny Blue slid into the transparent compartment and promptly found themselves hidden under some papers, back in the nightstand drawer.

"I can't wait for Evan to open this little package on Christmas Day." She beamed. "But, whatever am I going to say when he asks me how I obtained them? I'll have to think on it." She closed the drawer with one hand, while the other automatically positioned itself behind her back in readiness for the blarney to be executed in this explanation.

While the last load of washing drowned in the rinse cycle, the underwear spun out of control in the dryer. The vacuum sucked up the fir needles with such gusto, the Christmas tree feared for its life. Also in fear of the vacuum monster rearing its long, silvery body upwards, a terrified Mr. Spider escaped within the minutest crack between the skylight and the ceiling. In time, turmoil abated and a soothing cup of tea calmed the frazzled nerves of the Turner household. Bess took a sip of the aromatic Christmas blend and felt her body relax. Giving her neck a quick rub, she bent it backwards. Bess saw a relieved Mr. Spider poke his head through the crack and focus his little, beady eyes on her.

"You can come out now, Mr. Spider. You are safe for another day." She laughed.

As she put her mug down on the cluttered coffee table, she thought *I must drop these off in the book bin in the mall; maybe after lunch. While I'm there, I should look for some gifts for the Morton family.* She puzzled over this for quite awhile. Finally, she swung her arm across the table to pick up the books. A piece of paper floated to the floor. She picked it up and turned it over.

"It's the copy of 'White Christmas,' " she said as her head lifted to look at the mantel. Her eyes focused on the tea shoppe and Bess wondered ----- *will this sheet of music ever get to Miss Rose Water?*

"Miss Bess, how nice. You have managed to get me a copy of your beautiful song." Asweet voice interrupted her train of thought.

Bess found herself at the foot of the stairs, facing a familiar smile.

"Harriet will be pleased. Thank you so much."

"Your welcome, ----- Miss Rose Water." Bess uttered as she regained her composure. She handed her the Xeroxed sheet of music.

The door bell jingled and Mrs. Pennycroft came rushing into the tearoom all in a dither. "My, my, what am I going to do?"

"Whatever is the matter, Mrs. Pennycroft?" Miss Rose Water rushed over and put her arm around her. "Do come and sit down."

Mrs. Pennycroft plunked down on a chair, her hat all askew and with a shocked expression, she cried, "I cannot believe it. How could this happen to me?"

Lottie rushed out of the kitchen to see what and who caused all the commotion. "Dear me, Mrs. Pennycroft, what can be so important as to cause you such distress?"

"The most important dinner of the year and it is ruined, ruined I say."

"Bess, luv, get Mrs. Pennycroft a cup of tea."

Bess left the two ladies consoling a distraught Mrs. Pennycroft. As she reached the kitchen door, she looked to the left and noticed the quote of the day:

"The muse's friend,
Tea does our fancy aid,
Repress the vapours
Which the head invade,
And keeps the palace
Of the soul serene."

By Edmund Waller's "Of Tea" 17th century

*I do hope it works,* she thought and rushed into the kitchen.

Relieved to find a pot of tea steeping on the sideboard, she plunked it on a nearby tray. Tea came trickling out of the spout as she quickly carried it to the table.

"Here, luv." Lottie poured a cup, ignoring the flood of tea on the tray.

The three ladies stood motionless as the distraught one drank her tea. Time stood still. When the last drop disappeared, Lottie put her hand on the handle, ready to pour another cup, when the centre of attention relaxed and adjusted her hat. The other three ladies gave a sigh of relief.

"My dinner party is the social event of the season, and it cannot be cancelled. The Winter Solstice only comes once a year and today is the day. I have spent weeks planning the whole evening and this happens."

"Whatever is it?"

"My pianist has a severe case of the vapours."

"The vapours?"

"Yes, can you believe it, the vapours. Obviously, it is all in her head. Tobias, my butler, received the message, not more than an hour ago. How can I have a dinner without a pianist? It is impossible to get someone at the last minute and especially during the yule season."

'Oh, my dear, surely someone must be available?" asked Miss Rose Water. "What about Mrs. Wilmot's daughter? Mrs. Wilmot is always saying how well she sings and plays the pianoforte."

"Miss Wilmot's voice makes a squawking parrot sound heavenly."

"Oh my," exclaimed Miss Rose Water. "I know, what about Miss Bess?"

"Miss Bess?" questioned Mrs. Pennycroft. She turned to Bess, looked her up and down and said, "Well, what about it, Miss N-ike? Are you able to come and play for my dinner guests this evening?"

Bess looked at Lottie who nodded and said, "Yes, Mrs. Pennycroft, I would be honoured to play at your dinner party."

"Fine then, that is settled. My carriage will pick you up at half-past five." She gave a slight smile and got up to leave. At the door, she turned around and asked, "You do sing?" She opened the door, and as she stepped out she said, "I trust you do have another dress?"

After the overdramatic, Pennycroft dilemma, the morning rush came to a successful conclusion. Bess and Lottie sat at the kitchen table enjoying the peace and quiet. Even the gurgles, escaping from the kettle, sounded gentle as a babbling brook to their ears.

" 'Ere try one of me new experiments. I put ginger in me scones," said Lottie as she passed the plate to Bess.

Bess put down her teacup and picked up a flaky scone. "They smell delicious," she said as she took a bite, "and they are delicious." She continued with her mouth full, "There are so many flavours to enhance scones. Grated lemon adds a bite, especially when you spread lemon curd instead of jam on them."

"Lemon curd?"

"Lemony custard."

"I must try it. --- Ye know thick cream might be nice."

"Thick cream on top of jam --- Hmm --- Oh, be a devil."

"Speakin' of bein' a devil. Our Tom is gettin' pretty close to earnin' 'is 'orns. Why, last night I 'eard 'im goin' up to bed. It must 'ave bin goin' on midnight, an' 'im 'avin' to work in t' mornin'. 'E might as well move in wit' Robert. 'E spends all 'is time there. 'E thinks 'e's foolin' me, sneakin' past me bedroom, but I 'eard 'im loud an' clear last night. Thank goodness 'e didn't disturb ye. 'E didn't did 'e?"

"Tom? No, he didn't," answered Bess as stabs of guilt pierced her soul. "You mustn't be hard on him, Lottie. He has been very kind to me."

"Aye, so I've noticed." Lottie gave a chuckle. "That reminds me, I wanted to tell ye about The Eve Of St. Thomas, but I didn't get a chance last night. Oh well, 'tis too late now."

"Eve Of St. Thomas? --- What did you want to tell me?"

"I suppose if need be, it might cum in 'andy next year. First of all, The Eve Of St. Thomas was last night, the night before Winter Solstice. T'is a very old tale, that if ye take a St. Thomas onion, mind I don't know where ye'd get one, but I suppose a regular onion will do. ----- Well, ye peel it an' lay it in a clean 'andkerchief. Not that ye'd be usin' a dirty one. --- Lay it under yer 'ead an' as soon as ye lain down say these words ------

"Good, St. Thomas, do me right
An' bring me luv to me tonight.
That I may look 'im in t' face
An' in me arms may 'im embrace."

"Then in thy sleep thou shalt dream of 'im, that shall be thy 'usband."

"Lottie, did you do that?"

"Blimey, of course not. I told ye t'is an' old tale, an' I'm a modern woman. Besides, wot bloke in 'is right mind goin' want to embrace a woman wit' onion 'air?" They burst out laughing.

Bess cleared up the dishes and poured the dish water. She no longer worried about spilling the hot water and easily transported the heavy liquid to the sink. She proceeded to make a good dent in the pile of dirty dishes when Lottie spoke from behind.

"So, wot 'appened at t' steamship office, yesterday?"

Bess stopped in mid-splash and sunk her hands into the depths of the dirty water. *I knew she would ask me.* She took a deep breath. Her wrinkled hands rose to the surface. Grabbing a tea towel, she dried them, turned towards Lottie and automatically put her hands behind her back and crossed her fingers. Flour covered Lottie from head to foot. Bess felt she was about to address The Ghost Of Christmas Present, and anything she said would be held against her if it was not the whole truth.

Shaking the ghosts out of her head, Bess said, "The steamship office told me they had an idea my bags went on to ----- France. They should know more in a couple of days when the ship returns to Southampton."

"France? Well, let's 'ope yer luggage is 'avin' a bon voyage. Last summer, Bertie 'n' me were goin' to France fer a fortnight, but Mr. Brown cancelled 'is business trip, so we didn't go. ----- I know wot yer thinkin', but Mr. Brown promised Bertie a trip to France if 'e did well in school an' it worked. Bertie surprised us all. Of course, 'e was too young to travel wit'out 'is mum, so I couldn't disappoint t' lad. Mr. Brown kindly arranged fer sumone to work t' tea shoppe. Sadly, t' French businessman came 'ere instead. Maybe next summer." Lottie sighed.

Relieved the inquisition ended without getting herself deeper in hot water, she plunged her hands in the now, lukewarm dish-water. Bess uncrossed her fingers.

"Ye'll be needin' a new dress fer t'is evenin'. 'Tis a shame Mrs. Pennycroft saw ye at t' play, cause ye could 'ave worn t' same dress. Mrs. Pennycroft notices these things. After washin' up, go down to 'Taylor & Sons.' Lydia always 'as a few sample dresses she wants to show off. I'm sure she can fix ye up fer t'is evenin'."

"Good idea, Lottie. What would I do without you?"

"I'm sure ye would manage, but t'is nice to be appreciated."

Bess finished washing up and turned to put the tea towel on the rack to dry. Her eyes beheld a wooden rack suspended from the ceiling, full of undergarments hanging every which way. Silk toes pointed downward, pantaloons bottoms up, chemises bent over like rag dolls, and a mean looking corset, armed with bones sticking straight-out, ready to attack any invading foe. She managed to tuck it in a spot near the threatening suit of armour. *Naturally, this spot would be vacant, the corset would terrorize any cloth that came near,* thought Bess as she looked at the brave little tea towel shaking in fear.

As Bess walked through the doorway, Lottie shouted, "Mind

t' bodice, don't let Lydia give ye one too low. It wouldn't do to 'ave t' fine bred gentlemen be more interested in yer exposures than yer music." She laughed. "Mind ye, it would keep 'em awake."

Remembering the exposure angle, Bess covered her short hair with a bonnet Jo leant her. Buttoning the coat up to her neck, she proceeded to the front door.

Lottie came running to the kitchen door, wiping her floured hands on her apron and said, "I fergot to tell ye, Jo said to drop in t' book shoppe. Mr. Tell is givin' ye a good price on a book ye wanted. --- And that reminds me ---- Where is me 'ead? ---- Congratulations on yer lucky find in t' street yesterday. I 'ope ye don't mind Jo tellin' me."

"No, I'll drop in there on my way back from the dress shoppe. See you later," said Bess, as she closed the door and stepped out into the cold air.

She passed "Tellaway Books" and almost collided with two women coming out with brown paper, packages of books tied with string. She looked in the window and noticed a crowd huddled in a corner. *Hmm, must be a good sale on today,* she surmised and felt in her pocket to make sure she had her coins. Bess felt the cold metal slip through her fingers. She breathed a sigh of relief and mumbled to herself *later.*

An attractive building stood to her left. At first glance, Bess thought it strange to have a private residence in a business district. But, at a closer look, she discovered a business sign over two sets of double-wide oak doors, "Taylor & Sons." On the left, indented in the header over a large window, the word "Haberdashery" stood out in bold, brass letters. Over the door on the right, hung a sign, "Hats Off." An ornate, wrought iron railing, running vertically from the foot of the stairs to the building, separated the two doors.

In the bay window on the right, various women's hats with coloured feathers and bonnets of lace and muslin, stood perched upon short, brass poles. Three doll size dresses stood magically

165

upright, while a wire frame of a woman's torso stood behind. Bess walked up the stairs and opened the door.

The soft sound of the bell suited the pale colours and feminine furnishings of the intimate room. Tucked in the corner, between the front bay window and the smaller, side bay window, a fire glowed in the fireplace. Bright and cheery, the room smelt of fresh, spring flowers. A candle glowed in a delicate, china saucer. Bess moved closer and took another whiff of the scented candle.

A gentle humming came from behind a doorway, draped in a full-length, yellow brocade curtain. The sound intensified. A lady's hand appeared at the edge of the curtain, clutched the fabric and pulled it back, revealing the attractive seamstress.

"Oh--- I'm sorry, I did not know you were here. I do hope you have not been waiting long. I must get a louder bell. It is all fine and good to appear serene, but at what cost? --- Perhaps, some valuable business?" She smiled and her brown eyes grew wide. "Why, it is Miss Bess. I hoped you would come in for a fitting. I just received a bluebell silk that would go perfect with your beautiful blue eyes."

"Good afternoon, Miss Taylor."

"Do call me Lydia."

"Lydia? How interesting, my best friend is called Lydia. In fact, you remind me of her."

Lydia smiled and continued, "Did you notice, I was humming your beautiful Christmas song?"

Bess thought for a moment trying to recall the tune and finally took a guess, "Oh, you mean 'White Christmas'?"

"Yes, that is it. I am so glad I got the tune right. You must write down the words. My brother would love to hear me sing it all day long." She gave a hearty laugh. "Now, what can I do for you today?"

Bess explained the situation and added, "Lottie said you might have some samples available to model. I can't purchase a new dress, but perhaps I could rent one of your samples for the night?"

"Hmm ----- Take off your coat and let's have a closer look at you." Lydia helped her off with her coat and hung it on the coat-rack, by the front door. "Now, turn around once more." She stood back, surveyed Bess up and down and said, "Right, do sit down on the settee. I'll go see what I have in the back."

Bess sat down on the pink velvet seat. Strains of the unfamiliar version of "White Christmas" strained its way into the waiting room. Bess took this opportunity to look around the room. Encased in a gilded frame, a large pair of scissors, stitched in petit point, hung on the wall facing the front door. Lydia came in the room carrying a bundle of silks and brocades. She deposited them on the matching pink ottoman, covering the six inch, braided fringe around its edge.

"Let's see. Stand up, Miss Bess." Lydia picked up the deep-purple velvet off the top of the pile. "Hold it by the shoulders. --- That's it." Lydia stepped back to view her creation. "Sit down on this chair." Lydia put her finger to her chin. "No, too bright. It would detract from your performance." She rummaged through the pile and pulled out a pale-yellow silk chiffon. "Let's try this one." Up went the slender finger on her perfect chin. "Yes, definitely a mystical, muse like apparition. Now, let's go into the fitting room."

Through the draped doorway went the two ladies. A bay window made the larger room bright. On one wall, a black treadle, sewing machine looked right at home, wedged between bolts of material arranged upright and horizontal. The rainbow of colours of the brocades, silks, muslins and velvets, melded into each other, except where an independent, bold tartan caused the eye to take notice. Spools of thread stood on narrow shelves, while boxes of patterns overflowed from deeper shelves. A small fireplace in the corner, added just enough heat to make undressing bearable. A tall, silk screen stood to the left of the window.

"Off with your dress. Go behind the screen. We don't want the fellows from the firehall across the street, distracted. They have enough fires to put out, let alone their own." Lydia's hearty laugh made Bess laugh. "You can leave your undergarments on. I'll just get my pins and measuring tape."

Bess took off her dress. *What is she going to say when she sees my er --- undergarments?* Worried, Bess clutched the dress close to her body.

"Now, don't be modest. I won't see anything I have not seen before."

"Don't bet on it."

"Pardon, what did you say?" Lydia asked, as she extended her arm and took the dress from her. "Oh my." Her brown eyes almost popped out of their sockets. "I spoke too soon. Whatever do you have on? Whatever possessed you to cut off your pantaloons so short?" She waited for Bess to answer and when none came forward, she said, "I did hear you were seen in trousers when you had the spill outside the book shoppe, but I thought old Lily was telling tales."

"Yes, well, ------" Bess quickly crossed her fingers behind her back and said, "My pantaloons were making it very uncomfortable to wear trousers, so I cut them."

"So, it is true, but why would a lady wear trousers?" Lydia thought for a moment. "I suppose they do things different in America. Hmm ---- Did you cut your corset too?"

"Something like that, besides it too is much more comfortable. All those whale bones can get to you by the end of the day," said Bess and she murmured to herself *now that's a whale's tale, if ever I heard one.* She chuckled to herself and proceeded to uncross her fingers. "I do like this pale-yellow."

"Put it on and see how it fits." Lydia raised the dress over Bess's head and the dress slid down her shoulders. Lydia buttoned up the back and said, "Fits perfectly, in spite of the corset. Turn around and let me look at the front." Bess turned around and Lydia tsked. "Well, I don't know. ---- If we pull the shoulders up. ---- No, that will not do." Lydia unbuttoned the back and slipped the bodice down to Bess's waist. She reached over, opened a nearby drawer and pulled out the dreaded corset. "Sorry, dear, but you are going to have to put this on."

After five minutes of struggling with it, the corset overpowered Bess's upper torso. With a lack of unrestricted airflow, Bess pulled the dress over her quivering body.

"Much better. I should pin up the hem. Where are your shoes?" Lydia looked around to where Bess dropped her old dress. "No ---- Don't tell me." Lydia started to laugh and right away Bess got caught up in her infectious laugh. Lydia wiped the tears from her eyes and said, "Put them on. I will make the hem a little longer to hide the shoes."

A few pins here and there and the dress came off exposing one hundred and sixty years of undergarment fashion. "Don't take the corset off. You will survive. European women have survived for centuries. Besides, you will be going out shortly. Come back in an hour, I'll have the dress ready. With this new invention I just purchased, called a sewing machine, I can get the alterations done in no time."

"You are very kind. How much do I owe you?"

"It is a sampler, and besides it is good for business to have it modeled at Mrs. Pennycroft's annual dinner party. If anyone asks, give them my name. I should be paying you for the lesson you gave me on American unmentionables. By the way, they shall remain unmentionable. Only your haberdashery knows for sure."

Bess left the dress shoppe feeling a tight restrictive, but relieved. She would look presentable to Mrs. Pennycroft. *Now, what to do for the next hour?* Bess asked herself. Heading back to assist Lottie, she passed the book shoppe and remembered to stop by and see Jo. The crowd had dwindled, but still four ladies stood in line off to the left. Jo lifted her head and beckoned Bess over.

"I am so glad you came in. Mr. Tell would like to meet you. He is just at the back. I'll go get him," said Jo, as a tall lady, dressed in black came up to the counter.

"If you point me in the right direction, I'll find him. You wait on your customer."

"Thank you, Bess. He is at the back of the second aisle."

Bess walked down the narrow aisle, encased in bound books of all sizes and conditions of wear. Stopping to look at some of the titles, she noticed in gold letters "London Journal" J Boswell, 1762-63 and "The Life Of Samuel Johnson" J Boswell, 1791. Laying next to it, two huge books titled "Dictionary Of The English Language" Samuel Johnson, 1755, Vol.1 A-K, Vol.2 L-Z. Each book measured at least eighteen inches tall and close to two feet in width. *Good Heavens!* thought Bess. *One would need a library to keep them in.* Stacked higher, but in four volumes, a later edition of Johnson's dictionary, lay haphazardly on the shelf. *One would need an enormous table to view the contents; the weight alone could kill one. Thank goodness for pocket dictionaries,* she sighed. She forced herself not to touch their brittle jackets in fear she should destroy a part of written history.

Bess focused on the flickering light in front of her. In a small alcove at the end of her journey, stood a heavy desk covered in large, bound books and piles of paper. A magnifying glass wavered in the air as an unsteady hand grasped its brass handle. Covered in brown spots, the large hand put down the magnifying glass.

"Ah --- Good afternoon, miss," said the elderly man seated behind the desk. "Forgive me for not rising, but my legs are not as steady as they once were. By the time I managed to stand upright, you would be on your way. Miss Godale tells me, you are interested in the American author, Clement Clark Moore. I too have read his work, 'A Visit From St. Nicholas.' It is an amusing fairy tale, but do you think it will catch on?"

"Oh yes, Mr. Tell, I certainly do."

"Well, Miss ---Bess? I suppose everyone needs to believe in something, and he is a pleasant enough character. --- Since you are getting the book for Bertie and Artie, ---- I am rather fond of the lads. Artie reminds me of myself when I was a lad his age.

Likes to read, so I've been told." He parted his large puffy lips and smiled. "Yes, back to business. I will sell it to you for a tuppence."

"A tuppence?"

"Why yes, my dear, and not a penny less."

"Oh --- Mr. Tell, --- how many pennies are in a tuppence?"

"Why, two of course."

"Oh," said Bess as she breathed a sigh of relief. "I'll take it. Thank you very much."

She reached in her pocket and brought out her three coins. *The copper one is worth a penny; not enough. The silver one, --- ah yes, shilling,* she thought hard as she scratched her head. *Ten --- no, twelve pennies. ---- Yes, that's right. ----* She handed him a shilling.

"Thank you, but Miss Godale will give you your change. The book is up at the counter." He picked up the magnifying glass and handed it to Bess. "Have a look at one of my treasures." Mr. Tell opened a very old book. The pages of thick, yellow paper, crackled as he turned them over. "Notice the articulate writing." He pointed to the middle of the page. "The ink has faded, and the spelling much different from today, so use the magnifying glass. If you take your time and pronounce the words as they are written, you will understand the text."

As she looked through the large, brass rimmed glass, Bess discovered the beautiful, pen strokes. "Yes, you are right, strange how the spelling has changed, but the meaning stays the same. When was this written?"

"John Stowe, the leading antiquarian of his time, wrote 'A Summarie Of Englyshe Chronicles' in 1565. As an antiquarian bookseller, I was extremely fortunate to purchase this 1567 edition at an estate sale. It had been kept undisturbed for many decades in perfect storage conditions. After I authenticate it, it will be going to The British Museum for all to see for centuries to come." Mr. Tell smiled as he admired its creator's penmanship. He lifted his silver watch from his pocket and glanced at the time. "Now, my dear, it is time I get back to my task at hand."

"Thank you for sharing this piece of history with me, Mr. Tell." Bess handed over the magnifying glass to a shaky hand and left him to his love of books.

As she walked back up the aisle, she heard him say, "And -- thank you, Miss Bess for sharing your musical talent with Fetter Lane."

Back at the counter, Bess waited in line as Jo helped a customer. Looking around, she noticed the mysterious line had dwindled down to one customer. The lady turned and started to walk towards Bess. The stranger's face glowed as her eyes beheld the book in her hands. A man, with his head bent forward, remained seated at the mysterious desk. Bess watched as he put the quill down, flexed his fingers, raised his head and stared straight ahead.

"Why, Miss Bess. How nice to see you."

Bess left the line and walked over to the man. "Mr. Dickens, what an honour to meet you again."

"The honour is mine. I have been sitting here for, what seems like hours," He flexed his fingers again, "signing my books. I have only one copy left. Unfortunately, it is 'A Christmas Carol,' so you won't be wanting another copy."

"Oh yes, I would." She blurted out before thinking. "I aah --- have a friend back home who loves your book. Why every Christmas, he recites your dialogue word for word. "If they would rather die, they had better do it, and decrease the surplus population. Besides --- Excuse me ---- I don't know that."

"But you might know it," replied Mr. Dickens.

"It's not my business," continued Bess and they both recited in unison, "It's enough for a man to understand his own business, and not to interfere with other peoples'. Mine occupies me constantly. Good afternoon, Gentlemen!" They both laughed.

"I'm sure you wrote that passage explicitly for my friend. Like Scrooge, he too is a devoted accountant," said Bess.

Mr. Dickens picked up the quill, dipped it in the inkwell and opened the last remaining book. "Now, to whom shall I address this to?"

"Evan!"

Held closely to her heart, she carried the little, salmon coloured book up to the counter. Its gilded edges shone upwards upon Bess's already glowing face.

"How fortunate, Bess, you procured Mr. Dickens' last copy."

"Oh, Jo, I am so pleased. How much do I owe you?"

"Again you are fortunate, it is half price. Mr. Tell doesn't want any Christmas stock left over. He said there will be plenty on hand when next Christmas comes along. ---- That will be two shillings, eight pennies."

Bess felt in her pocket and came out with three coins, two shillings and one penny. "Oh no! I don't have enough. Oh dear! Jo, what shall I do? And Mr. Dickens already signed it. I can't put it back. ---- How stupid of me. I should have asked the price first, but oh no, I just lost all common sense when he spoke to me --- and I just had to have the book." Almost in tears, Bess looked longingly at both books. "I --- I ---- "

"Bess, calm down. --- Give me the two shillings, and you can pay me the rest when you get your money from the steamship company."

"Jo, I couldn't ask you to do that."

"You didn't ask, I'm just helping out a friend in need. Don't worry about it. How would you know 'A Christmas Carol' would be more expensive than all the other books. It is all this gild lettering and coloured illustrations that make it so expensive."

"Oh Jo, how can I thank you? Here, take the penny too."

"No, you best keep the penny, Bess. You don't want to be out without any money." Jo smiled. "Now off you go. Lydia Taylor doesn't like to be kept waiting. --- Don't forget your books."

Walking back to the dress shoppe with her parcel tightly clutched under her arm, Bess could not believe how stupid she'd been. She thought of Evan opening his present on Christmas Day *of course he won't think the signature to be authentic, but ---- it would make him wonder; especially after opening the little package containing the stamps.*

When she reached her destination, she noticed a man's three-quarter length, black suit, draped over a faceless, cloth mannequin. However, a few brush strokes of black paint, produced a most impressive moustache. Its bald head showed off a tall, silk top hat. Next to the man of cloth, stood another stationary figure, arms extended and head bent. This one had a nice crop of dark hair. *Now, this one is more realistic,* Bess thought. The arm reached up to take the measuring tape from its neck. The body turned and saw her staring in the window. A broad smile spread across its face. Sheepishly, she smiled and waved at Lawrence Taylor. *Serves you right for being caught in the act, peeping Bess.*

Embarrassed, she quickly moved along, colliding with the wrought iron railing. Fortunately, she stumbled forward and grabbed the railing. *At least I'm improving; I didn't fall backwards,* she mumbled under her breath. She glanced over to her left. Lawrence had disappeared. *I can only hope he didn't see my swan dive. Good Lord, every man I meet, I fall for. Heavens, if I'm not more careful, I'll be getting a reputation --- and that's not hard to procure in Victorian times.* She laughed as she opened the door to Lydia's dress shoppe.

"What's so funny? Are you going to let me in on the joke?"

"You wouldn't believe it if I told you." Bess quickly changed the subject, "Is my dress ready or am I too early?"

"Perfect timing. Come in to the fitting room."

Taking off her dress, Bess thought *oh, if only I could take off this blasted corset.* She laughed. *Well, I've just learned one lesson; never laugh in a corset.*

"Lift up those arms and I'll slip this over your head." Lydia moved the fabric skywards, and in the process smothered Bess as the layers of fabric fell downward, covering her face. "Breath in, while I button up the last couple of buttons. --- Good. ----Let's have a look." Lydia surveyed her masterpiece. A smile spread across her beautiful face. "Perfect. --- Come look in the mirror."

"The dress is lovely." Bess swirled around, catching the view from the back "Since most of Mrs. Pennycroft's guests will view me from this angle or the side, this is perfect." She swirled once more ending up face to face, bodice to bosom. "Oh my!"

"What is it?"

"It is a touch -- re -- vealing, don't you think? Ah --- Lottie told me not to expose more than my musical talents --- so to speak. -- Keep the audience focused on the music."

Lydia stood back. "Well, I suppose she does have a point, but it is a shame to cover up your other notes of interest." Lydia burst out laughing, and Bess got caught up in her infectious laughter. Tears ran down their eyes. Lydia took out a hanky and dabbed her eyes. "Here use this." While Lydia left the room, Bess dried her eyes. Lydia returned with a piece of lace. "Stand still while I tuck this inside your bodice. ---- There, that will make a respectable pianist out of you." She turned Bess around to face the mirror. A delicate inch and a half of creamy lace did the trick.

"Now mind when you bend over. We don't want it falling out."

"Thank you so much." Bess put her hand through her hair. "Now, if I could only do something with my hair."

"I'm not a miracle worker, but I can pin this lace rosette behind your ear."

As Bess rushed out the door, decked out in her yellow finery, she heard Lydia shout, "Don't bend over. ---- Don't forget to tell them where you got the dress."

She picked up her skirts, ran down the stairs and headed up the darkened lane to the tea shoppe. Just as she reached the corner of the shoppe, a magic coach with two white horses, stopped in front. Lottie poked her head out of the door and looked in Bess's direction. Frantically, she waved Bess near.

"Bess, t' coach is 'ere. Do 'urry. ---- Don't stand around, 'elp t' young lady up. ---- Oh, Bess, I did want to see ye all dressed up. Wot a pity. Oh well. -- Off wit' ye. Mustn't keep yer missus waitin', sir."

Bess accepted the extended hand of the young groomsman and entered the carriage without an incident. She breathed a sigh of relief as she sat down and thought *thank goodness, I didn't make a spectacle of myself in front of the servants. Why, I can just hear them talking in the kitchen, 'Blimey, ye should 'ave seen t' pianist; she stumbled when she entered t' carriage an' went straight through to t' other door. Knocked it open an' almost kept on goin'. If I 'ad nay grabbed 'er feet, she would 'ave landed 'ead first on t' street. Blimey, ye should 'ave seen t' shoes, ---- no, boots they were. Why, she could stomp a rat dead, she could wit' 'em. Lord knows where t' missus got 'er from.'*

The carriage swiftly moved along without too much turbulence. Bess sat back, exhausted from her busy afternoon. She rested her head against the velvet seat and closed her weary eyes. Thoughts ran through her mind *I'm getting hungry; probably for the best if I don't eat. This corset is killing me and food would only compound the problem. ---- What am I going to play tonight? Why did I say I'd do this favour for Mrs. Pennycroft? I don't even like her. ---- "White Christmas"? ---- "Silver Bells"? ---- Hear them ring --- ring --- ring.*

Bess opened her eyes. Mr. Spider looked annoyed.

"Mr. Spider?"

Ring ---- Ring ----- Buzzzzzz.

Bess looked around. She sprang from the chesterfield and ran to the utility room. The dryer did its last call for help, the zippers and buttons clanged for the last time and all went silent. She opened the door to find the poor, neglected victims huddled in a mass at the bottom of the dryer. She gathered them in her arms and carried them to the chesterfield. For the next hour, she lovingly folded and nestled them in their drawers and closets. Soon hunger took over. She went to the kitchen to prepare a hearty lunch, but felt a tinge of tightness to her upper torso, so opted for a light lunch of cottage cheese and salad. She washed it down with a cup of tea, which she decided to drink in the living room.

On the way to the living room, she passed the piano and picked up some sheets of Christmas Music. Sitting down, she thumbed through the familiar songs and placed them on her lap as she finished perusing them. She picked up the last one, read the words and looked up at the mantel.

"Silver Bells, silver bells, it's Christmas Time in the city. -- Ding-a-ling, ding-a-ling ---

Ding-a-ling ----- "

"Miss, we're here. Miss?" spoke a deep voice.

Bess took a moment to digest her surroundings and uttered, "Oh! --- I'm sorry. I must have been day dreaming."

"Quite alright, miss. The journey is quite long. Let me help you out, miss." A large hand appeared in the doorway, and Bess alighted the carriage, careful not to expose her footwear.

"Daniel, please assist the young lady to the front door. Mrs. Pennycroft gave strict instructions she was to enter through the front door and not the servants' entry. I'll take the carriage back to the stables to give room for the other carriages, then I'll be back to help you with the other guests."

"Right, gov'nor. --- Miss, t'is way."

The young footman guided Bess up the sprawling steps to the ornate, front door. Moments before reaching the top landing, she heard a succession of bells ting-a-linging to to a familiar tune. She turned around to see a large cart positioned at the foot of the stairs. Arched around the top of the cart, bells of various sizes, hung the length of the arch. A man, bundled up in dirty tweeds, gently swung a wooden mallet upwards, causing the bells to resound in melodious notes. The brass bells swung back and forth, mesmerizing Bess as they glittered under the flickering light of the gas streetlamp.

"Good evening, miss." A solemn, but polite voice announced, "Miss N-ike?"

"Miss --- Greaves is talkin' to ye." Bess felt a nudge at her elbow and turned to find young Daniel pivoting his head towards the front door.

"Oh, sorry." She smiled at Daniel and continued up to the front door.

An elderly gentleman stood motionless in the doorway. "This way to the drawing room, Miss N-ike. That will be all, Master Daniel." The door closed with a heavy bang.

Bess followed the servant, dressed in black and white, except for his deep, hunter green and maroon, brocade vest. The large entryway, encased in marble, echoed as the servant walked briskly to a double door. Only one set of shoes could be heard clicking on the cold marble, while Bess's runners politely remained silent. He swung the ornately carved door open to reveal a large room, the size of the entire first floor of Lottie's home. Around the perimeter of the gaslit room, stood numerous love seats of pale-pink and blue tapestries. A number of individual chairs and tables filled in any unused space. Two large, bay windows, draped in heavy, pale-blue velvet, hung from heavy brass poles. A grand piano took centre stage in front of the windows. A candelabra stood on top of the highly polished surface, casting willowy shadows to dance gracefully across its smooth exterior.

"Miss, let me take your music. I will put it on this table. It will be in easy reach for you whilst playing."

"Why, yes, thank you, sir." She handed them over, and he placed them on top of the table. "Silver Bells," she read aloud as the top sheet glared up at her. "Oh, my!"

"Is something the matter, miss?"

"Ah, no, sir. --- Yes, everything is fine, sir."

"Greaves, miss." Bess gave him a puzzled look. "My name is Greaves. I will take your coat, miss. The guests will be arriving shortly. Madam wanted you at the pianoforte, ready to play for her guests."

"Yes, of course --- Greaves."

"Will there be anything else, miss?" Bess shook her head. "Fine then, I must attend to our guests."

He exited the room, leaving Bess alone in the grand drawing room. *So, this is what a drawing room looks like. Hmm, not too comfortable looking. I much prefer Lottie's cluttered parlour,* she decided and proceeded to look around the room. The walls, covered in delicate, pink and blue flowered wallpaper, stood at least twelve feet high. Her eyes took in the numerous, gilded-framed pieces of art, from nymphs running through meadows to fat ladies, draped in silks, sipping tea on the verandah. Over the roaring fireplace, a painting of a hunting party, in coats of red, mounted on sleek, chestnut horses, whilst beagles ran to and fro, chasing the poor exhausted fox, heading for a thick forest of trees. *Just a few more strides. You'll make it, and then you will outfox them.* Bess silently gave encouragement, as she sat down on the piano stool.

Her back rested on a pink velvet, padded cushion, shaped like an upside-down pear. The stem end of the pear, served as the join between the back and the seat. A number of long curving, mahogany scrolls, further supported the back to the seat, thus keeping a lady's voluptuous skirts contained. *A woman must have invented this chair; the straight back keeps the pianist upright and helps alleviate the tendency to slouch forward whilst playing for any period of time. A woman needs all the help she can get to keep the stays from digging into her flesh. A man would never think of that,* surmised Bess. She took a deep breath and slowly exhaled, afraid she might burst her corset.

Her left hand dropped down on the table and her eyes followed. Her music sheets lay on its surface. She recalled how surprised she had been when Greaves mentioned them. Unaware of their presence, they successfully stowed away on her journey. *Thank heavens, I shall need my friends. How could I even think I could play all night without them?* She smiled, picked up the first sheet and began to play.

Music filled her thoughts as she played the finely tuned, grand piano. Lost in her music, she did not hear the room fill up with guests until she felt a tap on her shoulder.

"Ah, Miss Bess, we meet again. What a pleasant surprise. --- And here I thought I would be forced to enjoy the evening. At least now, I can enjoy the entertainment."

"Mr. Dickens!"

"Charles, do call me Charles, ---and if I may be so bold, Bess?"

"Why, I would be honoured, ---Charles. All my friends call me Bess."

Pulling up a chair, he continued, "I know why I am here, but how did you come to perform at this prestigious soirée?"

"Well, I could say the same to you, but being a lady, I shall not."

"Touché." They both burst out laughing, causing the guests to turn and stare at them.

They both explained why they were there, he as a guest speaker to hopefully loosen the purse strings of the guests and consequently spill into the pockets of the poor, and she as the substitute pianist. He excused himself, but not before he asked a favour of Bess, to which she agreed. In his gentlemanly fashion, he went off to mingle with the guests. She went back to entertaining the dozen or so well-dressed guests.

Various servants came in carrying trays of drinks. The large glasses of a dark brown liquid, disappeared very quickly. The gentlemen no sooner picked up a glass, swirled the golden liquid, took in the vapours and swallowed the contents in one large gulp, when another full glass replaced the now empty one. As gentlemen passed her way or stopped to compliment her playing, Bess got a whiff of brandy or rum. The ladies did not indulge in the golden liquid, but did take a sip of what looked to be small glasses of sherry. Through the chattering of guests, Bess overheard the phrase, coupe d' avant and translated it to be the Victorian custom of before dinner drinks, or to be more precise, the cocktail hour.

Presently, Mrs. Pennycroft wandered over to the piano and said, "My dear Miss N-ike, you are doing a fine job. After dinner, I do hope you will sing for our guests. We will be going in for dinner shortly. You may then take a break. Greaves will have a plate of food brought in for you. Now, if there is anything you need, do not hesitate to ask Greaves." She gave a feeble smile and turned to leave, but stopped and looked back at Bess. "I forgot to compliment you on your dress. It is lovely. Wherever did you get it on such short notice?"

"Why, 'Taylor & Sons,' of course, Mrs. Pennycroft," replied Bess as she gave an equally feeble smile. "You look lovely too, Mrs. Pennycroft."

Just when Bess felt her hands beginning to cramp, the dinner gong reverberated through the room, causing the guests to gasp and then laugh nervously. The women took the arm of the nearest man, and they exited the room, accompanied by the sounds of fabric swishing and endless chatter. As the last couple entered the dining room, the sounds dwindled to a soft drone of bees returning to their hive. The double doors closed and all became silent, except for the ticking of the clock over the mantel and the crackling of the fire.

Bess bent her fingers back and forth, stretched her neck up and down, left to right and hoisted herself from the chair. She lifted her arms above her head and in the same motion, bent her back forward and stretched her fingers to her toes.

"So, that is how pianists gets their exercise," echoed a loud voice, causing Bess to stand straight up. As she turned around, the familiar voice continued, "I must compliment you on your dress. I had not noticed it so lovely until now."

"Mr. Dickens ----- Charles, you have caught me at an embarrassing moment."

"Why, Bess, you must never be embarrassed about being natural. Natural beauty is a rare gift. --- Now come, my dear, dinner awaits us." He raised his bent arm for Bess to take.

"But, Charles, Mrs. Pennycroft is having dinner sent in here for me."

"Nonsense, my dear. You shall be my dinner companion. My wife conveniently ---- suddenly became ill and was unable to attend, so you will take her place at the table. Besides, we entertainers must stick together. Now, take my arm and say no more."

After a couple of taps on the door, it opened to reveal a glittering, dining room. Everywhere, candles flickered soft shadows on the pale-yellow walls. A hundred glowing candles, nestled in the overhead chandelier, bounced off the hanging crystals to the sparkling silverware and necklines of precious stones and diamond studded fingers. Twelve people sat at a long table of beautiful china and crystal, filled with rich, red wine. More candles stood upright amongst the lengthy arrangement of holly and red roses.

"Ah, Mr. Dickens, we wondered where you got to. Do come and sit down next to me," Mrs. Pennycroft spoke politely from the other end of the room.

As they made their way to the far end of the room, the men rose and the ladies gasped.

"Greaves, do help Mr. Dickens and Mrs. Di---- Oh ---- Miss N-ike to their seats." Mrs. Pennycroft caught herself and continued, "Miss N-ike, how nice of you to join us."

"Yes, I thought so. I knew you wouldn't mind, my dear Mrs. Pennycroft. Seeing as my dear wife is indisposed , I thought Miss N-ike could take her place at the table. We wouldn't want to be unbalanced at the table, man, woman, man, woman."

The men smiled at Bess, while the women remained purse lipped.

"Miss N-ike, my wife and I would be honoured to have you dine with us," said a large man with a bushy, grey moustache.

"Ladies and gentlemen, I should like to introduce you to Miss Bess N-ike. She is on a brief holiday from America and has graciously given of her valuable time to entertain us this evening." Mr. Dickens raised his glass. "To Miss N-ike!"

"To Miss N-ike!" The men smiled and the women reluctantly raised their glasses.

"That went quite well," Mr. Dickens whispered in Bess's ear as he put down his glass.

"Miss, would you like some beef broth?" A stern young waiter placed a small, white soup bowl on her plate.

No sooner did a waiter take away the empty bowl, when another presented her with a plate of fish. "Halibut, miss? Perhaps some oysters or lobster patties?"

"No thank you," replied Bess. She looked around to find the other guests refusing nothing and eating everything. *How do these women do it? I shall burst if I eat too much. I'll only eat what I truly like,* she reasoned, while adjusting her corset as discreetly as possible. *Not that anyone will notice. They are too intent on consuming all this food.*

The procession of food continued with roast beef, pork, venison, duck, pheasant and grouse. Numerous side dishes of vegetables filled the plates to overflowing. At that point, Bess thought *I'm going to explode all over this pristine, white tablecloth. ---- Dear Lord, contain me.*

"Miss N-ike, are you enjoying your stay in England?" a middle-aged man asked as his beady eyes peered over his wire-rimmed glasses.

"Oh yes, thank you for asking," answered Bess, relieved with a much needed break from eating. *If I keep talking, maybe the food will disappear.* With this food for thought, she continued, "Definitely an experience of a lifetime. Have you been to America, sir?"

"No, as a matter of fact I have not, but Lady Hadley and I are planning a voyage to the colonies next year. I have business to attend to in New York, and my wife has a niece in Boston, so we thought we would exchange a couple of months of London smog for your humidity." He burst out laughing. "Instead of ingesting it, we will be expelling it." His laughter turned into a coughing spell.

"Now, Hubert, it is not the weather that is the problem, it is your awful cigars," tsked a thin woman exposing a low neck-line, adorned with a large diamond necklace. Without hesitation, she lifted her hazel eyes in Bess's direction and continued, "Sir Hadley and I are leaving in June, after the dreaded icebergs have melted." She smiled. "My dear, how brave of you to travel in the winter months. Why, I have even heard of winds so fierce, they turn over a ship. What do they call them, Hubert, tornadoes?"

"No, my dear, they are called hurricanes. Named after a woman, so I've heard." He laughed. "Herr --- icane, get it , my dear." Once again, he started coughing.

"Waiter, get Sir Hadley some water," she shouted and in a whisper she said, "before he makes a complete fool of himself." She shook her head causing her diamond to sparkle as it swayed back and forth unabated, across her scant bosom.

"You have been to America, Mr. Dickens," said a man across from Mr. Dickens.

"Yes, Mr. Treadwell, I was there in '42. Unfortunately, I did not experience the herr --- icanes, but did run into a few head strong men of infinite power. You see, I went over there to stop them printing my books as I was not receiving a penny for my work."

"And what was the outcome of your venture?" asked Mr. Treadwell.

"They literally told me to jump in a lake." Mr. Dickens replied with a straight face as gasps could be heard up and down the table. "And --- have you seen the size of their lakes?" He laughed. "I'm not the best of swimmers, so I got on the first ship and came home."

"Mr. Dickens, I must apologize. America is like a child and is learning from its mistakes. Recently I read, that international copyright laws are now being recognized and soon to be strictly enforced. How unfortunate for you, but your visit was not in vain, others will benefit from your efforts." Bess touched his arm.

"Not to worry, my dear. I am taking swimming lessons and

shall one day return to America." The iceberg melted and they all laughed.

"Ladies, if you would like to make your way to the drawing room, Miss N-ike will entertain us. In the meantime, gentlemen, you can make your way to the library for a smoke. Greaves will announce when the dessert table is ready," announced Mrs. Pennycroft.

"Good timing," whispered Charles in Bess's ear.

Bess lost herself in her music, and did not notice the passing of time until she heard Greaves announce, dessert was being served in the dining room. Another dozen guests had appeared. The newcomers joined in on the procession back to the dining room. Bess remained at the piano and decided to take the opportunity to thumb through her music.

"My dear, you must not disappoint our guests. Do join us for some dessert." Mr. Pennycroft extended his arm and Bess accepted. "Besides, my dear wife takes pride in her dessert table. Her epergne is the finest display in London." He patted her arm. "So she tells me."

"Epergne?"

"Yes, I suppose you don't bother with them in America. You are too busy swimming." He gave a chuckle. "See that crystal, tree like mass in the centre of the table, that is what the French call 'epergne.' I don't know what's happened to plain old pudding and apple pie. Today, it's all got to be French this and that, with their Frenchie names, nobody can pronounce. See, each one of the branches holds a plate or basket of fruit, cakes or nuts. Nuts, who needs more nuts? There is enough around here as it is." They both looked around at the guests and winked at each other.

Extended to accommodate the new guests, the table had been stripped and replaced with fresh linen, a new floral arrangement, special dessert plates, cutlery and of course the elaborate epergne, showing off in the centre of the table. Bess thought *Mrs. Pennycroft is correct. This is the finest display in London. Mind, good old apple pie and ice cream wouldn't be too bad either.* She felt her waistline expanding just at the thought of it.

"Ouch," she uttered as a wayward, whale bone dug into uncharted territory.

"Sorry, miss," said a waiter as he breezed by her, carrying a plate of colourful ices.

"For our guests who have recently arrived, Miss N-ike from America, will be entertaining us on the pianoforte. Later, Mr. Charles Dickens will give us a Christmas reading," announced Mr. Pennycroft. "Miss N-ike, ladies and gentlemen."

"Thank you, Mr. Pennycroft. I will begin with a few familiar Christmas carols, and then I will play some of my favourite Christmas songs. I shall endeavour to sing a few verses. I would appreciate all the help I can get, so do join in whenever you feel the urge." Bess smiled and began to play "Silent Night."

After playing the first verse, she decided to sing it in hopes others would join in. Unfortunately, no one did, but she did receive a nice round of applause. However, when she sang "All Through The Night," a couple of brave souls joined her. By the time she played "The First Nowell," all joined in. A few guests huddled around the pianoforte. After a few more carols, she decided to introduce some lighter Christmas songs.

"Dashing through the snow -----"

Bess smiled and played an extra chorus, and finally a few burst into song, "Jingle bells, jingle bells ------"

Bess followed it up with "Silver Bells." All grew silent as she performed "White Christmas."

Just as she finished, a couple sitting by the window shouted, "Look, it is snowing."

The drapes drawn back, exposed the snow in all its beauty, falling like a shower of stars, glistening under the streetlight. Gasps spread throughout the room, so Bess kept the interest going by performing "Let It Snow! Let It Snow! Let It Snow"!

"Now, that we have officially welcomed winter, and before the weather gives us a blizzard, --- or one of Miss N-ike's herricanes, let us hear from Mr. Dickens," Mr. Pennycroft said in a joyous tone.

Once the laughter ran its course, the guests settled down and Mr. Dickens stood and took his place in front of the piano.

"On behalf of the guests, I would like to thank Miss N-ike for a most entertaining evening." Mr. Dickens turned and applauded Bess, and the others joined in with a loud round of applause. "To further your enjoyment, Miss N-ike has graciously accepted my invitation to provide background music for my Christmas reading. I hope this will help make up for my lack of a new Christmas book this year." A slight sigh went around the room. "My friends, I apologize for my lack of discipline to produce an annual Christmas book. I had every intention to continue my contribution to the Christmas festivities, but my latest novel has left me behind schedule. Came autumn, my ideas were well formed in my mind, but I was unable to put them to paper. My greatest regret is, I will leave a gap at Christmas firesides which I ought to fill."

Mrs. Hadley spoke up, "Now, don't you be hard on yourself."

"Here, here," repeated various gentlemen.

"Your sentiments are appreciated. If you will bear with me, I will draw from past books. I should like to begin with a passage from 'Pickwick Papers.'"

Bess quietly played "White Christmas," while Mr. Dickens recited thoughts of Christmas pasts.

"Many of the hearts that throbbed so gaily then (in the Christmas gatherings of our earlier years) have ceased to bear; … The hands we grasped, have grown cold: the eyes we sought, have hid their luster in the grave: and yet the old house, the room, the merry voices and smiling faces, the jest, the laugh, the most minute and trivial circumstance connected with those happy meetings, crowd upon our mind at each recurrence of the season, as if the last assemblage had been but yesterday. Happy, happy Christmas that can win us back to the delusions of our childish days."

"Going back to my younger days, when I was twenty-three, to be exact, I wrote my first Christmas passage. 'Christmas Festivities' appeared in 'Bell's Life In London,' in 1835. Basically, I wanted my readers not to forget painful memories, but to put them aside and count their blessings and rejoice in them. So, I give you my youthful ideals of Christmas festivities." Mr. Dickens smiled, as Bess began playing "The Christmas Song."

"Christmas Time! That man must be a misanthrope indeed, in whose breast something like a jovial feeling is not roused ---- in whose mind some pleasant associations are not awakened --- by the recurrence of Christmas. ----- "

Bess played another chorus of Mel Torme's classic, while Mr. Dickens continued, "Reflect upon your present blessings --- of which every man has many ---- not on your past misfortunes, of which all men have some. Fill your glass again, with a merry face and a contented heart. Our life on it but your Christmas shall be merry, and your New Year a happy one. -----"

Bess started to play "I'll Be Home For Christmas," when the paragraph of the Christmas party began.

"It is an annual gathering of all the accessible members of the family, young and old, rich or poor, and all the children look forward to it for some two months beforehand in a fever of anticipation. Formerly, it was always held at Grandpapa's, but Grandpapa getting old and Grandmamma getting old too, and rather infirm. They have given up housekeeping and domesticated themselves with Uncle George: so the party always takes place at Uncle George's house. ------ "

"See, dear George, even Mr. Dickens knows you're a kind and giving son." A woman was overheard shouting in her deaf husband's ear.

"Yes, quite right, my dear," George shouted back.

Snickers were heard. Mr. Dickens continued as if he had not heard the interruption. Every time Uncle George was mentioned, all would turn their heads in anticipation of further acknowledgement for dear George.

"As to the dinner, it's perfectly delightful. ---- nothing goes wrong, and everybody is in the very best of spirits, and disposed to please and be pleased. Grandpapa relates a circumstantial account of the purchase of the turkey, with a slight digression relative to the purchase of previous turkeys on former Christmas Days, which Grandmamma corroborates in the minutest particulars."

Bess started to play "Grandma Got Run Over By A Reindeer" and chuckled to herself, *This one's for grandpapas throughout time. Hey, the music is nice and besides they don't know the words.*

"Uncle George tells stories and carves poultry, and takes wine, and jokes with the children at the side-table ---- "

"My dear George, Mr. Dickens knows how good you are with the children," shouted the woman in poor George's ear. "But, carving the poultry? I shouldn't think you'd want everyone to know, you almost sliced off your finger last Christmas."

A moment later, Mr. Dickens resumed his sentence, "And winks at the cousins that are making love, or being made love to and ----"

"You are quite right, my dear. I'm very good at making love," an experienced George replied as his selective hearing picked up the good bits and discarded the rest.

By the time the guests composed themselves, George had nodded off, while his rosy cheeked wife, looked straight ahead.

Wanting to burst out laughing, but always a professional, Mr. Dickens controlled himself, opted for a little smile and continued, "And exhilarates everybody with his good humour and hospitality;" Chuckles disguised as coughs, echoed through the room. "and when ----"

"There are a hundred associations connected with Christmas, which we should very much like to recall to the minds of our guests;

There are a hundred comicalities inseparable from the period, on which it would give us equal pleasure to dilate. We have attained our ordinary limits, however, and cannot better conclude than by wishing each and all of you, individually and collectively, 'A Merry Christmas and A Happy New Year.'" Mr. Dickens bowed.

Bess ended with "We Wish You A Merry Christmas And A Happy New Year." All joined in singing and toasting each other. Even dear George's wife was seen to mouth the words, 'Merry Christmas.'

The aroused, dear George shouted out, "Happy New Year!" and downed his brandy.

Bess sat all alone in the coach as it quietly glided along the thin layer of snow, spread evenly on the deserted streets. *What a memorable night; I shall remember it fondly. No matter what generation, there will always be a dear George or a Hubert to add colour to what otherwise could be a dull night. Mind, if their better halves had not played a major role, the changing of the colours would have been lost amongst the other socially accepted guests. Thank heavens for unexpected guests to add interest to a formal affair.* She laughed.

A tap on the front window brought Bess back from her thoughts.

"Miss, is everything alright?" shouted the groomsman through the window.

"Yes, thank you," Bess shouted back, but suddenly an inspiration hit her and she shouted, "No, driver, stop please."

"Yes , miss. ---- Whoa!"

The carriage stopped and presently the groomsman opened the door. "Whatever is the matter, miss? Did you forget something? Are you not well?"

"Oh yes, I'm fine. In fact I feel like a child. ---- Would you be so kind as to let me sit up front with you?"

"Oh, miss, it wouldn't be proper. A lady like you and a night like tonight."

"But that is the point, sir. Tonight is the perfect night. Oh, please let me sit outside with you. I want to taste the snow, as it falls on my tongue and brush the flakes off my lashes. Oh, do let me ride with you. I could cover myself in this blanket if you were afraid I would get cold, or worse, if anyone saw me."

"Well ---- only if you promise not to tell madam."

"I won't, I promise. It's our secret, sir." Before he had second thoughts, Bess scurried out of the coach and ascended the side steps. "We haven't been properly introduced. My name is Bess ---- and your names is?" She extended a hand.

"Allen, miss --- Bess." He shook her hand and then said, "Wrap up now, Bess."

"Yes, Allen."

With a jerk of the reins, the horse bolted forward and they silently sped along. Even the horse's hoofs remained silent. Bess lifted her head towards the sky. The snowflakes fell upon her rosy face. She stuck her tongue out and received a cold flake of sheer delight.

"Bess, you remind me of my little sister. When I was a young fellow, I used to take my sister to school in our cart whenever the weather turned nasty." Allen tsked as he pulled his scarf up over his ears. "We did get blizzards in the Yorkshire Dales. --- No matter how terrible the storm, she would sit up with me, laughing and shouting encouragement to old Bessie. No offence, miss."

"None taken, sir." They both burst out laughing.

As they turned a corner, a dog sat in the middle of the street. Allen raised his left hand over his head and grabbed a leather strap dangling under a brass bell. He rang the bell, causing the startled dog to flee to safety.

"Whoa, Blackie ----" The horse snorted, but halted immediately. "Phew, that was close. Thank goodness, I decided to bring only Blackie out in the phaeton. A light cab and only one horse is easier to stop in these conditions. Those poor little blighters are roaming all over."

"Don't their owners have to keep them tied up?"

"No, there are thousands of strays all over the city. At night, they roam the streets in search of food. At least, he's made it through another night."

At the next corner, Bess reached over Allen's head and swung the leather strap. "Best to be safe than sorry." The bell jingled. "Jingle Bells, Jingle Bells, jingle all the way," Bess sang softly. "Oh what fun it is to ride in a one horse open sleigh."

Allen joined her and they sang until they turned the corner onto Fetter Lane. "The Goodale" stood in darkness. The street lay covered in a virginal blanket of snow.

"Whoa --- "

Blackie slowed down his pace as they drew up to the darkened "Lotatea Shoppe." Allen helped Bess down. She immediately went over to Blackie, patted his head and thanked him for a most pleasant journey.

"Let me help you to the door, miss." Allen took her arm. "It is best we be formal. The streets may seem deserted, but they always have eyes and ears lurking in the shadows." He smiled, doffed his hat and walked back to the cab. He opened the door and leaned inside. "Oh miss, you forgot your papers." He rushed back and gave her the bundle of music.

"Thank you, Allen." She reached up and gave him a kiss on the cheek.

"Goodnight, Bess," Allen whispered, turned around and disappeared down the lane, leaving only two tracks of wheels and a set of hoof prints in the snow.

Bess stood with her back against the front door and looked out at the peaceful scene. The snow fell softly, covering the only evidence of a recent intruder. Her eyes strayed across the street to the lamppost. The light flickered and went out.

"Darn, now I can't see to open the door."

Bess's right hand grasped for the doorknob, while her left hand held the bundle of papers. Losing her grip, the bundle fell to the ground. Fearing they would get wet in the snow, she bent over to pick them up. Fumbling around in the dark, she finally picked them up, surprised they were not damp. Her hand brushed the snow, making sure all the papers had been picked up.

"Snow? That's not snow. It's ----"

The light came on.

"It's carpet."

"Bong! Bong! Bong! Bong!" echoed the grandfather clock.

"Good thing Evan changed the timer on the lamp. Four o'clock and it's already dark. Dark? ---- Daah ----" Bess knocked the side of her head with her fingers. "It is December twenty-first, the shortest day of the year. ------ Welcome, Winter."

# CHAPTER XIII

Swirls of sandman ground into her eyes, as she desperately tried to remove the pesky objects. Gingerly, she made her way down the dark stairway. By the time she reached the bottom step, the sandman had resided in the corner of her eyes, and she managed to eradicate it from its hiding place. Relieved, she opened her eyes wide and saw a light coming from the kitchen. She distinctly moved toward the light.

"Good morning, Evan," she said loudly to Evan's back.

Evan jumped. "You startled me. I thought you were still up sawing a log. Do you want some tea? I just poured a cup. I can put some more water in the pot."

"No thanks, I'll wait. I'll just sit on the stool and finish my log."

"Log? ---- Very funny, Bess." He took a bite out of his toast. "Say, while I've got your attention ----- Bess? ---- Wake up."

"Evan? ---- Sorry, I'll hang up my saw. ---- You were saying?" She looked at him with bedroom eyes.

"Bess, you're so cute sitting there with droopy eyelids, spiked hair and pillow creases on your cheek."

"Thanks, Evan, you really know the right things to say to a girl."

He came over and gave her a kiss. "You're welcome, Sleeping Beauty."

"Is that raspberry jam?" Bess asked as she licked her lips.

Ignoring her question, he said, "Can you get a Christmas present for Sherry today? You know, something like you got her last year."

"I thought the secretary is supposed to get the wife a present?"

"Funny. I need to take it to work tomorrow; I've given her December twenty-fourth off."

"Nothing like giving me lots of time." She looked at Evan who gave her a pleading look. "Okay. I'll get her something nice. Do you want to pay me now or later?"

"Later, baby." Evan moved his eyebrows up and down.

His expression took her back for a moment. "Ooh!" she gasped. "Anything wrong?"

"No --- you just reminded me of something I'd seen recently." She shrugged it off and changed the subject, "Anything else you want while I'm out?" He shook his head. "Well, I'd better get started." She lowered herself off the stool and headed back up the dark stairway.

Bess arrived at the mall moments after the doors opened. The early hour proved beneficial in finding a parking place close to the entrance. As the automatic doors swung open, the familiar tune of "All I Want For Christmas Is My Two Front Teeth" greeted the eager shoppers. *Yeah sure. --- First, what kid's Santa's list has only front teeth on it??? And second, if front teeth were all we had to buy; why come in the mall??? We could pop into the hockey rink and pick them up for nothing. Come to think of it ---- who would pick a dumb song like that, especially for a mall?? If I was a merchant, I'd fire him.* Bess's blood pressure soared. *Just what I need to start my shopping.*

"Bah Humbug!"

"Lady, I agree with you," said a man laden with parcels as he passed her heading for the door.

*Okay, now that I've got that out of my system, it's time to get down to business. --- First, Sherry's present.* Bess walked into the first store she saw, stocked with miscellaneous travel accessories and leather goods. *A purse maybe too personal, but this may do,* she thought as she looked over at a rack of wool scarves. She thumbed through them, until she saw one in lovely shades of blue. *Yes, this will match her eyes. --- Well, I think they're blue. --- Oh well, no matter. --- Blue it is.* Bess took it off the rack and proceeded to the till, where she noticed a compact manicure set, perfect for a man. Without hesitation, she asked the saleslady to get it out from the glass cabinet.

"I'll take it and the scarf." Bess handed a credit card to the saleslady.

"A nice size for traveling," said the pleasant saleslady.

"Yes, I hope so," replied Bess with a faraway look in her eye.

Back in the mainstream of the mall, she passed a kitchen store and wandered in. Lovely pieces of Christmas china attracted her attention, but she soon left them for the meat and potatoes of the store, the utensils. She picked up a heatproof spatula and a matching, blue spoon. Not satisfied, she picked up two more, one red, one orange, along with a couple of different sized whisks. She turned towards the back shelf and spied some nonstick baking sheets. *Oh, these are so useful, but are they too big?* she reflected.

Suddenly she smiled. "Yes, this is perfect," she said out loud and then composed herself.

*I can roll it up --- no, two of them and put them into a stocking --- along with --- yes, of course, the spatulas. They can all fit into a large stocking. --- Oh, I do hope this works.* She took one more look at the baking sheets and thought *what have I got to lose? Heh, if it doesn't work out, I'll keep them for myself. Besides, I need some new baking sheets, and I've always wanted one of these Sil? ---- silicon sheets.*

Pleased with her purchases, she left the store laden with bulky parcels. Bess next entered a bookstore. Careful not to brush her parcels against the shelves full of books, she walked sideways to the children's section. She put her parcels down on the tiled floor and started scanning the titles, pulling out the odd one and perusing its pages. Bess came to the R's and pulled out JK Rowling's "Harry Potter And The Philosopher's Stone" and "The Chamber Of Secrets." After close scrutiny, she thought *the location and subject matter should be fine.* Pleased with herself, she took the two books up to the counter.

A display in the window of the sporting goods store, caught her eye. Two mannequins, decked out in brightly coloured sportswear, looked like they were enjoying a game of soccer. Suddenly, she realized why they attracted her attention. *Of course, why didn't I think of that? Thanks, guys.* She smiled and gave them a little wave of her fingers.

Inside the store, she searched the racks until she found exactly what she wanted. "I'll take these three shirts," she said to the young salesman, "and two of those, in a small size."

The last two items, she spotted while waiting in the line-up. At first she had been annoyed at the long line-up at the cashier's counter, but in the end proved the old adage, 'All things come to those who wait.' And with the wait came inspiration.

"Can I get names stitched on these?"

"No sorry, ma'am, but next door can do it for you."

Making her way back to the car, she stopped at the same shoe store she visited the other night with Evan. This time she made up her mind.

"Do you have these in size seven?"

Not wanting to put her parcels on the wet pavement, she rearranged them, as far up her thick,coat sleeves as possible and opened her purse. "Darn, where are my keys?" Bess fumbled in her purse, lifted her knee as a support for the purse and in the process lost her balance. "Oh!" she shouted. She promptly put her foot down in a most strategically placed puddle. "Damn!"

The jolt forced the keys to move into her fingers, and she

wrenched them out of the purse. Still mad, she took it out on the parcels by throwing them in the backseat. Bess lifted her wet foot into the car and grabbed the door handle.

"Shoot, darn, double darn. --- I forgot wrapping paper." Bess slammed her fists against the steering wheel. "No, I have to wrap Sherry's present. --- Darn Evan; it's all his fault." She grabbed her purse and keys, slammed the door and marched back into the mall.

Squish -- tap – squish -- tap, her feet hurried along the tiled floor. After leaving an impression on the Hallmark's floor, she decided to head back to the kitchen store. *Just one more thing; a Microplane is such a useful tool. How could I have passed it up? I'm already wet and cold. What's five more minutes?* Bess convinced herself. Twenty minutes later, after a visit to "The Body Shop" and the candy store, she exited the mall.

"I'm wise to you. You're not going to get me this time," she said to the innocent puddle as she skirted its depth and climbed into her car.

Parcels scattered all over the chesterfield, Bess plopped down. With bags still dangling from her outstretched arms, she rested her head on the back and sat motionless. Her legs spread far apart, with one dry and one wet shoe pointed upwards.

Her eyes beheld Mr. Spider looking down at her. "Don't you look so smug, mister. Just cause you're up there nice and dry and I'm down here, sopping wet. -- Okay, okay -- Well, one part of me is."

Taking a quick glance at the mantel, in hopes it would soothe her troubled soul, she quickly gave that idea up and closed her eyes. "I've got to take off this wet shoe." But did not move. "Tea, yes I need a cup of tea." Her head slouched forward.

"Tea, tea, oh for a cup of tea."

"Bess, luv, are ye alright?"

"Tea! Tea!"

"Aye, luv, I'll be right back."

"Bess, --- Bess, I've brought ye yer tea, luv."

Knock, knock ---

"What?"

"Bess, t'is me, luv. --- Lottie. I've brought ye a cup of tea."

"Lottie? -- Sorry, I'll be right there." Bess raised herself off the bed, covered in familiar parcels. She stuffed them under the bed, flattened down her hair, ruffled her dress and hurried to the door. "My foot feels wet." She opened the door to find a worried look upon Lottie's face. "Sorry, I must have been sleeping. Do come in. What time is it?"

"Ten past ten, luv. I just passed t' 'allway clock an' noticed t' time."

"I should be down helping you."

"Not to worry, I know ye got in late. Why, it must 'ave bin past one. That's t' last time I remember lookin' at t' clock before I fell asleep. I listened fer ye, ever so long. Now, 'ave yer tea an' then cum down. I must get back to t' kitchen. I've got bakin' in t' oven. --- Oh, I do want to 'ear all about yer evenin'."

"I'll be down in a few minutes." Bess accepted the tea and closed the door. "Why is my foot wet?" she questioned as she looked down at her foot. *If I didn't know better, it feels like I stepped in a puddle.* --- "Puddle?" Her eyes wandered along the floor to under the bed, where something white and plastic stuck out. "Plastic? --- Parcels? --- Wet foot?" Bess thumbed her head with her hand. "Now I remember."

She pulled the parcels from under the bed and quickly looked through them. *Well, the good news is, the manicure set is the right size for traveling. However, the bad news is, here is Sherry's scarf.*

"Bess, Mrs. Pennycroft t'is 'ere to see ye."

"Mrs. Pennycroft? --- Oh my--- I'll be right there." Bess threw the parcels back under the bed, stuffed the scarf in her pocket and ran down the stairs.

"Mrs. Pennycroft, is everything alright? I hope I didn't keep you waiting," Bess said between gasps of heavy breathing.

"No, no, my dear girl, everything is fine. In fact, last evening was such a success. Everything is perfect --- except for the weather," tsked Mrs. Pennycroft as she looked out the window. "I suppose even the weather was perfect. ---- Well, perfect timing that is. My guests thought I ordered the snow specially for the occasion." She laughed. "My dear girl, do sit down. Mrs. Morton, do bring us some tea and some of your delicious scones, I smell. I ran out before I had breakfast. Miss N-ike, I was terribly remiss in not thanking you last night. I was busy saying goodnight to my guests. I turned around, and Allen had taken you off in his chariot. I trust you had a pleasant ride home?"

"Yes quite, thank you. A most enjoyable one indeed. Your Allen is a fine driver." Bess smiled and looked out the window, easily spying Blackie in complete contrast with his white surroundings.

"Yes, indeed he is. Allen has been with us quite a few years, and I must say a most valuable employee." She smiled and too looked out the window. "But, don't you dare tell him, what I said. I don't want it getting out, I am an appreciative employer. It would be bad for my image." She gave a genteel laugh. "Oh, Mrs. Morton, do come and sit with us. If it was not for you, my dinner party would have been a disaster. I owe you my life for introducing me to this talented, young lady."

"Oh, Mrs. Pennycroft, you exaggerate my contribution to the success of your evening." Lottie blushed and without hesitation, brought another cup to the table and sat down.

"Do let me pour. It is the least I can do," said Mrs. Pennycroft.

"Would you mind if I take Allen a scone and a hot cup of tea? It is the least I can do to repay him for bringing me home, safe and sound." Before Mrs. Pennycroft could object, Bess was halfway out the door.

"Bess, --- don't you go out there without a coat," shouted Lottie to the back of her exposed dress. "--- And your feet are going to get wet. ----Mercy, girl---"

Bess closed the door on Lottie's unheeded concerns and

approached the carriage. She ploughed through the snow-covered sidewalk and stopped at the driver's seat, but found no Allen. At her approach, Blackie turned his head and cast a cloud of steam into the crisp air.

"Where's your driver, Blackie?"

In reply, Blackie snorted and reared his head around a couple of times. His large, brown eyes rolled upwards towards the carriage. Instinctively, Bess turned her head in the same direction. She gasped and the horse snorted when they saw movement within the carriage. She looked back at Blackie, who she swore, gave her a wink before she leaned up to open the carriage door. With a mighty pull, she opened the door.

"Ah, ha! There you are, Allen. I've brought you a hot cup of tea. ---Well, I hope it is still hot."

"Oh, miss, ---Why, thank you." Allen started to release himself from the bounds of the heavy, woollen blanket.

"No, don't get out. Eat your scone in there. Besides, Mrs. Pennycroft and Mrs. Morton are going to be awhile, discussing last night's dinner. ---And --- I must get back before I need to snuggle up with a blanket." She shivered, crossed her arms, and rubbed her hands up and down the length of her arms.

"You go in. Thank you, Bess, and Merry Christmas."

"Merry Christmas, Allen." Bess shut the door causing an avalanche to thunder down upon her head. Shaking off the wet snow, she ran over to Blackie. "Thanks for giving me a head's up in the right direction to Allen." She patted his silky neck. "Merry Christmas, Blackie."

Bess stretched out her hand, exposing three lumps of sugar. Blackie's velvety nose tickled her palm as he gently scooped up the sugar in one motion. He nodded in approval. She smiled and headed back to the warmth of the tearoom.

The door jingled and both ladies turned their heads towards the door. "Oh, you silly girl," chimed the two ladies.

"Come over by the fire." Lottie got up and positioned a chair in front of the fire. "Just look at you, why you have snow all in your hair. ----Sit down. --- Put your feet up here." She pointed to the raised hearth.

"Tea, dear girl." Mrs. Pennycroft handed her a steaming cup of tea. "Young folks, just do not think, these days." She shook her head.

"Bess, luv, Mrs. Pennycroft was telling me all about the dinner party. I am so proud of you. -- And to think Mr. Dickens asked you to accompany him." Lottie gave Bess a hug.

"Ladies, I must be off, but before I leave, I want to give you this small token of my appreciation." Mrs. Pennycroft handed Bess an envelope. "No, do not thank me, Miss N-ike. Just remember --- Don't let it slip, I'm an appreciative employer." She pulled on her gloves and headed for the door. "Mums the word, ladies."

Out on the street, the ladies heard her shout, "Allen, --- Allen, where are you? --- One just cannot get reliable help these days. --- Allen, -- what are you doing inside the coach? --- You good for nothing! ---- Heaven help me."

"Aye, she is a tarter."


No sooner did Mrs. Pennycroft depart and the door bell jingled to announce the arrival of the thirsty customers. Bess forced herself away from the comfort of the fire and moved over to the piano. Mince pies and scones disappeared as quickly as they were placed in front of the hungry ladies.

"Miss Bess, Harriet is ever so pleased with the music. Why, she has been at the pianoforte since early morning," whispered Miss Rose Water. "You and Mrs. Morton must come over on Boxing Day and hear her play. --- Yes, do come for tea, say two o'clock? Don't stop dear. I will mention it to Mrs. Morton."


Later on in the kitchen, Lottie put a fresh batch of scones in the oven, while Bess washed the dishes.

"If ye don't mind me askin', wot did Mrs. Pennycroft give ye?"

"I don't know. I haven't opened it yet. Let me dry my hands and we'll find out."

Bess picked up the tea towel, resurrected from a flour sack and dried her hands. From her pocket, she pulled out the envelope. She sat down at the table and opened it. A card escaped from its confines.

"Look, Lottie, it's a Christmas card." Bess exclaimed as Lottie pulled out a chair and sat down beside her. "How appropriate, --- a cheery family standing around the pianoforte."

"There ye be Bess, sittin' on t' stool playin'. 'Ow did she ever find such a card? Why t'is t' first Christmas card I've seen. Oh --- t'is lovely."

"It is, isn't it. I shall take it home with me and put it in a frame. I'll hang it on the wall, over my pianoforte. ---- You've never received a Christmas card?"

"Oh no, luv, only t' rich send 'em, an' that's only bin t' last couple years. They are so pretty. Maybe next year, I'll send 'em to me special friends."

"Good idea, Lottie. You send one and the next year your friend sends you one in return, and before you know it, you will be getting lots of lovely Christmas cards."

"Do ye think so, Bess?"

"I know so."

"Wot does it say inside?"

Bess opened the card and out fell a piece of paper.

"Bess, t'is a pound note. Wot's it say?"

"Miss N-ike, as I do not know you well enough to know what you would like, I have enclosed this note. Please get yourself something nice. Thank you for rescuing a desperate hostess from a disastrous evening. May you have a Merry Christmas in our England.

Sincerely, Williamina Pennycroft."

"My, wot nice words."

"A pound note?" said Bess.

"Wot ye goin' buy, luv?"

"That's what ---- er twenty shillings, right?"

"Aye, luv."

"That's twelve times twenty," Bess counted, "two hundred and forty pennies! Why, that will buy a lot."

"Aye, it will."

"Lottie, I want to give you half. Like Mrs. Pennycroft said, if it wasn't for you ----"

Lottie interrupted, "No, Bess, ye deserve it. Besides, Williamina will be beholden to me long after ye 'ave left England." She looked at Bess, and they both started laughing.

"Wot ye laughin' at?" asked Bertie.

"Just a private joke, son. --- Wot ye doin' 'ome so early?"

"Cause," answered a mischievous looking face, which turned to look at its partner in crime.

"Cause wot?"

"Cause it snowed an' cause 'tis Christmas."

Lottie looked suspiciously at both boys and they nodded. "Now, tell me t' truth." Artie and Bertie looked at each other and shrugged their shoulders. "I'm waitin'," demanded Lottie as she put her hands on her hips.

"Well, teacher said, since we wasn't learnin' today cause we was lookin' out at t' snow, we might as well go out in it. Maybe we'd learn a lesson there. He said Merry Christmas to us an' sent us 'ome."

"So, did ye learn anythin'?"

"Aye, 'tis cold 'n' wet. Can we 'ave summit warm to drink? --- An' summit to eat? --- Oh --- we learnt, t' snow makes us 'ungry."

"Off wit' yer coats an' wet boots. ---An' wash yer 'ands. I've got sum barley soup on t' stove." Lottie shook her head. " 'Ow about sum soup, Bess? Get four bowls down an' I'll join ye."

Bertie wiped the last of the soup off his mouth with his sleeve.

"Blimey, that were good, Mum. Now that me 'n' Artie ar' warmed up, can we go out an' make a snowman?"

"Aye, but mind, ye 'aven't got long before ye go over to Artie's. --- Button yer coats an' wrap yer scarves tightly around yer necks. I don't want ye cumin' down wit' colds fer Christmas," tsked Lottie. "Take t'is owlde 'at 'n' scarf. We don't want t' snowman to catch a cold."

"Yer funny, Mrs. Morton," giggled Artie.

"Miss Bess, cum 'n' 'elp us." Bertie pleaded, "Please, Miss Bess."

"Sure, why not. I'll be right out as soon as I clean up the dishes," said Bess as she carried a handful of dishes to the sink.

"Go on. Ye can wash 'em when ye cum in. Besides, ye'll be grateful to put yer 'ands in warm water after makin' a snowman."

Bess laughed and hurried out to help the boys. En route, she grabbed an old carrot, destined for the compost and a couple of small pieces of coal from the bucket by the stove.

"Button up yer coat. Ye don't want to ----"

"Yes, Mum," replied Bess. She opened the door. The jingling of the bell drowned out any further dialogue from Lottie.

"Miss Bess, cum quick, We need yer 'elp. T'is too big fer us to roll," the boys shouted.

Half an hour later, the boys tramped through the kitchen and clear out the back door. Moments later, each had an end of a shovel and reversed their routing, running out the front door. Fifteen minutes later, all three trooped in with the shovel and marched through the house, leaving the shovel leaning outside against the back door.

"Don't fret, Lottie. We'll clean up the floor," said Bess as the three quickly took off their footwear, lined them up against the stove and proceeded to wipe down the wet floor.

"Not a moment too soon, me afternoon customers ar' arrivin'. Go on upstairs an' get changed. Ye'll be goin' to Mrs. Doyle's soon. I don't want ye goin' over there in t' dark," said Lottie.

Immediately, a patter of stocking feet rushed through the kitchen and bounded up the stairs to Bertie's bedroom.

"I'll go and help them," said Bess.

"Oh, I fergot to tell ye, me 'n' Mr. Brown will be goin' to t' dance wit' ye tonight. Bertie's goin' stay overnight at t' Doyles'."

"Oh dear, I forgot about the dance. What will I wear?"

"That's another thing I fergot. Where is me mind? I was speakin' to Lydia Taylor t'is mornin', an' she said fer ye to wear t' dress ye wore last night. She's goin' too wit' sum posh gentleman, she is. She wants to show off 'er work," tsked Lottie. "Just like 'er always showin' off."

"So she should. What lovely work she does. I did have some nice compliments last night. Miss Taylor should definitely get some profitable business."

"Aye, t'is true, but wot a perfect model she 'ad."

"Oh, Lottie.----- Say, why don't I take the boys over to the Doyles' house. It would be nice to see Mrs. Doyle again. I might even spend some of this money." She patted her pocket.

Bess looked in on the boys, who ran behind the dresser when she caught Bertie in his drawers. She quickly closed the door and headed up to her bedroom. She looked in the mirror and thought *whatever am I going to do with this hair?* She reached in her pocket to get a comb and out came Sherry's scarf. *To heck with my hair, what am I going to do with this scarf?* Concerned, she sighed and laid it down on the chesterfield.

"Chesterfield? -- Oh, thank you --- We're both back. I'm going to wrap it right now."

"Where's the wrapping paper?"

She looked on the bare chesterfield. *Perhaps, it fell on the floor,* she thought as she searched the carpet. She saw a large bag on the coffee table and reached over to open it.

No wrapping paper, but two cookie sheets shouted, "You forgot us."

"Later," Bess replied. ----"Remind me." She looked up at Mr. Spider.

Bess got up and walked towards the cupboard of plenty, plenty of everything as Evan called it. *My feet are still wet. Now it is both feet. Hmm -- How water travels.* She bent over, untied her laces and straddled her shoes and socks over the register. Standing in her bare feet, she opened the overflowing cupboard of organized chaos. On the front edge of each shelf, a label described its occupants. Under wrappings, she found a small, red gift bag and green tissue paper. Out fell a small card, which she picked up.

Nonchalantly, she carried her stash back to the scarf, stuffed it in the bag and scrunched up a couple sheets of tissue paper on top. *Voila!* Pleased with herself, she put the finished present on the hall table, where Evan would find it when he dropped his keys there, along with anything else that lightened his load.

The clock struck two. *I'd better get the meat on and cut up the vegetables if I want to get the stew started,* she thought as she hurried to the kitchen. Out came the chunked beef. Down came the crockpot. Vegetables came flying out of the crisper. Peel, chop, chop, plunk. A glug of water and a drift of bay leaves covered the ingredients, before a heavy clunk sealed their fate inside the closed crockpot. Bess plugged in the pot and put it on simmer. The clock struck on the half-hour. *I'd better turn it up or it won't be ready for supper,* she decided.

Satisfied, she walked back in the living room. *Winter, ugh! It's getting dark already. I'll put on the village lights.* She reached down and plugged them in.

"That's much better, eh, Mr. Spider?" Bess looked up at a curled up man of leisure. "Now, if only my feet would warm up."

Bess walked over to the register and picked up her dry shoes and socks. Feeling a bit weary, she sat down on the chesterfield and proceeded to put them on.

"Ah, warm at last." She sat back and almost sat on the discarded cookie sheets. She plopped them on her lap and noticed the greeting card laying on the cushion beside her. "Darn, I forgot to put it with Sherry's present. I'll do it later."

She picked it up and looked at it closely. The scalloped edge along the top and down one side outlined a fancy cup and saucer, decorated with sprigs of holly and red berries. The cup sat upon a crochet tablecloth. *What a lovely card. ---- It would be perfect.* She smiled as she looked up at the tearoom. *What a shame. ---- I could just imagine ------ "*

"Miss Bess, me 'n' Artie ar' ready."

Knock, knock.

"Miss Bess, ar' ye in there?"

"Yes? ---- of course, Bertie. I'll meet you downstairs in just a few minutes."

"Aye, Miss Bess," replied Bertie, followed by the rush of footsteps down the stairs.

As Bess got up from the bed, the cookie sheets slid onto the floor. She bent over to pick them up, only to discover a card in her hand. *It's the Christmas card! I knew it was destined for Lottie. I'll give it to her later.* Excited, she stuffed the cookie sheets under the bed and thought *I must organize all this loot. I'll do it after I come back from Artie's.*

She put on the coat Lottie loaned her and stuffed her hand in the pocket. *What did I do with those books I purchased from Tellaways? --- Oh no, I hope I haven't lost them. I was so flustered, I could have left them anywhere.* She felt in the other pocket. No books; only a lonely penny rolled between her fingers. *Bless Jo for not leaving me penniless.* She quickly opened her coat and thrust her hand in her dress pocket and pulled out a pound note. She breathed a sigh of relief. *At least, now I can pay back Jo. ---- That leaves me 240 plus 1, ---- 241 minus 8, ---- 233 pennies left.* She thought for a moment *no, I'm not going to think how many shillings. The boys are waiting for me.* She tucked the pound note and one penny deep in her dress pocket, buttoned up her coat and headed downstairs.

The three bundled-up souls, forged out into the cold. Until they passed "Tellaway Books," their journey remained clear and dry. Their clearing of the snow in front of the tea and the book shoppes, not only paid off for the proprietors and patrons, but also for them.

"Maybe tomorrow, we can clear the snow off the sidewalk right to the Taylors'. Unfortunately, it won't help us now. Come on, lads, watch where you walk." Bess lifted her skirts, and off they plodded through the uneven trenches of footprints.

"Aye, then we can clean in t' other direction to Mr. Brown's. --- Artie, maybe Mr. Brown will give us a penny fer our efforts."

"An' maybe t' Peppers, Taylors, 'n' Fowlers," piped up Artie with a great deal of enthusiasm. " --- Four pennies! Bertie, we could buy sum sweets."

"Aye, gob stoppers. Ye get yer penny's worth cause they last ever so long," said Bertie as he licked his lips.

"Wot about sticks of rock? They last a long time an' 'ave sayin's inside 'em," blurted out Artie.

"Stop, Miss Bess. We turn t' corner 'ere. --- See our fire station." Bertie pointed across the street. "I'm goin' be a fireman. They 'ave excitin' lives, always goin' to fires an' rescuin' dogs 'n' cats. We 'ave lots of fires, so they need lots of firemen."

"I'd like to be a fireman too, cause I could ring t' bell all day long," added Artie as he pointed to the brass bell, suspended high up in the brick tower.

They trudged through the wet snow which felt crunchy underfoot. The temperature started to drop as the daylight gradually faded.

"Come, lads. I'd better get you to your house, Artie, before it starts freezing. How much further?"

"Not far, just t' next street. See t' red brick buildin' on t' corner?" Artie pointed straight ahead.

"Look, Artie. A fire wagon." Bertie beckoned Artie over to look in a shoppe window. "T'is 'orses 'n' firemen. -- Look, Miss Bess."

The three pressed their faces against the large window and viewed a great display of hand-carved animals, soldiers, carts and dolls.

"Oh, if only we 'ad more pennies," sighed Bertie.

"We don't 'ave no pennies, Bertie," replied the practical Artie.

"Ah, but it doesn't cost anything to dream and dreaming is as much fun."

"I suppose, Miss Bess," sighed Bertie. They reluctantly turned and walked up the street.

"Watch out, Miss Bess, 'im's an owler,' said Artie as he grabbed her arm.

"T'is true, Miss Bess. 'E's bad. 'E sells stolen goods. Uncle Tom told us to stay away from 'im," warned Bertie.

" 'E cums from just up t' street in St. Giles Parish. T'is very poor, St. Giles. Me dad won't let me go past Parker Street, cause t'is where t' Rookeries start, t'is part of St. Giles Parish. Lots of people from Ireland live in t' Rookeries. So, when we moved 'ere, me mum 'n' dad wanted to live close to our old friends. Me dad says t'is t' luck of t' Irish, we found a place right on t' edge of St. Giles."

" 'Ow cum if it be t' luck of t' Irish, so many of 'em live in t' middle of t' Rookeries, Artie?" asked Bertie.

Artie looked crossly at Bertie. "Maybe cause t' Irish are lucky to escape t' famine. Sum of us ar' just luckier Irish."

"Aye, t'is true, Artie." Bertie stopped to think for a moment. "That makes me an even luckier Englishman to 'ave ye as me friend, Artie." Bertie smiled at Artie and looked up at Bess. "An' ye too, Miss Bess."

"We are all lucky to have each other." She smiled and grabbed Bertie's hand.

The three skipped down the street. Suddenly, they stopped and wiggled their noses.

"Chestnuts! Get yer 'ot chestnuts 'ere!" shouted a young man.

Bess remembered her lone penny burning a hole in her pocket. She reached down, pulled it out, and gave it to the street vendor who gave her a warm bag, full of chestnuts.

"By the time we get to your house, Artie, they should be cool enough to eat."

"Let's 'urry." The boys quickened their pace, dragging Bess across the slushy, cobblestone street.

They crossed the corner and turned right on Parker Street. Bess noticed the stark contrast in architecture from Fetter Lane to Parker Street. Tall, forbidding buildings lined both sides of the street. No gaslights guided the leery victim down the street of ugly giants. Artie's hand gripped tighter as they passed the third house. A vacant lot strewn with rubble and litter, lay on their left.

" 'Urry Miss Bess. T'is ghosts in there. Sumtimes I see 'em runnin' around an' makin' 'orrible noises," said Artie. "That's why they tore t' 'ouse down at number seven, but t' ghosts ar' still there." Artie's wide eyes looked up at Bess. "I always run past 'ere, so they won't catch me."

They stopped at number fifteen, a five-storey building blackened with time. Some of the upper windows were boarded up, others had tattered pieces of cloth hanging from the soot, encrusted windows. Black smoke drifted out of the numerous chimneys, causing their eyes to sting and their breathing to labour.

"See four 'ouses down, t'is ghosts there too. Lots of people 'ave seen 'em in t' attic of number twenty-three. Me dad made sure we was on t' ground floor, far away from 'em," said Artie. He lead her along a narrow path to a small door on the right side of the building. "Mither, --- Me 'n' Bertie 'n' Miss Bess ar' 'ome," shouted Artie as he opened the door.

The pleasant smell of baking entered their nostrils and the warmth of the roaring fire, invited them in from the cold. The room looked worn, but cosy. Secondhand furniture dotted the living room. A dining table and a beautiful, handcrafted hutch stood in the far corner. Other handcrafted pieces of furniture stood out against the thread-bare material of the chairs and sofa. Throws tried in vain to cover them. However, the room had a homey, comfortable appearance about it.

"Miss Bess, cum an' see." Artie grabbed her hand and lead her over to the fireplace. "Look." Proudly, he pointed down to a covered, wicker basket. He fell down on his knees and lifted the knitted blanket, exposing four kittens. "Aren't they smashin'?"

Bess knelt down and smiled at the little balls of fluff. "Oh, Artie, they are lovely. What are their names?"

"We 'aven't named 'em yet. Me mum says I can only keep one. Even t'ou they be good mousers." He sighed, "I 'ave to find 'omes fer t' other ones."

"I'm goin' ax me mum if I can 'ave t' rest," announced Bertie.

"Where's the mother cat?" asked Bess.

"Me 'n' Patty 'eard 'em meoowin' in t' vacant lot at number seven. Patty wouldn't go in, cause she thought t'is ghosts makin' ghost sounds, so I ran fast an' picked 'em up. No mum were wit' 'em."

"My, you were very brave, Artie." Bess gave him a pat on the hand.

"We all bin feedin' 'em warm milk."

"You are doing a fine job. They certainly look and sound healthy," congratulated Bess as the kittens started a chorus of meows.

"Ye can 'old one," said Artie. He picked up a black and white kitten.

Bess opened her hand and a soft little ball of fur curled up in her palm. "Look at his little face. Why, he can't be more than a couple weeks old."

"Artie,-- put t'ose kittens down," ordered Mrs. Doyle as she came in through an open doorway. Bess turned towards her and Mrs. Doyle looked startled. "Oh, Miss Bess, sorry I didn't know ye were here. I swear Artie's goin' kill t'em wit' kindness. Poor little ones."

Bess gave the kitten a kiss and reluctantly laid it in the basket with its siblings. Artie covered up the basket, and the three got up from the floor.

"Miss Bess, how nice of ye to bring t' lads. I do worry about t'em walkin' about t' streets. T'is not a safe neighbourhood." Mrs. Doyle rubbed her red, chaffed hands on her apron and brushed a lock of red hair away from her rosy face, while little Patty clung to her mother's skirt.

"You have a nice place, Mrs. Doyle."

"T'ank ye. We do the best we can. Mr. Doyle t'is a godsend with his carpentry skills."

"Yes, I was just admiring this hutch ---- and this bookcase is beautiful."

"Would ye like a cup of tea?"

"I would love some, but I must be on my way."

"Aye, yer goin' dancin' tonight. T'is been a while since we last did a jig." She laughed. "Maybe next time," she sighed.

As Bess turned to leave she remembered, "Oh, there's some chestnuts in the bag. Share them with your little sister, now."

Artie shouted from the doorway, "Don't ferget to run past number seven, Miss Bess."

Bess waved and headed back along the street, quickening her pace past number seven. At the toy shoppe, she stopped and peered in the window. A beautiful, little shiny face looked back at her. She opened the door to the sounds of cuckoo, cuckoo. She looked up to see a cuckoo bird welcoming her into his shoppe. His curiosity satisfied, the cuckoo went back inside his house and slammed the door shut.

"Gud tag, Fraulein," a deep voice greeted Bess.

She looked around the shoppe full of stationary toys. Not a wooden mouth moved. Suddenly, behind a large, wooden box, a body jumped up. A jovial, round face surrounded by a wreath of white whiskers, turned towards Bess.

"Ja, fraulein, may I help you, please?"

"Oh, yes, ---- sorry. You startled me. For a moment I took you for one of your toys. Pardon me for asking, but is your name Jack?"

"Jack?" He looked over the box in front of him. "Oh, Jack, dhet

213

is gud." He gave a hardy chuckle. "Nein, Jack --- Klaus ---- Klaus Sievert --- Herr Sievert, fraulein?"

"Bess N-ike, ---- ah --- Fraulein N-ike."

"Ja, dhet is gud. The Fraulein Beethoven of America. --- I was at Frau Morton's tea party on Sunday. You play very gud."

"Danke shoen, Herr Sievert. We were looking in your window earlier and a couple of toys took our interest."

"Ja the kinders, Artie and Bertie, gud boys. I saw your happy faces through the window."

"They liked the fire wagon and I liked the doll."

"Ja, let me get them from the window so you may see them better." said the shopkeeper. Coming back with his hands full, he laid the toys on the counter. "It comes with these firemen with their horses." He placed the four finely, hand-carved firemen alongside the wagon and positioned the horses, two by two, in front of the red wagon. "They are from the finest wood from The Black Forest. Dhat is gud, ja? Mein cousins back in Germany, carved all these." Proudly, he swung his arm around the cluttered room, surrounded with shelves of toys. "I just received a shipment today." He disappeared behind the large, wooden box and instantly reappeared with his hands full. "Mein cousin, Helmut carved these. Gud, ja?"

"Ja --- yes, they're toy soldiers ----- nutcrackers."

"Ja ----Nussknacker. How did you know? Not many people know of them. Dhet is mein first shipment."

"Er ----- I have a German friend who told me about them. He described them so well that I guessed what they were," said Bess as she crossed her fingers behind her back. "You are wise to introduce them to England. I am sure they will be popular."

"Popular you say?"

"Oh yes, you will sell many. How much are they?" Bess asked right away, not wanting to get into the same trouble with the books. "And --- how much are these?" Pointing at the fire set. "And the doll? Did your cousin make her too? Her face is so lifelike."

"Mein cousin, Gretchen paints the faces and Cousin Hilda sews the clothes and Cousin Wilhelm carves the body." He smiled and started counting in German. "How many of these do you want?" He pointed at the toy soldiers.

Bess thought for a moment. "Four," she blurted out.

"Ja, dhet is gud." He smiled and went back to his counting. "Ja, dhet is zwel crown."

Dead silence enveloped the shoppe. Bess gave a puzzled look at Herr Sievert. *What is a swell* crown? *I don't even know what an ordinary crown is worth,* she frantically thought.

"Ah, fraulein ---- Dhat is two crown. ---- Ja, okay?"

"Ah, two crowns," repeated Bess. She tried to recall how much a crown equaled. *Yes, --- I found a half-crown. ---- Two --- No, two and a half shillings. So, one crown is five shillings.* "Yes, ten shillings."

"Ja, zehn shillings. Dhat is right."

*I hope he said ten shillings. Let's see, that leaves me ten left, minus eight pennies for Jo,* she calculated and said, "Ten shillings. Dhat is gud. I'll take them."

She reached down in her skirt pocket and brought out the pound note and handed it to

him. *Why do I have so much trouble with their money? I just can't keep pennies, twopence, farthings, crowns, shillings ---- straight. Why can't they all be pennies?* Pennies I can relate *to,* pondered Bess, as she watched him bundle the wooden pieces into paper packages and tie them with string. He handed her four silver coins.

"Oh, half-crowns?" She thought for a moment. "Two crowns ---- ten shillings, right?"

"Ja, dhat is right, fraulein." He smiled at her. "I too had trouble with English money when I first came here, what zehn years ago." He helped her to the door and handed her the parcels. "Danke shoen." He nodded as he opened the door, where upon the cuckoo immediately sprung into action and started cuckoo ---- cuckoo.

"I noticed your Christmas tree in the window. Where did you get it?" Bess asked over the repetitive cuckooing.

"Ja, they are not easy to find here in England. Back home in Germany, we all have a Christmas tree. I am sorry, a customer gave it to me and I do not know where he got it."

"Well, thank you --- and Merry Christmas, Herr Sievert."

"Fröhliche Weihnacten ----Auf wiedersehen, Fraulein N-ike."


Pleased with her purchases, she merrily walked down the street, stopping at the corner to look over at Firehall Number Eight. Firemen spread long, heavy muslin hoses along the snow covered ground, in hopes of rewinding them on the large, wooden wheels, whilst others checked for punctures. All this activity heightened her senses, and she sniffed the air.

"Fire, do I smell smoke?" Bess looked at the firemen who continued their duties. She looked up at the silent bell hanging motionless in the tower. "Obviously, the power of suggestion."

She turned the corner and headed up Fetter Lane passing "Taylor & Sons". She glanced over at Lydia's display window and saw two arms frantically waving. She waved back.

"Bess, ---- Bess, come in. I have something for you," shouted Lydia through the opened doorway. "I'm so glad I saw you. Come in out of the cold. Soon as it starts to get dark, the temperature drops." Lydia shut the door.

"I didn't realize how late it is. I've been out longer than I expected. I can't stay long, but I must thank you for loaning me the dress. It was a great success. I mentioned your name a few times to ladies who I hope will become new customers."

"How delightful. I look forward to opening my doors to wealthy ladies." Lydia's smile lit up the room's fading light. "Now, I must not forget why I summoned you. In the excitement yester-day, you left your parcel in the dressing room." Lydia ran into the back.

"My parcel?" queried Bess.

"Here it is," announced Lydia. She handed it to Bess. "I think it is books."

"My books! Oh, thank you. I wondered where I mislaid them."

"They must be important, you look very happy."

"Yes, very important, and I am very happy." Bess reached out to grab the parcel and dropped another from her hand. As she bent over to pick it up, something caught her eye in the display case. "My, that is beautiful."

"I only got these in this morning. I'll show them to you." She bent over and pulled out two woollen shawls. Lydia unfolded one and placed it over her shoulders, swinging around to show Bess the back, which draped to her waist.

Bess gently brushed her hand across the fabric. "It is so soft. The colours go with everything. How much are they?" Bess held her breath.

"Three shillings each." Lydia looked at Bess's face which suddenly projected a far away look. "I have some nice scarfs for two shillings." She bent down and brought out a black and red tartan one with black woollen tassels hanging from the two ends. She handed it to Bess to feel its soft surface.

"What colour would suit Lottie best?" asked Bess, looking over at the two shawls.

"Definitely the cream coloured one. It will contrast with her dark-brown eyes and hair. Besides, it will go with everything. She would look lovely in the deep-blue, but it would not be as serviceable." Lydia thought for a moment. "I don't think ---- no, she does not have a blue gown." She looked at Bess. "However, it would look lovely on you. What with your blond hair and these beautiful, blue eyes." She saw the hesitation in Bess's face. "I just remembered, I have two more out back."

Left alone, Bess pondered and calculated *I'd love that blue one, but I don't have enough money, but I could buy ----*

"Are these not lovely?" Lydia interrupted Bess's train of thought. "Now, I personally love this white one with the black threads running throught it. Too bad Lottie does not have black hair."

*Ah, but Lydia does,* Bess thought and blurted out, "I"ll take it and the cream one." She stopped and did a quick calculation *that's six ---- and if I buy the scarf for Jo,---- that's eight shillings. That will leave me one shilling --- four pennies left, after I pay Jo.* Once more she blurted out, "I'll take the scarf too. Don't you think it would look nice on Jo?"

"With her black hair, the colours will look stunning on her. Are you sure you don't want the blue one, rather than the black and white one?"

"I'd love it, but I don't have enough money. Besides the black and white one is for my friend back home. Like you, she has black hair. In fact, you remind me of her."

"I understand. --- That will be eight shillings." Lydia received four coins from Bess and gave her two shillings in change. While putting the woollens in a parcel, Lydia said, "I noticed you have a doll in one of your parcels. I have the perfect gift to put with it. My supplier always gives me miniature samples so here, take these two. Perhaps your friend in America has a daughter."

"Thank you, Miss Taylor. My friend will be pleased. --- I must go and thank you again for allowing me to wear the dress tonight. I hear you are coming too. I shall see you later."

"Lydia, do call me Lydia. Remember, don't wear the lace cover-up. The young men like to have something interesting to look at." She laughed as she opened the door for Bess.

Walking back towards the tea shoppe, Bess still smelt smoke. She looked back down the lane, but noticed no movement from the firehall. *It must be my imagination,* she shrugged. As she passed the book shoppe, she saw a very busy Jo attending to a lineup of Christmas shoppers, buying that special book for someone. She wanted to go in and pay her debt of eight pennies, but decided to give it to her at home. With all the parcels hanging from her arms and not a free hand to open the door, let alone dig in her pocket, she would only cause a commotion in "Tellaway Books."

Bess picked up her pace and within minutes reached the tea shoppe. Fortunately, a patron opened the door from within, just as Bess attempted to rearrange her load. She thanked the woman and hurried inside. Lottie, busy in the kitchen did not notice her arrival, so Bess headed up the stairs. Moments earlier as she looked for Lottie, she noticed the saying on the chalkboard and recalled those words of wisdom by Tien Yiheng.

"Tea is drunk to forget the din of the world."

*How true*, she thought as she vividly recalled her journey to Artie's neighbourhood and remembered Mrs. Doyle's unselfish offer of a cup of tea.

Safely inside her bedroom, grateful for a reprieve from Lottie's curious eyes, she plunked the parcels on the bed. Attempting to disengage the last couple of parcels from her arms, she heard a loud clanging outside her window. Bags dangled from her arms as she rushed over to the window. With a free hand, she managed to open the window. The sound, now very loud, she looked down and saw the fire wagon go speeding by.

"I knew I smelt smoke." She breathed in the smoky air. "It must be close, definitely something burning."

Beep, Beep, Be—eeeep!

"What is that? It doesn't sound like a bell. I sounds like a ---- smoke alarm!"

Bess's eyes opened wide. They burned from the smoke engulfing the living room. She blinked.

"Living room? Smoke alarm? --- Oh no ----- The stew!"

She ran into the kitchen, banging the parcels on the door frame. She ripped them off her arms, deposited them on the counter and unplugged the crockpot. Black soot, escaping from the lid gone askew, ran down the sides of the pot onto the counter. Grabbing a nearby pot holder, she lifted the lid to discover a blackened mass of unrecognizable stew. Immediately, Bess slammed the lid back down and ran for some water. The pot sizzled as she poured water on the charred remains. Nothing to rescue there, she hustled over to the back door, opened it wide and fanned out some of the smoke. Leaving the door open, she opened the windows, desperately fanning the smoke outwards.

"Shut up! I'm doing my best," she screamed at the beeping smoke alarm. In frustration she yelled, "I'll fix you." She grabbed a chair, stood on it, pulled off the plastic cover and ripped out the batteries.

Her knees buckled. She sat down on the chair and put her head in her hands. "What am I going to have for supper now?" Bess asked a silent house.

An hour later, the house felt darn cold, but at least it smelt fresh. Bess closed the door and windows. Once again, the kitchen sparkled. Forlorn, the crockpot lay in the garbage. *It has served us well, but all good things must eventually come to an end, albeit, a tragic end, but still an end.* She sighed, grabbed the parcels off the counter and headed for the doorway.

"I see you're still Christmas shopping. Stop, oh do stop. I don't deserve anymore," pleaded Evan as he entered the living room.

"Evan, I didn't hear you come in. We have to go out for supper. I bur ---"

"Burnt the supper. I thought so. I smelt the faint odour de smoke when I came in. Day-dreaming again?" He laughed.

"Oh, Evan, I'm sorry. I murdered the crockpot."

"Better it than me. ---- Get your coat and I'll get the car out."

"I'll just get rid of these parcels."

"Close the living room window while you're at it, Bess."

"I didn't open any windows in here. I'm sure I didn't. I only opened them in the kitchen and dining room. I ----" She looked towards the mantel and spied the tea shoppe's third story window open. "Oh!"

❆

"Not a bad dinner, but I would have preferred stew," said Evan as they entered the hall.

"Oh, Evan," cried Bess.

"Just kidding. Here give me your coat." Evan took the coat and opened the closet rather boisterously.

Crash! Down went the shelf of shoes.

"Evan! ---- How many times have I told you the shelf was wobbly? --- Look shoes all over the floor."

Evan picked up a couple of runners and stacked them on top of each other. "I"ll fix it this weekend. He picked up a pair of high heels. "I haven't seen you in these for a long time. Why don't you wear them anymore? I always did like you in high heels. You know I've always been a leg man." He looked up at Bess and winked.

"They are my dancing shoes --- and --- you never take me dancing anymore. Remember when we used to go dancing almost every Saturday night?" sighed Bess.

"You're right. Tell you what, go put them on and we'll have a spin around the floor," announced Evan in a vain attempt to get Bess's mind off the collapsed shelf.

"Don't be silly."

"Put these shoes on, woman. I'll put on some music."

Before Bess could protest, Evan hightailed it into the living room and turned on the radio. She picked up the cream coloured, leather pumps, sat down and untied her runners.

"Come on, woman, let's see a bit of leg." Evan waltzed over to Bess. "That's more like it," he proclaimed as Bess rolled up her pant legs. Extending his hand, he asked, "Miss, may I have this dance?"

Bess laughed and said, "What the heck. --- Why certainly, sir." She gave him her hand and he helped her off the chesterfield.

"May I have this dance for the rest of my life ----- " sang Evan as he pulled her in his arms, and they twirled around the floor.

Three songs later, they fell exhausted onto the chesterfield. Legs spread out before them, they sat back and listened to the music. Five minutes later, Evan's heavy breathing turned into a muffled snore. Bess tried to keep her eyes open or look at the mantel, but even that did not keep her eyelids from shutting.

Suddenly, she felt cold and shivered. She opened her eyes to see a blast of snow come through the window. Bess quickly closed the window and rubbed her arms. Turning away, she saw a bed full of parcels.

Knock, knock.

"Bess, do you need any help?" asked a gentle voice.

"No --- ah ---- Yes --- Just one minute, Jo," said Bess. She ran over to the bed and stuffed the parcels under the bed. "You can come in now."

Jo opened the door and looked surprised. "Bess, you are still in your day dress."

"What time is it?"

"The men will be here in fifteen minutes. Come on, off with this dress. Where's your corset and petticoats?"

"Jo, I just can't get the hang of this torture chamber," tsked Bess as she pulled the monster from the drawer.

"Take off that strange contraption."

Bess gave her an odd look. "Oh, you mean my bra."

"If that is what you call it, yes. --- Good ---- Now put this on and I will tighten it up."

"Do you have to?"

"Lottie," shouted Jo. "I need your help. ---- Breathe in Bess. -----More."

"What's all the noise. Can I help?"

"Tom ---- stay out of here ---- and no you cannot help." Jo shut the door in Tom's face.

"Get out of t' way, Thomas Evans," demanded Lottie as she came puffing up the stairs. "I'm cumin', Jo, as soon as I get t'is big bloke out of t' way." She barged past a smirking Tom, opened the door and shut it before Tom could take a peek inside.

"Lottie, can you get her dress? It is hanging up in the wardrobe," Jo asked as she tightened up the corset with one last pull.

"There, all done." She tied the ends into a bow. "You can breathe now, Bess."

"Breathe? I'll never breathe again. Jo, you're worse than Lydia."

"Bess, you've torn yer dress," said Lottie.

"Oh dear, I must have done it on the carriage last night."

"Good Lord, wot was ye doin'? 'orsin' around? Just look at it, Jo."

"Let me have a look," said Jo. "I can mend it. I'll go and get my sewing basket. In the meantime, you two can put on the dress." Jo hurried off, checking to make sure the coast was clear of a peeping Tom.

"Lift up yer arms so I can slip it over yer 'ead. ---- Turn around an' I'll button it up."

Jo came back into the room carrying a wicker basket. "I know I have some yellow thread in here." She rummaged through the assortment of threads. "Perfect, this will do. Now, do I have a fine needle for this delicate chiffon?" Eventually, Jo mended the tear, while Lottie finished dressing Bess. "Now, where are my scissors? I am forever misplacing them. If I had ten pair, I would still lose them."

"Come on, ladies, your escorts are waiting downstairs," announced Tom.

"Give us two minutes an' we'll be right there," shouted Lottie. "A fine job, Jo. No one would ever know t'is bin torn." She gave Bess a stern look. "Let's 'ave a final look." The women made Bess twirl around. "Oh, t' lace, we'd best get rid of it," said Lottie. She swooped the lace piece away from Bess's bodice. "Pinch 'er cheeks, Jo. Perhaps a flower in 'er 'air will 'elp," tsked Lottie.

Each lady made a grand entrance into the dining room, accompanied by cheers from the three spit and polished gentlemen. After placing a coat over the lady's shoulders, each took his lady's arm, and off they went into the snowy night.

This time, Bess sat between Tom and Sean and so did not afford a view of the city's vistas. The temperature had dropped.

Bess enjoyed the warmth of the two manly bodies, shielding her from the winter chills.

The men spoke of their upcoming football match, a week from Sunday. From the conversation, it sounded like Tom and Sean looked forward to their weekly match and were disappointed Sunday's match had been cancelled due to Christmas. Mr. Brown enjoyed football, but preferred the new version called rugby. Being a baker, he felt more at home handling the ball rather than kicking it and thought Sean should feel the same way. Tom further voiced his displeasure at missing last Sunday's match due to Lottie's neighbourhood tea. Lottie put in her two pennies worth and told him life was not all play; he had a duty to his fellow neighbours. After a yes, Sister Dear, they all laughed and the conversation changed to something they all could agree on, the weather. They all turned and looked out the carriage windows and observed the snow fluttering down. They shivered and moved a little closer to each other.

The carriage came to a halt, the door opened and out jumped Tom. He extended his hand to Bess who extended her foot, revealing a delicate, dancing shoe. Tom smiled and literally swept her off her feet, carrying her to the entrance of the dance hall. Seeing Tom's chivalrous act, the two other men picked up their ladies and plodded through the snow-clad walkway to the entrance. After much giggling, the ladies' feet gently touched down on the marble floor of the majestic Vauxhall. Music and laughter filtered into the foyer, enticing all to abandon their hats and coats and proceed to the dance floor.

Bess marvelled at the sight before her. Women in gaily, coloured gowns, swirled around the dance floor with their handsome partners, dressed in the finest, evening attire. In the maze of dancers, she spied Lydia Taylor, smiling at a handsome, blond-haired gentleman, holding her at arm's length as they waltzed around the dance floor. The orchestra, of perhaps a dozen musicians, performed on the centre stage. The music came to an end and the dancers took to their seats, lined up against the walls. A harpist began a lilting sound. The violinists positioned their instruments under their chins, picked up the bows and began to accompany the harpist. A beautiful sound waft across the room, and the dancers alighted to fill the floor with swaying feet.

"Miss Bess, may I have this dance?" asked Tom as he put out his hand.

"Why, yes, sir," replied Bess. Daintily, she offered her hand.

"Isn't the Viennese Waltz delightful?" Lydia remarked as they waltzed by.

"Yes indeed." Tom gazed into Bess's eyes and graciously swung her around.

Bess thought *Tom is very light on his feet.* Gradually a warmth spread over her. She wanted the dance to go on forever. Unfortunately, all too soon the music ended, and they made their way to the rest of their party. No sooner did they reach them, and the orchestra leader announced the next dance.

"The Lancers ---- Oh, we must get one more pair." Lottie scouted around the bustling room. "There's Lydia and ---- Who is that, Jo?" Not waiting for a reply, she waved and beckoned them over. "Lydia, do join us to make a set."

"How kind of you to ask. Yes, of course we will join you," replied Lydia and gave one of her sparkling smiles to the men. "Mr. Brown, Tom, Sean, I would like to introduce you to Wilbur Carlyle, The Earl of Farnham."

"How do you do, sirs. ---- And the charming young ladies are?" The debonair earl smiled at the women and bowed just as the music started up, preventing any further introductions.

The four pairs arranged themselves in a square and began to dance. Bess thought *it's like a slow square dance without the caller.* ---- *Too bad there isn't a caller telling me to allemande left and do-si-do, cause I don't know which way to go.* She struggled through most of the song, but by the end, got the hang of it. By the third dance, she was really into the swing of it, but all good things must come to an end and the music stopped.

225

After a brief intermission, they caught their breaths and soothed their parched throats with liquid refreshments. The music began in full force with a polka. *Now, this one I can do. Why, I can polka with the best of them,* chuckled Bess to herself.

"Miss Bess, would you do me the honour?" asked The Earl of Farnham. "You don't mind, do you, guvnor?" He looked at Tom.

"Of course not, Wil, old boy," answered Tom with a grin and a wink at Bess. "Lydia, shall we?"

Fortunately, the polka left little time for chitchat let alone breathing, so Bess did not get involved with small talk which would get around to questions about America. The polka ended up as a change your partner, and Bess clung breathlessly to Tom as the last chord finished.

At midnight, the orchestra hung up their instruments and the weary, but happy dancers headed home. The snow had stopped. Without having to avail the gentlemanly services of their weary partners, the ladies managed to make their own way to the carriage. All started to nod off on the return trip. More than once, Bess found her head resting on Tom's warm, broad shoulder. The next thing she knew, her shoes were being removed.

"Bess, don't curl your toes. I can't get your shoes off."

"Huh," Bess replied dreamily. "My shoes?" She opened her eyes.

"Didn't you just ask me to take them off? You said your feet ached," said Evan. "Good heavens, Bess. We only danced a couple of dances. I guess I'd better take you out dancing more often, old girl."

"Yes, you should. Great fun. Let's do it real soon," muttered Bess as she whispered, "Tom."

# CHAPTER XIV

The snow fluttered down, as Bess woke from a long winter's nap. She opened her eyes and focused on the white flakes floating before her. *Am I here or there?* Bess asked herself. On a quick peruse of her surroundings, she recognized the Turners' bedroom. She left the warmth of her bed and made her way to the window.

Evan always opened the drapes as soon as he got up. His structured occupation left him no margin for error, so it spilt over in his off hours. Each morning, he needed to know what Mother Nature had in store so he could prepare accordingly. From his first observation, he picked out his clothes and footware. He then planned his departure time related to weather conditions.

"Ouch, my feet ache," groaned Bess.

"I thought I heard you," said Evan as he poked his head around the bathroom door. "I groaned too when I saw the snow. I'm going to have to hurry. I want to leave myself lots of time to drive to work. The traffic is going to be slow going. ---- What's wrong? You look like you're walking on a bed of coals. Did I step on your feet last night?"

"No, Twinkle Toes, don't worry. I'm sure I'll survive. I'd forgotten my shoes rub a little. I think I have a couple of blisters." She hobbled back to the sanctuary of her bed.

"Bess, I'm leaving."

"Evan --- Oh, I must have drifted off."

"Thanks for getting Sherry's present. I hate to ask you, but I need another favour. My special order is in at Wilson Office Supply. Would you pick it up for me? Go early before the snow starts laying." He leaned over and gave her a kiss goodbye. "Oh, I put some weight in the trunk, so you should be okay. But, take your time. Leave lots of room between you and the next car." At the bottom of the stairs, he shouted, "Drive carefully."

A thin layer of snow lay on the side of the street. No snow adhered to the wet pavement as Bess entered the parking lot of the small strip mall. Wilson Office Supply and Harry's Hardware attracted the di-hard locals, while the drugstore and liquor store attracted both the young and old. The advent of the computer and the big box stores, forced many small office and stationery stores out of business. Fortunately, Wilson's loyal customers kept its doors open. Whenever possible, the Turners gave their business to the independent owners. Besides, they loved the feel of walking into an intimate room filled with shelves of neatly stacked supplies. They never felt overwhelmed by the long, imposing rows of the big box stores. If they needed advice, an experienced sales person stood ready to assist.

While looking around, Bess noticed boxes of ballpoint pens on sale. She picked up one. *The way Evan loses them, I might as well buy two. Besides, the price is right.* Further down the aisle, she picked up a box of Wite-out. *He goes through that as much as he misplaces his pens,* she mused. At the back of the store, the children's section caught her eye. She arrived at the counter with her arms full. She plunked the three boxes, along with three boxes of crayons and three colouring books onto the glass counter. As Mrs. Wilson rung in the items, Bess spotted an old fashioned, fountain pen in the display shelf.

"Could I have a look at the fountain pen?"

"Of course, Mrs. Turner. You don't see them anymore.

Remember when we were kids, our hands were blue from the ink spills."

"Not only our hands, my clothes were permanently dotted with ink spots."

"Surprisingly, we only have two left. I guess it shows the age of our customers," laughed a white-haired Mrs. Wilson.

"I'll take both of them," said Bess pleased with her decision. "Oh, I almost forgot the reason I came here, Evan's special order."

"Yes, I have it right here. Your husband said you'd be in today."

Arms full, she passed Harry's Hardware and suddenly stopped. The fountain pen inspiration gave her other ideas, so she retraced her steps and went into the hardware store. *Now, what can I get the men? Something useful, something not too hard to explain, but not yet invented?* Bess wondered as she headed towards the tools. Looking up for the tool signage, she bumped into a bin. She looked down at the object that jumped in front of her.

"Yes, of course," she shouted, "everyman's fixer-all, duct tape."

"Can I help you, ma'am?" asked Harry's son. "Oh, Mrs. Turner."

"I'm looking for something for someone who lives in the past." She looked at a puzzled face. "No electronics or power tools."

"Ah, how about one of these? They are always handy." He pulled out an Exacto knife from the next bin.

"Excellent, I'll take one --- two --- four of them, Jason." As she walked behind him to the cash register, she noticed something else. "Perfect for Mr. Doyle --- And these for Mrs. Doyle."

A quick stop in the liquor store for brandy for the Christmas pudding and the drugstore for toothbrushes, she headed back to the car. After depositing her bags in the backseat, she brushed the snow off the windows. While reaching across the windshield, her eyes caught sight of The Stitch In Time. Ten minutes later, accompanied by all her prized parcels, including one from the sewing store, she drove out of the parking lot. She made one more stop at the grocery story and headed home.

Back home, safe and sound, she sorted out her purchases: groceries put away in the kitchen, Evan's special order laid out on the hall table, and the rest still in bags, awaited her inspection. While in the kitchen, she had plugged in the kettle. It now whistled at a high pitch. She rushed back in and remedied the situation.

A mug of steaming tea in one hand, she sat down amongst the parcels and sighed. "Where do I begin, Mr. Spider? Just hanging out; sure, ignore me in your webbed hammock. It does contrast nicely with the white film of snow laying on the skylight." She looked at the mantel. "I've been buying so many presents for them, I need to start a list."

On the coffee table, she found a pen and a notepad. After opening each parcel, she wrote down the article and who would receive it. Suddenly she stopped. *I'd better check what's in those parcels I brought home last night.* She scratched her head. *Now, where did I put them? Evan went to the garage --- and I didn't have time to --- I know.* She leaned over the back of the chesterfield and the parcels stared up at her. Rummaging through them, she discovered the two nutcrackers, Lydia's shawl and doll and Evan's "A Christmas Carol." However, to her dismay, " 'Twas The Night Before Christmas" also came along for the journey.

"It will be the night before Christmas before I get this back where it belongs, and that is if I'm lucky." Bess laughed. "Before I have anymore mixups, I'm going to take you lot upstairs." She picked up Lydia's presents. "Here's the doll's shawl. --- Hmh --- Where's the other one? I must have left it behind." She put a note on her pad to check for it. "I'm keeping one and Bruce can have the other nutcracker." She put the regal king in the bag and stood the wooden soldier on the coffee table. She opened the book and admired the inscription, "Evan, you won't believe it, but I'll know." She smiled as she picked it up and trotted upstairs to hide her gifts.

Bess hurried back downstairs and plugged in the lights on the mantel. She did enjoy her arrangement, so sat down to bask in its glow. She picked up " 'Twas The Night Before Christmas," glanced over at her parcels laying beside her and picked up the list.

*"Bertie & Artie --- colouring books & crayons"* She glanced at the nutcrackers. "Nutcrackers ---- I hope." She gazed at the tearoom and smiled. *"Nutcrackers"* she wrote down and thought *I must check the other purchases when ----*

She picked up a discarded parcel on the bed and looked inside. Two nutcrackers looked up at her. *I just put them under the bed. --- No, I put one under the bed and the other on on the coffee table. Right?* She immediately looked under the bed. Many parcels lay jammed under the bed. *No, I definitely only put one parcel under the bed.* She looked up.

"Bed? No, living room, I'm supposed to be in the living room not the bedroom." She looked at the four-poster bed. It finally dawned on her. "I'm back in Fetter Lane."

Bess sat back down on the bed and noticed the list. She shrugged *I might as well finish my list here.* After completing the list, she separated the presents into individual piles, placing them in the wardrobe and stuffing some under the bed. She found the other shawl for the doll and laid it on the bed beside " 'Twas The Night Before Christmas." She picked up the book and laid it on the dresser.

"Thank goodness, now you are where you belong." She smiled as she lovingly touched its jacket.

One last look around, she noticed Lottie's Christmas card laying in the cookie sheet. She opened the card, read the verse and signed it. Just then, she heard a noise coming from Jo's room. She slipped the card in her pocket and felt for some coins, nestled deep within.

"Jo," she shouted as she popped her head out the door. "I've got your money for you."

"Good morning, Bess. --- Money?"

"Yes, the eight pennies I owe you for the books." Bess reached down and brought out a shilling.

"Give it to me later. I do not have any change on me. I'll bring the change home later. I do not want you going out without any money in your pocket. See you later."

"Ah, there you are, Miss Bess. I thought you'd be sleeping after our evening out on the town," said Tom cheerfully.

"Good morning to you too, Mr. Evans."

"I'll come home at noon so I can deflect my sister, while you sneak out in your finest to assist Ivan Williams with his Christmas deliveries." Tom gave her a wink. "Don't forget your cap."

*Cap? I forgot all about my job this afternoon. I wouldn't let you know, but bless you, Thomas Evans,* she said to herself and said to him, "Thank you, Tom, I'll be ready to go on my appointed rounds." They walked down the stairs, and at the front door she gave him a parting thought, "Hey, Tom, --- you cut a mean rug."

"You're welcome. ---- I think?" answered Tom. He doffed his cap and headed out the door muttering, "A mean rug? Hmh."

The familiar sound of the kettle beckoned her near, so she made her way to the kitchen. At the door, she looked up to her left and read:

"Come oh come ye tea thirsty restless ones.
The kettle boils, bubbles and sings musically."
------ Rabindranath Tagore

"I'm coming," sang Bess as she entered the kitchen.

"Bess, luv, I thought I 'eard ye. My, yer in a good mood t'is mornin'."

"Good morning, Lottie. Is that tea I smell steeping?" Bess sniffed.

"Sit ye down an' I'll join ye."

"Finish your baking; I'll see to the tea." Bess took two cups off the shelf and poured the tea into the cups, being careful to avoid too many tea leaves.

"Yer gettin' pretty good at pourin' tea. I may 'ave to 'ire ye." Lottie laughed. She put the currant buns in the oven and walked over to the table. " 'Ow did ye enjoy t' dance? 'Twas a grand time."

"Yes, I did enjoy myself, especially after I got the hang of the dances."

"Hang? --- Aye, t' way they swing us around, t'is looks like we're 'angin' from their arms." She laughed.

"Yes, it took me some time to figure out the moves. One cannot just step into a dance. For instance, could you do the twist or jive right away?"

"Of course I could, luv. Why I did t' gallop an' t' Roger de Coverley after just one turn around t' floor. ---- Wot's t' twist 'n' jive?"

"I'll show you one of these days."

"Aye, I'd like to know wot ye dance in America, so when I go visit ye, I will fit right in."

"I'm sure you'd have no trouble with the Macarena."

"Of course not, I pride meself on me meringues an' me lemon meringue pie. T'is delicious, so Mr. Brown says. I shall bake ye one." Lottie puffed out her ample chest.

Bess could hardly stop laughing. She reached in her pocket and pulled out an envelope. " I almost forgot, I have something for you."

"For me?"

"Open it, Lottie."

With eager fingers, Lottie opened the sealed envelope and took out the card. "Oh, a Christmas card!" Her hand trembled as she studied the card. "Oh, t'is beautiful. Look t'is a cup 'n' saucer. --- Oh my, me first Christmas card." She opened the card and read the inscription:

"Lottie,
Merry Christmas Time
'Tis time to share precious moments
and have a cup of tea,
Just you and me.

*Thank you for your kind and generous spirit.*
*Love always,*
*Bess xx000"*

"Oh, Bess." Lottie wiped the tears from her eyes and gave Bess a hug. "Wot a perfect Christmas present. I shall cherish it always. Thank ye, luv."

"You are most welcome. Now enough of this --- You're going to make me cry." Bess laughed instead and wiped a tear off Lottie's cheek. "What can I do for you?"

"Yer quite right. T'is time fer business. There won't be any money made sittin' 'ere." Lottie got up and positioned her card high up on a shelf out of harm's way. She took one more glance at it. "Oh, t'is beautiful." She smiled. "I've sum 'olly sittin' outside t' back door. Would ye bring it in? I want to put sprigs of it on t' tables an' around t' tearoom."

Bess opened the door and found a huge bundle laying under the overhang of the roof. "Ouch!" she hollered as her hands scooped up the branches.

"Nasty little buggers, but once ye get 'em on t' tables, no one's goin' touch 'em, so their worth t' pain. --- 'Ere, I'll 'elp ye." She grabbed the ones escaping from Bess's grasp.

"Beautiful but deadly." Bess groaned as she sucked her scratched fingers. "Look at all these red berries." She picked up the empty vases, standing on a side table and started filling them with the sharp foliage. "Ouch!"

"Be careful, I don't want me pianist's 'ands to be scarred. It wouldn't look good fer business, especially fer our genteel patrons." Lottie laughed. "Mrs. Pennycroft would be 'orrified if she knew 'er 'olly was responsible fer disfigurin' 'er favourite pianist's 'ands. 'Twas Mrs. Pennycroft's driver who brought 'em yesterday afternoon."

"Allen? I'm sorry I missed him."

"Now, don't ye be gettin' too friendly wit t' 'elp. Artists don't mix wit' servants."

234

"Why, Lottie, I'm surprised at you. You, who invite Lily, the flower woman and Sam, the chimney sweeper, to tea."

"They's business people not servants."

"I see, ---- different strokes for different folks."

"Summit like that."

They both kept busy, Lottie preparing more goodies, and Bess putting the arrangements on the table. Bess artistically arranged the extra sprigs of holly around the room: on the counter, mantel, piano and window sills. Amazingly, she still had a couple of sprigs left over, so she rushed upstairs and placed them on the mantel in the parlour. Coming back down the stairs, she heard the door jingle. To her surprise, two gentlemen stood in the doorway.

"May I seat you, gentlemen?"

"No thank you, miss. Is Mrs. Morton here?" asked a white bearded man in a brown tweed overcoat. He took off his top hat and smiled at Bess.

Just at that moment, Lottie came rushing into the room, brushing flour off her apron. "Oh, Mr. Weatherby, Mr. Dinsdale, how nice to see you."

"Mrs. Morton, it is always our pleasure. We know you are a busy woman, so we shall get right to the point. We are collecting funds for the poor."

"Aye, I didn't think you were coming for tea. One minute please." Lottie turned and went back into the kitchen.

"You are the young lady from America, I presume," said the gentleman with the handlebar moustache. "My wife comes here quite regularly and is very impressed with your musical abilities."

"Mr. Dinsdale and I go door to door at Christmas, endeavouring to give our unfortunate poor a bit of the Christmas spirit. From generous donations from people like Mrs. Morton, we are able to give blankets, clothes and food to many."

"Ah, Mrs. Morton, Mr. Weatherby was telling the young lady of our Christmas Charitable Door To Door Collection For The Poor."

"Put this in your purse, kind sirs. Now don't look at Bess like that. Like the poor, she too has come on some hard times and is unable to give you any money. Perhaps, she will come with us on Christmas morning and help serve the poor."

"You could play the pianoforte, while the poor partake of our charitable meal?"

"Why yes, I could certainly do that." Bess released the last coins in her pocket.

"Thank you, ladies. Until Saturday." They doffed their hats and then tapped them lightly onto their heads. "And, Merry Christmas, ladies."

"Merry Christmas," returned Lottie. The door closed and she turned to Bess. "Their fancy coats ar' worth more than t' poor's lodgin's; if 'em's lucky enough to 'ave 'em. --- An' they think they're doin' summit wonderful fer t' poor. One day a year, i'nn't enough." She shrugged her shoulders. "I suppose t'is better than nut'in'. --- Poor blighters." She sighed and then brightened up. "Speakin' of 'ard times, ye best go see if yer luggage 'as cum."

Before Bess could put her crossed finger behind her back, the door jingled and in walked the first parched ladies of the day. 'Twas a busy morning with many shoppers coming in to revive themselves before continuing on or returning home. At first glance, the regulars appeared miffed with the strangers taking over their holy space, but soon settled in nearby tables. They viewed the newcomers with curious glances and then carried on their bits of gossip with their friends. Surprisingly, a number of gentlemen accompanied their wives and sent appreciative looks towards Bess and Lottie.

More than one gentleman was overheard to say, "Mighty fine scones and the music most pleasant, indeed. Perhaps, we should see if the young lady could play at one of our dinners, my dear."

Most of the customers had left, when in charged Artie, brushing past a lady with her hands full of parcels. "Young man, where are your manners?" squawked the lady as she readjusted her load.

"Sorry, ma'am." Artie doffed his cap and rushed to the piano-forte. "Cum quick, Miss Bess." He grabbed her arm.

"What is it, Artie?"

"Miss Bess, please cum quick. I don't want ye to miss 'em." He took her hand and dragged her out the door, brushing past the same lady.

"Well, I never." She pursed her lips and shuffled her poor parcels.

"Artie!"

"Listen, Miss Bess. --- 'Ear 'em?"

Bess listened intently and finally heard a faint ringing of church bells.

"T'is t' Bells of St. Giles in the Fields, they is. 'Em ring ev'ry Thursday at noon. I wanted ye to 'ear 'em cause 'em's just up t' street from me 'ouse. Me dad don't let me go up there cause t'is a bad area, but I still like to 'ear t' bells. --- Do ye like 'em, Miss Bess?" Artie looked up at her with an expectant look of approval.

"Yes, Artie, they are lovely. Perhaps someday, we can go look at the church together."

"I'd like that, Miss Bess. --- Just me 'n' ye?"

"Yes, just you and me."

"I 'ave to go 'ome now. Me mum's expectin' me." He squeezed her hand and ran down Fetter Lane. "See ye tonight at t' pantomime."

"Young lady, what are you doing out here without a coat? You'll catch your death," asked a male voice doing a poor imitation of a female.

She spun around to see Tom walking down the lane with a big smile on his cheeky face and wagging his finger. "Tom, you devil, Artie wanted me to hear the Bells of St. Giles in the Fields. --- And for your information, you do a poor imitation of your sister."

"Ah --- but you did recognize it was my dear sister I was imi-tating. Do I need to say more? Huh?" Tom gave her a smug look.

Before Bess could come up with a comeback, a bell rang loudly. They both turned and saw Sadie and Jim pull up alongside.

"Miss Bess, --- Tom, --- I just won t' goose. After months, no years of puttin' in me name fer t' draw, I finally win t' Christmas goose. Mary will be so excited."

"Congratulations, Jim. --- What time's dinner?" Tom patted Jim on the back and shook his hand. "You've got one over on old Lily now."

"Aye, that I 'ave. -- But -- ye know, I'm goin' ax Lily 'n' Sam to share t' goose wit' us."

"What a nice gesture, Jim. Lily will be so happy." Bess smiled.

"Ye best get inside, Miss Bess, before ye catch yer death," advised Jim.

"See, what did I tell you?" Tom winked as he wagged his finger at her.

"We best be on our way, Sadie 'n' me, fer there's still deliveries to be done --- an' I want to go in an' see Mr. Brown to reserve me oven fer t' goose."

"What did Jim mean by reserving an oven?" Bess asked Tom.

"Most people don't have ovens in their lodgings, so at Christmas, they pay the baker to roast their bird for them."

"Oh, I never imagined they wouldn't have ovens. --- What about stoves?"

"Well, they either cook on a pot bellied stove or in their fireplace."

"My, my." Bess looked astonished.

"Bess, don't you think it's about time you changed into Ben?"

"Ben? Oh dear. What time it it?"

He pulled out his pocket watch. "It's half-past twelve and I want to be out of here in twenty minutes. Off with you. I'll keep my dear sister occupied till then." He opened the door and gave her the all clear sign. "Don't forget your cap and don't say much. We don't want Ivan asking questions later. Do we, Ben?"

Back in her room, she opened the wardrobe. On the hanger, she spied her familiar attire, trousers and warm sweater. Having become quite good at removing her dress, she quickly slipped out of it and into her comfortable jeans. Bending over to lace up her runners, she heard a loud ringing. *Jim is still celebrating,* she smiled. Straightening up, she found herself back in her living room with the ringing still blaring in her ears.

"Oh, the telephone." She picked it up. "Hello?"

"Bess, I swear you're going deaf. I let it ring ten times."

"Lydia --- Sorry, I was occupied."

"Aren't you always these days. I won't keep you, I know you have a busy schedule."

"Well actually --- " Bess looked at the clock, "I only have five minutes."

"If I didn't know you better, I'd think you were giving me the brush off. However --- I'll be brief. I'm just doing the final arrangements for Christmas dinner."

"Do you need me to cook the goose, since you have no oven?"

"Bess, where have you been? The oven was fixed two weeks ago. --- And, what's this about a goose? You turkey! Naturally we're having turkey. It's been years since we cooked a goose --- literally that is. Besides, where would one find one these days? --- Mind you --- everywhere you look there's Canada Geese waddling and pooping all over the parks. Hmh --- Come to think of it ---- maybe a goose would be a good idea."

"Lydia! ----- The reason for your call?"

"My, my, it's so unlike me to digress."

"Yes, Lydia."

"I just wanted to remind you to bring the cranberry sauce and the Christmas pudding."

"I haven't forgot. In fact, I bought the brandy this morning, so we'll have a flamin' good puddin'."

"Always prepared, that's my Bess. We'll eat about four on Christmas Day, but come early. You know, I can always use the help." She laughed. "Just kidding, but come early, so we can open our presents first."

"Bye, Lydia."

"Ta ta for now." The phone went dead.

"Darn the cranberries. --- I forgot them. Maybe I have a jar in the cupboard." Bess looked at the time *12:48* and ran to the cupboard.

No cranberry sauce in sight, but another jar caught her attention. She lifted the cream coloured paste from the shelf and the light went on. *Perfect, now, where is that recipe book?* she puzzled. Rummaging through her recipe box, she sighed when she pulled out the small booklet on sourdough. With one minute to spare, she rushed into the hall closet, pulled out her boots and ran back to the mantel.

"Please don't let me let Tom and Ivan down," she begged as she concentrated with all her might on the tearoom.

"Bess --- Bess, come on. Lottie's gone out to the shed."

"Oh, Tom --- Right ---- Good ---- I'm coming --- I just have to put on my --- " looking down, she saw her boots in her hand and continued, "boots." Her other hand still held the jar of sourdough starter, so she put it on the dresser, grabbed the cap, lying on the dresser, her coat and ran out the door.

Out of breath, she puffed as she closed the front door, narrowly escaping Lottie, who she heard bang the back door shut. Out in the cold, she put on her cap, tucked in her blond hair and buttoned up her coat.

Clop, Clop.

"Whoa! --- Aye, Ben, my man, you're right on time. Hop up!"

Ivan moved over and Bess looked up at him. *And, here I thought Lydia's minivan was high above the ground,* she muttered as she attempted to hop up. *Hop up ---- that's a laugh.*

"Give me your hand, mate. You'll soon get the hang of it."

*If I don't, I'll be hanging from it, mate,* thought Bess as she clumsily climbed up.

With a quick flick of the reins, off they went down Fetter

Lane. Riding on a carriage in the daylight provided Bess with a completely different view of the streets of London. The narrow side streets and alleys, covered in shadow, still looked sinister, but they did not trigger her imagination to deeds of evil. From her vantage point, she saw a city bustling with activity. Street vendors parked their carts along the curb: selling fish, vegetables, flowers, --- Performers darted in front of their carriage, and when lucky, drawing a crowd on the sidewalk as they juggled balls and sang and danced for pennies. Turning the corner, they came across a group of carolers, bundled in warm coats and muffs. They inspired Ivan to sing a few carols. His beautiful voice drowned out the sounds of shouting, horses' hoofs upon the cobblestones and the bells and whistles of passing carriages.

"Whoa, Billy!" Ivan pulled the reins tight and stopped at an entrance to a small circular street. "Right, Ben. Off we go." He alighted from the carriage and headed to the back. "Quickly, Ben, bach."

Bess looked down at the far distant ground and dangled her legs over the edge of the seat. With a deep breath, she closed her eyes and jumped down. Fortunately, Ivan occupied in the back of the carriage, did not notice her landing. Brushing off the snow from her bruised knees, she slowly made her way along the dark-green cab to the back door. Ivan filled her arms with parcels and boxes.

"Ben, bach, the two top parcels go to number eleven and the last three boxes, number six. They're already paid for so just deliver them. I'll turn old Billy around and meet you back across the street." Ivan gave Bess a hearty slap on the back. "Don't you be talking to the pretty young maids. We've got lots more to deliver." He gave a hearty laugh and closed the back door.

Thankful she had her boots on, Bess struggled through the slushy walkway. At number eleven, a small gate greeted her which caused her some distress. She balanced her load with one arm and struggled with the latch with her vacant hand. The deed accomplished, she made her way up the slippery staircase. As she reached the top landing, her foot slipped on an icy patch and down she came, landing at the bottom of the door. Before she could get up and retrieve her scattered parcels, the door opened.

"Yer a fine one --- cumin' to t' front door an' spillin' t' parcels all over. T'is a good thing madam didn't see ye. I saw ye cumin' through t' gate, strugglin' even then wit' t' parcels. Yer lucky I got to t' door before ye rang t' doorbell, cause if madam 'eard t' bell, she'd surely ax who were there an' I'd 'ave to tell 'er it were t' clumsy delivery boy." The young maid grabbed the parcels before Bess could stand up straight. "Off wit' ye." The door slammed in her face.

Along with her bruised ego, she added a bruised shin to her person. Clutching the three boxes close to her chest, she gingerly walked down the icy stairs and muttered, "Well, maybe madam should get the man servant to clean off the stairs if madam wants her parcels delivered in one piece." She straightened her back and marched through the open gate to number six.

Just as she reached number six, a carriage pulled up and a woman tapped on the window. Bess turned to see the driver jump down and open the cab door.

"Wendell, fetch the boxes from the young man." She pointed towards Bess. "What good timing. Wendell take them around the back. I don't want the children to see them. --- Young man, ---- come here." She opened her velvet bag and gave Bess two coins. "Share with the driver. ---- And Merry Christmas."

Bess tightened her fist around the coins. "Why, thank you, madam." Running back towards the delivery carriage, she passed number eleven. "See that, madam, -- my first tip. ---- And Merry Christmas to you too."

The green, delivery carriage with the words "Williams & Sons" boldly printed on the side, stood waiting for her. Feeling quite smug, she hopped up onto the seat and off they went. She handed Ivan one of the coins.

"What's this for?"

"T'is yer tip," she whispered.

"What did you say, lad? --- Speak up --- Ah, tip did you say?" He laughed. "Good for you, Ben, bach. Keep it. I get paid from the stores for delivering their parcels, but thanks for offering. You're a good lad, Ben, bach."

Over the course of the afternoon, another dozen or more stops, the descent and ascent became easier and Bess quickly learned to head for the servants entrance. Soon her pockets jingled with pennies. When coins were not forthcoming, a piece of fruit or an edible Christmas goody exchanged hands, which Ivan did not refuse.

"Aye, there's Alwyn, the milkmaid. We'll stop and get some milk to have with our mince pies. Whoa, Billy!" The carriage stopped in front of a cart carrying containers of milk.

A young lady with rosy cheeks looked up at them. "Aye, Ivan, bach, nice to see you." Her smile lit up her face. "And who is this young lad?"

"Alwyn, my luv, don't be getting any ideas." Ivan laughed. "This is Tom's mate, Ben."

"Ben, nice to meet you. Ivan and I knew each other in Cardiff. My dad runs a dairy farm nearby. I came to London to sell the milk, and who should I run into? In fact, Ivan nearly ran me over. If it weren't for Billy warning him, he would have run me over. The Williams Brothers think they own the streets with their big, fancy delivery wagons and their name written in fancy letters. Why back in Wales, they're just ones of thousands of Williams, no better, no worse. Now take a name like Evans, why just ask Tom, bach."

"Hush, girl, why there's more Evans' in Wales than sheep."

"I haven't seen Tom lately. I hear he's sweet on an American lady. Please tell me it's not true." Alwyn pouted.

"Aye, so I've heard, but I've not met her. Have you, Ben?"

Bess choked on her pastry and coughed up, "No."

"I'll be seeing him at football next week, so I'll ask him for you since your so interested."

Alwyn poked Ivan in the arm and said, "I was only asking, Ivan, luv."

"Come on, Ben, bach, let's get a move on. We've got a couple more deliveries. I don't want to be late getting back. Tom's nephew, Bertie is performing in the pantomime tonight, and I promised the lad I'd be there."

They had only gone a short distance, when they stopped in front of Ashleigh Terrace. A neat row of red brick houses, encased in four-foot high, split-rail fencing, flanked both sides of the narrow cobblestone street. A man with a long pole entered the deserted street and began lighting the gas streetlamps. The temperature dropped a degree as each lamp stole the daylight. They both hopped off the carriage, and Bess ran to the back, rubbing her hands together to keep warm.

"Ben, we don't need to open the door, the boxes are on top."

"Huh?"

"Being a little fellow, you probably couldn't see the boxes stacked up there. No mind, your size is going to come in handy now. You're going to be part of my human ladder. Give us a foot and I'll hoist you up. You can hand the boxes down."

Bess looked straight up the side of the carriage and groaned *what have I got myself into or onto, this time? Doesn't he know I'm a middle --- mature woman?*

"One, two --- three ---- up you go, Ben, bach."

"Thanks, Ivan," she muttered as she ejected into the air. She grasped the iron railing around the top of the cab and clung to the cold metal. Gingerly moving on all fours, she handed the boxes to Ivan. "Oh my gosh!" she muttered as she looked past Ivan's open arms. The hard ground lay far below.

"Did you say something, Ben, bach?"

As Bess cleared the top of the boxes, the carriage began to sway. She crouched down on her stomach and shrieked, "Oh Lord, I'm not meant for this world."

"Steady, Billy. ---- Almost done. ---- Swing your legs over the edge. I'll grab you," shouted Ivan.

"Easy for you to say," she muttered. Reluctantly, she moved her

244

spreadeagled form over the side. She stopped to calm her shattered nerves when the rocking became too much.

"Let go of the railing, Ben, bach."

*Didn't he say he played football? Oh no, that's English soccer, not American football. They don't use their hands. --- Oh, if only he played baseball,* she mused as she let go.

"See, I told you I'd catch you. Now deliver these boxes to number seventeen, twenty-two and --- let's see--" Ivan pulled out a piece of crunched paper from his pocket. "Aye, number fourteen."

The night was drawing in quickly so Bess used the gaslights to pick out the house numbers, *number twelve ---- thirteen.*

"Wot yer lookin' fer, mate?" A young voice startled Bess.

She looked around to see a young boy and girl sitting on the fence. When she approached them, she noticed their dirty faces and tattered clothes. A sole dangled from one of the girl's boots. The other boot had no laces.

"Yer lost?" asked the girl.

"Number fourteen?"

"There 'tis, mate." The boy pointed his bare finger through his worn glove. "Give it to me, I'll take it in fer ye. T'is a vicious dog livin' there. 'E knows me."

"Thanks anyway, mate ---but I 'ave to deliver it, personal like," replied Bess.

"Good luck. ---- Ye can't say we's dinn't warn ye." They both laughed.

As Bess put her hand up to ring the door, a large woman in an apron opened the door and brandished a rolling pin. "Off wit' ye, scalliwags. 'Ow many times 'ave I told ye not to lay about? --- Blimey ---An' wot do ye want? --- Oh, yer deliverin' t' parcels. Madam said ye'd be cumin." She reached in her pocket and gave Bess a couple of pennies, took the box and slammed the door shut.

"Sees, I told ye there were a vicious dog 'ere." The boy giggled and stuck his tongue out at Bess who returned the gesture. The two urchins ran down the street.

When she finished her deliveries on Ashleigh Terrace, Bess found the two urchins hanging around the back of the carriage. "Nice wagon yer got. Can we 'ave a ride?"

"Sorry, mate, but 'ere." Bess reached in her pocket and pulled out two pennies. "That's fer 'elpin' me." She handed them each a coin.

"Anytime, mate." They grinned and took off before Bess could possibly change her mind.

"Poor mites. They'll get you everytime. They respect an older mate who will stand up to them, --- in their native tongue – so to speak." Ivan laughed as he untied the reins. "That's why they were hanging around the carriage --- to have one more jaw with you. --- Come on, Billy, let's go home."

The carriage turned onto Fetter Lane. "Ye can let me off here."

"Right then, Ben, bach. Thanks for the help. I enjoyed your company, even though your a man of few words. Anyway, actions speak louder than words." Bess started to slide down to the ground when Ivan tapped her shoulder. "Here's a shilling for your time. Thanks again, Ben, bach. ---- Nosta!" Ivan shouted as he and Billy headed up the lane.

"Nosta to you too, Ivan. --- Hmh, I think that means good night. --- I hope so."

"T'is ye, Bess?" shouted Lottie from the kitchen as the door jingled.

"Yes, Lottie --- Give me five minutes and I'll join you," shouted Bess as she ran up the stairs, taking them two at a time so Lottie wouldn't see her in her working attire.

Without encountering anyone en route, she breathed a sigh of relief and closed her bedroom door. *I'd better get out of these clothes.*

"Luv, I fergot to tell ye," said Lottie as she knocked on the door.

Bess opened the door and poked her head out. "Yes?"

"Yer only got 'alf 'n' 'our to get ready. We're goin' to t' pantomime.

T' lads ar' in t' play, so we mustn't be late. --- No need to dress up, t'is only at their school. We'll walk over, so bundle up."

"Yes, Mum." Bess shut the door and opened the wardrobe. As she took her dress off the hanger, she spied Lydia's yellow dress. "Darn, I forgot to take it back. ---- Shoot."

She quickly changed, put on her boots, grabbed the evening dress and ran down the stairs. She heard Lottie in her bedroom, so slowed her gait to a tiptoe until her feet reached the lower stairwell. Off on a run, she flung the front door open, caught the bell before impact and tore down the lane. At the haberdashery, she knocked on Lydia's door, but no one answered. She peeked through the window and noticed a closed sign hanging in the corner.

"Darn."

"Can I help you?"

Bess spun around to see Lawrence Taylor leaning over the railing. "I guess I missed Lydia. I wanted to return the dress she lent me."

"Miss Bess,--- I didn't recognize you. Here, I'll take it. Lydia's gone to the theatre. She's always off socializing, not like us married folks."

"Actually, I must be off too. Thank Lydia very much for her kind gesture. I appreciate it very much."

"I'll tell her. ---- I don't want to keep you.---- You young folk are always in a hurry. -- Oh, to be single again." He gave a hearty Taylor laugh. "Only kidding."

Bess said goodbye and rushed back to the tearoom. *My gosh, I'm running around here just like at home. Hmm? --- And people say our lives are too busy these days. --- Little do they know. It's never changed.* Out of breath, she entered the tearoom.

"Who's there? Mr. Brown, t'is ye?" Lottie's voice became louder. "Oh, Bess, where's Mr. Brown?" Lottie looked around the room as she stood on the bottom step. "I thought I 'eard t' door jingle. Must be 'earin' things."

The door opened and in stepped Mr. Brown. "Ladies, are you ready?"

Back outside went a breathless Bess. The rapid breathing caused a great cloud of vapour to follow her. The two ladies, each grabbed an arm and the trio walked down the lane. A couple of blocks down, they turned a corner, and moments later another. Fifteen minutes later, they reached their destination.

A tall, brooding building peered down at them. *Typical school,* shivered Bess. Through its shadowy recesses, Bess saw a light flicker. Sounds of laughter escaped through the stone walls. As the light grew stronger, they quickened their pace. Mr. Brown grabbed the iron handle and the large, wooden door creaked open. Children ran everywhere; adults lagged behind, while voices gave fruitless demands to squeals of laughter. Inside the large hall, a young boy ushered them to a row of wooden seats.

"Oh --- there's Tom ---- You hoo -- Sean." Lottie waved and made her way to the seats, the fellows held for them. "Jo, did ye 'ave any trouble wit' their costumes?" Lottie turned to Bess. "Jo came earlier an 'elped t' teacher wit t' costumes. Artie's tail okay?" Jo nodded and they both chuckled. "Don't sit 'ere, luv. T'is a seat by Tom."

They all sat down and in walked Ivan. "Sorry I'm late. By the time I got Billy settled, it was going on half-past six."

"No worries, mate. Saved a seat for you. Say how did it go with old Ben?" asked Tom. He winked at Bess who lowered her head.

"Aye, now he's a funny, little bloke. Never says a word. A hard worker though --- well he tries." Ivan broke into a hearty laugh. "For an Oxford rower, he's not too agile." Ivan could hardly contain his laughter. "You should have seen him hanging on to the top of the carriage. His poor hands were white from gripping the railing. I felt sorry for the little bugger. ---- But, he never complained. Generous too. ---- Why he offered to share his tips with me. Not many lads do that. To make him feel good, I did take some of the sweets."

"Not too agile? You don't say. That surprises me." Tom laughed and nudged Bess in the ribs, while poor Bess tried to disappear into the woodwork. "Tell me more."

"He got back at a couple of street urchins. Stuck his tongue right back at them. As you said, 'He's a feisty little bugger.' "

"Where are my manners? Ivan, I'd like you to meet Miss Bess. --- Miss Bess, -- Ivan." Tom winked at Bess who kicked his leg with her heavy boot. "Ouch! Definitely a feisty little --" He gave another wink; Bess graciously accepted by sticking out her tongue.

"Pleased to meet you, miss. You're the young lady from America." Ivan reached out to take her hand. She glanced at him, smiled and lowered her head. "Have I met you before?" You do look familiar. Funny ---"

Saved by the school bell. A stern looking schoolmarm rang the brass bell several times, until the buzz from the audience faded. She parted the centre of the dark-blue curtains another couple feet and in perfect diction announced, "Ladies and gentlemen, children ---- Parker Street Primary presents 'Dick Whittington.'"

She groped her way back through the curtain and moved faster and faster off the stage as the curtain followed her in close pursuit. Immediately a young boy,carrying a stick over his shoulder, entered the stage. On the end of the stick, a small bundle of cloth bobbed up and down as the boy marched towards the centre of the stage.

"Aye, we ar' 'ere," shouted the boy.

"Here," corrected the schoolmarm's voice from behind the curtain.

The boy looked around. "Right ---- Aye, we ar' here." A broad smile broke out upon his little face. The audience chuckled.

"It's Bertie!" shouted Bess and promptly put her hand over her mouth.

"We're 'ere --- here," repeated the boy loudly and looked behind.

On all fours, a fuzzy creature stumbled onto the stage. His tail kept getting in the way. In frustration, he got up on his hind legs, picked up his tail and ran across to the boy. The audience burst out laughing.

"Where ye bin, Cat?" scolded the boy. "Cum on. --- We've cum from Gloucester an 'ere ---- here we ar's in London." A bell rang. "Listen, Cat.--- 'Em's Bow Bells. Ye can 'ear 'em all over London, so they say."

"Meooow!"

The boy and the cat exited the stage to the clapping of the smiling audience.

As they left the school, Bertie ran up to Bess and took her hand while Artie took the other one. All smiles, Bertie said, "Did ye like t' pantomime, Miss Bess? --- 'Ow about when I became t' Lord Mayor of London?"

"You were definitely the best Dick Whittington and Lord Mayor of London I've ever seen."

"'Onest, Miss Bess?"

"Honest, Bertie." She smiled and lowered her head toward Artie. "And a most handsome cat I've never seen. You played your part so well, I didn't recognize you, Artie."

Artie looked fondly up at Bess, exposing his charcoal whiskers. "Thank ye, Miss Bess. I spent a lot of time watchin' t' kittens, --- to get it right. Did ye like me meooows?"

"Purrfect, Artie." They all laughed.

They said their goodbyes to the Doyles and headed back home. "The Lotatea Shoppe" greeted them with shelter from the cold night air and the pleasant smells of baked goodies yet to come.

"Stay fer tea, Sean, Mr. Brown," said Lottie as she put her coat on the hook and made her way to the kitchen. "We'll 'ave our tea in 'ere. T'is warmer. Tom, stoke the fire."

"Aye, sister dear, I'm doing it as you command."

The men moved the tables closer to the fire, while Tom added more coal. The chill soon left their bodies. The platter, overflowing with food, arrived from the kitchen. They devoured every last crumb and washed it down with numerous cups of hot tea.

"That was good. I didn't realize how hungry I was," proclaimed Mr. Brown. He pushed his chair away, stretched his legs and rubbed his stomach. "Mrs. Morton, if you keep feeding me like this, I shall be as rotund as Basil Pepper."

"Never, Mr. Brown. Ye'd 'ave to eat 'ere ev'ry meal to catch up to 'im an' then sum." She blushed when she realized what others may think she implied. She quickly changed the direction of the conversation. "Besides, t'is all ale 'n' spirits sloshin' inside 'im."

"You're right there. Everyday I see Basil passing the bakery right on the dot of noon. Lord knows he isn't going for a walk," said Mr. Brown.

"Robert says he is his best customer," spoke up Jo.

"Aye, old Basil's there whenever I'm in the pub," confirmed Sean.

"T'is makes me fat just thinkin' of 'im. --- Tell ye wot, let's do sum dancin'."

"Dancing?"

"Aye, Bess told me about sum new dances they do in America. 'Ow about it Bess?"

Bess checked out the group, who except for Lottie, looked like they were ready for bed, not the dance floor. "I do think the dances I mentioned are a bit too energetic, especially after we just ate."

"Oh, Miss Bess, can't we? I'm not too full," jumped up Bertie.

"Perhaps yer right, Bess, besides 'tis Bertie's bedtime."

"Oh, Mum."

"Tell you what, Bertie, why don't I play the music and maybe tomorrow night we can try the dancing?"

"Good idea," The others moaned in unison.

"This song will be the easiest to learn, but by the tempo, I think you will agree it is best tackled on a light stomach." She flexed her fingers and proceeded to play a rousing version of "The Twist." "Anyone want to get up and dance?" Bess asked. She

251

turned around to see twelve, motionless wide eyes staring back at her.

"Aye, ye were very wise to delay t' lesson. Even tomorrow might be a bit soon," stated Lottie.

Dead silence prevailed for what seemed a lifetime until they burst out laughing. Wisely, Sean and Mr. Brown got up and put on their coats before anyone changed their mind.

"Aye, tomorrow then. --- Good night and thank ye for tea," said Sean as he neared the front door. "Good job, laddie. Ye did us proud. --- Good night, Jo."

"Hold up, Sean," hailed Mr. Brown. "I'll walk with you. --- Good night --- and --- ah— interesting music, Bess."

"Tom, luv, will ye take Bertie out back before 'e goes to bed?"

"Come on, Bertie, old man. We'll leave the women to clean up." Tom herded Bertie through the kitchen and out the back door. "Burr, it's cold out here. Don't be long, mate."

The three women cleaned up the dishes, while Tom put the tables and chairs back. By the time they climbed upstairs, the days activities caught up with them. The thought of stretching out in bed, overwhelmed them. Bess plopped down on the bed, bent over and pulled off her boots.

"That's better." She wiggled her toes and let her feet rest on the carpet. "Oh, the warmth of a plush carpet." Her neck jerked upwards. "Mr. Spider, t'is ye I see before my weary eyes?" Mr. Spider ignored her ramblings and nestled into his web. "Sure, easy for you to do. ---- Okay, I'm jealous." The darkness through the skylight alerted her. "What time is it? I'd love to join you, but I'd better get supper on. Evan won't want to eat out two nights in a row."

Bess lifted her boots off her lap and deposited them in the closet. She snatched up her runners and headed for the kitchen. En route, she plugged in the Christmas lights. *I do love the lights. Too bad they don't have them in Olde London. Oh well, what they don't know, they don't miss. --- Peace of mind; that's a good thing.*

Fifteen minutes later, the chicken, accompanied by potatoes

and turnips, roasted in the oven. While cleaning up the counter, Bess came across her abandoned, plum pudding recipe. *I'd better measure out the raisins and currants,* she reminded herself.

Rinsed and sufficiently dried, the fruit went into a large bowl.

"I'd better keep you singing a sweet song," she said to her captive audience as she opened the bottle of sherry. "One for you and one for me. -- We'll both be singing a sweet song." Bess laughed, took a sip and poured the rest over the dried fruit.

"Whoa, whoa,--- I heard it through the grapevine. --- Honey, honey. Y -- a--h!" "That should keep you happy and plump. ---- Yah, yah ----"

# CHAPTER XV

Christmas Eve: the last day of anticipation, the last day the children desperately try to behave, the last minute shopping, the last minute wrapping, the last minute preparations and the last minute house cleaning.

Bess decided to give the house a quick clean before tackling the Christmas pudding. Fortunately for her, only the Turners would view the house, but still they must wake up to a clean house on Christmas morning, at least until the presents were opened. Evan left early for the office in hopes of getting finished early. They planned a quiet evening at home before heading to midnight service.

The vacuuming done, she headed for the kitchen. She noticed Mr. Spider scurrying into the recesses of the skylight. "You do hate that vacuum, don't you? It must be an hereditary thing. --- Not to worry, it's Christmas."

She sprung the lid from the bowl and breathed in the intoxicating aroma of plump raisins, marinated in sherry. The aroma escaped into the kitchen. On the top shelf of a cupboard, she found the canner and nestled behind, her old heat-proof bowl. Being careful not to drop it, she generously greased the half-egg shaped bowl and set it aside.

Into the mixing bowl, the aromatic spices drifted down upon the the snow-white bed of sifted flour. Careful she did not include unwanted portions of her fingers, Bess grated the carrots. Successful, she tackled the mixing with brute strength, first the sugar and butter, then the eggs, flour and the best for last, the fruit. Her arms ached from the constant turning of the wooden spoon. Finally, she scooped the heavy mixture into the greased bowl and sealed it off from invading moisture. She placed the bowl inside the canner and poured hot water down the interior sides of the canner, being careful not to pour any directly on the top of the bowl. Bess took one last sniff and lowered the lid. She turned on the element and reluctantly cleaned up the mess.

The dreaded deed done, she remembered, "The hard sauce!" Out came the icing sugar. "I knew I left the butter out for a reason. Thank heavens." She flexed her overworked muscles once more, and beat the two ingredients into a smooth paste. "Brandy! --- Yes! --- I'll mix some brandy into it."

She put the finished sauce into the refrigerator which twigged her memory. "Cranberries! Darn I forgot. I'll have to run to the store." She gave the canner a questioning look. "Should I? --- No, I'd better not." She turned off the stove, grabbed the car keys and headed up to the store.

Forty minutes later, cranberries in hand, she cut open the plastic bag and poured the hard, bright red berries into a saucepan. She turned the knob to medium and placed the saucepan on the burner. Twenty minutes later, the cranberries bubbled and the water in the canner gurgled, causing pressure to repeatedly lift the lid. Soon the bowl of pudding started to do "The Percolator Twist."

Bess placed a bunch of Japanese oranges in a decorative Christmas bowl and poured unshelled nuts into a wooden bowl. One in each hand, she headed for the coffee table, but as usual, the mantel drew her attention. "Is old Dickens' London as busy today?" She gazed deeply into the tearoom, expecting an answer.

"Bess! --- Oh, Bess, ---- cum quick. T' postman 'as sumthin' fer ye."

"Ah ---- Yes, I'll be right there." Bess went to open the door, but her hands held bowls of oranges and nuts.

She put them on the dresser, and ran down the stairs holding her skirt well above her knees. At the bottom, she dropped her hands. Her skirt began to float to the floor. Directly in front of her, with his mouth wide open and his eyes riveted at her skirt drifting down to the floor, stood a motionless, Harry Topham.

" 'Arry Topham, don't ye stand there wit' yer mouth open."

"Miss Bess," he blushed, "I have a special delivery for you." He extended his hand.

"Thank you, Harry." Bess took the card. "It's a Christmas post-card." She turned it over. "Look, Lottie, it's from Bertie and Artie."

"The lads came into the post office yesterday. They said you really liked the Christmas postcard, so they pooled their pennies and bought it. I said I'd deliver it, so they wouldn't have to pay for a stamp, but they wanted a stamp on it. They said you liked the stamp as much as the card. I said I'd special deliver it today so you'd get it in time for Christmas."

"Why I never. --- T' lads ar' always surprisin' me."

"What a perfect Christmas present," choked Bess as she turned the card over and over.

"A cup of tea, 'Arry?"

"Sorry, Mrs. Morton, I must be off. I still have lots of mail to deliver. -- Merry Christmas ladies."

"Merry Christmas to you and Mrs. Topham." Bess returned the greeting.

"Aye, an' tell Millie I'll need 'er to clean on Monday," shouted Lottie. "Nice young man 'e is. Millie's a lucky girl to 'ave 'im. --- Cum in t' kitchen an' 'ave sum tea, Bess, then ye can 'elp me wit' t' dressin' fer t' turkey. --- Blimey, I fergot to remind 'Arry about t' goose. I 'ope 'e 'asn't fergot to bring it over after three. I can't put in t' oven before three cause I'm still bakin' fer t' tea shoppe. Millie said it were alright, cause they'll be eatin' their Christmas dinner around eight tonight. I wish I 'ad more ovens, I could roast at least three or four more. --- But, at least I 'ave an oven an' a good one at that ---- thanks to Mr. Brown." Lottie began to hum a Christmas carol, whereby, Bess joined in and they burst into song.

Over many carols, they ripped the bread into tiny pieces and spread more sage and thyme on themselves than on the naked bread. Over in the corner, hung the featherless turkey awaiting his fate. Not that he cared, his spirit had long since flown the coop. The coal bucket spilled over with nature's black gold, in preparation for the long hours of cooking ahead.

The door bell jingled and so began another busy day. Miss Rose Water reminded them of her invitation to tea on Boxing Day, while expanding on her niece's progress on the pianoforte. Mrs. Wilmot never stopped talking, for fear her latest gossip would not be heard before the Christmas festivities began. Mrs. Pennycroft acknowledged Bess and actually requested a few Christmas songs. Bess noticed a rhythmic movement under Mrs. P's skirt as Bess played "Jingle Bell Rock."

"Why, you're the quote of the day, Miss Bess --- and a very nice one indeed," said a smiling Miss Rose Water as she returned from paying at the display counter. "Thank you, Mrs. Morton; everything was lovely as usual." She put on her fur hat and gloves. "Merry Christmas, ladies."

Bess's curiosity got the better of her, so she hurried over to the chalkboard. Sure enough, written in Jo's handwriting ----

> "Merry Christmas Time
> T'is time to share precious moments
> And have a cup of tea
> Just you and me." By Bess Nike

Bess felt a soft pat on the arm. "Lovely, dear." Miss Rose Water turned and walked out into the snowy outdoors.

Chubby Mrs. Pepper and her neighbour, Mrs. Fowler got up to leave. They came in together, found a nice table for two by the fireplace and partook of one too many goodies. The two ladies left with rosy cheeks covering their happy faces.

"Now don't ye ferget dinner's at six on Sunday. Cum wit' a good appetite. Mr. Fowler 'as sum choice mutton set aside. Merry Christmas, ladies."

Out waddled the two ladies, and headed up the lane with their bell-shaped skirts swaying, oblivious to everything and everyone, who unfortunately enough got in their way. *They look like two bowling balls making a strike in Fetter Lane,* thought Bess as she watched their backsides. She smiled and closed the door.

"They ar' a sight, ain't they?" chuckled Lottie. "Did I tell ye, we're goin' to t' Fowlers' fer dinner on Boxin' Day? So much goin' on, I can't remember."

"Like you said, so much going on I can't remember myself," replied Bess.

"Mrs. Fowler's a great cook an' very 'ospitable. Unfortunately, 'er father, t' captain is summit else, but still a 'armless owlde pirate. Besides, 'e nods off before 'is yarns get too long." Lottie shook her head and laughed. Turning back towards the tearoom she said, "Ah, Mrs. Pennycroft, you are leaving us?"

"Yes, Mrs. Morton, I have things to do, but thank you for a lovely tea."

"Wait, Mrs. Pennycroft, I'll be right back," said Bess. She high-tailed it up the stairs to her bedroom. Two minutes later and out of breath, she returned giving her a small decorative bag. "Thank you for including me in your Winter Solace Dinner Party."

"You shouldn't have, Miss N-ike."

"It is just a little something I brought from America."

"From America?" quizzed a curious Lottie.

Bess hesitated a moment and slipped her hand behind her back. "Yes, I didn't get a a chance to tell you, I got one of my bags back from the shipping company." She crossed her fingers.

"May I open it now?" asked Mrs. Pennycroft and Bess replied with a nod. She removed the red tissue paper and lifted out a pretty bar of mauve soap. "Oh, how lovely." She breathed in the scent. "Lavender --- and not too strong. It is shaped like a flower. Have you ever seen such soap, Mrs. Morton?"

"Indeed I have not, Mrs. Pennycroft."

"Thank you, my dear." Mrs. Pennycroft's voice cracked. "I shall use it for special occasions. Merry Christmas." She smiled and opened the door.

On hearing the door jingle, Allen came running over to assist her. Bess waved.

"Oh, go on --- give 'im one of t' cakes," ordered Lottie. Before she could change her mind, Bess ran over to the counter and picked up an eccles cake. "Give 'im two an' one of t' mince tarts. T'is Christmas."

Bess put them in a little box and hurried out the door which Lottie just happened to leave open. "Allen! Oh, Allen!" Bess rushed up to him just as he lifted his leg up on the carriage. "Merry Christmas, Allen."

Allen doffed his hat. "Merry Christmas, Bess."

"You old softie." Bess tweaked Lottie's cheek when she entered the warm tearoom.

"Mind t'is only cause it be Christmas." Lottie headed towards the kitchen. "Bess, luv, bring in t' dirty dishes."

Bess no sooner gathered up a tray when the door jingled. Surprised that customers would be coming that late for morning tea or so early for afternoon tea, she turned around. "Mr. Dickens!"

"Merry Christmas, Bess," he regaled, entering the room with his arms around a large box.

"Put your parcel down here." Bess cleared a nearby table of its contents.

He released his grip. "Ah, that's better; not that it is heavy. Most of it is "The Times" crunched up to fill the empty spaces." He removed his hat and gloves.

"Let me hang your coat by the fire, Mr. Dickens."

"Charles --- Bess, --- and yes, thank you. It feels a bit damp; what with all the carriages heaving water up on the sidewalks. Puddles everywhere."

"How about a cup of hot tea? We don't want you to catch your death as Mrs. Morton would say." They both laughed.

"Splendid idea, will you join me?" He looked around the empty room. "Perhaps Mrs. Morton would like to join us since the tellers of tales have departed."

"Nicely put, Charles. Take this table by the fire. I'll be right back." All excited, Bess charged into the kitchen. "Lottie, Mr. Dickens is out front and he wants us to join him for a cup of tea."

"Oh my, don't keep 'im waitin'. Fill up t' teapot an' I'll bring sum scones; just out of t' oven, not five minutes." Lottie brushed off her apron and gathered up the loose strands of hair dangling in her face.

"Mrs. Morton is delighted you are here and will be joining us in a minute." Bess smiled and brought the tray of dishes and teapot to the table.

"Let me take that." Mr. Dickens sprung from his chair and took the tray. "Sit down, my dear. You ladies must be tired. --- A busy time of the year. I do admire women who run a household and a family, let alone ones who run a business. My dear wife, who I love dearly, has a maid, a cook, a manservant and --- " He counted them off on his fingers. "And still she is too exhausted to come calling on the neighbours."

"Ah, good afternoon, Mr. Dickens. And how is Mrs. Dickens?" Lottie put down the plate of scones and a bowl of jam. "Still poorly? Why, I haven't seen her in here for such a long time."

"See." He looked at Bess. "Mrs. Morton, you are looking lovely today as always. I don't know how you manage to be so busy and yet always look so fresh and lovely."

"Flattery will get you anything, Mr. Dickens. Have a scone, right out of the oven." Lottie passed him the plate. A slight blush appeared on her cheeks.

They laughed and chatted for some time until Lottie said, "You will have to excuse me, Mr. Dickens. I must get back in the kitchen. The afternoon crowd will be arriving soon."

"Of course, but before you go into the kitchen to conjure up your magic, I have a little Christmas gift for you." He put his hand in his suit pocket and pulled out a tiny box. "You are a fine lady, Mrs. Morton."

"Oh, Mr. Dickens, ye needn't 'ave." In her excitement, she reverted to her easy manor of speaking. With trembling hands, she lifted the lid. "Oh, t'is lovely. Look, Bess, t'is a teapot." She picked up the brooch. "'T' flowers painted on it, look like t' ones on me big teapot." She pointed to a large, china teapot on the side table. Tears filled her eyes. "Oh, thank ye, Mr. Dickens." Lottie leaned over and gave him a kiss on the cheek.

"Thank you, Mrs. Morton. A fine lady like you deserves a fine, china teapot." They all laughed.

"Merry Christmas, Mr. Dickens --- an' bless ye." Lottie made a quick exit, in fear he would see her womanly tears of joy.

"Charles, what a nice gesture. You have certainly made her day." Bess touched his hand. "Don't move --- I'll be right back." She ran upstairs before he could reply.

Returning out of breath, she said, "Charles, a small token of all the pleasure you have given me over the years." She handed him a long, slim box.

"Dear Bess." He opened the box. A puzzled look appeared on his face. "It's grand --- It is a ---?"

"A fountain pen."

"A fountain pen?"

"It will make writing so much easier for you. Let me show you." She took the bottle of ink off the counter and brought it to the table. "See --- You dip the nib --- " She saw confusion written all over his face. "Ah, the quill, into the ink --- then gently clasp this gold bar with your fingernail, moving the bar to a horizontal position ---- like this." He nodded. "Now, slowly return the bar to the vertical or closed position, thus causing the ink to draw up into a little reservoir. If you want to empty it, do the opposite. Keeping in mind to drain it over the ink bottle. You try it." He took the shiny, black pen from her and repeated her instructions. "Good, now here is some paper. Try writing with it."

He wrote her name on the blank paper. "This is smooth and quiet. Why I can write all night and Mrs. Dickens will not be disturbed from the constant scratching noise."

"Hmh, that's true. Plus, you can write a lot faster. The reserved ink in the fountain pen keeps flowing. You won't need to dab your quill in the ink all the time."

"Fountain pen --- hmh ---- just like a fountain."

"I hadn't thought of it like that, but yes, I suppose it is. ----- After you are finished using it, screw the top back on and it will not leak." She demonstrated. "It is very handy when travelling. You don't need to have an ink bottle on hand to write down something."

"Marvelous. Wherever did you find it? Why I've never seen one, let alone knew of its existence."

Stunned by his question, she thought *I should have anticipated this.* "In America," she blurted out. "Yes, in America."

"America? I thought you said you lost all your luggage." He thought for a moment. "Ah, the steamship company found it?"

Bess took her hand off the table and placed it behind her back. The fingers had the routine down pat so automatically crossed. "Yes, that's it. --- I received one of my bags. It happened to contain a couple of fountain pens. When I left home, I thought they would make nice gifts if I should meet some kind people."

"When were they invented? America is becoming a progressive nation. If they keep going the way they have, they will surpass us. --- And to think, we thought they were crazy savages when they threw us out."

"Still miffed about the Boston Tea Party?"

"I suppose you could say that." They laughed. "If more people could meet people like you, they would think differently about folks from America. Take Mrs. Pennycroft for example, since her dinner party, your name has graced many a social function."

"Well, my dear Bess, this brings me to why I stopped in today. Naturally, I wanted to bring Mrs. Morton's gift, but I also wanted to give you a small token of my gratitude for your assistance in entertaining the elite." He got up and walked over to the large box on the nearby table. "This is for you."

"For me? --- A small token?"

"Yes, yes, now open it, girl." She moved over to the box and stopped. "Here, let me help you." He grabbed a knife off the table and cut the heavy string. On her tiptoes, Bess tried to lift the top of the box. "At this rate, we'll be here till Christmas." He lifted the lid and exposed a wad of packing. "You'd think I was giving you The Crown Jewels, the way it is packed."

"Oh, you didn't?" Bess tried to sound surprised.

They promptly lowered their heads into the depths of the box and proceeded to bang them together. "Ouch!"

"Perhaps to prevent any further injury, I shall lift my head out first and you can lift out the contents," echoed Bess, rubbing her forehead as she surfaced.

"Got it!" Charles reappeared holding a wooden box.

"Charles, are you sure it doesn't hold The Crown Jewels?"

"Sorry to disappoint you, my dear, t'is only a writing desk."

"A writing desk?"

"Yes, a travelling writing desk. I thought it would come in handy on your journey home. See the top comes down to form a desk, and inside the little compartments hold inkwells, quills, paper and a few of The Crown Jewels."

"It is lovely, Charles."

"Yes, and quite useful. Why, when I'm strapped for space, --- which often happens on the train, I can put it on my lap. See." He sat down and demonstrated.

"Ah, a laptop."

"I suppose you could call it that."

Bess chuckled and gave him a kiss on the cheek. "Thank you, Charles. It is much better than The Crown Jewels."

"Of course, that is why I got it for you." He looked at her and they both burst out laughing. "Well, I must be off. I have to pick up a Christmas tree. Ever since Prince Albert introduced the Christmas tree to court, Mrs. Dickens demands one each Christmas."

"Christmas tree? Where would you purchase one around here? I'd love to get one for the Mortons."

"Well, get your coat and come with me."

Bess picked up her writing desk and hurried upstairs. She placed it on the dresser, moving a bar of decorative soap out of the way. Not knowing where to put the soap, she stuck it in her pocket and heard the jingling of money inside. She grabbed her coat and bonnet and hurried down the stairs to find Mr. Dickens waiting at the door, holding the empty box under his arm.

"I'm just going out on an errand, Lottie. I'll be back soon," shouted Bess.

He hailed a passing carriage and off they sped down Fetter Lane. After four or five turns down narrow streets, the carriage came to a stop. Mr. Dickens alighted the carriage and gave Bess a hand out.

"Do ye want me to wait fer ye, guvnor?" asked a toothless driver.

"Yes, please, sir. --- Bess, this way."

He extended his arm, which Bess accepted, and they walked into a fenced-in yard. Shovels and buckets lay strewn everywhere. At the end of the short pathway, a glass building stood out of character to the surrrounding brick buildings. Inside, they found themselves surrounded by small Christmas trees. On a nearby table, stood stacks of pottery.

"Merry Christmas, Mr. Green. The young lady and I would each like one of your best trees. Go over to the table and pick out a pot for your tree, Bess. Mr. Green will pot it for you." Bess picked out a green and white ceramic bowl, and Mr. Dickens carried it to the counter. "Only one potted, Mr. Green. Mrs. Dickens has the pot we used last year, cleaned and waiting at home."

Mr. Green, dressed in a worn leather apron, placed the tree in the pot and packed down soil around its base. Satisfied the tree would not move, he looked up and smiled, showing teeth as dirty as the soil. "That'll be two shillings fer t' lady an' one fer ye, Mr. Dickens."

Bess reached into her pocket and brought out two silver coins. *They look like quarters,* she thought as she handed them over to the man. *After I pay Jo, I'll have one shilling -- ah --- four pennies left. Boy, I'm getting good at this.* She smiled.

Back in the carriage, filled with the scent of fresh evergreens, they headed back to the tea shoppe. "Sorry about the high price of the tree. Mr. Green's an honest merchant, but Christmas trees are a rare item, and he knows only the wealthy can afford them. So, he makes his profits when he can."

"Thank you for your concern, but I earned a couple of shillings helping a friend, so I am more than happy to share my wealth with my dear friends. I am delighted to give them something they have not had before. I hope my small gesture will be the beginning of a new Christmas tradition for them. There is nothing like a beautiful Christmas tree to brighten the dullest of winter days and complete the magic of Christmas."

"I agree. Maybe someday soon, all homes will have a Christmas tree."

"I'm sure they will, Charles." Bess smiled.

They pulled up to "The Lotatea Shoppe" and Mr. Dickens lifted her potted tree out of the carriage. "Wait for me, sir. I'll only be a minute."

"Right, guvnor," replied the driver.

Bess rushed ahead and opened the door. "Put it on the table by the piano. I'll clear it." Quickly, she moved two cups and saucers off the tiny table. "Oh, that's perfect. Lottie will be able to show off her tree to passersby."

"I'll move it a foot closer to the window. We want them to have a good view. If you want to show it off, might as well give them an eyeful." They laughed. "Besides, it will bring pleasure to those who have never seen a Christmas tree."

Bess studied the tree. Its branches hung perfectly spaced around the trunk, with no bald spots to hide. Suddenly, she looked perplexed.

"What's wrong, Bess?"

"How do you attach the candles?"

"Very carefully. Fire is definitely the biggest worry. Ah, there is a toy merchant around the corner who can help you."

"Ah, Herr Klaus Sievert?"

"Why yes, you do get around. He may still have a few candle holders left. The Germans have been lighting Christmas trees for a long time. They know how to keep the tree lit and keep the house from burning down." He gave her a devilish smile. "Well, my dear, I must be off before the driver takes off with Mrs. Dickens' Christmas tree."

"Thank you so much for your gift and spending a memorable Christmas Eve with me. Merry Christmas, Charles." Bess gave him a hug. "In America, we like to hug."

"A nice custom indeed." He kissed her hand. "Merry Christmas, dear Bess." He opened the door and shouted at the driver, "Doughty Street, my good man."

"Bess, t'is ye?" Lottie shouted from the kitchen.

"Yes, Lottie, I have one more errand. I'll be back in a few minutes before the afternoon customers arrive."

"Right, luv."

As she ran down the lane, she looked back to see the tree's silhouette in the window. *Definitely needs lights,* she thought. When she passed "Tellaway Books," she spied Jo through the window and thought *I'd better pop in and give her the eight pennies I owe.* Two minutes later, back outside, debt free, she felt relieved and walked with her head held high and her steps a little lighter. Turning the corner, Bess saw the toy shoppe.

Inside, the cuckoo announced her arrival. Herr Sievert looked over and smiled. She strolled over to the Christmas tree to check out the candle holders, while he finished with a well-dressed gentleman buying a large doll. The individual candle holders, made of tin, perched securely on the branches. The small, saucer shaped base had an angel cutout backing to stop the flame from reaching the bare branch. Peering under the saucer, Bess noticed the branch had been slipped through a narrow tin loop, attached to the underside of the saucer. The candle stood snugly in the jaws of the tin clasp.

"Ja, Fraulein, can I help you?"

"Yes, I hope so. Mr. Dickens told me to come and see you. Can I buy some of these candle holders?"

"Herr Charles Dickens? Ja?"

"That's right. We were out and bought Christmas trees. I am without any lights, and I do want it to look nice for Mrs. Morton."

"Ja, Frau Morton." He stopped and thought for a moment. "Ja, dhet is gud. I have some in the back." He hurried through the back door returning with a small box of tinkling metal. "I have ten candle holders. Will dhet do?"

"Oh yes, how much are they?" asked Bess, putting her hand in her pocket.

"Five pennies."

Bess pulled out five coins, one shilling and four pennies.

"Give me the four pennies and I'll give you the candles too. Ja, dhet is gud?"

"Very good. Thank you and Merry Christmas, Herr Sievert."

"Danken shoen and Fröhliche Weihnachten."


Her little box rattled as she hurried back to the tea shoppe. Bess turned the corner onto Fetter Lane and noticed Lydia Taylor in her shoppe window. Seeing Lydia reminded Bess, so she put her hand in her pocket and headed up the walkway. Lydia opened the door just as Bess put her hand on the door handle.

"Bess, dear, how nice to see you. Lawrence gave me the dress. Sorry I missed you."

"I just wanted to thank you again and give you a little gift for the kindness you showed me." Bess pulled out the soap, she had put in her pocket earlier.

"My, how nice. --- Why, it is a bar of soap." Lydia put the round bar up to her nose. "It smells like raspberries. Wherever did you get something so delicious? And, how did you know I love raspberries?"

"Actually, I brought it from America. I thought, perhaps if I met someone nice, I could give it to them. --- A token of faraway places."

"And did you know you would be meeting a dressmaker?" Lydia laughed. "It looks like a pin cushion."

"Of course, I'm psychic," replied Bess.

"Oooh ---- does that mean you can see into the future?" Lydia smirked.

"I suppose you could say sooooo."

"Soooo --- do you see the earl in my future?"

"Ah ---- speaking of the future, what time is it?" Lydia pointed at the clock on the mantel not taking her eyes off Bess. "Oh no. I have to run." Bess grabbed the door handle. "Merry Christmas." Before Lydia could say anything, Bess ran down the stairs, tinkling her tinware.

"It's me Lottie. I'm just going up to my bedroom. I'll be down in a minute."

"Right, luv."

Up in her bedroom, Bess took off her coat and stopped to touch the writing desk. She smiled, as her hand swept across its smooth surface. Hearing a loud, tinkling noise, she looked around. *No, I left the candle holders downstairs.* The noise got louder. *It sounds like a lid over boiling water.*

"The Christmas pudding!"

She ran into the kitchen to find the pot gasping for water. Quickly she filled the kettle and poured the water down the inside of the pot. The pot hissed as the water reached its parched interior. Silence filled the room. She exhaled and broke the silence. The Christmas pudding was saved and just in the nick of time.

"Thank you, Santa." Bess wiped the moisture off her forehead, obviously left over from the last remnants of steam escaping when she lifted the lid and not from sheer perspiration. She noticed the pot of cooked cranberry sauce on the counter. "Thank goodness, I took it off the stove before I travelled to Olde London Town. Anymore disasters and Mr. Spider will be dining alone. --- You hear that, Mr. Spider?" shouted Bess. "Tea, I need a cup of tea. This double life is too stressful."

She plugged in the kettle and put a small, rump roast into a pan, surrounding it with fresh vegetables. She popped it in the oven, set the temperature to 350F. Bess poured the steeped tea into one of her favourite Christmas mugs, holly boughs entwined in a poinsettia. Headed for the living room with her tea, she hesitated *no, I'd better be safe than sorry.* She reached over and turned the oven knob down to 325F and the stove element to simmer. Sitting down on the chesterfield, she almost sat on Mr. Dickens' travelling desk.

"Look, Mr. Spider, the desk did live up to its name. I'd better put it away before it makes another journey."

She rushed upstairs and put it under the bed, thinking *I'll explain this later to Evan.* Back on the chesterfield, she sipped her tea and looked at her village. *I couldn't explain this in a million years, let alone a hundred and fifty years, back then or now.* She laughed.

"Wot yer laughin' at Bess? Ye got sumone in there, I don't know about? Sum deep, dark secret?"

"Ah ---- something like that, Lottie." Bess hurried to the staircase. "I'll be right there." Not a moment too soon, she reached the bottom step, and the door jingled announcing the first ladies for afternoon tea.

Bess sat down at the pianoforte and stayed engrossed in her music, only to stop to take requests and acknowledge the patrons. From the background, the continuous jingling of the door, accompanied her sleigh bells and jingle bells, while silver bells competed with ladies' laughter.

"Miss Bess, ---- Artie! Look! T'is a Christmas tree."

"Hush, wot's all t' noise?" Lottie came running into the room.

"Mum, look ---- t'is a Christmas tree."

"A Christmas tree? Don't be daft, lad." Lottie came over to the pianoforte. "Oh my, yer right, t'is a Christmas tree." She put her hands on her cheeks. "Where'd it cum from? Bess, ye know anythin' about t'is?"

The door jingled and in came Harry Topham carrying a stark-naked goose.

" 'Arry, look --- a Christmas tree."

"A Christmas tree, how did you get it, Mrs. Morton?" Harry and the goose took a gander at the bare tree. "Only rich postees have Christmas trees; you must be rich, Mrs. Morton."

"Rich in miracles, 'Arry." Lottie laughed. "Cum on let's get t' goose dressed an' in t' oven."

Bess got off the stool and went over to the boys. She gave each boy a large hug and a kiss on the forehead.

"Wot's that fer, Miss Bess?"

"It's my way of saying thank you for your Christmas postcard. You couldn't have given me a better present. I'm going to keep it in my pocket so it will be close to me."

"We knew ye liked 'em, cause ye asked a lot of questions about 'em at t' post office. Me 'n' Artie knew ye mustn't 'ave 'em in America, so's we got one fer ye. Mr. Topham said 'ed deliver it to ye on Christmas Eve. Do ye like t' stamp cause ye were very interested in 'em?"

"When I go home, I shall show all my friends." She smiled at the boys and their faces beamed with pride. "Now, how about we decorate this tree? It looks a little bare."

"Aye, aye." Bertie clapped his hands.

" 'Ow, Miss Bess?" asked a puzzled looking Artie.

"We could make some garlands and string them around the

tree. --- I know, I have some coloured paper in my bedroom. We'll cut them into strips and paste the ends together to to make a chain."

"Let's get 'em, Miss Bess." They ran up the stairs, with Bess following in close pursuit.

"Wot ar' ye doin' to me tearoom?" asked Lottie as she frowned at a pile of coloured paper, strewn all over the tables and floor.

"Look, Mum, we're makin' paper chains fer t' Christmas tree. Do ye want to 'elp?"

"No, but I'll pick up t' paper off t' floor, so ye can make more chains. 'Eaven ferbid, if ye 'ad to stop yer work to pick up off t' floor." She shook her head and winked at Bess.

The door jingled and in walked Jo, brushing the snow off her coat. "My, what is going on?"

"Look, Miss Jo, t'is a Christmas tree an' we're decoratin' it. Want to 'elp?"

"I'd love to, Bertie. Why, I've never decorated one. Let me take my coat off."

The over-worked bell jingled again and this time Tom appeared. "Bedlam? Is that bedlam I've come home to after a hard day at the office?"

"Uncle Tom, yer so funny. Cum see our very own Christmas tree. Cum 'n' 'elp us."

"Right, Bertie, old man, soon as I get rid of my boxes. I'll run up and tuck them away."

"Wot's in t' boxes, Uncle Tom?"

"Never you mind, lad," Tom shouted down the stairs. Bertie giggled.

"I'll go an' make us a cup of tea. Ladies, why don't ye clear another table an' we'll 'ave it 'ere whilst we decorate t' tree?" Lottie headed for the kitchen.

"Let me help you. I'll move these tables around. I'll have to do it for Christmas dinner anyway. Come on, lads, take one end," said Tom, slightly out of breath.

Job accomplished, he threw some coal on the fire. "Since it looks like we are going to be down here for a while, it might as well be warm."

Lottie poked her head around the kitchen doorway. "Tom, do ye remember t' old star we kept since we was kids? Wot about puttin' it on top of t' tree?"

"I think it is in the attic. Come on, lads, let's go see if we can find it." Tom lead the charge up the stairs.

"Where did the tree come from?"

"Mr. Dickens and I went out and bought one each. Jo, don't ask me where, because I have no idea where I ended up. All I know it was a glasshouse and --- oh yes, his name was Mr. Green."

"How appropriate." They both laughed.

"Did I 'ear ye say ye bought t'is tree, Bess?" Lottie shouted from the kitchen.

"You heard correctly. Do you need any help?"

"Oh, ye dear girl. 'Ow kind an' no I don't need any 'elp."

"We's found it," shouted the boys as they ran down the stairs, covered in cobwebs.

"It is a bit thread worn, but I think I can attach it to the top of the tree," said Tom. He brushed a cobweb from his face. "Darn spiders."

"Don't blame them," replied Bess. She thought of Mr. Spider. "You invaded their space. Stand still." She picked off the wispy threads of webbing off Tom's hair and shoulders and received a wink in return."

The door jingled, interrupting their private moment. In walked Artie's dad and sister. "Artie, come on, lad. T'is time we got ye home. Yer mit'er's been worried about ye."

"Look, Father, a Christmas tree, an' me 'n' Bertie ar' decoratin' it. See wot I made, Patty." Artie grabbed his sister's pudgy little hand and showed her the green and red paper chain.

Patty examined the chain. "Look, Father."

"Well, t'is a fine job, son."

"T'is that Mr. Doyle I 'ear?" Lottie poked her head out once more. "Yer just in time fer tea."

"T'ank ye, Mrs. Morton, but we should be off."

"Come in, Michael, my man, and warm yourself by the fire. Besides, Artie's not finished his work yet. Right, Artie?" Tom pulled out a chair for his friend.

"Maybe a hot cup of tea t'will warm t' old blarney stone."

"Besides, Maureen could do wit' a bit of peace 'n' quiet away from ye lot," said Lottie as she brought in a tray filled with buns and cheese.

"Since ye put it t'at way, let me take t' tray, Mrs. Morton." Mr. Doyle grabbed it from her and set it down on an empty table.

The excited children ignored their food and concentrated on the decorations. The adults sat back and watched the energy exude from the children. They drank their tea and munched on buns while discussing local affairs. Lottie proudly showed off her teapot pin. They all agreed Mr. Dickens to be a very kind and generous man. However, Christmas did bring out the generous nature in people, of which they all agreed. During the second cup of tea, the children became bored with the conversation and demanded the adults' assistance in decorating the tree.

"Right then, lads, let's put the star on first. --- Hand it to me, Bertie," ordered Tom. "You did a fine job of cleaning it up. Can you give me a hand, Michael?"

"After several attempts, they secured the star on top of the tree. "Not as easy as it looks, Tom," laughed Mr. Doyle. "Hand us t' paper chains, Artie. ---- I'm ready when ye are."

The two men wound the chains around the branches, standing back to look it over.

"What do you think?"

"Ye need sum around t' back."

"It looks a little lopsided on this side."

"No, a wee bit higher, Tom."

"Let me do it, Uncle Tom."

"Bertie, stay away."

"Well, I did ask," chuckled Tom.

"Oh, I almost forgot. --- The candle holders." Bess looked around and spied the box, abandoned in the corner. "Luckily, I managed to get these from Herr Sievert."

"Let's see, Miss Bess." Bertie ran over to Bess.

They all huddled around the table. Bess opened the box and lifted out a shiny angel.

"Oooh! T'is pretty," gasped little Patty.

"Come on, Bertie, you can hand them to me." Tom took one over to the tree and examined the holder. "Right, I think the branch must go inside this loop. What do you think, Michael?"

"Me thinks we best leave t'is to t' men. 'Ow about sum music, Bess? Nuthin' like Christmas carols to put 'em in t' right frame of mind. Might even get 'em workin'."

"Hush, woman." Squeals of laughter exploded from the children.

They all sang carols as they worked around the tree. The three children handed the the candle holders to the men. Soon angels took wings and sparkled in the fire's light.

"Can we light t' candles, Mum?"

"Be careful. Let yer uncle 'elp ye."

Standing around the tree, they all held their breath as Bertie lit the first candle.

"OOOOH! AAAAH!"

"Come on, Patty, your next." Tom lifted her up. Both the candle and her face lit up at the same time. "Artie, my man. ---- Bess, your next. Shall I lift you?" He whispered in her ear.

"You wish." Bess smiled demurely and struck the match.

"I like a woman with fire." He winked.

She carefully brought the match over to the wick and lowered it onto the tip. "It's beautiful. Look how it makes the angel glow. Jo, your turn."

Jo found a candle at the back of the tree and proceeded to light it. Her brown eyes turned to a liquid amber as the flame reflected on her porcelain face.

"Miss Jo, ye look like t' angel cum alive," said Bertie.

"Don't move, angel. Come, lads, Patty, let's see if the tin angel is still on the tree."

On tiptoes, six little feet followed two large feet around the back of the tree. All went silent. With serious expressions on their faces, they searched upwards.

"Still there."

"You're sure?" asked Uncle Tom. They nodded. "Good then. Jo, you can move." He turned and winked at the children.

"Ah, Uncle Tom, yer foolin' wit' us."

"Sister dear, I believe there is a candle waiting to be lit."

"Oh Tom,--- Oh Bess, 'ow lovely." Lottie's teardrops sparkled in the candlelight. She regained her composure. "Mr. Doyle, do cum an' light a candle."

"T'ank ye, Mrs. Morton. I'll get t'is one up here." He chose one near the star. "Tom, let's make the star shine."

Tom lit the candle on the right. The star began to twinkle. They all stood back and took in the beautiful glow emanating from the tree. Their angelic faces looked upward.

"T'is t' North Star."

"T'is t' Star of Bethlehem."

"Our first Christmas tree. Thank ye, Bess."

Tears ran down Bess's cheeks. "You are most welcome."

The jingling of the doorbell broke the blessed silence.

"What are you all looking at?" asked Mr. Brown, holding a large box.

"Mr. Brown, good evenin'. Tom, 'elp Mr. Brown." Lottie's face glowed a darker shade of red.

"Cum see, Mr. Brown. T'is our very own Christmas tree." Bertie grabbed his hand.

"Why, Bertie, my lad, what a sight to behold."

"Miss Bess got it fer us an' we made decorations. See 'em." Bertie pointed his finger at the chain of red and green paper.

"What a clever piece of artistry." Mr. Brown patted Bertie on the head, while Bertie stuck out his chest. Artie came closer. "Good work, Artie."

"Can Mr. Brown light a candle?" asked Bertie.

"Let's see. ---- Aye, there's two left. Bertie, give Mr. Brown a match." As he lit his candle, the door jingled and in walked Harry Topham. "Just in time, Harry. There's one candle left."

"Well, I hope my goose looks half as good as this tree," laughed Harry.

"Cum on, 'Arry, let's get t' goose 'ome fer Millie," said Lottie.

"Goose, home, that reminds me. I'd better get back to 'The Brown Bread.' I left Sean in goose grease up to his elbows. Everyone wants to use our ovens. Why, there's five baking right now, with another five laying in wait. I don't think either one of us will get much sleep tonight. Five more coming at four in the morning and the last five mid-morning."

"Aren't ye cumin' to church wit' us?" asked Bertie.

"Yes, Sean and I will be there. We'll put the last ones in the oven before going, and they will be ready by the time the service is over."

"Don't ferget Mum's turkey dinner after."

"We'll be there. Don't you worry, lad." Mr. Brown saluted to Bertie. "I almost forgot why I came. Give this to your mother. I managed to get these buns baked before Goose Bedlam started. See you tomorrow. Merry Christmas."

Lottie came out of the kitchen , giving Harry a hand. "Merry Christmas, 'Arry. Enjoy yer dinner." Lottie looked around the room. "Did Mr. Brown leave? Wot a pity."

"We should be leavin' too, Mrs. Morton," said Mr. Doyle.

"I've just made sum chocolate. Ye can't leave yet."

"Please, Father," pleaded Artie.

"P'ease, Father," repeated Patty.

"Alright, since it bein' Christmas, only a half-hour mind. Yer mit'er will worry if we don't get home soon."

While the chocolate was being served, Bess ran upstairs. Two minutes later she returned. "Children, I'd like to read a Christmas story to you that my mother read to me, when I was Patty's age."

"Cum sit by t' fire, Bess. Give 'er t' cup of chocolate, Tom. Children, sit beside Bess. Bertie! Where's yer manners? Ladies first."

They all sat in a semi-circle around the fire, each holding a cup of hot chocolate. Eyes riveted to the little, red book, cupped in Bess's hand, they sat motionless. The Christmas tree glistened in the candlelight. Through the branches, silent snow flakes fell and gathered to watch the interior's celebration. Bess opened the book and flipped a couple of pages. Their gilded edges shone in the firelight.

" 'The Night Before Christmas,' by Clement Clarke Moore. ---- 'Twas the night before Christmas and all through the house not a creature was stirring, not even a mouse." Bess looked up at six-wide eyes. "All the stockings were hung by the chimney with care ---"

"Why, Miss Bess?" asked Bertie. "We don't put ours on t' chimney."

"We do when they're wet. Was they wet, Miss Bess?" asked Artie.

"Hush!"

Bess smiled. "No, Artie, they were not wet. Listen and I'll tell you why." When they nodded, she continued, "All the stockings were hung by the chimney with care ---- In the hope that Saint Nicholas soon would be there." She looked up to see puzzled looks on their faces, but they did not interrupt. "Then, what to my wondering eyes should appear, A minature sleigh and eight reindeer."

"Reindeer? Wot's that?"

"They are cousins to the deer in the park. They live way up north and like myself, only visit at Christmas."

"Oh."

"A little old driver so lively and quick,

I knew in a moment it must be Saint Nick.

And more rapid than eagles his reindeer all came,

As he shouted, 'On Dasher,' and each reindeer's name.'"

"Ru --- Rudolph that's one, inn'it, Miss Bess. I remember cause ye sang a song about 'im." Bertie smiled.

"Very good, Bertie." When the children settled down she continued, "And so up to the housetop the reindeer soon flew, with the sleigh full of toys and Saint Nicholas too."

"Does that bloke, Nicholas, live up north too?" asked Bertie.

"Yes, way up north, in the North Pole."

"Don't ye be interruptin', Bertie," scolded Lottie.

"Down the chimney he came with a leap and a bound,"

"I'd mighty well leap and bound if I came down this chimney." Tom laughed, and the childrens' eyes diverted in the direction of the blazing fire. They started to squirm.

"He was dressed all in furs, ----"

"Scorched," mumbled Tom.

Bess gave him a dirty look and continued, "And his belly was round. He spoke not a word," She hesitated and dared anyone to speak. "But went straight to his work

And filled all the stockings, then turned with a jerk

And laying his finger aside of his nose,

Then giving a nod up the chimney he rose.

But I heard him exclaim as he drove out of sight,

'Merry Christmas to all and to all a good night'! " Bess gently closed the book.

"Miss Bess, if we put our stockings up will t'is bloke, Nick-o-las, fill 'em wit' toys?" asked Bertie.

"From t' sleigh?" added Artie.

"Does 'e go to America sumtimes?"

"Yes, children, every Christmas Eve, he comes to every child and fills their stockings. Mind you, if they have not been good, he does not come."

"Blimey!"

"Can we 'ear it once more? Now we knows wot it means, we can listen better?" asked Artie.

Bess looked at Mr. Doyle who shrugged his shoulders and nodded.

" 'Twas the night before Christmas and ---------------------- 'Merry Christmas to all and to all a good night'! "

Silence prevailed. Slowly, the adults came back to reality and stirred. Three little bodies, huddled next to Bess, did not stir. Smiles covered their faces and their eyes held shut.

"Oh look, they have fallen asleep," observed Jo.

"I'd best wake t'em."

"Leave 'em be, Mr. Doyle. Take 'em up to Bertie's room," said Lottie.

"Right t'en. We'll bring t'eir church attire around in t' mornin'." After tucking them in, he buttoned up and said, "T'anks for a most enjoyable even' --- and ---- 'Merry Christmas to all and to all a good night'! "

"Good night, Michael."

"Are ye cumin' up to bed, Bess, luv?"

"In a minute, I just want to take in this lovely moment."

"Good night then."

Bess focused on the candles, now reduced to a low burning stub. Gradually, one by one the flow of melted wax extinguished its flame. The silent room went dark.

# CHAPTER XVI

*B*ess crept downstairs. Evan's persistent snoring followed. *As long as the snoring continues, the task at hand will not be interrupted,* she smiled. Squealing in protest, the closet door opened. She held her breath and thought, *another item to add to Evan's to do list.* The snoring continued. Bess breathed a sigh of relief and quickly rummaged behind the coats. She pulled out a brown bag and very slowly closed the closet door. She tiptoed to the living room.

Except for a sliver of light coming through the skylight, the room stood in darkness. Bess did not want to turn on the light in fear Evan would wake, but the way his snoring came down the staircase like a wind tunnel, chances of him waking up seemed highly unlikely. Looking around the room, her eyes automatically focused in on the mantel. Dickens Village stood in darkness. *Of course, I'll plug in the lights. Evan won't notice them.* She bent over, fumbled for the wall plug and made contact. The village glow spread shadows over the wall. High above, Mr. Spider stirred.

"Sorry, but --- let me be the first to wish you Merry Christmas, Mr. Spider," whispered Bess.

Settling back on the chesterfield, she pulled out the contents of the bag. Bess thumped her head. *Where is my brain?* Annoyed with herself, she got up and unhooked Evan's stocking from the mantel. *It's hard to believe we've had these over thirty years.* Her mind went over their earlier conversation.

"Remember when we got these Bess? It seems like only yesterday. We hummed and hawed over which ones to buy; you wanted the velvet and I wanted the felt."

"Yes, I remember --- and you won."

"Yeah and it was the last time I won."

"Evan!"

"How much did we pay? Ninety-nine cents?"

"That's why we didn't buy the velvet ones. Even then you were accounting every penny."

"Why spend a dollar forty-nine when ninety-nine cents looked just as good. Besides, look how long they've lasted; good as new!"

"Yes, Evan. Let's hang them up. I'm tired."

"Tired? You were sound asleep when I came home. It took me ages to wake you; mumbling something about candles."

Bess smiled as she sat back down on the chesterfield. She stuffed the toe with a pair of new socks. Then came the toothbrush, candy bars, oranges, bag of Licorice Allsorts and a couple of handy gadgets, which she hadn't a clue of their usage, but Evan must surely know. They were guy things. At the top, she stuffed in a crossword book, a Christmas tie and card. She hung the stocking on the vacant hook. *Yes, I think this will hold for another year. Hmh, this felt has grown on me, but I will never tell Evan that,* Bess chuckled. Lifting her head, she looked straight into her bedroom window above Fetter Lane.

The lights became dimmer, the snoring fainter and the room colder. Her eyes squinted.

The mantel disappeared. A large cabinet hovered in the darkness. Shadows flickered.

"Clop, clop clop!"

"The stockings! I must get them filled."

Bess opened the wardrobe and brought out the boxes of goodies and emptied the contents on the four-poster bed. The red velvet stockings, purchased at the drugstore, she spread out on the bed. Overwhelmed by the piles of goodies surrounding the stockings, she scratched her head. *Where's my list?* Nothing in her pockets except a single shilling, Bess panicked. *It's here somewhere.* The poor lighting made it impossible to see, so she lit the candle on her nightstand. Searching around the room, she spied a piece a paper on the dresser and smiled.

Bess started to fill the stockings. Bertie and Artie got the same: candy, chocolates, nuts, crayons, colouring book and a toy soldier. Patty's did not have a toy soldier, but contained a bar of smelly soap and bubble bath. The adults' stockings had more useful items. The women's held soap, bath bubbles, deodorant. The men's bulged with duct tape, an Exacto knife, aftershave, deodorant and manly soap. She then put in a few personal items pertaining to each individual. She carefully reread the list.

In Lottie's, Bess slid a microplane, heatproof spatulas, spoons, two rolled up Sil sheets and two whisks. In Jo's, a pair of sewing scissors and a thread picker nestled into the empty crevices. A pair of rubber gloves kept popping out of Mrs. Doyle's stocking, while a bar of Irish Spring, a small bottle of Bailey's Irish Cream and a retractable measuring tape weighed Mr. Doyle's down. Tom's received a tube of Chapstick, Wite-Out and a compact manicure set. A small bottle of Scotch Whiskey and a box of MacIntosh Toffee completed Sean's stocking. With only a few things left, Bess stuffed O'Henry Bars, the sourdough starter and accompanying recipe into the top of Mr. Brown's. To finish off the stockings, each received the traditional standbys: toothbrush and a Japanese orange.

Even in the dim light, they looked impressive all laying in a row. Immediately, it hit her *will they know which one belongs to them? Why they've never hung a Christmas stocking.* Pondering this dilemma, she stared at the them. An idea unfolded and she rummaged in a couple of stockings, pulling out a red crayon and Jo's scissors. She cut ten strips off the bottom of the list and with the crayon wrote a name on each piece. Bess pinned the appropriate name to the cuff of the stocking. The crayon and scissors went back to their rightful stockings and the whole lot carefully placed in a discarded box.

Out in the hallway, arms stretched around the heavy box, she crept over the creaky floorboards. Bess listened for sounds. Tom's snoring kept pace with her heartbeat. Cautiously, she made her way down the two flights of stairs. *Thank goodness, I've got my pyjamas on. In that long dress, I'd trip for sure. --- Pyjamas? Please don't let anyone see me.*

The dying embers gave off just enough light to prevent Bess from walking into anything. *No hooks? Shoot!* She took out each stocking and laid it out on the hearth, keeping them out of the way of flying embers. Satisfied with the arrangement, she picked up the box and took one last look at the ten beautiful stockings all in a row.

"One, two ---- one, two?"

*Ah, right; one for Evan, one for Bess,* she smiled, put the empty bags in the box and took it out to the recycle bin. She crept back upstairs towards Evan's or Tom's snoring.

"Merry Christmas, Bess." Evan leaned over and gave her a kiss.

"Merry Christmas, Evan. What time is it?"

"It's eleven o'clock."

"Eleven? We're supposed to be at Lydia's at two."

"Well, if you didn't insist we go to midnight service, we wouldn't sleep so late Christmas morning. We're not getting any younger. We need our beauty sleep."

"Speak for yourself. Why, I'll have you know I feel like twenty-one."

"Could have fooled me; you're sound asleep everytime I come home."

"Go have your shower. I'll go down and start breakfast."

To drown out the rattle of the water pipes, Bess turned on some Christmas music. On the way to the kitchen, she plugged in the Christmas lights. Soon the smell of bacon permeated the air.

"Smells good. I'm hungry," announced Evan, as he came in wearing a red, fleece robe and rubbing his wet hair with a white towel.

"Good timing, Santa," laughed Bess. "Put down the towel and carry the plates into the dining room. I'll bring the toast."

"Dining room? ---- Oh right, we always have breakfast in there on Christmas morning."

"Right, now get a move on before everything gets cold."

By the time they finished their second cup of Christmas Spice, the clock struck half-past twelve. The two stockings hung undisturbed on the mantel, and presents laid unopen under the tree. Dirty dishes went flying into the dishwasher.

En route to the bedroom Evan said, "We should at least look in our stockings."

"Good idea. We can open our presents later."

Out came the contents of the stockings.

"What a beautiful pair of blue earrings."

"They match your eyes. Santa sees all." Evan winked. "I needed a magnetic screwdriver to keep all those annoying screws from falling into crevices I can't reach."

The clock struck one. "We'd better get dressed. We still have to pack up the car and Lydia did want us there early."

"Yes, dear."

The Escape left two tire tracks in the fresh snow as they drove up the street. The vehicle smelt of Christmas pudding, while the rustling of wrapping paper brushed against the presents. Evan turned the dial until he came to "God Rest Ye Merry Gentlemen."

"One of these Christmas days, we're going to spend it at home; just the two of us. We'll sit by a blazing fire, feet up, eggnog in hand and take in the smell of roasting turkey wafting through the air."

"Maybe next year?"

"Maybe."

Just after two, they drove into the Stevens' driveway. A large, inflated nutcracker greeted them. Escaping his massive plastic arm, they carefully walked along the edge of the brick sidewalk. Every guarded step crunched the salt crystals into tiny, glittering specks. Arms full, Bess barely managed to ring the doorbell.

"Bess, let me get that," Bruce shouted over the boxes. "Anything else?"

"Take this, Bruce. I'll go get the Christmas pudding." Evan handed over the box of brightly, wrapped presents.

As soon as the door closed, they exchanged Merry Christmas hugs and kisses. Coats hung up in the closet, boots exchanged for slippers, presents tucked under the tree, and food relayed to the kitchen, they finally sat down. Lydia brought in a tray of festive Christmas mugs filled with hot chocolate and a heaping plate of shortbread and minced tarts.

"Hmm, smells good, Lydia," said Evan. He took in a deep breath.

"She's been starving me all morning. Don't touch the shortbread," complained Bruce. "Lydia, where's those cherry bars you made?"

"I'm getting them. I can only carry so much. If you'd get those big clod-hoppers moving and help me."

"Now you two lovebirds, t'is Christmas," piped up Bess.

Bruce jumped up, tripped on the leg of the end table and landed at Lydia's feet. "You sit down, I'll go fetch the sweets for my sweet." They all groaned. "No, don't anyone move. I can manage with only nine and a half fingers."

Lydia shook her head. "It's not your nine and a half fingers I'm worried about, it's your ten clumsy toes that concern me."

"Cruel."

"Bruce, can you turn on the burner under the canner? I want to warm up the Christmas pudding," shouted Lydia at his retreating back.

"The tree looks good," commented Evan when Bruce returned.

"Yeah, it should. It's one of those damn expensive, cultured ones. Nothing but the best for my Lydia," Bruce said sarcastically.

Ignoring his remark, Lydia said, "Let's open our presents. Bruce, dear, you can be Santa."

"Santa? With that bald head?" Evan roared, "How about his helper, the giant elf?"

Bruce got down on his knees and handed Lydia a present. "For you, my sweet, --- and here's another one. --- Bess, this one is for you. --- Evan --- What's this? One for Bruce?"

The meticulous wrappings disappeared into a pile of torn paper on the floor. Busy hands ripped stubborn, scotch tape from its victims, exposing the contents to its eager recipients.

"Oh, what a beautiful shawl," said Lydia as she unfolded it. "Feel how soft it is, Bruce."

"Hmm," replied an uninterested Bruce. When she put it around her shoulders, he took an interest. "Brings out the black in your hair --- and the white."

"Bruce!"

"In a complimentary way that is." Bruce corrected himself and wisely changed the subject. "A real nutcracker; what a masterful piece of art." He turned it upside down. "Not made in China or Japan either. --- The real McCoy; has to have been made in Germany."

"Yes, the Nussknacker was handcrafted in Germany in the mid-eighteen hundreds, I believe. That's what Herr Sievert told me."

"Bess, a real antique? You shouldn't have."

"Nothing but the best for our friends," said Bess. Bruce got up and gave Bess a hug and a hearty pat on the back to a speechless Evan.

"Oh, Bess, this doll is precious. Look at the expresssion on her face, Bruce," said Lydia.

"Hmm, real nice."

"Herr Sievert's distant relatives, Gretchen, Hilda and Wilhelm made this lovely doll."

"An old family affair in Germany, I assume?" quipped Bruce.

"Ja, dat is gud," laughed Bess. Evan gave her another puzzled look.

"Look at the tiny shawl. It matches mine," declared Lydia. "Open yours, Bess."

As Bess removed the last of the wrapping, she announced, "It's a Dickens church. Oh, how perfect and I'm supposed to go to church -------"

"Church? We've already been. We're not going again?" Evan sounded alarmed.

"Of course not. It's still shaking from our visit last night. We wouldn't want to be responsible for it falling down from another visit. Help me open this box." She shook her head and thought *keep these things to yourself, girl.*

As she lifted the lid, a grey stone cathedral lay in the recesses of the styrofoam. "Look at the strong columns flanking the entrance."

"Let me take it out, Bess." Evan lifted the church out by the columns.

"Be careful, Evan."

"It's as heavy as it looks. Definitely a solid place to worship; no fear of this one falling down. Perhaps,we should go to this church."

*Perhaps, we shall,* smiled Bess.

"Anymore room on the mantel?"

"I'll make room."

"Come and help me in the kitchen, Bess." Lydia looked around. "The guys can clean up the mess."

Lydia set an elegant table. Candles glowed in the muted light and turned the wine amber in colour. Christmas crackers laid ready for pulling. They held hands and Lydia said grace.

Their hands released from the circle of friendship and grabbed the beckoning crackers.

"Let the fireworks begin," they shouted in unison.

The numerous plates of turkey and vegetables disappeared within the stretched walls of their stomachs. No matter how bloated they felt, they saved room for the flaming Christmas pudding. The men unbuckled their belts, while the ladies undid the buttons on their waistbands.

At seven o'clock, Evan said, "Come on, Bess, time to head home."

Bess rushed into the house with her church, while Evan put the car away. She plugged in the lights of the Dickens Village and pondered *where will I put the church?* She took it out of the box. *No too big, maybe it will fit on the bookcase.* Bess moved a few books and set it down between the remaining books. Satisfied, she plugged it in. *It definitely has an etheral appearance, especially since the rest of the room is in darkness.*

Evan interrupted her moment of serenity. "Here's the bowls of cranberry and hard sauce. I would have preferred the turkey and pudding." He handed them to her.

"I'd better put them in the fridge."

"No, they can wait. Let's sit and bask in the silence for a few moments." Evan breathed a sigh of relief, and plunked down on the chesterfield. "Such a peaceful scene on the mantel." They both closed their eyes as the clock struck eight.

"Miss Bess, Miss Bess, get up yer Saint Nicho-las 'as bin 'ere. Cum quick."

"Wha --- What time is it?"

"'Tis eight o'clock," replied Bertie through the closed door.

"At night?"

"Nay, eight in t' mornin'."

"Maybe Miss Bess is still sleepin'," joined in Artie. "Suppose we'd better bang 'arder?"

"Aye." They proceeded to bang harder and faster.

"I'm coming; hold your horses."

"'Old yer 'orses? See I told ye she were still sleepin'," said Artie.

Bess jumped off the bed, looked down to make sure Victorian attire covered her body and noticed a bowl of cranberry sauce in one hand and hard sauce in the other. She put the bowls on the dresser and wondered --- *no they won't go off. It's as cold as a fridge in here.* She straightened her skirt and put her fingers through her hair.

"Dickens Christmas, here I come."

As soon as she opened the door, the boys grabbed her hands and dragged her down the stairs. Little Patty followed closely behind.

"What's all the racket?" Tom's door opened.

"Cum quick, Uncle Tom, Miss Jo. Saint Nic-ho-las bin 'ere."

"Saint Nicholas, you say. Woooooo a cousin to Scrooge or Marley?" moaned Tom.

"Uncle Tom, don't be silly. T'is Miss Bess's Saint Nic-ho-las from America."

"Ah right, the bloke from ' 'Tis The Night Before Christmas.' Can't miss that. I'll be right down." Tom closed his door. "After you, Jo."

Thundering footsteps bounced down the stairs.

"Blimey, wot's all t' noise?" Lottie shouted up the stairs. Six tiny, bare feet and a pair of runners entered the tearoom, almost trampling a stunned Lottie. "Wot's t' rush?"

"Mum, look. Saint Nic-ho-las ---- 'e brought us all stockin's."

"Stockin's?"

"Over 'ere, Mrs. Morton, by t' 'earth." Artie rushed towards the fireplace with Patty and Bertie in tow.

"My, my, wot's all t'is 'ere?" Lottie cupped her hands on her cheeks. "T'is stockin's. Blimey."

Bess took in the astonished looks on each face. The children's faces beamed magically; the adults' faces showed true wonderment. They all stared at the sight before them. No one blinked in fear the row of stockings would disappear. *My journey has a purpose after all. Just to see the amazement on their faces, is the greatest gift I could ever receive. Thank you, Lord,* thought Bess as she looked up.

"Can we 'ave 'em, Mum?"

"Wot?"

"Let me see." Tom bent down and checked out the stockings. "Why look, this one says Tom. Being the man of the house, I should start."

"Uncle Tom," groaned Bertie.

"No? Well let's see. ---- Patty --- Girls first." Tom picked up her stocking and put it on the table. "Sit down so you can open it, Patty." Moving back to the hearth, he stopped at the boys' stockings for a second, but reached for Jo's instead. "Ladies first, lads. Jo, this is for you and Lottie this is yours." Tom returned to the hearth. The boys stopped breathing. "Bess, where's yours? I see Mrs. Doyle's, but no Bess'."

The boys looked perplexed. " 'E couldn't ferget ye?" They turned and looked at Bess.

Taken off guard, she thought *well that was dumb.* She put her hands behind her back, crossed her fingers and waited for instant inspiration to smite her. "Ah ---- mine's in my bedroom. I think -- er --- Saint Nicholas couldn't squeeze another stocking on the hearth, so he laid it at the foot of my bed. He does that when there are no fireplaces, so I've heard."

"Well in that case, can me 'n' Artie 'ave ours now? Please, Uncle Tom."

"I hate to see two lads cry. Okay --- Artie, Bertie here you are."

The lads didn't need to sit down to dive into their stockings. "Look, a toy soldier."

At the same time, Jo said, "How handy; scissors. --- And what's this?"

Bess came to the rescue. "I believe it is a thread picker. See it pulls up the stitched threads and cuts them; see." She demonstrated on a piece of her hem.

"What a good idea. Oh, how I shall enjoy using this. Saint Nicholas sure knows what to bring us. ----- Lottie, what have you got there?"

"I'm not sure. Bess, wot do they use t'is fer in America?" Lottie picked up the Sil sheet.

"It's a Sil sheet. I've not seen one, but they say it prevents baking from sticking to the pan. It's heatproof; like these spoons and spatulas."

"Ye mean to tell me, t'is floppy sheet won't melt? Hmm --- it feels funny. Feel it, Jo."

"It does feel funny; almost like a thin wax. What did you say it was made of, Bess?"

"Silicon and these spoons are made of teflon. They are a new invention, but I can't tell you what they are made of or why they are heatproof. All I've heard is they work."

"Silicon, teflon, blimey ---- t'is sumthin' from another world."

Bess laughed, "Ours is not to reason why, just do and try. I'm sure you'll love them."

"Wite-Out?" Tom looked at the small container.

Acting surprised Bess said, "Oh, this is perfect for you. It's very popular in America. When you make a mistake with your sums, you can put some on it and the mistake disappears. You can write over it. I'll show you later." Bess winked at Tom and turned to Patty. "What have you got there? Why it's nice smelly soap and bath bubbles; little girls love them. Wait to you have your bath." Patty replied with a shy smile.

The church bells started to ring. Within seconds, church bells chimed all over London. "Cum, children. Get ready fer church. There be plenty of time to play wit' our stockin's later. Put 'em away fer now." Lottie managed to order them upstairs over the overwhelming ringing of the church bells. "Tom, can ye put t' turkey in t' oven fer me?"

The door jingled and in walked Mr. and Mrs. Doyle. Christmas greetings exchanged, along with Artie's and Patty's regular clothes for their Sunday bests, the group left the tearoom fifteen minutes later.

Church bells guided them along the snowy streets. The louder they rang, the closer they got. At the end of a narrow lane, a tall steeple housed the incessant bell. Rich and poor alike shook hands and wished each other a Merry Christmas. The Doyle and Morton households made their way inside the huge, stone church. The noise from the parishioners bounced off the high ceiling and reverberated through the air. Even with rows filled to capacity, cold air whistled down the long aisles, causing the candles at the altar to flicker.

Two-thirds the way down the aisle, Sean managed to hold a row for the group. Covered in sweat, the poor fellow's brow told the tale of his plight to keep the row empty. Many a dirty look and comment passed his way. The Christmas spirit only went so far. They had only sat down when Mr. Brown managed to squeeze in on the aisle.

The organist, far above the congregation, gave a heart throbbing pounding of the keys and the service began. Bess looked in the direction of the droning sounds coming from the pulpit, but only ladies' hats and the back of men's heads could be seen. As the deep voice echoed through the church, she lifted her head for an unobstructed view towards heaven. A mellow fresco of numerous cherubs dancing on the ceiling, confirmed her direction. Satisfied, she lowered her head taking in the grandeur of the tall, stained-glass windows. Colourful scenes of angels and robed men with arms outstretched, dominated the arched alcoves surrounding the perimeter of the church. Mesmerized by the beauty, she sat motionless. A crescendo from the organ jolted Bess's attention back to the service.

Just when her eyelids began to close, the choir began to sing a hearty chorus of "Hark The Herald Angels Sing" as they filed past her row. Suddenly, the jerking of drooping heads caused a domino effect along the pew. They composed themselves, stood up and joined the the congregation as the choir passed their row.

Out in the crisp air, they parted company. Mr. Brown and Sean carried on to the bakery as the ovens remained in hot demand for the cooking of the Christmas goose. The rest of the party made their way around the side of the church and entered a large hall, jutting out from the rear of the church. Inside, row upon row of tables set with white tablecloths and boughs of holly, stood ready for the less fortunate.

Bess took her appointed position at the pianoforte. For the next hour she played Christmas music, while the others served Christmas dinner to the poor. Even the children did their part by handing out sweets to the smiling waifs, dressed in rags. Lily, the flower lady, looked like a queen compared to the poor of London, sitting at the tables. Bess wondered *where have they been hiding? Oh, I've seen a few on the streets, but nothing like this. Right before my eyes, I'm seeing Dickens' London. Here they sit in their dirty rags called clothes, faces drawn and taut, and questioning eyes piercing deep into my soul asking, 'Why me and not you'?* Bess could look no more. She bowed her head and concentrated on the ivory keys. She prayed her music would bring a glimmer of hope to some of the vacant eyes, drawn deep within their sockets.

"Bess, luv, t'is time to go. We've done our part," said Lottie.

Bess got off the stool and spun around. An old woman looked up and gave her a toothless smile. "Bless ye, luv."

Tears came to Bess's eyes as a nearby table temporarily stopped their ravenous intake of food, to smile or give her a salute. Some poor souls grabbed her hand and echoed a Merry Christmas.

As they left the warmth of the church hall, a long line of Londoners, in sparsely covered garments, huddled together, waiting for their Christmas dinner. A young woman grabbed Bess's hand, said nothing, but looked deep into her eyes. Bess saw hopelessness and fear reflected from within the tormented soul. The woman opened her mouth to expose oozing gums of rotten teeth.

"Cum, Bess, luv." Lottie put her arm around her, causing the woman to release her hold.

In a daze, Bess walked back to the tearoom. She kept seeing those desperate eyes. Her hand ached from the bony hand that squeezed all the warmth out of Bess. She shivered.

Heavenly smells of turkey, roasting in the oven, greeted them as the tearoom door opened. "Cum by t' fire, Bess, luv. Yer freezin'. Tom, stoke up t'fire. Let's get sum life back in our Bess."

The warmth of the fire and the children's laughter soon brought Bess around. *I must enjoy the moment and be thankful I am not that young woman,* she told herself. Soon the hustle and bustle of the last minute preparations for the Christmas dinner, took precedence over her earlier experience. Jo and Bess laid the table with fine, white china and sparkling silverware. Lottie and Maureen Doyle busied themselves in the kitchen. Tom continued to add coal to the fire, while Michael Doyle contained the children.

Just as the ladies brought out the bowls of steaming vegetables, the door jingled and in walked Mr. Brown and Sean. "Ah, Mr. Brown --- Sean, perfect timin'. I thought ye'd be late, wot wit' all yer oven demands."

"Mrs. Morton, you don't think we'd miss a minute of your famous Christmas dinner?" replied Mr. Brown. He took off his heavy coat and Sean emptied a bag under the tree.

"While yer standin', Mr. Brown, would ye cum into t' kitchen an' fetch t' turkey?"

"At your service, my lady." Mr. Brown bowed.

The children giggled. " 'Urry, we're 'ungry."

The chatting stopped when Mr. Brown carried the golden turkey into the room. "Where do I put this fine bird?"

" 'Ere." Lottie took the plate away from the head of the table. "Tom will carve." She smiled at her brother. "Sit down everyone." The two boys made a mad dash to sit on either side of Bess. Lottie gave Bertie a stern look and shrugged her shoulders. "T'is Christmas."

Tom took his job seriously and did a fine job of carving the turkey. Sean said grace. The bowls of vegetables circulated around the table. Bess barely found room on the plate between the mashed potatoes and brussel sprouts, to lay her turkey.

"Gravy please," asked Bertie.

Bess poured it over his plate and then on Artie's before pouring some on her plate. *Something's missing,* she thought as she looked at her heaping plate. *Dressing? No it's under the beans.* Suddenly, she remembered. Bess got up and ran upstairs, leaving all surprised.

"Wot's wrong wit' Bess?" asked Lottie. "Did she spill sumthin' on 'er dress?" She looked at Bertie who shook his head.

A moment later, Bess came down the stairs carrying a bowl. "Sorry for being rude, but I just remembered, cranberry sauce."

"Cranberry sauce, wot's that?" asked Bertie.

"Christmas dinner is not complete without cranberry sauce." Bess looked around a table full of puzzled faces. "You don't know what cranberries are? Don't you have them here?"

"Never 'eard of 'em? 'Ave ye, Mr. Brown?" Lottie looked directly across at Mr. Brown and then to her left. "Did ye 'ave 'em in Ireland?"

"No," replied the Doyles.

"I'm sorry, I just assumed you knew. Cranberries are very popular in America. They are a tart berry, but when you add sugar and cook them, they are delicious and very healthy."

" 'Ow'd ye get 'em 'ere, Miss Bess?" asked Bertie.

Stunned for a moment, Bess put her hand behind her back,

crossed her fingers and said, "Why ----- why, Saint Nicholas, of course, brought them. He knows how I love cranberry sauce."

" 'E put 'em in yer stockin'?" Bertie crunched up his face.

Bess laughed. "No, he put the bowl on my dresser."

"Smart as well as generous," chided Tom.

"Take a spoonful and see how you like them." Bess handed it around. "No, not all at once, Artie, just a little at a time with your turkey. ---- That's better."

"Hmm ---- tastes good."

Maureen Doyle put a small amount in her mouth. "Tart and sweet at t' same time. What do ye t'ink, Michael?"

"Interestin'."

"Aye, indeed, it certainly adds flavour to the turkey," added Sean as he smacked his lips.

"Now that I think about it, I did read about cranberries in one of our American books. I had trouble envisioning them. Thank you, Saint Nicholas for clearing my vision and my taste-buds," laughed Jo.

"Well, let's make a toast," chimed in Mr. Brown. He lifted his goblet of red wine. "To the cranberries."

All around the table, they lifted their glasses. "To the cranberries."

"To Saint Nic-ho-las," toasted Bertie with his glass of milk.

"To Saint Nic-ho-las!"

"Sean, 'ave sum more turkey," said Lottie as she pointed at Tom to pass the platter.

"Aye, only if there be any cranberry sauce left."

The plates licked clean, they all inched their chairs away from the table. "Oh, I'm full," groaned Tom.

"Me too." Bertie rubbed his stomach.

"Well, I 'ope ye left room fer t' Christmas pudding?" Groans and moans replied to Lottie's statement. "Not to worry. --- By t' time t' dishes ar' cleared off an' t' tea brewed, ye'll be ready fer puddin', right?"

"Right." They all groaned.

The men sat around the table discussing politics and sports, while the ladies cleared off the table. Even little Patty did her part, by bringing in Bess's empty bowl. Her finger took a swipe of the red remains of the cranberry sauce and landed the sweet nectar in her mouth.

"Patty," scolded her mother.

"Maureen, let 'er be. T'is Christmas an' 'er only chance of ever 'avin' cranberry sauce." Lottie smiled, "Patty Doyle, suppose there be a lick fer me?" Lottie put on the kettle and prepared the pudding, while Jo and Maureen started washing the dishes. "Bess, can ye get me t' brandy from t' cupboard? Jo, bring me t' silver platter lyin' on t' drawin'board."

"Let me help you," said Jo as she rushed over to Lottie who held the steaming pudding in her towelled hands.

"Thank ye, luv. I'll just untie t' wet cloth an' we can turn t' puddin' upside down on t' platter," said Lottie as steam rolled down her rosy cheeks. "One --- two --- three." Lottie lifted the bowl off the half-moon shaped pudding.

"Perfect!" They inhaled the pleasant aroma. "It smells delicious!"

"Jo, can ye an' Bess take in t' tea trays? Maureen, can ye get t' pitcher of custard sauce? I'll bring in t' puddin'."

"I'll bring in t' brandy too," said Maureen as she took the simmering brandy off the stove.

"Right then, let's go, ladies. Patty open t' door, luv."

The traditional procession began. The men stopped talking. The boys licked their lips. Teapots and cups placed on the table, custard jiggled in its pitcher and all eyes looked on in anticipation. Lottie came into the room proudly carrying the dark, plum pudding. Maureen poured the steaming brandy over the top of the moulded pudding. It ran down the sides and ignited into a bluish flame as Tom lit the brandy. Oohs and aahs erupted. The flame subsided and Lottie scooped the pudding into small, crystal bowls. The pitcher of custard became the centre of attention as each poured a generous amount over their pudding.

During the excitement, Bess ran upstairs and retrieved the hard sauce off the dresser. Lightly touching the sauce, she exclaimed, "Still hard; good."

Back downstairs, a breathless Bess said, "Try some of this."

"Wot's it, Miss Bess?" asked Bertie.

"It's hard sauce; very sweet , so take just a little."

"Hard sauce?" asked Bertie.

"Did Saint Nic-oh-las bring it?"

"Indeed he did, Artie."

"He's good." Tom winked.

"Look, Mum, it melts into t' puddin'," said Bertie.

"Hmm," the children murmured through mouthfuls. "Do ye think Saint Nic-ho-las could bring us sum next year?"

The dishes washed, the women came into the tearoom to find the tables returned to their original spots, and the men sitting around the fireplace, engrossed in their sports talk.

"Aye, the lads will be in good shape for next Sunday's match," said Sean.

"Well, I don't know. After Christmas feasts, they could be in more shapes than they expected," laughed Mr. Brown.

"That's true. I wouldn't want to be playing tomorrow after tonight's feast. At first I was disappointed the game had been cancelled; especially as I missed last Sunday's game. Now I'm glad I'm not playing, but I'm sure looking forward to kicking the ball around next week." Tom stopped and jumped up to offer chairs to the ladies. As he held the chair out for Bess, he whispered in her ear, "You are coming to see me play next Sunday?"

"Providing it's not snowing, I'll come to see all you men play."

"Bess, do t'ey play football in America?" asked Michael Doyle.

"Well, yes and no --- they play football, but it is a completely different sport; albeit an extremely popular sport. It's more like a combination of rugby and your football. As for your football, it too is popular, but is called soccer."

"Strange. What about cricket?" asked Mr. Brown.

"Very little is played there."

"Cricket takes too long," piped up Lottie. "Men should be spendin' their time doin' sumthin' useful; not playin' wit a blimey wicket. --- Wicket it is." She gave a hearty laugh.

"Lottie, you say that about football."

"T'is almost as bad. A waste of time, I say, but blokes will be blokes."

"Mum, can Mr. and Mrs. Doyle 'n' Sean 'n' Mr. Brown open their stockin's from Saint Nic-ho-las?"

"Why of course. I fergot all about 'em," said Lottie. "Lads, ye can 'and 'em out."

" 'Ere, Mither, Father. Saint Nic-ho-las brung 'em fer ye." Artie carefully carried them over.

"Fer ye, Mr. Brown, Sean," said Bertie. --- "Wot's that?" asked Bertie as Mr. Brown extracted a metal object.

"I'm not sure." Mr. Brown examined it. "It's called Exacto ---- hmm?"

Bess piped up, "I think it is a knife. --- Yes, see the little lever slides up and yes, a sharp blade appears. I've been told it works very well cutting straight lines or tape."

"What's this, Bess?" asked Sean as he picked up a round, grey ball.

"Ah, everyman's secret weapon in America, duct tape. Why, it wraps pipes, covers holes and even mouths when people talk too much." Bess looked at Tom who looked like he was going to interrupt.

"Wot's this, Father?" Artie looked closely at his father's stash.

"I don't know, son." Michael examined the round object. "Well look, t'is a -- ah, yes, a measure."

Bess interrupted, "By pulling this lever down, it will hold the measuring tape still. When your finished, lifting the lever will release the tape back into its case."

"'T' leprechauns must have had somet'in to do wit' t'is. It's magic." Michael sprung it back and forth while Artie laughed. "Look here, Maureen; Irish Spring and Bailey's Irish Cream. Hmh, one's a soap and one's a spirit."

"Don't get them mixed up, Michael," laughed Tom.

"Look, Michael, I too have some soap ---- and gloves?" replied and uncertain Maureen.

"Gloves? I never seen any like 'em," puzzled Artie.

"They're rubber gloves, so when your mom washes clothes, she can wear them. They are water and heatproof. And ---- since you have some lotion there," Bess pointed, "your hands will be soft in no time." She smiled.

"Oh, how useful."

"Sourdough starter?" Mr. Brown opened the little book, attached to the bottle. "Very interesting. I'm going to try this tomorrow. ---- O'Henry?"

"It's a very popular chocolate bar in America."

"Well, I must be very popular in America." Bess looked at him strangely. "It is my Christian name ---- Henry, that is."

"Blimey, your Saint Nicholas even knows secrets we didn't know," chided Tom, "and even nationalities; Irish for the Irish. Hmm --- What's for the Scotsman, Sean?"

" 'Ow about Scotch Whiskey 'n' MacIntosh Toffee?" Sean lifted up a bottle in one hand and a red box in the other.

"Bloomin' marvelous!" Tom winked at Bess.

"Aye, speaking of marvelous, I 'ave a present for ye, I've ne'er seen before." Sean went over to his coat pocket and brought out a small wooden box. He handed it to Lottie. "I 'ope we 'ave room."

Lottie slipped the loose paper off the box and read it out loud, "'Fry's Eating Chocolate.' Eatin' chocolate?"

"Aye, Fry's just introduced it. We can eat it without putting it in baking or warming it for a drink. The salesman said 't'is a bonny treat.'"

"Open it, Mum." With Bertie's encouragement, Lottie opened the box to find a dozen, individually wrapped packages. She unwrapped one to discover a solid, brown slab of chocolate.

"Go on, Lottie. Try it," urged Tom.

All stood still as she took a bite. "Oh my, t'is delicious. --- Blimey, t'is good."

Each took a piece and experienced their first taste of eating chocolate. Bess thought *a bit grainy --- somewhat of a bitter taste, but for a first try, not bad. Eventually, they'll get all those ten letter preservatives in there, and it will taste just right.*

"Thank you, Sean, for giving me the opportunity to taste Fry's, first eating chocolate. It is very good, indeed," said Bess.

"Do ye 'ave eatin' chocolate in America?"

"Yes, we do, Bertie. It tastes different and doesn't smell as strong."

Everyone took a whiff. "Hmmm."

"I think ours doesn't smell so ---- chocolatey because they add other things, like nuts and flavoured creams. Why, Mr. Brown's O'Henry bar has both in it."

"Well, I shall certainly enjoy it then." Mr. Brown smacked his lips.

"Me 'n' Artie can 'elp ye, Mr. Brown."

"I'm sure you could, but since it has my name on it, why, it would be rude of me not to eat it all. Besides, lads, I don't want to disappoint Saint Nicholas. He might not come back."

"Yer right, Mr. Brown," said a crestfallen Bertie.

"But I do have something that will sweeten your mood." Mr. Brown reached in his jacket pocket and pulled out three sticks of hard candy. "Here you are, Patty, Artie, Bertie."

"Rock candy! Oh goodie!"

"Wot do ye say?"

"Oh --- thank ye, Mr. Brown," the three echoed as they sucked their candy.

"I also have some twists of barley and ------ "

"Gob stoppers!"

"I luv 'em. They change colours as I suck 'em," declared Artie.

"They sound like our jaw breakers. ---- Yes, I'm sure they are. When I was your age, I would get a small bag full of them. I don't know if I liked them that much, but when I got four for a penny, I loved them," recalled a smiling Bess.

Bess got up and went over to the Christmas tree. Careful to avoid the flickering candles, she squeezed her body behind the tree and bent over, exposing her petticoat and runners. She picked up two presents.

"Can I help you?" asked Tom with an evident gleam in his mischievous eyes.

"Oh, yes, you can take these. Er --- Thank you, Tom." A blushing Bess stood up and straightened her skirt.

"At your service, miss." Tom winked. "Why, whose this for? Is there a Bertie or an Artie here?"

"Uncle Tom." The boys rushed over. "For me?"

"Well, let's see." Tom looked up at the presents, deliberately held high above the boys' heads. "Hmm – they both say to Bertie and Artie ----- Love Bess xxooo."

"Wot's xxooos?"

"Hugs and kisses," piped up Bess, still stuck behind the Christmas tree.

"Well, if you insist." Tom moved closer to Bess.

"Uncle Tom."

"Okay, take your presents and I'll help Bess out from behind the tree." Tom extended his hand towards Bess.

"Look, Artie, t'is t' fire wagon in t' toy shoppe window."

"Wot's in t' bottom?" asked Artie. He dropped the other present to help Bertie unwrap the rest of the box. "Look, t'is a fireman."

" 'Ere's a 'orse --- an' another ---- an' ----- "

"Aye, what ye got there, laddies?" asked Sean as he bent down.

"Look, Sean, t'is wot we's bin wantin' ferever." Bertie showed him a wooden horse.

"Bertie, old man, it looks like Sadie," commented Tom, kneeling down beside them.

"T'is me favourite, cause it looks like 'er an' cause if it weren't fer Sadie, Miss Bess would never of cum to live wit' us." Bertie grinned at Bess.

"What's in the other present, Artie?" asked Jo.

Artie ripped it open and out fell three books. "Books! I luv to read, I do, Miss Jo."

Jo cocked her head towards the floor. "Let's see them, Artie. I don't recognize them."

Artie picked one up, while Bertie came to the rescue and picked up the other two. "La-st of t' M-o -----"Artie put his finger under the h.

"Mohicans, Artie. I've heard of it." Jo looked at the author's name. "Yes. Of course, James Fenimore Cooper; he's an American author. Did you bring this over with you, Bess?"

"Actually, I did. A friend gave it to me to read on the journey." Bess thought for a moment and put her hand behind her back. With crossed fingers, she said, "Infact, he said it was a great adventure for a young boy's imagination." She winked at the boys. "Luckily, it was in the luggage I got back the other day."

"Wot's a mo-e-can?"

"Mohicans are American Indians, Bertie."

"That sounds exciting. Maybe I could read it too," said Tom.

Jo picked up the other two books. "I've not heard of Rowling." She opened the book.

"Strange, it's published here. I thought the author was American."

" 'Arry Po-ot-ter," read Artie, "an' t' pi --------"

"Let me read it, Artie: 'Harry Potter And The Philosopher's Stone' and 'Harry Potter And The Chamber Of Secrets.'"

"Look at t' picture on t' front, Mum." Bertie handed the book to his Mom.

"Blimey, t'is looks like ye 'n' Artie."

"Where did you get them, Bess?" asked Jo.

Fingers still crossed, which Bess worried she may soon become permanently deformed, she said, "I saw the colourful front covers in a shoppe window and immediately thought of the boys. Er --- unfortunatley, I didn't notice the name of the shoppe or what street it was on." She looked at Jo. "Sorry, Jo."

"No matter, I will ask my suppliers."

"Well, lads, what do ye say to Miss Bess?" said Michael Doyle.

They both jumped up and gave Bess bearhugs. "Thank ye, Miss Bess. We luv 'em."

Michael looked at Maureen and said to Patty, "We were goin' to give ye your present t'is mornin', but since ye slept here last night, we brought it wit' us. Since t' lads have presents, we didn't want our lovely girl left out. He reached over the counter and brought out a large parcel. "Merry Christmas, Patty."

Her face lit up as her little hands pulled out her gift. "A dolly!" Patty held her precious present close to her. "Thank ye, Mither, Father 'n' Artie.

As they crowded around to view the doll, Bess remembered something and slipped up the stairs. Rummaging around her bedroom, she found the object of her search and headed downstairs. "Patty, I think this might fit your dolly." Bess handed her the miniature shawl, orginally destined for Lydia, which miraculously kept skirting the journey to the future.

"Oh, t'is pretty. Thank ye, Miss Bess."

The time came for all the guests to depart. Michael cleared his throat. "Since I'm goin' to have to carry your sister home, ye can help and carry t'is." Michael reached behind the counter and threw out a ball.

"A football!" Artie squealed.

"Laddie, ye can come play with us on Sunday." Sean shouted, "Watch out, Tom; he may just replace ye."

Laughing, Tom opened the door. " He might as well start practising now." The ball flew out the door with Artie in hot pursuit.

"Merry Christmas," shouted the Doyles. They trodded into the snowy night, arms laden with presents and one sleeping child, cuddling her dolly.

"Bess, luv, ye was too kind wit' t' lads." Lottie closed the door and shivered.

"Mrs. Pennycroft was too kind. I just shared her kindness."

"Speakin' of sharin', 'ere's sumthin' ye was interested in." Lottie handed Bess an envelope.

Hidden in the bottom corner, lay a small piece of paper. Bess lifted it out. "A Penny Black."

"Aye, remember I told ye I 'ad an extra one and since ye was so interested, I want ye to 'ave it."

"Lottie, are you sure?" Lottie smiled and nodded. "Thank you."

"Well, since it is your turn." Tom gave Bess a neatly, wrapped parcel. Bess untied the red ribbon and out drifted the scarf she admired at "Taylor & Sons." "Lydia said you really liked it."

"Oh, I do. Thank you, Tom." Bess gave him a kiss on the cheek.

"Thank you, Bess," said Tom as Bertie giggled.

"One more," said Jo. She pulled out a present from behind the velvet drape.

"It's beautiful. I have a perfect spot to hang it." Bess lifted the piece of cross-stitch. "Did you do this?"

"Yes, I've always liked lighthouses and I wanted this to help guide your journey home."

"It will be my guiding light." Bess gave Jo a hug. "Now, I have three more presents to give out. Jo, this is for you. Lottie ---- Tom, this is for you."

Jo opened her's first to reveal a scarf. "Thank you, Bess. It is lovely." She put it around her neck.

"Oh, my, wot a beautiful shawl." Lottie wrapped her gift around her shoulders. "Oh, I shall look posh when we go fer tea tomorrow, Bess. Thank ye, luv." The ladies hugged.

"Wot yer got, Uncle Tom?"

"Well, I know it's not a shawl; it's too small and too hard." Tom winked and Bertie laughed. He opened the sprung loaded box and said, "Why, it's a ------- "

"Fountain pen." Bess came to the rescue.

"Wot's a fountain pen?"

"A fountain pen, you know, Bertie, old man." Tom turned to Bess. "It's a ----- "

Bess demonstrated the use of the pen. "See how much faster you will be able to do your accounting."

"Well, I never."

"Another new invention from America?"

"Yes, I brought it with me."

Tom scribbled some letters on a piece of paper. "I think this too is an American invention." He handed it to Bess.

She read, "XXOOO." Tom winked, Bess blushed and Bertie giggled.

"Bess, wake up. We should open our presents."

"We just opened them. I love my shawl."

"Shawl? Who gave you a shawl?"

"You ----- " Bess opened her eyes to see Evan staring at her. "Er ---- I must have been dreaming. I did get a new shawl, but I got it myself."

"Show it to me later. Let's open our presents before Christmas is over."

"What time is it?"

"Eleven o'clock."

"Right then. You be Saint Nicholas."

"Saint Nicholas? I haven't heard Santa referred to that for a long time. Why, it is almost ancient."

"Actually, I've heard him called that quite often lately," smiled Bess. "I've forgotten a present. I'll be right back." She ran upstairs and thought *how often have I done this today? Well, at least it's good exercise.*

Bess opened the drawer of her nightstand and lifted out a small present. She carefully peeled the tape off the wrapping paper. Within the folds of the paper, the little, red book appeared. Tucked between the cover and first page, a tiny, glassine envelope crinkled when she picked it up. Holding her breath, she plunged her hand into her pocket and pulled out its contents. Bess exhaled. *Yes, the Penny Black has made the journey to the twenty-first century.* As she opened the wrinkled envelope, young Queen Victoria's profile stared back at her. Gently, she removed the stamp and placed it in the glassine envelope alongside the Penny Red and Two Penny Blue.

Bess smiled as she relived the moment Lottie gave her the stamp. Even after she said goodnight to the Morton household and closed her bedroom door, she felt the excitement. She couldn't wait to give it to Evan and now the time had come.

"Bess, it's eleven-fifteen. What are you doing?"

She placed the envelope back in the book, quickly rewrapped the present and ran downstairs.

"Saint Nicholas leave a present upstairs?"

"He certainly did. It's addressed to you, Evan."

Bess's heart stopped as he ripped open the silver paper. "A book, a small, red book. Hmm, it looks old." Evan put it under the light. "'A Christmas Carol.'" Bess continued to hold her breath. Evan opened the book and read, "'To Evan, Charles Dickens --- December 21, 1847.'" He gave her a strange look. "No, couldn't be," he remarked. The transparent envelope fluttered to the floor. "What's this?"

The room grew silent. Only the sounds of crinkling paper could be heard as Evan's fingers picked up the envelope and eagerly opened it. His plump fingers drew out a blue postage stamp. He went over to the light and examined it.

"Is this what I think it is?" He rushed over to the drawer and brought out a magnifying glass. "Damnation, I think it is." In his excitement, he gripped the envelope tighter, causing a crunching sound. Evan looked down to see red and black. "There's another one. A red ---- a black ---- A Penny Black! No couldn't be." The magnifying glass went into overload. "Bess, do you know what this is?" Bess shrugged her shoulders. "But --- where did you ever come across the first postage stamp? And a Penny Red and a Two Penny Blue? My Lord, Bess, I can't believe it and this book too. If they are authentic, do you realize how old they are?"

"Well, you did say that it was a very long time since Saint Nicholas' day. Maybe he's been saving it for you."

Evan looked at Bess with a peculiar expression. Regaining his composure he said, "Open your presents, Bess."

She ripped away the wrapping on the first present to discover a styrofoam box. Upon lifting the lid, her eyes grew wide as they gazed upon a Dickens building. "Oh, Evan, 'The Old Curiosity Shoppe.' What a coincidence; we both got something from Charles Dickens." The styrofoam screeched as she lifted the ceramic building from its tightly moulded box. "It's beautiful, Evan. I can just imagine walking through the angled doorway and entering a shoppe full of curiosities. Perhaps, your book laid upon its table or your stamps laid ready to be attached to an important letter or parcel."

Evan looked through its window. "I didn't realize you had such an imagination. Very curious. Maybe that's why it is called 'The Old Curiosity Shoppe.' " He gave her another strange look and said, "Open your other present." Absent-minded, Bess took the slim, red box from Evan and continued to stare at the shoppe. "Bess, your present."

"Oh, yes ---- sorry, Evan. My, it is small. Hmm, what can it be?" She untied the gold bow and lifted the lid. "A piece of paper; just what I always wanted."

"Bess, ---- look at it."

She unfolded the legal-size paper and read, "Cruise away?" Her eyes went down the page. "Hawaii? ---- What is this, Evan?"

"Pack your bag, Bess. We're going cruising through the Hawaiian Islands."

"When?"

"December 27."

"December 27? This year? Like two days from now?"

"Yes, isn't it great? I saw an ad in the paper, phoned and luckily, they had two tickets."

"Hawaii? ---- In two days?" ----- *great.*

# CHAPTER XVII

*B*ess tossed and turned. She tried to close her eyes, but like a sprung loaded coil, they remained open. Her mind kept switching from the warm sands of Waikiki to the warmer embers of the tearoom's fireplace. One minute the smell of coconut oil filled her nostrils and the next, the smell of fresh baked scones overpowered her senses. The sound of waves crashing on the shore almost put her to sleep, but the persistent clip clop of horses hooves would awaken her.

*Why did he pick now to go to Hawaii? Doesn't he sense I'll be going on an ocean voyage to America in a couple of weeks? He knows I get seasick. I don't want to disappoint Evan, but I don't want to leave my friends in Fetter Lane. I'm not ready yet.*

"Oh, Evan!"

"Snoort, snoort ---- What?"

Bess laid motionless in bed until Evan's snoring remained constant. She slipped out of bed and crept downstairs and plugged in Fetter Lane. With a heavy heart, she plunked down and absently stared at the Hawaiian cruise itinerary. In desperation, she cast her eyes skyward for inspiration and saw a worried Mr. Spider.

"What do I do, Mr. Spider?" When nothing was forthcoming, she continued, "I know I should be ecstatic, being whisked off on a tropical cruise in the middle of winter, but ---- oh, Mr. Spider, I don't want to go. I am on a journey of a lifetime, and I don't want it to end. It may never come my way again."

Bess looked across at the tearoom and said, "How can I tell them I'm leaving so soon? Why, I haven't seen Tom play soc -- er football yet and Lottie needs my help. --- And the boys. --- I want to read "Harry Potter" to them --- I ----- "

"Bess, luv? Whose in there wit' ye?"

"Ah ---- no one. I'm just mumbling to myself."

"Well I 'ope yer gettin' sum good answers."

"I wish."

"Pardon."

Bess opened the door, and Lottie's smile turned to a frown. "Bess, luv, ye look like ye 'aven't slept a wink all night. Anythin' wrong?"

"Too much Christmas dinner."

"Well, let's 'ope it settles to the bottom cause we've got lots more eatin' to do today; wot wit' Miss Rosewater's tea an' t' Fowler's dinner." Lottie patted Bess's hand. "We'll be goin' to church first thin' t'is mornin'. T'is Boxin' Day and t' church will 'ave lots of boxes to give out to t' poor. Bess, go wash yer face; ye'll feel better. 'Ere's a warm pitcher of water." Lottie handed the white, china pitcher to Bess. "But, do 'urry, luv. We don't want to be late."


Bess held Bertie's hand tightly and pressed her arm closer to Tom's as they walked to the church. When they reached their seats, she didn't want to let go.

"I should give you a shawl everyday." Tom winked at Bess as her arm slowly slipped from his.

The sermon focused on giving to others, hence the boxes filled with food and essentials for the poor. The sermon took another direction and the vicar said, "Do not disappoint those who give themselves to you; even though your heart is not glad."

At that moment, Bess knew she must go with Evan to Hawaii.

She looked at her new family and wondered *how do I tell them I'm leaving?* As they knelt to pray, Bess asked for guidance. Like with Evan, she did not want to disappoint them.

After church, Lottie stayed behind to help sort out the boxes. Tom took Bertie and Bess back to the tearoom. Jo went off to the pub to help her brother. The tearoom felt empty.

"Tell you what, Bess, why don't you change into your trousers and come along and help Bertie and me? Bertie can keep a secret, can't you, lad?" Bertie nodded his head. "No one must know Bess is a girl ---- and no telling your mother."

"I promise, Uncle Tom."

"Right then, off you go. Ivan will be here in five minutes to pick us up."

"What are we doing, if I might ask?" Bess shouted from up the stairs.

"Delivering boxes to the poor."

"On Boxing Day. Hmm --- Now that's a novel idea." Bess looked down the stairs and winked at Tom.


A "Williams & Sons" green, delivery carriage stopped at the curb. Bess went over to the horse, patted his head and gave him a lump of sugar. He gave her a thank you nod.

"Nice to see you, Billy," she whispered in his flickering ear.

"Aye, Tom, bach, I see you've brought along some helpers. Bertie, bach, what's this? You've grown since I last saw you. You'll have no trouble hopping up on the seat. Up you get, lad." Ivan extended his hand, while Tom gave Bertie a boost from behind. "Aye, Ben, bach, good to see you, mate."

"Ben? T'is Mi -- " Bertie started to say when Tom cleared his throat. Getting Bertie's attention, Tom zipped his mouth shut. "Aye, Ben." Bertie giggled.

"Tom, you and Ben get in the cab." Ivan clicked his tongue. "Billy, wake up."

Billy sprinted off and Bess landed on Tom's lap. "I always liked

Billy; a horse after my own thought." Tom snorted. "Ben, mate, don't move on my account."

After a few more close encounters, they arrived at the church. "And I was just starting to enjoy this ride." Tom waved his eyebrows up and down as he opened the door.

"Sorry for tossing you around in there. These delivery wagons don't have the comfort of a coach," remarked Ivan, as he followed Bertie. "Aye, perfect timing." A group of men, arms full of boxes, emerged from the church. "Open the back door, Tom, bach. We'll fill it up first."

They left the church, with Tom and Bess snuggled together amongst the boxes. "This is even better." Tom put his arm around Bess. "Ah, that's better; I was getting a cramp in my arm."

Bess replied, "Sure, sure." However, she did not remove his arm. *Boxed in is not such a bad idea.* She smiled.

The first delivery came all too soon. In spite of the cramped quarters, Tom jumped down and opened the back door, leaving the stacked boxes in the cab untouched. Bess followed his example and ignored the obvious lack of space in the cab. Loaded with boxes, the three of them headed towards a dilapidated building.

"Happy Boxing Day!" heralded Ivan from his high perch.

Windows opened and expectant faces stared through grimy panes of broken glass. The creaky door swung open, and calloused hands reached out to Tom. Skin and bones clung to Bess's arms as she handed over the boxes. Small hands pushed their way passed dirty skirts and trousers to grab the boxes from Bertie. Within seconds, they stood at the door empty handed.

"My gosh! What's in those boxes? Gold?"

"You might say so: some contain food, others clothes, even blankets. They'll sort it out. If it's something they can't use, they'll barter or exchange it." Tom shook his head. "Come on, lads. Our job is not done yet." He gave them a smack on the backside.

Within the hour, all the boxes found a home. Overwhelmed, they returned to the sanctity of "The Lotatea Shoppe."

"See you next Sunday, Ivan."

"Aye, I hope t'is not snowing, Tom, bach. No decent Welshman should be out in the freezing snow playing football. Rugby, maybe." Ivan laughed. "That reminds me, did you give our Bertie his Christmas present?"

"Blimey, I forgot."

"Uncle Tom," whined Bertie.

"Thought as much since he only talked about toy soldiers and firemen." Ivan laughed at Bertie and Billy snorted. "And, horses."

As he left, Ivan shouted, "Nice seeing you, Ben, bach."

Inside the tearoom, Bertie grabbed his uncle's arm. "Wot about me present?"

"Ah, your present, I almost forgot."

"Uncle Tom."

"Come on up to my room." The two started up the stairs and Tom suddenly stopped.

"Bess, you go first. I think I hear Lottie in the kitchen --- and we don't want her to see you in your trousers. We'd all have too much explaining to do." She squeezed between the two of them and they charged upstairs.

Bess no sooner got her trousers off and her dress back on, when Bertie banged on the door. "Miss Bess, football boots. Cum see." With one hand on the doorknob and the other manoeuvring the button of her dress through the buttonhole, she opened the door to a wide-eyed Bertie. "See wot Uncle Tom got me." He thrust a black boot at her. "T'is 'ere cleat 'elps a bloke from slidin' an' fallin' in t' mud. Not many mates 'ave 'em."

"Bertie, you are a lucky boy to have a thoughtful uncle."

"A rich one too. Blimey, 'em cost more in me school boots."

"Wot's all the noise?" Lottie shouted up the stairs.

"Mum, cum see wot Uncle Tom got me fer Christmas." Bertie rushed to meet his mother in the hallway. "Look, Mum." Bertie handed a boot to Lottie. "Inn't smashin'?" His face beamed. "Can I take 'em over to show Artie? We could play wit' 'is new ball. Can I, Mum?"

"Ye could drop 'em in t' snow an' ruin 'em."

"I'll take him over there. It will give me a chance to chat with Michael," piped up Tom through his bedroom door.

"Can we, Mum?" Bertie stared at his mother.

"Oh, off wit' ye, but 'ave 'im back in time fer 'is bath cause me an' Bess ar' goin' out fer tea soon."

"Sister, dear, don't fret. I'll take care of it while your at tea." Tom came out of the room. "Come on, Bertie, my man. Let's be off."

"Speakin' of tea, we best get ready. Miss Water is expectin' us."

Bess ran upstairs to get her new shawl. She placed it around her shoulders and felt its softness comfort her body. She looked in the mirror and agreed with Lydia; it did enhance the blue of her eyes. She ran her fingers through her hair, grabbed a small parcel off the dresser and headed downstairs.

They flagged a cab and took off for Miss Rose Water's tea. The journey took them through a nicer part of town. Bess picked out a couple of familiar landmarks she had seen on her delivery service with Ivan. To her surprise, the cab turned into a square of lovely, brick houses, where she had delivered parcels only three days before. The carriage stopped in front of a three-storey, pink house. A bright pink door awaited their arrival. Along the walkway, bare sticks of rose bushes poked through the blanket of snow. *I bet they're pink too,* smiled Bess. The door opened and a young woman dressed in a black dress, white apron and cap greeted them.

"Miss Water is expectin' ye ladies. T'is way please."

"Mrs. Morton, Miss Bess, do come in. I am delighted to see you. Come sit by the fire. Marie, please take the ladies coats."

"Thank you, Miss Water. This room is lovely," said Bess as she took in the feminine ambience.

Soft shades of pink covered every corner of the room, from the flocked wallpaper, to the drapes, upholstered chairs, pillows, the rug, they stood on and even the pianoforte said, 'Rosewood.' Pleasantly surprised, Bess found the room void of clutter; very few knick-knacks adorned the tables and mantel. The cozy room needed little candlelight to make it bright and cheery. The room's hostess looked right at home in her surroundings.

"Marie, will you let my niece know our guests have arrived --- and let Mrs. Hudson know, we shall want tea in about twenty minutes." Miss Rose Water waited until she left the room. "A lovely girl. Marie came to us a year ago. Poor thing; no family. We are most fortunate to have her. She is a great help to dear Mrs. Hudson, who has been in our household since I was a young girl. We both needed some young blood here."

"Auntie, I'm sorry, I didn't realize our guests had arrived." A pretty, fair-haired young woman entered the room.

"Harriet, dear, do come and meet Mrs. Morton and Miss Bess."

"Nice to meet you. Auntie has told me much about your lovely tea shoppe. --- And Miss Bess, thank you ever so much for the music. Will you play for me. I do want to know if I'm playing this correctly."

Bess and Harriet made their way to the grand piano, while the other two remained chatting by the fire. Impressed by the beautiful tone of the piano, Bess played "White Christmas."

When she finished, she said to Harriet, "Your turn."

The two exchanged positions. Harriet played very well. Time went quickly by as they got caught up in their choices of music; each giving the other a chorus of the latest song.

"Tea is served, miss."

"What a treat to be served, instead of serving the tea. Why yes, Marie, I would like another cup, please," said a delighted Lottie. "I do hope your Mrs. Hudson will give me the recipe for these tarts. They are delicious."

"Bakewell tarts. Mrs. Hudson is from Derby. I think it is an old local recipe. She has baked them for our family for years. I do admire good cooking. Poor Mrs. Hudson tried to teach me to cook, but somehow I manage to burn everything. Harriet is a much better pupil." Miss Rose Water smiled proudly at Harriet, sitting on a pink, tuft ottoman.

"Ah, but no one can grow roses like you, Auntie."

All too soon the ladies rose to leave. They thanked the hostess and headed for the waiting cab to take them back to their work-a-day world.

"A small token for your kindness, Miss Water." Bess handed her a pink, satin satchel containing a bar of rose scented soap.

Miss Rose Water gave her a kiss on the cheek. "Thank you, my dear. It has truly been our pleasure to spend the afternoon with you."

"See you at the tea shoppe."

After a pleasant ride back, they opened the front door to gales of laughter coming from the kitchen. The ladies poked their heads in the doorway to find Bertie soaking in the tub and Tom performing a bizarre interpretation of a powwow dance. On the table, "The Last Of The Mohicans" lay open.

" 'Ave ye started to read t' book?"

"Ladies, we didn't hear you come in. No, we haven't started the book yet. I'm just setting the stage for Bertie. We have to be in the right frame of mind."

"You'd better hold onto that mind of yours. When you get to the middle of the book, them there Indians grab you by the hair and scalp the mind right off you."

"Miss Bess, yer spoofin', right?" Bertie turned his head.

"You'll have to read the book to find out." Bess produced an evil smile. "Oh, you missed a spot on your neck, Bertie."

"Miss Bess, yer not supposed to be lookin' at me."

"Don't worry, Bertie, old man. The way your huddled in that bathtub, she can only see your neck."

"That reminds me, when do you have your bath, Tom?"

"Why, Miss Bess, I didn't think you were interested."

" 'E 'as it on Tuesday night," giggled Bertie.

"Oh, not tonight? I thought after your football match, you'd be needing one," said a disappointed Bess. *I'm going to miss it; no thanks to Evan.*

" 'E wants to be manly in front of 'is mates, so 'e 'as a cold one at t' football field," teased Lottie.

"Blokes 'ave cold baths. Only ladies 'n' children 'ave 'ot baths."

"Right, Bertie. Nothing like a cold bath to make a man out of you." Tom smacked his chest.

"T'is funny on Tuesdays, 'ow t' 'ot water disappears, when yer 'avin' yer cold bath," tutted Lottie.

"Ladies, out with you. It's time for Bertie to get out. --- Listen, I hear the clock strike five." Tom put his hand up to his ear.

"Blimey, Mrs. Fowler t'is expectin' us fer dinner. 'Urry, Bertie." The ladies stepped back into the dining room to give Bertie some privacy. "Me baby is growin'. 'Ere 'e is talkin' about bein' a man already. Why, 'e's still wet behind t' ears."

Through the closed kitchen door, they heard Tom scold Bertie, " Your hair's still wet. Come on, lad, give me that towel. Your mum is going to blame me if you catch a cold."

"Literally, I'd say, Lottie." The two ladies looked at each other and burst out laughing.

"Can't stop time; can we?"

"True, but when we least expect it, time can stop us," replied Bess thinking of the last ten days. "Sometimes, we can even go back in time."

"Pardon, wot did ye say, luv?"

"Miss Bess, can ye lace up me boots fer me?" Bertie interrupted as he barged through the door.

"Where's yer uncle?"

"Uncle Tom's throwin' out t' bath water."

By the time Bess managed to lace up Bertie's boots, Tom entered. "Ladies, let me help you with your coats."

"Oh, I fergot a Christmas cake. Mrs. Fowler luvs me cake." Lottie ran into the kitchen.

"Oh, I forgot something too." Bess ran up the stairs. Tom shook his head.

On her dresser, Bess grabbed the last bar of scented soap and slipped it in her pocket. A box of chocolates lay unopened. She had planned to give it to the Mortons as a Boxing Day gesture, but when Sean proudly presented his first box of "Fry's Eating Chocolate," she changed her mind. Somehow her every day chocolates, however tasty they may be, should and would not interfere with that historical moment. She picked up the box. *Yes, this is an appropriate hostess gift on Boxing Day.* She turned and said to herself *I'll take it.*

"Ladies, come on. We'll be late."

The gaslights lead them safely past "Basil's Spice & Mustard Shoppe." Bess took a deep breath. The spices lingered in the crisp, night air. *Perhaps I will not smell them again,* she sighed. *In fact, where will I ever smell such intensity of herbs and spices? The spice section of the supermarket? Huh --- with the bottles all hermetically sealed; I think not. And, what's the chances of being there when one of them accidentally falls and breaks on the floor? Hmm ---- that's an idea.*

As they reached "The Brown Bread," Mr. Brown stepped out. "I've been watching for you. I thought I might have missed you, and was just about to leave when I saw your happy faces."

"Good even', Mr. Brown." Lottie smiled demurely.

"Mr. Brown, guess wot Uncle Tom gave me fer Christmas?" Bertie grabbed his arm.

"What is it, lad? It must be grand."

"Aye, t'is t' best. Football boots."

"That is grand, Bertie." He patted him on the back.

"Hush now, Bertie. Remember, t' captain doesn't like a lot of noise," scolded Lottie as they stood on Fowler's doorstep.

"Welcum, do cum in from t'cold." A friendly smile greeted them.

They entered through the butcher shoppe. The room smelt of fresh antiseptic and cleaning fluids. Not a dead thing hung from the empty hooks. In the display counter, no remnants of ground or cubed meat lay in the clean trays.

"My, Mr. Fowler, t'is looks like a different place. I've never seen it so clean. Not that ye don't keep it clean, mind," said Lottie as they made their way to the back of the shoppe.

"Aye, wot wit' two days off, I've given it a right owlde clean, if I do say so meself." He pointed towards a set of stairs, hidden from view of the shoppe. "This way, ladies. Mrs. Fowler t'is waitin' fer ye."

"I 'ope she 'asn't gone to any trouble."

"Ye know Mrs. Fowler; she bin cookin' an' cleanin' all dye. Don't tell 'er I said so," he laughed.

As they climbed the dark, narrow staircase, the heavenly smell of lamb roasting, became stronger. More than one stomach gurgled in anticipation of what awaited them. They neared the landing and the warmth of the room flowed down to greet them.

"Where's me supper, woman?"

"Not long now, Father; our guests will be 'ere any minute."

"'Ere we ar', Mrs. Fowler," shouted Lottie.

"Ah, Mrs. Morton. Mr. Fowler, do take their coats." Mrs. Fowler gave a welcoming smile. "Cum sit by t' fire; ye must be cold."

"Woman, ye don't know wot cold t'is. Why, I remember t' time we was sailin' on t' North Sea an' 'em icebergs ----- why, t'was big as mountains, they was."

"Aye, Father. --- 'Ave a stick of barley sugar. 'Twill tide ye over to supper."

"Tide? --- Did I tell ye about t' time we got in to port in France an' t' tide went out so far, we waited days before we could set sail."

"It used to be 'ours, now t'is days." Mrs. Fowler shook her head. "Mrs. Morton, I do luv yer shawl."

"Aye, t'is lovely. Bess gave it to me fer Christmas."

"Oh, wot a luv. My, yer shawl is a pretty blue, Miss Bess."

"Uncle Tom gave it to 'er fer Christmas," piped up Bertie.

"Oh, did 'e now? My, my." Mrs. Fowler looked at a blushing Tom and giggled.

"Don't tease 'im. Why, if I found one to match yer green eyes, I'd buy ye one." Mr. Fowler smiled down at his jovial wife. "Men do t'is coind of thing, right Tom?" Tom nodded. "Tell me, Tom, 'ow's Mr. Turner treatin' ye?"

"Such a gentleman." Mrs. Fowler smiled.

The captain nodded off, while the three men sat in the corner and discussed Mr. Turner's virtues. *I wonder if Evan's ears are burning,* mused Bess. The women talked about Christmas Day and the latest fashions seen at church. Bess took the opportunity to look around. The small parlour appeared even smaller with every inch taken up with tables, covered in knick-knacks, chairs adorned with embroidered pillows, crochet throws and cabinets filled with books and china. A large, red plaid ottoman, surrounded by a skirt of silk tassels, left little walking space. Near the front window, a large terrarium confined a potted plant. Seascapes hung from the planked walls. *The captain's influence, no doubt.*

"Is this your needlework, Mrs. Fowler?" asked Bess.

" 'Eavens no, luv. T'is Mother's work. She's always got a needle in 'er 'ands. Me, on t' other 'and, were all thumbs," giggled Mrs. Fowler. "Innit right, Mother?"

"Aye t'is right. It weren't lack of tryin'. Why, I gave 'er music lessons. Stone deaf she were. I tried paintin'; thought she might take after her father. 'E painted all these." Mrs. Fowler's mother pointed to the ones on the wall. "Seems she be colour-blind. I tried to teach 'er needlework, but after a short time I gave up. I were afraid there were no blood left in 'er pricked fingers. Thank goodness, Mr. Fowler didn't notice 'er lack of parlour skills."

"Mother, I weren't that bad."

"Ah, but put 'er in t' kitchen, she excels. If she isn't cookin' delicious meals, she be workin' on t' shoppe books."

"Ah, Mrs. Fowler is a jewel; she keeps me fed 'n' rich." Mr. Fowler proudly patted his protruding stomach. "An she's pretty as a lilac in May. Wot more could a man want?" He gave his wife a loving smile.

"Oh, Mr. Fowler, after all t' years, ye still make me blush." She raised her well-fed body off the chair. "I'll just go in an' see 'ow dinner's progressin'."

"Dinner? Blimey, innit ready yet?" asked the captain as he stirred from a nap. "Five bells an' we'd eat; not like 'ere 'n their fancy ideas. --- Eatin' at five bells, nay six or seven bells. I'm goin' back to t' Victory. Nelson ne'er let us wait six bells fer our even' meal." He squinted at Bertie. "Cum 'ere, lad. I'll tell ye about T' Battle of Trafalgar. Nelson 'ad just given 'is famous signal, 'England expects ev'ry man will do 'is duty,' when they started firin'."

"Weren't ye scared?" asked a wide-eyed Bertie.

"Nay, not I; not wit' Lord Nelson givin' t' orders. Why ----- "

"Dinner is ready."

"Wot? T'is about time. I'll tell ye later about Nelson losin' 'is arm in '97."

"Father!"

They entered the dining room, all aglow in the flickering light of the massive candelabra, suspended over the large table. Great care had been taken to set the table, adorned in pristine, white linen and fine china of pink roses. On the sideboard, bowls of vegetables stood steaming. At the end of the table, the largest roast, Bess had ever seen, waited to be carved.

"Mrs. Fowler puts on a fine spread. We don't do it French style, wit course after course. We like to put it all out at once. Nothin' like getting' all t' flavours mixed in together."

"Mr. Fowler, would ye please carve t' lamb before t' dinner gets cold."

"Aye, Mrs. Fowler. Nothin' like a good piece of mutton."

"Carrots, Mr. Brown?"

"Mrs. Fowler, you've cooked the roast to perfection."

"Thank ye, Mr. Evans. More potatoes?"

"Puddin' where's our puddin'?"

"Dessert is cumin', Father."

"Let me help clean up the dishes." Bess got up and gathered a pile of dirty plates and used cutlery.

"Mrs. Morton, do sit. T'is nice to wait on ye fer a change. Miss Bess 'n' me will be back in a moment wit' t' dessert."

"Bertie, luv, 'elp Bess. Ye can take t'is bowl. Mind ye don't drop it."

"Mum!"

"Our Bertie is grown' up. Won't be long fer 'e's a man," observed Mr. Fowler. "Why I were tellin' Mrs. Fowler, only t' other dye, 'ow Bertie 'n' Artie 'ave grown. -- An' so mature. You've done a fine job wit' 'im, Mrs. Morton. Can't be easy raisin' 'im wit'out a father. But, Tom 'ere is a big 'elp. Bertie's very proud of 'is Uncle Tom; always talkin' about 'im when 'e cums into t' butchery."

"Aye, I'm very thankful fer me two men." Lottie smiled at Tom and Bertie, while at the same time, giving Mr. Brown's hand a squeeze under the table.

"Anyone fer puddin'?" Everyone's eyes shifted towards the sound of Mrs. Fowler's voice.

"Is that apple vapours I smell?" Mr. Brown took a whiff of the steam rising from the suet pudding.

"Aye, ye 'ave a good nose. I found sum apples in t' cellar. A wee bit passed their prime; sumwot like us. But, after a bit of soakin' in sherry, they plumped right up; again, sumwot like us. I steamed 'em in t' puddin' wit' sum raisins an' Basil's spices."

"It sure smells good, Mrs. Fowler." Bertie took in a good whiff. "Can I 'ave sum?"

"Bertie!"

"Please." He looked at his scowling mother.

"Aye, ye can, Bertie." Mrs. Fowler cut into the pudding releasing the accumulation of cinnamon, nutmeg and cloves to permeate the air.

"Ah!" Everyone inhaled the aromatic spices.

"Mother, can ye pass t' custard?"

"Good idea, but I'll pass t' custard t'is way, so yer father gets it last."

"Custard? Nary a man who doesn't luv 'is custard. Where's t' custard, woman?"

"Hold yer sails, Captain. T'is cumin' "

The last traces of pudding scraped clean from their bowls, the men retired to the parlour. The ladies cleared the table and headed to the kitchen where a sink full of dirty dishes, awaited their attention. The kitchen, situated at the back of the lodging was well stocked with shelves and cupboards. A large stove took up a good portion of the room. Steam spewed from the large pot boiling on its shiny, black iron surface.

"Stand back, ladies. I'll pour t' 'ot water in t' sink." Mrs. Fowler grabbed a couple of muslin tea towels off the sideboard and lifted the heavy, tin pot off the stove. "I swear t'is gets 'eavier ev'rydye." She poured the water into the sink, causing steam to envelope her. "As if I don't get enough water seepin' from me pores already. Middle-age steam engine, I call meself." She took a hankie from her pocket and wiped her brow.

Bess smiled and recalled a similar fate, middle-age bestowed on her. "Do sit down, I'll wash up," she sympathized.

"I'll be alright in a minute, dear. Like t' train, it passes quickly," she laughed. "Mrs. Morton, don't ye get yer 'ands wet. Sit down wit' Mother. Yer always workin', dear. Although ye be young, it do ye good to get off yer feet."

Bess washed, while Mrs. Fowler dried and put the dishes away.

"Mrs. Morton, ye 'ave a lot in common wit' me mother; both bein' seamen's wives."

"Aye, I'd fergotten yer 'usband is at sea." Mrs. Fowler's mother shook her head and tsked. "T'is a lonely life wit' out yer man an' 'ard to raise a family alone. Why, I raised four babies whilst 'e were sailin' around t' world. --- An' who gets all t' glory, Lord Nelson. T'is us women keepin' t' 'ome fires burnin' an' raisin' t' families that deserve t' praise. Where's t' justice? 'E gets 'em when their young 'n' fit an' we get 'em when their owlde, an' their minds 'ave sailed out of port once too often."

"I never thought of it that way, but yer right," frowned Lottie.

"Take an owlde woman's advice, dear; don't deprive yerself of t' company of a good man, like Mr. Brown. Cause ye can be sure yer seaman, so far away from 'ome, is enjoyin' t' company of young ladies, if that's wot one calls 'em."

"Mother!"

"Don't ye, Mother me, child. I know wot I'm sayin'."

" 'Ow about makin' t' tea, Mother. We're almost finished wit t' dishes." Mrs. Fowler abruptly veered her off course.

" 'Ere let me 'elp," said Lottie and turned her red cheeks towards the stove.

The women entered the parlour to find the men deep in conversation. " 'As T' Corn Laws bein' replaced 'elped ye any?"

"Well, I was beginning to wonder, but the wheat harvest was better this year, so hopefully the price and the rationing will come down soon," said Mr. Brown. "Mr. Peal had no choice; the corn restrictions had to come off. Unfortunately, the timing was bad. Who can predict what Mother Nature has in store for us? Poor crops and higher prices effects us all."

"Aye, it cost Mr. Peal 'is job. Say, wot do ye think of John Russell?"

"He's just got in as Prime Minister, so we'll have to wait and see," said Tom.

"Wot do ye think of t'is upstart, Disraeli, Tom?"

"Well, he certainly is making a name for himself. I read his book."

"Aye, I 'eard a great deal about it. Wot did ye think of it?"

"'Sybil'? Well, it certainly gave the reader a look at our society from the rich to the poor. It gave one something to think about; that's for sure."

Mr. Brown added, "Your right, Tom. I don't think we have heard the last of Benjamin Disraeli."

"Gentlemen, enough politics. Time for tea."

"Aye, t' women aren't interested in politics. We best change t' subject."

"Ye men say we aren't interested in politics, but we ar' interested in t' new 'Ouse of Lords." Mrs. Fowler poured the tea. "Bess, 'as Tom taken ye to see it? I 'ear t'is grand, wit' plush, red benches an' furnishin's."

"Aye, ye'd think they 'ad enough red, when it burnt down?" Mr. Fowler laughed.

"T'is about time they got it finished. Why, when did t' owlde 'Ouses of Parliament burn down?" asked Lottie.

"1834, I believe. --- Yes, I had just arrived in London," answered Mr. Brown.

Tom shook his head. "And it still isn't finished. I read in the paper they've started the Common Chamber. Rumour has it, they are going to built a clock tower."

"Wit' all t' delays an' overcosts, it will be ten years before that's done," piped up Mr. Fowler.

"Do ye think it will ever be done?"

"That's a good question, Bertie. The way the government works, not in our lifetime," answered Mr. Brown.

"Now if Nelson were in charge, it'd be finished 'n' done wit'."

"Aye, yer quite right, Captain."

"England expects that ev'ry man will do 'is duty."

"Aye, Father."

Back in the tearoom, Tom carried a sleeping Bertie up to bed. Lottie rushed into the kitchen. The back door creaked; followed by the sound of footsteps running along the gravel path. *Good idea, Lottie. What with all that tea we've drunk today.* Bess smiled and headed up to her room.

Inside the dark room, Bess's thoughts returned to her dilemma *how am I going to tell Lottie, I'm leaving? What am I going to say?* She lowered her face into her cupped hands. *I don't want to leave. I'll miss Tom's bath, his football match, his -----*

"Bess, have you been here all night? Couldn't you sleep?" Bess felt Tom ---- Evan's breath on her cheek. He put his arms around her. "Is something wrong?"

After reassuring him everything was fine, she patted his leg and got up and switched off the village lights. "I'm just excited about our trip. Come on, let's have some breakfast. We've got a busy day ahead of us."

Boxing Day had always been a day to put up their feet, peruse their Christmas presents, partake of left over turkey and indulge in tasty squares and mince tarts. Never a thought was given to the origin of Boxing Day or what it truly represented. This Boxing Day Bess found out the true meaning; the giving of boxes of useful items to the needy. *Not in my wildest dreams did I ever imagine I would participate in the giving of them, but I did today. If people only knew, they would say it did happen in my wildest dreams. I have no intention of telling anyone. It's my secret; my Dickens' world.* She looked up at the mantel and smiled *my world.*

No time for carefully going over their presents; instead, they stacked them in a corner to await their attention on their return from Hawaii. Evan brought down the empty boxes from the attic and brushed spider's webs off his shoulder. Bess smiled as she looked up at a smug Mr. Spider. Soon the decorations, wrapped in their protective coverings, rested peacefully in their familiar boxes for the next fifty weeks. Evan took the jam-packed boxes back up to the attic. Out of breath, he returned and unscrewed the bolts supporting the tree. He lifted the sad looking tree from the stand and took it outside. Bess followed close behind with the broom and swept up the fallen needles.

"Shouldn't be too many. We haven't had it up long," shouted Evan from the backyard.

"True, but it's a shame though. I do enjoy the tree more after Christmas when there is time to sit back and admire it."

"I agree with you there; no time before Christmas. But, just think of us enjoying the palm trees, swaying in the warm, ocean breezes. Not a bad compromise, I'd say."

Bess went over to the mantel and gave a sigh. She fondly touched her village.

Evan put his arm around her. "It's getting late and we still have to pack. Why don't you leave these till we get back?"

Bess immediately brightened. "Oh, Evan, that's a good idea. I do hate to put them away. I've grown very fond of them."

"I know, Bess, dear."

Packed and ready to go on the early morning flight, they crawled up to bed. Set to go off at 5:00 A.M., the alarm clock ticked off the seconds. Bess watched the luminous hands go slowly around its face; one o'clock, two o'clock. Every other tick, Evan inhaled a loud snort and blew out a whistle on the third tock. *This is ridiculous. I might as well get up.* She eased her body out of bed; being careful not to waken Evan. She crept downstairs. *I'll make myself a cup of tea. It will probably be the last one I have until I get back home. Can't get a good cupper in Hawaii. They don't boil the water. Nothing worse than lukewarm tea.* Bess shuddered and walked into the kitchen. She watched over the kettle until the boiling water bubbled over the spout. Satisfied, she made the tea and retired to the living room.

Automatically, Bess plugged in the Dickens' lights. They shone like a halo hovering over Fetter Lane. Her eyes followed the glow upwards and discovered poor Mr. Spider, blinking in astonishment at the sudden stream of light invading his dreamland.

"Sorry, Mr. Spider. I'm going to miss our little chats, but I'm sure you'll enjoy the peace and quiet." Bess looked down on the mantel. "I'm going to really miss all of you." A single teardrop slid down her cheek.

"Bess, luv, wot ar' ye doin' down 'ere in t' dark?"

Bess brushed the second tear from her eye. Grateful for the darkness, she said, "Oh, sorry; I hope I didn't startle you?"

"No, t'is okay. I came down fer a cupper and saw ye way off in another world. 'Omesick were ye?"

"Home is where the heart is; yes, you could say I was homesick."

"I see ye 'ad t' same idea. I'll go get me tea an' join ye." Lottie hurried off. Bess felt something warm in her hand; a Santa Claus mug full of hot tea.

"Summin' botherin' ye, Bess?"

"Actually there is. I don't know how to tell you this."

"I knew it. Ye were so quiet tonight. Best to get it out. Wot is it?"

Bess put the mug down on the hearth and in the next motion, put the same hand behind her back. Fingers crossed, she announced, "I have to go away."

"Aye, luv, I've bin dreadin' t' day ye leave."

Bess looked into Lottie's eyes. "Tomorrow."

"Tomorrow?"

"Yes, very early tomorrow. I ----- er ----- went by the steamship company after church and ---- and they found my bag with my travel ---- tickets."

"Oh, no, yer goin' tomorrow? Oh, Bess, I wanted t' 'ave a proper goodbye fer ye."

"No, I'm not going home yet. Remember I said when I arrived here, I planned on doing some touring. My ticket is for…" Bess frantically looked around the dining room and in desperation closed her eyes. Suddenly, the Fowlers' plaid ottoman came to mind *plaid* ---- *tartan.* "Scotland!"

"Scotland, but that's so far away. Why, it will take days to -- ah, yer ticket is fer t' train. 'Ow excitin'."

"Train--- er --- yes, train. I'm taking the train to Scotland first thing in the morning. I've always dreamed of seeing the palm trees ----- er heather on the hills."

"Well, ye won't see much 'eather on t' 'ills t'is time of year." A cheeky smile spread across Lottie's face. "Nor t' strappin' young lads in their kilts."

Bess looked at Lottie's rosy face in the fire's glow. "You should be blushing, you naughty woman." Bess burst out laughing and Lottie followed suit.

"Hush, woman. Ye'll wake up t' 'ouse. Oh, Bess, luv, I'm goin' miss ye. 'Ow long ar' ye goin' fer?"

"About two weeks."

"A fortnight?"

"Well, maybe not two weeks; ten days I think. I'll be back January fifth."

"Ye'll miss New Year's Eve wit' us. Mind ye, I 'ear they do sum fierce celebratin' in Scotland. Ye'll 'ave to tell me all about it." Lottie thought for a minute. "At least ye will be back fer Twelfth Night."

"Twelfth Night?"

"Aye, t'is a grand celebration. I think t'is better than New Year's Eve, in England, anyways." Lottie laughed. "Twelfth Night goes back to medieval times. "T'is t' last celebration of t' yule season. Like t' Scots, we eat, drink 'n' be merry. Ye will 'ave to try sum twelfth cake."

"You have a special cake? Like Christmas cake?"

"Not exactly; t' bakers make t' cakes an' put in a lucky bean or pea. Why, we've a King of T' Bean 'n' a Queen of T' Pea.

----- Before ye ask, I don't know why; t'is one of those things we don't question, we just 'ave. T'is like yer Saint Nicholas."

"I see."

"T' next day, bein' Twelfth Day, is t' beginnin' of Opentyde, when we get down to serious business. T'is also called Feast of Epiphany. T'is time fer weddin's." She looked at Bess. "'Ow long will ye be stayin' in England? T' weddin' period goes till Ash Wednesday."

"Ah, that's around Valentine's Day, I believe." Bess chuckled. "I bet cupid's a busy fellow in England. Sorry, I'll miss all the action. I will have left for America by then."

"Oh, Bess, I did 'ope they'd never find yer ticket. Why, Bertie 'n' Artie will be so disappointed." Lottie tsked. "Well, they do say t'is better to marry one of yer own country-woman than to marry a foreigner." She lowered her voice to a whisper, "Tom will be so disappointed."

Bess ignored the last remark and turned the subject back onto Lottie, "Mrs. Fowler's mother is a wise woman. You should heed her advice."

"Wot advice?"

"You know what I'm talking about. You couldn't get a better man than Mr. Brown. He's crazy about you; I know you feel the same."

"Don't be daft. I'm a married woman wit' a child."

"That's true, but you are a beautiful woman full of life. It is time you thought of your happiness. It won't be long before Bertie becomes a man and leaves home. Will his father return home then, crippled and diseased? Another captain to haunt your remaining years. Oh, Lottie, you are so spirited and full of life. Don't rob yourself of a beautiful life with Mr. Brown."

"But divorce, Bess? I couldn't . Women don't divorce their 'usbands. Why, men 'ardly ever divorce their wives. Society doesn't allow it. An', I couldn't live in sin: we'd be outcasts. I 'ave to think of Bertie."

Bess unlocked her fingers, took Lottie's hands and smiled, "Remember, the love of a good man far outweighs society's wrath." She patted Lottie's cheek. "Think about it." She brushed a tear from Lottie's cheek. "I'm off to bed. I won't wake you . Please tell Bertie, Artie and Tom, I'm sorry I didn't have a chance to say goodbye. I didn't want to spoil the evening at the Fowlers. When we got back here, they went to straight to bed. Tell them, I'll see them on Twelfth Night."

"Goodnight, Bess. 'Ave a good journey, luv."

Bess followed Lottie up the stairs, remembered her Santa mug and went back down to get it. She took a final look around the tearoom, she had grown to love. The angel, nestled on top of the Christmas tree, caught the light from the outside gaslamp and sparkled. She smiled in appreciation. Bess glanced at the counter and her eyes looked up at the saying of the day:

"Tea ---- that best of all travelling liquors"
Jane Austen

# CHAPTER XVIII

"Hawaii is very selfish. You'd think after all the money we spent there, it would at least given us a tiny portion of its weather to bring back with us," grumbled Evan as he brushed the snow off his coat and kicked his shoes on the door step. "Fat lot of good all those pineapples you brought home, do to keep us warm."

"Perhaps next time, we should stay in a five star hotel."

"Nice try, Bess."

"And I'm sure if we went in August, Hawaii would be much more accommodating. I hear they are quite selfless during the summer months."

"Close the door."

"What about the pineapples?"

"Serve them right for being Hawaiian pineapples. ---- Okay, I'll get them. You turn up the furnace and I'll bring in the luggage --- and the pineapples." Evan sighed as he walked towards the garage, leaving a pool of melting ice on the floor.

En route to the cupboard to get some towels to mop up the floor, she turned up the thermostat. Arms full of fluffy towels, she detoured by the living room and stopped in front of the mantel.

"I hope you missed me as much as I missed you." She plugged in the lights, smiled and cast her eyes upward. "I missed you too, Mr. Spider. Did you look after them while I was gone?" Mr. Spider opened one eye, squinted and stretched his spindly legs. "I bet you haven't moved since I left." He nodded his head as Bess continued, "Get that scowl off your face. I thought you'd be glad to have company." He slowly shook his head. "Were you shaking the cobwebs out of your head or was that a no? Okay, I get the hint, I'll leave you alone."

"Who were you talking to?" asked Evan as he came into the room laden with suitcases.

"The soon to be Ghost of Christmas Past." Bess stuck her tongue out at the spider who disappeared under the skylight moulding. "Coward."

"Sorry, what did you say?" Evan came down the stairs empty handed.

"Are you really going to work today?"

"Yes, it is only ten o'clock. I better go in for a couple of hours. The work will be piled up to the ceiling. Will you get me one of those pineapples? I'll take it to Sherry as a peace offering."

Bess opened the box of four pineapples, and their scent permeated the air. She inhaled the fruity perfume, causing her to recall the warm, tropical breezes that caressed her body as she laid on the deck chair. The waiter, dressed in white, refilled her empty glass of ice tea. The juicy spear of pineapple bobbed up and down in the icy, amber liquid.

"Ice! Watch the ice on the walkway, Bess. ---- Bess?"

"Ice?"

"Yes, ice. I'd better throw some salt down. Maybe I should shovel the driveway."

"No, you go. You've done enough shovelling for one day. Next time, we must do valet parking. I'm surprised we even found the car under all that snow."

"Thank goodness I had the shovel and broom in the trunk." He creaked his neck. "Valet parking? Not a bad idea, Bess."

"Off with you so you can come home before rush hour. Don't fall asleep. Don't forget we only slept a couple of hours on the plane."

"See you later, Bess." Evan leaned down and gave her a kiss.

"Oh, the pineapple." He grabbed one and headed for the car, leaving deep footprints in the snow.

"I'd better get out there and shovel the driveway." She looked up at Mr. Spider who reappeared from his hiding place. "Thanks for the offer, but I can manage."

An hour later, a red-nosed Bess stumbled into the house. Numb fingers, fumbled with the obstinate buttons on the parka. Success at last, she hung the wet coat on a hook and tackled the next task, the boots. Bess bent over, but her back ached so she sat on the floor and pulled them off. She wiggled her frozen toes. *Ouch, that hurts, but at least they're here and functioning.* She placed her wet boots and socks on a sheet of newspaper. Passing the hall mirror, she noticed the tuque still on her head. Lifting it off, Bess tsked; her hair lay flat against her skull due to tuque compression. *Oh, to be back in Hawaii, now that winter's here.*

"Tea, that's what I need; a cup of hot, steaming tea."

Bess wrapped the patchwork quilt around her frigid body and sat down on the chesterfield. She encased the mug of tea in her hands. The steam wound its way up her nasal passage. She took a sip of the hot liquid and felt its warmth go down her throat. Her droopy eyes glanced at the mantel before the lids closed.

"Bess, oh, Bess, luv, did I 'ear ye? Bess, ar' ye 'ome?" Lottie knocked on the door.

Bess pried her heavy lids open. "Lottie is that you?"

"Aye, luv."

Bess threw back the quilt and rushed to the door. She flung it open and flew into Lottie's arms. "I've missed you. I'm so glad to be back."

"Yer shivering; ye didn't get a cold in Scotland, did ye?"

"No, I'm fine."

"Wot 'appened to yer 'air? T'is all stuck to yer 'ead? --- An' yer nose t'is red."

"Oh, I must have dozed off and slept on my face."

"I know, luv; me 'air is a mess in t' mornin' if I don't wear me nightcap." Lottie smiled at Bess. "I'll go make us a cup of tea an' ye can set yerself right." She headed for the stairs. "I want to 'ear all about yer trip."

Bess looked in the mirror. Hair, plastered to her head in one spot, stood straight up in another. She touched her nose which no longer felt numb, and rubbed off flakes of dead skin, left over from her sunburn. She breathed a sigh of relief when she found herself dressed in her dirty old, wrinkled dress. *Thank goodness I don't have to explain my clothes.* Bess brushed and teased the matted hair until a respectable shape appeared, straightened out her skirt and walked out of the room.

From the stairs, Bess heard Lottie singing, "O ye'll tak t' 'high road an' I'll take t' low road an' I'll be in Scotland a fore ye."

Bess stopped on the bottom step and looked around the room. The tables stood ready for the morning patrons. Over by the window, a vacant table looked forlorn. *Something is missing ---- the Christmas tree. I too shall soon be a distant memory,* she thought. Her heart became heavy. Following the melodious sounds erupting from the kitchen, her eyes stopped at the counter. Curious, they lifted to see what saying Jo had penned on the board.

"We drank tea as soon as we arrived and so ends the account of our journey" Jane Austen

Bess smiled. "How appropriate."

"Did ye say sumthin', luv?" Lottie came out of the kitchen with a tray, humming "My bonny lies over t' ocean." " 'Ere we'll sit by t' fire. Scotland, aye t'is a mighty cold place in winter. No wonder ye look under t' weather. Mind, I can't say ye look pale." Lottie took a good look at Bess. "Cum 'ere, luv, so I can see ye in t' fire's light. ---- Why, ye look brown. Blimey, wot was ye doin' in Scotland?"

"Well --- actually, I did manage to get some sunshine."

"Off wit' ye. In Scotland? Blimey! Wait till Sean 'ears about t'is; 'e'll want to go back 'ome." Lottie laughed as she poured the tea.

"Perhaps we better not mention it, for Jo's sake, that is."

"Blimey, yer right. T'is a shame they're both so shy. We should 'elp 'em along, right?"

"You, who can't even work out your own love life ---- and me, who will be leaving tomorrow?"

"Bess, luv, I was 'oppin' ye'd changed yer mind."

"Sorry, Lottie, I must get back home."

"I know, luv, but still I was 'oppin'."

"So tell me about Twelfth Night." Bess changed the subject.

"Well, a few friends will be droppin' in, so I've done sum extra bakin'. We'll play sum games and do sum dancin'. Maybe ye can teach us yer American dances. Wot were they called? Maca ---- Blimey, I'm getting' me tongue all twisted. Twist! That were one."

The door bell jingled. They both looked up to see two ladies storm in, leaving the door wide open.

"T'is a shame ye didn't tell me about Scotland," tsked Lottie. She picked up the tray.

"Bess, be a luv an' close t' door. Blimey, sum people 'ave no manners."

Bess rushed to close the door and heard Lottie say, "Good morning, ladies. Here's a nice table for you, close to the fire."

Bess reached the door and heard horses' hoofs thunder along the lane. She looked out to see Jim and Sadie go by. She waved, Jim doffed his hat and Sadie bowed her head. The two trotted past the book shoppe and the haberdashery, disappearing in the fog enveloping the firehall. A whiff of cinnamon willed her head in the other direction, where she caught sight of Basil sneaking out of his shoppe. He promptly straightened his back and with a steady gait he passed the bread and poultry shoppes. He did not veer off his path until his stout legs turned into "The Goodale." *Truly a man with a mission,* laughed Bess and took one last look knowing it might be her last one at Fetter Lane. With a sigh, she closed the door on Fetter Lane.

Bess strolled over to the pianoforte and caressed the smooth wood. *If it wasn't for you, I wouldn't have met Miss Rose Water, Mrs. Pennycroft and Mr. Dickens. Thank you for opening the doors to an exciting, musical journey. And --- most important of all, the chance to repay a small portion of Lottie's kindness.* She smiled at the ivory keys and started to play for the patrons of "The Lotatea Shoppe." *No, I can't play Christmas music; that's over. Think, girl.* She played a few chords until her thought process and fingers became in tune with each other. Bess played "Loch Lomand," much to Lottie's delight, followed up with "My Bonny Lies Over The Ocean" and finished her Scottish ballads with "Danny Boy."

"Luv, 'aven't 'eard of that one before; t'is new?" asked Mrs. Fowler as she put her hand on Bess's shoulder. "I may not be able to play, but I 'ave an interest in music. I thought I knowed most of t' Scottish ballads, since me father's family cums from Glasgow."

Surprised Mrs. Fowler did not know this famous song, Bess puzzled over this revelation. *Of course, the lyrics for "Danny Boy" weren't written until the early 1900's.* "Yes, I recently heard the song on my trip."

Bess had not told a lie and thus saved herself from crossing her fingers behind her back; a feat most difficult whilst playing the piano. She smiled as she recalled an Hawaiian singer, Danny MacKilani come on stage, dressed in a tartan, aloha shirt and sing his theme song, "Danny Boy." *Apparently, he too had relatives from Glasgow.* Not surprisingly, peals of laughter bounced off the rustling palm trees. With a captivated audience, he went on to enrich the luau further with the historical beginnings of "Danny Boy." Bess clearly heard him say, ' The music, originally known as 'Londonderry Air' was composed in 1855 and the lyrics for 'Danny Boy' were not written until 1913.' *Well, his performance and my trip were not in vain, after all,* she chuckled.

"Well, I shall keep an' ear out fer it; not me deaf one either." Mrs. Fowler burst out laughing. "Rosemary, luv, 'ave ye 'eard t'is song? T'is lovely," she said as she walked back to her table where Mrs. Pepper sat munching on a mouthful of scone.

To be on the safe side, Bess finished up playing soft ballads from her era. If anyone asked, she could honestly say they were songs from America. Miss Rose Water asked her if Harriet could have a copy of "A Wonderful World."

Bess played well into the afternoon until Lottie said, "Bess, luv, go up an 'ave a rest. Ye must be tired after yer trip an' 'ere ye bin playin' fer 'ours. Go on wit' ye. Rest up fer there'll be lots of celebratin' tonight."

Inside the bedroom, Bess shivered. *I haven't felt this cold since I got here.* She looked in the mirror. *Nah, it couldn't be my age. Like Evan, I'll blame it on Hawaii. Right, I must get to it.* She reached down and opened the dresser drawer and laid its meagre contents on the bed. From under the bed, she pulled out the two baking sheets and proceeded to the wardrobe. Perched on the bottom shelf, a pair of snow-white runners anxiously awaited their calling, truly the forerunners of their brand. She plopped them on the cookie sheets and sat down on the bed. Narrowly missing the two novels for Jo, Bess picked up Jo's lighthouse wall-hanging. Hidden underneath, lay the boys' Christmas postcard. She placed Jo's needlework on her knees and lifted the postcard to her chest. A warmth, unequal to anything she felt in Hawaii, spread over her.

"I can't leave these behind." Taking another look around, she saw the three shirts for Bertie, Artie and Tom. "Tom's! Oh, that reminds me."

With eyes wide open, she stared at the mantel. "The mantel? Shirts?" Gradually the the confusion cleared. "I'm home. --- Right, the shirts. I need to unpack the suitcase."

Immediately, Bess started to get up, but something weighed heavy on her legs. Looking down, she saw the lighthouse beaming up at her. She reached to pick it up, but the postcard hindered her movement.

"Oh, I'm so pleased you've made the journey with me." She carried them upstairs, where the postcard went in the drawer of her nightstand and the lighthouse on the bed.

Surveying the bedroom walls, Bess smiled when she found the perfect spot, directly across from their bed, to hang the lighthouse. *When I first awake, I will see my guiding light. It will remind me of my family far away.*

Ten minutes later, the lighthouse hung straight on the wall. Bess stood back to admire her handy-work. *Nice job, if I do say so myself. And to think if I left it for Evan to do, it would be on his to do list for ages.* Turning around, she almost stepped on an abandoned suitcase. Luckily, she caught herself and sighed *isn't this where I came in?--- That reminds me* and pointed at the suitcase.

Bess put the menacing suitcase on a chair and unzipped it. Rummaging through the contents, her hands forged to the bottom. Turfed soiled garments landed in a heap on the floor. Out came a large, plastic bag; inside, Bess found a number of identical shirts. She recalled her secret purchases and smiled. Thankful for Evan's afternoon nap, Bess went shopping at Macy's in Waikiki. In an after Christmas bargain bin, she found the same all-weather shirts, she had bought for Tom. She couldn't pass up such a deal. Besides, she had planned on buying one for Sean and Ivan at home; at that price she bought all six. To justify her whim, she would give one to Michael Doyle and Constable Hunter. They played football. Of course, Mr. Brown would get one , although she couldn't remember if he actually played the game or only spoke of it. If not, he could wear it when he played rugby. The sixth shirt would be a spare, in case she forgot someone.

When Bess returned to the hotel room, Evan's snores greeted her. She quickly placed them at the bottom of the suitcase. She always unpacked them, so Evan would not notice a plastic bag. And, if he did, she would say it contained dirty underwear. Case closed.

Bess took out the toiletries, placing the suntan lotion at the back of the cupboard. *Won't be using this for a long time.* She took a whiff of the boxes of complimentary soaps, they confiscated from the cruise ship. *I'll keep one and ---- I didn't notice the picture of the old cruise ship on the box. Why, it could be a scene from the 1840's.* She stuffed the boxes in the plastic bag, containing the shirts and gathered up the pile of dirty clothes. En route to the laundry room, she dropped the plastic bag on the chesterfield.

While the clothes washed, she finished unpacking and took the empty suitcases to the cupboard. While rearranging space for the biggest suitcase, she accidently hit an upper shelf which caused an empty box to fall. Lying at her feet, "Basil's Spice & Mustard Shoppe" looked up at her. Bess's heart stopped.

"Oh, I guess it's time."

With trembling hands, she picked up a box and reluctantly opened the lid to expose a lonely cavity. She walked over to the mantel and unplugged "W.H. Turner Counting House."

"It's about time you called it a day, anyways, Tom."

Bess carefully dusted off the counting house and placed it in the styrofoam enclosure. Each subsequent building became a little easier, until only two remained on the mantel. "The Lotatea Shoppe" and "Tellaway Books" stood in the centre of the bare mantel, along with a single streetlamp left to guide the passerby. Her hands cupped Sadie and Jim. They eased the wagon into its compartment, making sure Jim felt comfortable and then guided Sadie into her stall and with one finger stroked her head. With a tear in her eye, she closed the lid.

Bess sat down on the chesterfield and brushed the tears from her eyes. A crinkling noise made her aware of the plastic bag, she half sat on. She pulled the rest free and placed the bag on her knees, causing a whiff of pineapple to drift up her nose. She reached over to the box and lifted one out, to discover a soft, juicy bottom. *I'd better check out the other two. We may have to eat them right away and give one to Lydia tomorrow.* She grabbed another by its sturdy growth of sharp leaves and pulled it out of the box.

"Want some, Mr. Spider?" Bess lifted one towards the skylight. Getting no response, she lowered it and looked at the mantel. "How about you?"

"Miss Bess, ---- Miss Bess, yer back." Artie banged on the door.

Startled, Bess jumped. The plastic bag slid onto the floor. The pineapples banged into each other, causing a slight leak to seep out. She stepped over the bag, deposited the wet fruit on top of the bag and hurried to the door.

"Oh, Artie, ---- Bertie, I missed you."

The boys grabbed her around the waist so tightly, the breath leapt right out of her mouth. "Miss Bess, we missed ye too."

Bertie sniffed. "Wot's t'is smell?"

"I can smell it too. Hmm, t'is smells good."

Bess smelt her hands. "Oh, it's pineapple. It is a special treat for later."

"Pineapple? I never 'eard of it," said Bertie. "Where'd ye get it?"

"Scotland, didn't ye, Miss Bess?"

" 'Ow do ye know, Artie?"

"Cause I read "Rob Roy" an' they grow lots of funny things: 'aggis, 'eathers, Lock Ness monsters."

"Did ye really get it on yer trip, Miss Bess?"

"Well yes, actually I did, Bertie."

"See, I told ye."

"Cum on, Miss Bess." They each grabbed a sticky hand and dragged her downstairs. On the first landing, they bumped into Uncle Tom coming up the stairs. "Uncle Tom, look whose 'ere."

"So I see. Welcome home, ---- Miss Bess. The two lads certainly did miss you."

"Only two?" Lottie's voice echoed up the staircase.

Tom made a slight cough. "Right then, lads, take Miss Bess downstairs and I'll join you in a minute." As the two adults tried to pass, their bodies grazed each other. Tom whispered in her ear, "Nice perfume; Scottish is it?" He winked.

"Cum on ye two, wash up."

"Ah, Mum, do we 'ave to. Smell me 'ands. Miss Bess got us sum pin ---- apples."

Lottie tsked, but took a whiff of Bertie's outstretched hand. "T'is don't smell like apples. Wot yer talkin' about, lad? Any excuse not to wash yer 'ands. Go on wit' ye."

"Can I help you, Lottie?"

"Aye, Tom will be down in a minute to 'elp move t' tables. ---- Oh, Tom, let's put t' tables in a circle so we can dance an'----- "

"Play games," shouted Bertie running in with wet hands.

"Aye, that too. We can lay t' food on one of t' long tables an' t' wassail bowl on t' side table." Lottie pointed her finger here, there and everywhere.

"Here, lads, go fill the coal bucket," ordered Tom.

"Oh, Tom, they just washed their 'ands."

"So, they can wash them again. Besides, a little dirt will make men out of them," laughed Tom. "Off with you then, before your mum makes you put on your Sunday best." Scuttle in hand, the boys disappeared through the kitchen.

"Tom, yer a bad influence on t' lads. Wot will Maureen say when she sees Artie?"

"I'm sure Maureen Doyle has seen worse."

"Men!" Ignoring Tom, Lottie turned to Bess and asked, "Luv, would ye mind playin' fer us. Maybe ye could play sum of that American dance music. T'is time we learnt sum new steps."

"Ah, you've got some new moves to show us, have you?" Tom gave Bess a wicked smile.

The door jingled and in walked Jo. "Bess, how nice to see you. How was your trip?" Jo rushed over and gave Bess a hug. "I'd love to see Scotland."

"Maybe Sean will take you," said Bess before thinking. Jo blushed.

"Come warm yourself by the fire, Jo," said Tom without looking at her. "I'd better go and see what's holding up the lads." He made a quick exit.

"I'm sorry if I embarrassed you, Jo. I was only teasing."

"I know. It's not your fault. For some reason, I blush whenever Sean and I are mentioned in the same sentence. I just don't understand it."

"Perhaps someday you will," Bess replied , while at the same time thinking *before it's too late.* "Feeling any warmer?"

"Oh, good even', Miss Jo. We bought ye sum more coal."

"I can see that, Bertie." Jo ruffled his hair and rubbed the black soot off his nose.

"Blimey, Tom, wot did I tell ye? I knew they'd get black. Cum on ye two. Back to t' sink." Lottie grabbed the two boys by the back of their collars and herded them into the kitchen. "Did ye get t' twelfth cake, Jo?" she shouted from the doorway.

"No, Mrs. Fowler is bringing it over."

"Is Mr. Tell cumin' over?"

"I'm not sure. We got a new shipment in today and he wants to look it over."

"Do you need a hand, Jo?"

"Thank you, Bess," said Jo as she picked up an armful of books. "We've been so busy in the shoppe, we haven't gone through them. Mr. Tell is sorting them, and I brought some home to read. We like to be aware of what we are selling our readers. It's difficult to keep up with the latest books. Why I heard yesterday, Bell and Dickens are going to release new novels this year. Speaking of Bell, there are rumours going around in the publishing world that the Bells are going to be making a big announcement. Strange, up to now there is little known about them, but with the success of their books, they can't keep hidden for long."

Bess grabbed an armful of the heavy books and followed Jo upstairs. "I just remembered something in my room. I'll see you downstairs in a few minutes."

Her bedroom looked a mess; what with the bed full of gifts and the plastic bag securely planted on the floor, thanks to two plump pineapples. Feeling a bit chilly, she grabbed her blue shawl and wrapped it around her upper body. She bent over to pick up the pineapples, but decided to bring the plastic bag along. It was one thing to have juice on her hands, but a trail of sticky juice, albeit fragrant, all the way down the stairs would not be acceptable. She scooped up the bag, surrounding the ripe fruit. Careful not too get any juice on the shirts, she slipped them out of the bag. Before leaving, she took one last look. Bess had everything she needed, on the bed.

"Tom, will ye carry t' wassail bowl." Lottie pointed at the punch bowl full of floating apples.

"Hmm ---- smells good." He turned as Bess walked into the kitchen. "Almost as good as Bess." He winked. "What are these fierce looking weapons you're carrying?"

"Pineapples."

"'Ow did ye ever cum across 'em? Captain Morton brought one 'ome once; carried it all t' way from t' West Indies. 'Ad a whole bunch when 'e left there, but wot t' sailors didn't eat, t' rats ate. T' smell attracts 'em. Give us a whiff, luv." Lottie inhaled. "Blimey, I don't blame 'em."

"Miss Bess got 'em on 'er trip."

"In Scotland?"

"Well you see, a ship docked --- and ---- I bought these off the crew." She told a half truth. She did buy them from the crew, but in Hawaii not Scotland.

"Blimey, yer lucky to 'ave found 'em."

Bess chopped off the heads of the pineapples, and slid the knife lengthwise between the hard skin and the juicy fruit. The boys' mouths watered as each slice released the aromatic juices. She scooped out the hard cores and sliced the golden fruit into chunks.

"Do you have a bowl I can put them in?"

"Aye, give Bess that crystal bowl; t' one wit t' scalloped edge."

"Anything you desire, Miss N-ike." Tom bowed and passed her the bowl.

"Thank you, Tom."

"The pleasure's all mine." He winked. "The way you swing that knife, I wouldn't want to get on your bad side."

"Can we 'ave a piece?"

"Why, I just happen to have five ---- six pieces left on the cutting board." The boys rushed to the counter and each took a piece, popping the succulent fruit in their mouths before Lottie could object. "Lottie, Tom have a piece. --- Ah, Jo, you're just in time; have a piece of pineapple."

"I've read about them, but I've never tasted them." She took a bite. "Oh, it's delicious --- and the smell, hmmmm."

"Don't waste any of the juice, Bess; pour it in t' wassail."

"Mr. Brown 'n' Sean ar' 'ere, Mum."

Lottie removed a strand of loose hair from her face, took off her apron and waltzed into the dining room. "Aye, Mr. Brown, ---- Sean, we didn't 'ear ye cum in. We was busy in t' kitchen."

"Mrs. Morton, you look lovely this evening." Mr. Brown stared at her. "Ah -- yes, here's the buns. Sean took them out of the oven not twenty minutes ago."

"Ye must be tired. T'is a busy day fer ye, wot wit' all t' parties tonight."

"You sit down beside Mr. Brown, Lottie. We'll look after the buns."

"Bess, don't encourage her; she's a married woman," whispered Tom.

"So --- she's entitled to some fun." This time she winked at a startled Tom.

"Bess, do cum sit down an' tell us all about yer trip." Lottie patted the seat next to her. "Sean, sit beside Bess. I'm sure ye've got lots of questions to ask 'er."

Reluctantly, Bess sat down and thought *now I'm in trouble. I've never been to Scotland.* In readiness to cross her fingers, she put her hand behind her back. The door bell jingled and all heads turned towards it. Literally saved by the bell, she breathed a sigh of relief and laid her hand back on her lap.

"Ah, t'is t'Doyles. Warm yerselves by t' fire. Let Mrs. Doyle sit down, Bertie. Take yer mum's coat, Artie. Tom pass 'em a cup of cheer."

"I've brought ye some soda bread, baked t'is mornin' in my own oven," proudly said Maureen.

"New oven?" queried Bess. "Did you get a new stove?"

"Aye, t'is grand. Michael and t' wee ones gave it to me for Christmas. I still cannot believe it. Instead of havin' to bake on top of t' stove, now I can bake t'ings proper like in an oven. Michael worked such long hours to buy it."

"Now, Maureen, I can not take all t' credit. If it wasn't for Mr. Brown, I could never have bought it. He managed to find one at a very reasonable price."

"And it has a hot water boiler just like Lottie's. Ye can not imagine how helpful 'tis for my washin' all t' laundry. ---- And, t' gloves I got are a godsend for my hands. T'is t' luck of t' Irish; I'm the luckiest washer-woman in London." Maureen got up and planted a big kiss on Mr. Brown's cheek.

"Thank you, Mrs. Doyle, but what did I do to deserve this pleasure?" smiled Mr. Brown.

"Ye've helped Michael make my life so much easier. I want ye to come over for Sunday supper. We'll have a roast."

"It is not necessary. You need not go to all that trouble. It was just by chance I heard about the stove and I thought of you."

"I won't hear no for an answer. Do bring Mrs. Morton and Bertie."

"Well, when you put it like that, ---- I'd -----" Mr. Brown looked at Lottie who nodded, "we'd be honoured to come for supper."

The door jingled and in walked Mr. and Mrs. Fowler, arms full of trays and parcels. "Where do ye want t' food, Mrs. Morton?"

"My, wot all ye got there?"

"Sum nice cheese an' Mrs. Fowler cooked up sum meats 'n' fowl."

"T'is t' twelfth cake ye 'ave on yer tray, Mrs. Fowler?" asked Bertie. His face lit up when she nodded. "Can we 'ave sum?"

"Soon as we're all settled." Lottie took the cake and put it on the table. "Oh, t'is lovely, an' I can smell t' plums. Wherever did ye get fresh plums at t'is time of year?"

"When Mr. Fowler went to buy t' chickens at t' market, a merchant were sellin' plums, just brought in from Spain."

"Blimey, Bess bought sum pineapples, just shipped in from t' West Indies."

"Pineapple?" My I 'aven't 'ad any since I were a child. Father brought sum 'ome after a sea voyage from t' Indies. Must be goin' on forty years. Hmm, I can still smell 'em."

"Ye should, Mrs. Fowler, cause we got a whole bowl full. 'Ere 'ave sum." Bertie lifted the bowl to her.

"Give Mrs. Fowler a fork. Ye don't want to get 'er 'ands all sticky."

Not waiting for a fork, Mrs. Fowler popped a chunk in her mouth. "Oh, t'is delicious." She licked her fingers. "An t' smell, t'is as good as before."

"Bertie, pass the bowl around."

"Ah, Mr. Tell, I didn't see ye cum in; glad ye could make it. Yer just in time fer tea. Tom, take Mr. Tell's coat. Cum all, 'elp yerselves, there's lots to eat. ---- No, Bertie, we'll cut t' twelfth cake after." Lottie rushed around making sure everyone had a plate.

The door opened and in popped a friendly face. "Just checkin' to make sure t' party is under control."

"Constable Hunter, do cum in. Please join us for a bite of food," smiled Lottie.

"Sorry, Mrs. Morton, I'm on duty. Just makin' me rounds."

"Well then, let me get ye a bun 'n' sum tasty 'am. Ye can take it wit' ye."

"Thank ye. Good even' to all." The constable doffed his hat.

"See you Sunday, Charlie. Sean and I have a few tricky moves to show you," said Tom.

"Can I bring me football, Father?" asked Artie.

"T' way 'em two blokes shoot, we'll be needin' yer ball, Artie." Constable Hunter laughed as he closed the door behind him.

"My, t' 'am is tender. Ye can cut it wit' a fork. Can I cut ye sum, Mr. Brown? Mr. Tell?" Lottie piled a couple of thick slices on the fresh buns. "Chutney or mustard?"

For the next while, they feasted, diminishing the quantity of food spread out on the long table by a considerable amount.

"Aye, that was a bonnie meal, Mrs. Morton."

"Thank ye, Sean, but we all contributed, so we should all be toasted." She smiled and looked at her brother. "Tom."

"Right." Tom stood up and cleared his throat. "As man of this house, it has been bestowed upon me, by my lovely sister, to toast the occasion. First of all, does everyone have a full glass?" He looked around the room. "Good, then raise your glass and let's begin. First, my family and I want to thank you for sharing Twelfth Night with us ----- and bringing all this delicious bounty. --- To friends."

"They raised their glasses and shouted, "To friends!"

"Just little sips, lads; there's more to come," said Tom as the group laughed. "Next, let's toast the end of a grand Christmas time. May we continue with the new traditions, introduced to us this past Christmas."

"Aye, 'ear ye, 'ear ye," shouted Bertie. He took another large gulp of wassail.

"To the new year, 1848. May it bring happiness and prosperity to us all."

"Aye, Aye."

"Be patient, Bertie old man, I know you are anxious to bite into the twelfth cake, but I have one more toast to make." Tom's face grew serious and all became silent. "As we all know, Bess will be leaving us tomorrow. She suddenly appeared from no where, invaded our lives, of which I must admit has been a most enjoyable invasion, and just as suddenly will be departing our shores, but not our hearts. ---- Bess, we wish you a safe journey home and a speedy return to Fetter Lane. To Bess N-ike."

"To Bess N-ike!"

Speechless, Bess sat, while everyone watched a single teardrop slide down her cheek.

"Cum on, Bertie, time to cut t' twelfth cake." Lottie wiped her eyes as she picked up the knife.

"Now mind ye don't swallow or bite down on t' pea or bean. I'm not sure which one is in 'ere, cause I made three cakes: one fer 'ere, one fer t' Peppers an' one fer me parents. I 'ad two peas 'n' two beans, so I put a pea in one, a bean in one an' both in t' third cake. An' cause they all look t' same, I don't know wot is in where," giggled Mrs. Fowler.

Everyone took their task in hand and ate their cake slowly; to be a king or queen for the night was a great honour.

"Bean! I've got it!" shouted Bertie as he jumped up and down.

"Wait now, Bertie, t' ladies aren't finished; maybe one of 'em 'as a pea."

Bertie looked intensely, as each woman took a bite of cake. Time stood still. One by one, they finished their cake. With bated breath, Bertie watched the last remaining piece enter Jo's mouth. Her jaw moved in slow motion. Finally, she swallowed.

"Sorry, Bertie. ----- You will have to ----- rule all by yourself. I too did not get the pea."

"Yeah!" Bertie smiled from ear to ear.

Uncle Tom placed a crown of gold paper on Bertie's head. "King Bertie, we are at your mercy; be kind."

In a stern voice, Bertie commanded, "Me servants, we shall play blind man's bluff."

Yeahs and groans followed, until someone shouted, "Anyone got a scarf?"

"Artie, ye go first."

"Aah, Bertie."

"King Bertie!"

For the next half-hour, the dining room turned into a speed-way of bodies, trying to escape the open arms of the blindfolded assailant. Victim after victim fell into its evil clutches. Even poor Mr. Tell did not escape the outstretched arms of a timid Patty. Mr. Tell almost smothered Jo, who in turn smacked a startled Tom right across the face. In retaliation, he grabbed the leg of Bess's chair, causing it to tip over, landing Bess on the floor, with Tom on top of her.

"At last I have you where I want you, wench." He wrenched off his blindfold.

"Oh, Uncle Tom, yer so funny."

" 'Ere, 'elp t' lady up. T'is time fer sum music, King Bertie," strongly suggested Lottie.

"Music, wench," demanded Bertie.

His mother put her hands on her hips and opened her mouth to utter a reprimand, but Bess jumped in. "Yes, your majesty." She gave her king a curtsy and walked over to the pianoforte.

"How be if I play a few slow songs so you can catch your breath, and then I'll charge your batteries with some livelier music?" Bess looked at her exhausted audience who nodded their heads in agreement.

She started off with "Moon River" and by the end, their heavy breathing quieted down, so she sang "What A Wonderful World." By this time, she had their undivided attention and stepped up the tempo with "Tie A Yellow Ribbon."

"Do they really tie yellow ribbons around oak trees in America?" asked Artie.

"Ar' they goin' to 'ave 'em tied fer ye, Miss Bess, when ye get 'ome?"

"Of course, a whole forest full, Bertie my man," laughed Tom.

The children's faces took on a far away look into the yellow forest. A few bars of "The Sting" and they were back. Their little feet started tapping. Cheers erupted when she finished "Alexander's Ragtime Band." *Thank goodness I didn't sing the words because inquisitive little minds would certainly ask, 'What's a ragtime band'? And, I don't have an answer. How does one explain something after their time and before my time?* Bess laughed.

"Are you warmed up yet? No? Well, this should do it." Bess rolled her hands along the keys. "Goodness gracious, great balls of fire."

"Since ye all be up on yer feet, let's get Bess to show us sum of t' dances from America."

"Yeah! Great balls of fire!" shouted a hyper Bertie.

"Wot about t' twister one?" asked Lottie.

"Okay, I'll play the song through first, so you get the beat and then I'll show you the twist." By the time she finished the song, the children's bodies twisted in all directions, while the adults stood dumb-founded with eyes wide-open. "Now, everybody, let's do the twist." Bess looked at her hesitant pupils. "Everyone in a row, facing me. --- Come on, Mr. Tell; you can use your cane as a support. --- Good. The idea is to twist on the balls of your feet and your body will follow. --- Pay no attention to anyone else but me." Bess lifted her skirt to reveal her runners. Those not familiar with her strange footwear, gasped. "You're right, I should take them off; I can twist better in my stocking feet." Quickly, she bent over, untied her laces and slipped off her runners. "That's much better." She twisted her feet back and forth. "See, as you twist, your body will move."

"Yes, indeed! We can certainly see your body moving." Tom moved his eyebrows up and down while the children giggled.

"Oh my." Mrs. Fowler put her hand on her mouth.

"Remember, only look at me. Don't worry about anyone looking at you. Think of all the exercise you are getting." Bess smiled. "Now, let's try it."

Amused, she watched her pupils attempt the first moves. Skirts swished back and forth, while the men's waistcoats slapped the sides of the ladies' skirts.

"Good. See how easy it is. Now move your arms ----- no bend them. That's right. --- A little lower in front of your chest, Sean."

"Oops, sorry, Jo."

"Space yourselves out a little more. ---- That's it. ----- Now twist."

"Oh my," squealed Mrs. Fowler.

"I'm going to play the music. I want you to twist your feet and arms together."

As Bess played, she heard giggles, a lot of puffing and the accompaniment of clashing cymbals of swishing fabric and grinding of leather shoes upon the hardwood floor. Every time she turned around, a maze of twisting material flashed before her eyes. She finished the song and swung around on the stool. *I'll be; they are all still standing, albeit rosy cheeked. Is that a smile upon their faces?*

"Oh my," puffed Mrs. Fowler.

"Blimey, t'is time fer a cup of tea."

"Aye."

"Aye."

"Miss Bess, wot smashin' fun!" The children ran up to her. "Can we do it again?"

"No, I think you have had enough." Bess looked at three disappointed faces. "But, I'll show you one more move." She got off the stool. "We are going to twist right to the floor. Twist both feet together --- the the same direction --- like this. --- Good Patty. Now, bend your knees. --- Lower ----- lower. That's it, right to the floor. Now, start to come back up --- not so fast Bertie. ---- that's it."

"Yeah! That was fun. ---- Look, Mither, Father."

"You can show your parents how to do it when you get home."

"T'anks, Bess!"

"Tea's ready," announced Lottie as Jo and her came in carrying trays of goodies.

"I dinae think it will catch on 'ere, but I did enjoy it," remarked Sean.

"Aye, mate, it's just a twist-e-er version of your highland fling," mocked Tom.

"Ye know, Tom, it brings back memories of our Irish jigs. Don't ye t'ink, Maureen?"

"Well, maybe t' feet, Michael, but not t' hips."

Everyone burst out laughing.

"Before I depart, Miss Bess, could you indulge an old man the pleasure of listening to you sing and play one more song?" asked Mr. Tell. "Preferably a slow one."

"It will be my pleasure." Bess put her cup down and moved to the piano. She smiled at Mr. Tell and began, "When I grow too old to dream, I'll have you to remember --------" She followed it up by singing, "I'll see you in my dreams. Hold you in my dreams --------"

The room became silent, except for the movement of the hot coals as they smouldered and fell into the bed of ashes.

"My friends, please take heed the words in this, one of my favourite songs." Bess played the intro and sang the chorus with feeling, hoping each would get a subtle message:

"For all we know ----- we may nev-er meet a-gain.
Before you go --- make this mo-ment sweet a-gain.
We won't say good-night until the last min-ute.
I'll hold --- out my hand and my heart will be in it.
We come and go --- like a rip-ple on a stream.
So love me to-night, to-mor-row was made for some.
To-mor-row may nev-er come, for all we know."

Bess slowly looked around at a pensive group, smiled and said, "I would like to end with this song, which has ended many a dance in my country:

Good – night sweet-heart,
Tho' I'm not be-side you,
Good – night sweet-heart,
Still my love will guide you.

Dreams en-fold you, in each one I'll hold you.
Good -- night, sweet-heart, good -- night --------"

Bess wiped a tear from her eye and turned around to see glim-mers of liquid glistening on each cheek.

Mr. Tell pulled out his silver pocket watch. "Right then." He cleared his throat. " It is time to say goodnight, sweetheart."

"Aye, we must be off. Cum, Mrs. Fowler."

"Artie, Patty, put on yer coats."

The departing guests thanked the hostess, wished Bess a safe journey home and gave her a lengthy hug. Bess saw them off at the door, waving at them long after they disapppeared in the fog.

"Don't ferget, Artie," shouted Bertie as he tucked under Bess's arm.

"I won't," a faint reply echoed through the fog.

Sean came behind her and said, "Aye, yer a bonnie lassie, Bess N-ike. T'is been a pleasure to know ye." He gave her a big bear hug.

"Don't let her get away; Jo's a real prize." Bess smiled and gave him a wink.

"Aye, that she is."

"What's all the whispering? Secret plotting?" joked Mr. Brown.

"No, just giving Sean a little advice. In fact, the same advice I'm going to give you."

"It does sound serious. What parting advice do you have for me?"

Bess grabbed his strong hands and held them tight. "Don't give up on Lottie; she's worth the wait."

Mr. Brown put his arms around Bess, held her close to him and whispered, "I know, my dear. Sometimes, we have to fight for the ones we love and I am a fighter."

Without another word, the two gentlemen stepped out onto the sidewalk and disappeared into the enveloping swirls of fog.

"Cum in, Bess, luv, we don't want ye goin' 'ome wit' a cold. Blimey, wot would they think of us? ---- Bertie, luv, give Bess a hug an' off to bed wit' ye."

"Goodnight, Miss Bess." Bertie rushed up and almost bowled her over. They held onto each other, neither wanting to let go.

"Goodnight, dear sweet Bertie," a lump in her throat caused her to hesitate, "sleep tight, don't let the bedbugs bite."

"Cum now, Bertie, luv." His mother took him from Bess's embrace and lead him up the stairs.

"I'll practise me twist, Miss Bess, ---- so ye'll be real proud of me when ye cum back."

The lump grew bigger as Bess watched the two figures climb the stairs. After one last look around her favourite tearoom, she proceeded up the stairs, smiling through her tears, with each creak of the stairs. Jo stood waiting by her bedroom door and gave her a hug. Without saying a word, Jo sped off to her room. Bess turned the glass doorknob. Suddenly, she swung around. She felt a presence behind her. She looked up and down the hallway; nothing. The door to Tom's room stood firmly shut. Bess sighed, walked into the lonely darkness of her bedroom and closed the door.

"Bess, ----- Bess, why are you sitting in the dark?" spoke a familiar voice from far away.

Suddenly, a bright light appeared. "Oh, Evan, it's you," replied Bess as she blinked.

"And, who else would it be?"

"Tom --- er – it would only be you, my love."

"Day dreaming again?" He gave her a peck on the cheek. "I see you've packed up the village." Evan looked at the boxes, piled on the floor, and then at the mantel. "Well, almost." He gave her an unexpected hug. "Come on, let's go out and get a bite to eat and call it an early night." He yawned. "I'm exhausted; must be jet lag. ----- Leave those two buildings, they can wait until tomorrow." Evan held out his hand.

"Perhaps, tomorrow may never come ------- for all we know." She slipped her hand in his warm palm and their fingers entwined into one.

# CHAPTER XIX

*B*ess dreaded this day with all her heart and soul. She knew, as soon as her foot touched the carpet, that first step would initiate the end of her glorious journey. Oh, how she wanted to lie in bed forever, but being a practical person, she reasoned *if I did that, Evan would put me in the luny bin for sure. Mind you, bedlam would be better; at least I'd still be safely tucked in bed and the Mortons could visit me.* Desperate thoughts called for desperate thoughts. *Don't be crazy. ----- Crazy? ---- Well, if they only knew where my mind has been these last few weeks; both this world and that world would definitely think me crazy. Oh for heaven's sake, Bess.* She threw back the covers and planted both feet on the carpet. *Now, get on with it.*

Bess trembled as she approached "The Lotatea Shoppe." Her hands enfolded the minature building. She tried to lift it off the mantel, but it resisted her feeble efforts. Her eyes peered deep inside the bedroom window.

"Why can't I let go?"

In desperation, Bess looked around. Suddenly, she knew why. Strewn all over the four-poster bed, lay the parting gifts, she planned to give to her Dickens family. The journey could not end until she performed one more task.

Bending over to pick up two books, the blue in her sleeve caught her eye. With a sigh, she unbuttoned the dress and slipped it off.

When the wardrobe door opened, Bess gently put the well-used garment on a hanger, next to the evening dress, Lottie loaned her weeks ago. *I'll not be needing you anymore,* she sighed. At the far end of the closet, the turtleneck sweater hung next to her jeans. Reluctantly, she took the sweater off the hanger and pulled it over her head. Moments later, she hoisted the jeans up her legs, held her breath and zipped them up.

Bess scribbled a few notes:

*Jo,*

*I thought you might enjoy reading these two novels. I read them on my voyage over.*

*I had forgotten they were in my luggage. One of the books is set in the future, but who knows what may take place in twenty years; stranger things have happened. Oh, yes, the heroine's name is JO. Enjoy and thanks for being my English friend.*

*Love Bess XXOOO*

Bess opened the bedroom door and tiptoed along the dark hallway to Jo's room. She laid "Little Women" and "Gone With The Wind" on the floor in front of Jo's door and tucked the note between the novels. Bess hurried back to her bedroom, scooped up two parcels and went across the hall to Tom's room. She lifted her hand to knock, but slowly put it down and sighed. She bent down and placed the parcel with the shirts inside, in front of the closed door. Pinned to it, a note read:

*To my football team, Sean, Tom, Ivan, Michael, Henry & Charlie,*
*Sorry I won't get to see you play, but knowing these will keep you dry and warm, will make me happy.*
*Love Bess XXOOO*
*P.S. There's one extra, in case I've missed someone. Otherwise, be good sports; don't fight over it.*

She gently laid the box with Tom's name on it, beside the parcel. The attached note read:

*These ballpoint pens are the newest invention. Well, that's what the man told me from the same sailing ship I bought the pineapples. The ink is already inside. Since you can't refill them like the fountain pen, you will just have to throw them away when empty.*

*Heaven forbid if you should make a mistake in your figures, but amazingly, the man also had wite-out, so here's a bunch more. Not that I'm saying you make lots of mistakes.*

*Thank you for rescuing me from the dreaded hoofs of wild Sadie, my shining knight,*
*Sir Tomolot.*
*Love always, Bess XXOOO*
*P.S. I'll see you in my dreams.*

Bess crept back to her little sanctuary for the last time. She picked up the remaining parcels and double checked to make sure she had everything. *I'm sure I've forgotten something.* She took one final look around and finding nothing, quietly closed the door and walked down the stairs. By this time, Bess knew which stairs creaked, so gingerly placed her foot on the tattletalers, silencing their fun.

After successfully descending the first flight of stairs, she crept along the second-floor hallway, pausing in the doorway of the parlour. *How can such an overcrowded room be so still?* She listened to the silence and recalled the animated conversations held in the cozy room. Smiling, she carried on to Lottie's bedroom. At the foot of her door, Bess laid the two non-stick baking sheets. On top, she placed a shoe box, tied with raffia and a small parcel.

A note accompanied the items:

*Dear Lottie,*
*I noticed your baking sheets needed replacing, so I hope these will do. They*

*are the Latest in bakeware and I was assured they are designed not to stick. What will they think of next? Hope they work.*

*I'm sure your patrons will enjoy these recipes. Make sure you try the one for Nanaimo bars (Have fun pronouncing this one.) Some of the ingredients are included:*

*Bird's Custard Powder, chocolate. And of course, another non-stick pan. When I looked around, it was surprizing what I found. Sorry, but I can't remember where I bought them, so I can't give you a name or address of the company.*

*The shoes are designed to give you comfort at day's end. When I retrieved my luggage, I noticed these new shoes (of which I had forgotten about). Luckily, we are the same size and since you can't get them here and I can back home, they're yours.*

*These little gifts are a small token of appreciation for your kindness and gener-osity you have shown a stranger. I will not forget you.*

   *Love Bess XXOOO*

   *P.S. Remember what I said about Mr. Brown.*

Her last stop before descending the final flight of stairs, found her in front of Bertie's room. Slowly, the brass doorknob turned until the door opened. Bess poked her head inside the dark room. Following the soft whistles, emanating from Bertie's breathing, she cautiously tiptoed up to his bed. His lovely, little face looked so innocent, framed within the folds of the feather pillow. She bent down and gave him a kiss on the forehead. He did not move. Bess took one last look at her dear, little friend and slowly crept towards the open door. Stopping at the dresser, she placed two sweatshirts. On top of each, she put a baseball hat. Now accustomed to the darkness, her eyes caught the yellow embroidery written on the hats and corresponding shirts: "Bertie" and "Artie." Bess knew they were correct. Along each name, a checkmark appeared. Satisfied, she smiled and closed the door.

Her task completed, she hesitated on the last step, sighed and descended onto the floor of the tearoom. Before her, tables stood draped in crisp, white tableclothes. Mrs. Pennycroft's table stood alert, awaiting the arrival of its best patron. Over in the corner, Bess could see sweet Miss Rose Water nodding at her. She walked over to the pianoforte and silently touched the ivory keys. As her hand automatically reached down to the piano stool, she felt something soft and warm. *Tom's shawl! I knew I was missing something.* Bess wrapped it around her shoulders and brought it up to her cheeks. She breathed in the subtle smell of the wool, hoping to capture a small essence of Tom.

Bess gathered her courage, walked to the front door and turned around for one last look. Her eyes scanned the room, stopping at the counter. In anticipation, she looked up. Jo had not disappointed her.

"𝕿ea ---- 𝕿hat best of all travelling liquors."
𝕵ane 𝕬usten

Bess turned the door handle. The bell jingled.

"Darn, I forgot."

"So, you thought you could leave without saying goodbye."

Startled, Bess turned around to see Tom at the foot of the stairs.

"What, no goodbye kiss?"

She let go of the door handle and walked towards Tom; not taking her eyes off his handsome face. Each step seemed like an eternity. She felt his warm breath as she reached up and touched the frown lines, etched on either side of his mouth. Bess's eyes met Tom's. Time stood still. He placed his warm hand on her trembling hand and gently kissed each finger.

"Oh, sweet music, thou doth play," he whispered as he looked into her eyes. Slowly, he lowered his head. Their lips met. The kiss, soft and warm lingered for a long time. Neither wanted to let go. As their lips parted, they held each other tighter.

Softly, Tom said, "For all we know --- we may never meet

again. Before you go ----" he hesitated and Bess joined in, "make this moment sweet again." They kissed once more.

It was time.

Bess left his embrace and looking straight ahead, walked to the door. Her hand reached out and grabbed the handle. Without hesitation, she opened the door, oblivious to the jingle and stepped out into the cold, damp air. Hand behind her, she pulled on the cold, iron handle.

A second before the door closed, she heard Tom say, "Bess N-ike, I knocked on your door last night."

Her heart stopped. *Oh, Tom!*

"Miss Bess, Miss Bess," a breathless voice echoed up the street. "I were afraid I'd miss ye."

"Oh, Artie." Bess closed the door.

"Miss Bess, ye 'ave a big fog drop under yer eye. 'Ere let me get it fer ye." He reached up and brushed a tear from her cheek.

"Thank you, Artie." Bess gave him a long hug as he wrapped his tiny arms tightly around her.

"Goodbye, Miss Bess. I luv ye," shouted Artie as he disappeared into the fog.

"Did ye get 'em, Artie?" Bess looked up to see Bertie hanging out her bedroom window.

"Aye," a feeble reply uttered down the fog laden lane.

"Get inside, Bertie, you'll catch your death in this damp air," Bess shouted up at him and smiled. *Blimey, I sound like Lottie.*

"Goodbye, Miss Bess. ---- Please cum back. ---- We luv ye, Miss Bess."

"I love you too, Bertie."

With a heavy heart, she hurried into the fog. Suddenly, she stopped at "Tellaway Books." Taking a last look in the window, Bess saw the reflection of the gaslamp flickering through the swirl of fog. *Will Tom's lamppost be standing two centuries from now?*

Clop, clop. ------ Clop, clop!

The sounds became louder. Bess's foot touched something. She jumped.

Clop, clop!!

The gaslamp went out.

Clop, c –l – o – p.

Sweat rolled down her face. Her clammy hands began to shake. Something moved. Bess's eyes flew open. She looked down at her clenched hand. Releasing her grip, she saw a brown snake.

"Snake! ---- Snake? ---- Cord ---- It's an electrical cord, dummy."

Regaining her composure, Bess's eyes followed the swaying cord to its plug. Back and forth, it hit the rocks on the fireplace.

Clop, clop.

"Meow, meoooow."

Startled, Bess felt a movement in her pocket. Gingerly, she slid her hand inside and felt something warm and silky; out came a rusty, coloured kitten. Alert, green eyes looked up. Before she could react, another movement occurred in her other pocket. Her vacant hand scooped out a black and white kitten. Sleepy eyes barely opened.

"Artie, you Artful Dodger, you slipped them into my pocket." She put them up to her face and kissed them on the tops of their heads. "Whatever am I going to call you, you little dickens?"

Bess thought for a moment as the wee ones purred. Focusing on the mantel, the answer struck her. She looked the wide-eyed kitten in the face.

"How do you do, Dickens."

Satisfied with her first choice, Bess looked around for inspiration. The rain beat against the skylight. Looking up, she thought *Mr. Spider will know.*

"Mr. Spider, what shall we call this kitten? ---- Hey, Mr. Spider, where are you?" She narrowed her eyes and searched above. Her silent companion had disappeared. "Mr. Spider?"

The kitten's sleepy eyes opened wide. "Mr. Spider, it is then."

She gave the kitten a hug. "Okay, lads, well I hope you are boys, make yourselves at home. I have to put our buildings away and then we can start our present life together. We'll start off with some milk and tea."

While the kittens huddled around her legs, Bess opened the last two boxes. Carefully, she picked up "Tellaway Books" and leaned down to put it in its private library.

"What the Dickens!" she laughed. "Come on you little devil; out you get. I know you know from whence you came, but this is your new home." She scooped up the mass of rusty striped fur and sent him off in search of his brother.

Unimpeded, Bess gently wedged the building into its styrofoam confines. "You can squeak all you like, but you're in here until December." She plunked the lid down.

Reluctantly, Bess picked up "The Lotatea Shoppe" and laid it in its box. The tip of her finger caught in the door handle. She thought of Tom standing in his nightshirt.

"Oh, Tom, we may never meet again." She closed the lid down on Dickens' World.

Bess stared at the bare mantel. Her eyes wandered around the well-used living room. Lifting her misty eyes, she searched one last time for Mr. Spider.

"Oh, Tom, if only I heard you knock." ----- *But, would I have opened the door?*

A sharp bite of reality brought the answer. The kittens nipped her feet as they rolled in and out of Evan's, once perfectly aligned slippers, now scattered at the foot of the stairs.

"Oh, boys, have I got some more explaining to do and this time it's to Evan. Come on, you two. Another time. Another adventure. Life's awaiting us."